**Also available from Jen Doyle
and Carina Press**

Calling It
Called Up
Called Out

To Rachel. Dancing on tables with you is the best.

JEN DOYLE

Called Up

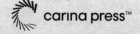
carina press™

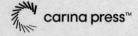

carina press™

ISBN-13: 978-1-335-00620-2

Recycling programs
for this product may
not exist in your area.

Called Up

www.CarinaPress.com

Printed in U.S.A.

Called Up

Chapter One

There were four women dancing on his bar. Max Deacon was a happy man.

"*Dude*," his buddy Jason said, holding up his Bud in a toast.

"Life is good," Deke answered, holding up his water in response.

Not that he was checking the women out, of course. Ladies One and Two were his sister and her best friend, Lady Number Three was the fiancée of one of Deke's best friends, and Lady Number Four was one of his own best friends. Off limits, every one.

The front doors swung open.

"Tuck!" Fitz yelled, throwing her arms up in rock concert-style greeting with enough enthusiasm she almost spun herself off the bar.

Tuck, who also happened to be Officer John Tucker of the Inspiration Police, folded his arms across his chest as he looked over at Deke. "Is she drunk?"

The woman wasn't a big drinker. Really, Fitz wasn't big on letting herself go in any particular way. Seeing her having a good time dancing and hanging out with friends was very much a "life is good" moment. But

Deke preferred his information from the source. "Are you drunk, Fitz?"

Shimmying as she danced, she turned to him. "Just high on life." She laughed as she was pulled back around by Dorie.

"You ready for the first wave?" Tuck asked as he came over, happily accepting the Coke Deke had waiting for him. "They'll be naming the King and Queen soon."

Tonight was the night of the senior prom, an all-hands-on-deck type thing, and for this one night, the bar was open all night, to high school kids only. They could order anything they wanted off the menu, any drink on the list—the list, of course, consisting entirely of mocktails with an alcohol content of zero.

Deke loved prom night. The kids had fun playing at being adults, the parents were happy, and Deke was happy. Yeah, it irritated him that the comments he got from the parents tended to be more along the lines of *Good ole Max, still partying it up old school,* rather than, *Thanks for being an upstanding citizen and keeping the kids sober and off the streets,* but whatever. He had an image he played up, so he couldn't blame them.

"Hell yes, we are," he said, nodding his head at the women. "Can't you tell? Our crack staff is ready to go."

"We heard that!" Fitz shouted. Since she was head of the Iowa Dream Foundation, which was bankrolling the night, not to mention the woman whose idea the whole thing had been, it wasn't a surprise she hadn't let him get away with that.

Then again, she wasn't in the habit of letting him get away with anything, no matter the circumstances. "Maybe I should turn up the music a little bit louder."

"Funny," she said, turning her back to him and thrusting her ass in his direction, in a "kiss my…" sort of way.

"You wish," he called back.

She thrust her ass back again, which of course meant he had no choice but to smack it with his towel.

"Ouch!" she yelped, rubbing where it stung. "Why do you always have to hit so hard?" Glaring down at him, she said, "I'm not really into the spanking thing."

That was all kinds of wrong.

He was about to say so when she stripped off her T-shirt and exposed the tank top underneath. A tight one. Tight enough for the thought of an actual spanking situation to flash through his mind.

Damn. Apparently his dick didn't seem to care that it was Fitz's ass he'd just smacked. Definitely wrong. It had clearly been far too long since he'd gotten laid.

Wash Fairfield, the last of tonight's helpers, strode through the bar's front door and stopped short. "For Christ's sake. You ladies do realize a hundred horny boys and girls are about to walk through these doors, don't you?"

The comment only served to prompt Dorie i.e., the fiancée, to strip down to her own tank top and throw her T-shirt at Wash's head. "Key word being 'about,'" she said. "We've still got ten minutes and we're making 'em count. Right, ladies?" As the women whooped and hollered their agreement, she ran her hands down to her thighs and danced her way into a crouch, jiggling everything she had.

"I can't look." Wash averted his eyes as he beelined it to the stool next to Tuck. "Is Nate aware this is happening?"

Called Up

"Nope." Deke jerked his chin up at the TV. It was the bottom of the ninth and Nate, Dorie's fiancé and also currently one of the highest paid players in Major League Baseball, had just tossed his catcher's mask and was running for a foul ball.

Wash shook his head. "I can't decide if Nate would appreciate a picture of—" He waved his hand in the general direction of the dancing. "Or if he'd just have my ass for noticing."

The four men turned their heads simultaneously, just as Dorie raised her hair off her neck and arched her shoulders back in order to catch the air of the ceiling fan.

"Have your ass," three of them said, looking back at Wash, who just sighed and nodded. "Give me a Sprite. And keep 'em coming."

"Gladly." Deke placed the drink in front of Wash.

But with the hordes about to descend, he did need to call an end to the fun. The ladies all groaned when they saw the look he gave them, knowing exactly what it meant.

"One more!" Lola shouted, jumping off the bar with the ease of someone who had been doing it her whole life. Which she had, in fact, since she and Deke had pretty much grown up here. She ran to the jukebox and queued up...

Yep. The dulcet tones of Salt-N-Pepa's "Shoop" came over the sound system and all four women went wild.

Deke leaned against the counter and smiled. They were having a good time. Jules was going through a messy divorce, and Lola didn't get much time in the way of girls' nights. Fitz wasn't *ever* this relaxed, although there was that time she'd fallen asleep with her head on his shoulder during movie night and totally drooled all over him. But, hey. If the four of them wanted to milk it for one more song, who was he to say...

Oh, hold on a minute, though. He was *totally* the one to say, "That's not the line, Fitz." He considered it one of his prime directives in life to correct her whenever she was wrong, especially since it happened so rarely.

"What?" she snapped, hands on her hips, as she stood above him. "Of course that's the line."

Pushing off the counter, he said, "It's 'lick *him* like a lollipop.' Not them."

"It's lick *them*," she insisted.

"What exactly do you think she's licking?" he asked, his gaze coming up to meet hers.

"His. *Balls*." Fitz not only enunciated clearly, she also held up her hands in such a way as to, well, hold a guy's balls. Then she stuck her tongue out and licked at the air.

He rolled his eyes. "It's his dick, Fitz. 'The bow-legged one'? You do get the reference, right?"

She crouched down in front of him on the bar. "And he can't be bowlegged because he has huge balls? You know that for a fact?"

Since they were all close friends here, that comment set off a round of guy vs. girl trash talk in which Deke would normally be fully involved. But as Fitz shifted to put her own two cents in with Jason, it occurred to Deke she was now perfectly placed for him to do some licking of his own. If she were any other woman in the world, of course.

Shaking it off, he brought his head up, right as she turned back and—

He took a step back before any part of him came into contact with any part of her. Except now he was at eye level with her chest and couldn't help but notice how truly excellent it was.

Jesus.

She was one of his best friends. Noticing *anything* about any one of her attributes was wrong in a big way. Her being Nate's baby sister made it even worse. But since these thoughts would never again see the light of day, that was neither here nor there.

Like her tank top.

He squeezed his eyes shut for a second.

"Deke? Are you okay?" she asked, her head cocking to the side.

Making sure to keep his eyes from roaming anywhere south of her neck, he got himself back into the flow of conversation. "Why?" he asked. "Do you need a demonstration?" No one needed to know that his dick jumped a little at the thought. Before she could respond in any way whatsoever, he went back to wiping the counter down. "Lola, are you hostessing? Time to get our asses in gear."

Yeah, at the first possible opportunity, he was going to get himself laid.

What was *that*?

Fitz straightened up, then carefully got herself down from the bar. Time to get to work. The tables had all been set and there were stations for appetizers distributed throughout the room, but it wouldn't hurt to get the water glasses on the tables. Not the way the waitstaff ordinarily would have done it, but it wasn't ordinary to be slammed with a hundred hungry teenagers at once.

With Jules and Lola handling appetizers, Fitz and

Dorie headed to the waitresses' station to start in on the water and ice.

"Does Deke seem okay to you?" Fitz asked.

Dorie cocked her head. "What do you mean?"

Well, he seemed fine *now*, joking with the guys as he cut up some limes. Still… "I don't know. He was just…"

Well, she didn't want to go into details because then she might have to mention there'd maybe been a moment when he couldn't take his eyes off her boobs. Yes, he was a breast man; everyone knew that. But they'd gone running together yesterday and she'd been wearing a sports bra without a shirt. He hadn't even looked twice. He never had.

"He just seemed off."

Dorie swung her head to look at Deke and then back to Fitz, a big smile on her face.

"No," Fitz said immediately. It had been the heat of the moment. The highly un-family-friendly song.

"Maybe you shouldn't have pretended to lick his—"

"I didn't!" They had conversations like that every day. The guys had stopped censoring themselves around her, oh, probably fifteen years ago. Honestly, she'd been hearing things she'd wished she hadn't since the night Deke had an unfortunate manscaping incident back in college and Fitz was the only one who could handle the trauma of taking him to the emergency room.

"I was making a point." Then she smacked Dorie on the shoulder. "And nice way to blame the victim. Geez."

Dorie laughed. "I was making a point."

For the most part, the evening went on as usual, the number of kids growing as the night went on and chaperones switching in and out. To her surprise, Fitz was having fun. It wasn't exactly a specialty of hers. Not that she was against having a good time, she just didn't tend to do it very often. At least not in a dance-like-you-don't-care-who's-watching kind of way. Not after spending seventeen years being highly aware that everyone in Inspiration *was* watching her, and making sure to give them absolutely not one reason to raise their eyebrows.

"I can't believe we danced on the bar," Lola said a few hours later as she, Jules and Dorie joined Fitz in the back office for a well-earned break.

"Me, neither," Jules said. "But I'd totally be up for doing it again." Then she giggled and turned to Dorie. "Oh, my goodness. When you told Deke you'd pull up the official ASCAP lyrics? I almost peed my pants."

It made Fitz smile. Jules was the kind of woman whose hair would never dare be out of place and who'd had to go out and buy a tank top in order to waitress tonight because the closest she'd had was her silk shells. They weren't the closest of sisters—half sisters, to be technical—but their relationship had definitely improved over the past couple years and Fitz wanted her to be happy, especially now that she was free of her jerk of a husband.

Sitting back in her chair, Jules added, "I'm just not sure the guys can handle it again any time soon."

"Honestly?" Lola answered. "I don't think there's a lot out there that fazes my baby brother anymore. But the whole 'Shoop' thing took the cake."

Fitz ignored Dorie's glance as they all leaned forward to clink their glasses together. Deke had *not* been checking her out. She forced a smile.

As the evening came to a close, however, and things began to slow down, she couldn't quite get it out of her head. Like Lola said, Deke was rarely fazed. He'd been charming women for as long as Fitz had known him, with those eyes of his promising he knew exactly what to do with his freakishly amazing body and cover-model-meets-boy-next-door looks. He was probably also one of the nicest guys on the planet, making him that much more of a catch. That he'd been caught by pretty much every single woman in town between the ages of twenty-two and forty-five, very possibly the only exceptions being Jules, Fitz and Dorie, seemed to matter to no one. It certainly didn't matter to him.

But whatever. She was getting worked up about nothing. Looking over at him now, there was nothing to indicate anything out of the ordinary. He was making a final round of drinks, shaking his head as he laughed at something one of the boys said.

"You guys make a good team," Lola said, coming up behind her and, obviously, noticing where Fitz's attention was directed. "This has been such a great night. It just gets better every year. I'm so glad you convinced us to do it."

Fitz turned her head to Lola. "It wasn't my ide—"

"I was there when you came up with it," Lola reminded. "After that car crash messed up those kids a few years back. You were the one who said there had to be something the foundation could do."

"But Deke…"

Lola rolled her eyes. "Yep. I remember that, too. You came up with it and he got all these crazy ideas on how to make it happen and then you reined him in and made it something that would actually work."

Well, yes. That was true. So true in fact, Fitz had decided to add it to the portfolio she was building for the headhunter she was working with. Not that she hated her job by any means. She loved it. Mostly. She'd just been thinking maybe it was time to spread her wings a bit. Be a little more challenged. Head off to pastures unknown. Or, rather, pastures where *she* was unknown, rather than keep on doing the same old thing in a town where, for going on seventeen years now, everyone's first thought was "half-sister of the Hawkins clan" rather than "Fitz Hawkins."

"Like I said," Lola continued, "a great team."

Letting herself look at Deke again, Fitz allowed, "Yes. We are."

It was true. So when he also looked up and their eyes met, she was relieved that whatever that strangeness had been before was gone. Instead, he just cracked a smile and held up a finger, mouthing the words, *Lick him.* Emphasizing the "him," of course. *As in one.*

She held up a finger of her own. Then, when he laughed, she went back to her business, a smile on her face.

Chapter Two

A few days later Deke found himself on the ball field, one of his favorite places on earth. Granted it was a Little League field rather than Yankee Stadium, where Nate was playing tonight. But that was fine by Deke.

He'd never wanted Nate's life. Or envied Wash's days playing basketball in Miami. Or felt the call toward the military that Cal had, or even to teaching like Jason. He liked being behind his bar and he liked playing ball. Hell, he even liked coaching Little League. As kids started to filter onto the field, he smiled and thanked God for the gift of baseball. Life didn't get much better than that.

"Call it, Uncle Deke!" Jimmy Fielding yelled from second base.

Deke wasn't actually Jimmy's uncle, but since he was coaching the team because of his nephew, Silas, that's what all the kids called him now.

With a grin, he put his hand to his ear. "What was that?" he shouted. "I couldn't hear you!"

As a few other kids came onto the field, they picked up what Jimmy had started, chanting, "Call it! Call it! Call it!"

So, with all the theatrics of a coach whose Little

League team consisted of seventeen overly enthusiastic six- and seven-year-olds, Deke Babe Ruthed it, raising his hand and pointing up the third base line. "Coming at you, Portia!"

The girl gave a toothy grin, setting her shoulders with grim determination as she held both her hands out, ready to catch. He threw up a ball and swung the bat. The soft lob fell right into her glove, pretty much against every natural law that existed.

To the cries of "Me next!" he did the same thing to each player who managed to stick to their position.

As more kids drifted onto the field, the moms started to gather, too, piling into the bleachers angling up the third base line, the knitting needles going as they arranged themselves into a virtual MILF buffet.

"Looking good, Deacon!" Peggy Miller shouted, to a smattering of giggles from the other moms. "Jeans today, huh? No baseball pants?"

"Time and a place, Peggy." For fuck's sake.

"You know it, Deke," she said to more giggles. "Oh, how you know it."

It wasn't that he minded the attention. That was a lineup he'd enjoyed in the past, but lately it was falling flat. Even Peggy, who he'd hooked up with off and on since she'd moved back to town following her divorce, wasn't doing it for him these days.

Since he wasn't about to announce in front of his kids he'd stopped wearing his baseball gear because their moms were paying too much attention to his ass, however, he just nodded and gave as genuine a grin as possible. Then he threw another ball up in the air and hit a first grade appropriate line drive to Jimmy and scanned the field. Silas wasn't there yet, even though

Lola defined "on time" as twenty minutes before any-one else expected her to arrive, and Deke was trying not to think about Si being late. Not that he worried.

Lola's Suburban rolled into the lot just as practice was officially getting underway.

"Hey, guys," he said as Silas and Jules's son, Matty, jumped out of the car and ran onto the field. "Every-thing okay?"

Before Silas could even respond, a strange sensation ran down Deke's spine. As he straightened up and turned, he only vaguely heard Si say, "Mom asked Auntie…"

"Fitz."

Wearing, thank God, a running shirt and jogging shorts. Much less revealing than the tank top from the other night.

Not that he *cared* what she was wearing, he just hap-pened to notice.

"Hey." She smiled distractedly as she rummaged through Silas's bag and pulled out a bright red bottle. "Don't forget your water, hon." After brushing back the hair blowing around her face, she put her hand on Si's shoulder and directed him back to the outfield.

"Heads up, Si!" Deke called out, and hit one just far enough for the kid to have to dive for it. He hit another out toward center field, and the kids all went running for it. So much for keeping them in their positions. Deke took the opportunity to pair them up and get them going on some drills before turning back to Fitz.

The sun caught the reddish highlights in her dark-brown hair, but he focused instead on how unusual it was for her to be doing the Little League run, even though she'd been living at Lola's for about six months now and playing nanny.

He and his parents had done whatever they could to help Lola in the two years since Dave had run off an icy road a few months after returning from deployment. She'd been coping okay until the triplets had turned three and hit a whole new level of hellion. She'd had a major breakdown at Thanksgiving dinner, saying something about parties and presents and, if memory served, *Santa fucking NOT coming to town if one more kid asked one more time if he could eat his* fucking *pie before dinner.*

Fitz had moved into Lola's house two weeks later. Her job running the foundation meant she made her own hours, and, since the new librarian in town had needed housing she'd offered her apartment for rent. "Two birds with one stone," she had said back then.

"Is Lola okay?" he asked now, leaning his bat against the fencing behind home plate.

"What?" Fitz seemed oddly fidgety. Distracted, even, as her gaze came back to his. "Oh. Yes. Jules's doctor's appointment got cancelled, so your mom said she'd take Lola's hostessing shift and I said I'd take the boys to practice." All of which sounded perfectly normal.

So why was there this strange vibe going on?

Shit. Was it because of what he'd said the other night? The whole lyrics thing? Or, of course, maybe she'd noticed he...

Fuck.

What the hell were you supposed to say when you'd been caught checking out your best friend's tits?

"Look, Fitz, I, uh…"

But she was focusing on something in the stands. He turned to look. Peggy Miller and crew? Frightening in their own way, but harmless. Unless you were wearing baseball pants, that was.

Still, something wasn't right. He took a step closer and murmured, "Are you okay?"

Fitz snapped her head up, a tight smile on her face. "Can you get Si and Matty home? I'm meeting Dorie and then I have to get the boys from daycare."

"Sure," he said. "We're on for Monday night, right?"

Although if anyone asked, Deke would say it was solely to help Lola out by giving her one night a week to be completely free, watching *The Voice* with Fitz and the boys every week had become one of the highlights of his week. Especially as Fitz would get Silas and the triplets engaged in a trash-talking ticklefest more often than not. It was highly amusing.

The smile she gave him was genuine this time. "Watch out, Team Blake. Team Adam is going to whip your ass."

Not if I get to yours first, he almost said, except he was suddenly worried she might take it the wrong way.

Worried maybe he *meant* it the wrong way.

With a hasty wave, he turned back to the field. "Okay, kids. Time to play ball!"

Talk about a flashback from hell.

Deke at home plate plus Peggy Miller and her mean girl crew sitting in the bleachers watching him? Yeah. That was some déjà vu Fitz could do without. Because once upon a time in high school Fitz had shared her teenage Deke-appreciation thoughts with Peggy, who, as it turned out, was the exact wrong person to confide in. Lesson learned.

And thanks to that lesson, Fitz's high school Deke-crush was over almost as soon as it began, although that was probably a good thing. Competition for the man's attention was fierce. Honestly, sometimes Fitz thought Deke had more fans than Nate did. Not in numbers, of course—her brother had stadiums full of women screaming his name. But they were faceless, nameless. They either kept their distance or the distance was kept for them.

Deke, on the other hand, had a following. And, defying all reason, they all seemed to have slept with him and then parted on completely fine terms. In all of Fitz's years in this town, since the moment she arrived at her foster home and he'd been helping Mrs. Jensen haul mulch for the garden, Fitz had never heard a bad word said against him. Not even Lola, Fitz's only true friend in the months after her parents had died, even so much as hinted at something bad.

With a shake of her head, Fitz opened the door to Lola's Suburban and climbed in. He was pretty to look at, sure. She loved him, absolutely. But she knew the brand of underwear he wore—and not because she'd been the one pulling them off of him. No. She had that intimate piece of knowledge because she'd accompanied him on a ridiculous number of shopping trips for new underwear. He hated doing laundry so much that he'd rather buy new. Sometimes she'd even pick up a few packs for him if she was out on her own and there was a sale. Of course, she'd make sure at least one pair had purple polka dots, but still.

Her phone rang as she was about to leave the ball field parking lot, and since she still had time before she had to meet Dorie for their run, she pulled over and parked. It was a Chicago number, not one she recognized. "Hello?"

"Fitz, it's Doug Blackler." The headhunter she'd signed up with. "You're never gonna believe where I'm calling from."

Um, okay. "Where?"

"I'm in Sam Price's bathroom."

"TMI, Doug." She did *not* need to know that.

"Not *going* to the bathroom," he replied. "*In* his bathroom."

Sam Price was the GM of the Chicago Watchmen, aka her big brother's team. Fitz sighed. Not the kind of news she was looking for.

She hadn't told Nate she'd put herself on the job market—hadn't told *any*one. She'd get to that part if and/or when it became necessary. Plus, the whole point of using a headhunter was to be anonymous. If she'd wanted to use Nate's name to get a new job, she would have done it already. "You've been talking to Nate?"

"Of course not," Doug snapped. Most likely because he'd assured her he wouldn't share her name with anyone until the time came to do so. "The reason I'm *calling* from the bathroom is that there's a very private meeting happening right now. And the people in that meeting, which includes your brother, by the way, would kick me out if they knew I was on the phone with you. I just want to know if it's worth my throwing your hat into the ring for the head of the private foundation they're all brainstorming right now."

"What?" She sat up straight. Talk about burying the lead. "You have details?"

"Only that the numbers they're talking are about ten times bigger than anything else we've looked at to date."

Since the other jobs he'd put in front of her had been on the same scale of what she already did, they hadn't been quite what she was looking for. Somewhere new was important, but she needed a challenge, too. Since "ten times bigger" put them in the hundreds of millions of dollars range, it definitely counted. Hell, yes, she wanted her hat in the ring. The bigger question was whether they'd even consider her.

That would be the test, she supposed. And if they didn't balk at her qualifications as the head of a small-ish community foundation, then there was no reason she should. Right? "You won't give them my name?"

"I'd keep that secret wrapped up until the second I put you in front of them."

Which would be an absolute necessity because Nate would raise holy hell if he knew she was thinking of leaving Inspiration and the foundation they'd started together almost a decade ago. She couldn't even imagine what the others would say.

But there was a buzz of excitement running through her nevertheless. "I'm definitely interested."

As she hung up, she happened to look up to see Peggy staring at her from across the parking lot with a not very nice look on her face. Same old, same old. Except then Fitz turned her head and realized it was because *Deke* was looking at her in a way she wasn't used to. And This was…not like that.

With a shake of her head, she lifted her hand in a quick wave, then hightailed it out of there.

Chapter Three

Fifteen minutes later, Fitz arrived at the library. She parked the car and got out, turning to head inside, and almost collided with… "Mrs. Bellevue."

The other woman was big, both wide and tall, and her booming voice actually sent fear running through Fitz's veins.

Maybe if Fitz hadn't spent the first fourteen years of her life on an isolated homestead with only her parents for company, things like that might not bother her quite so much. Or maybe if her parents hadn't then died in the same tornado that destroyed Inspiration, sparking a scandal that left her the object of town-wide scrutiny and speculation for over half of her life, she would have been able to brush it off.

But when this morning's statement was, "Hello, Ms. Hawkins. I'm glad to see you're wearing clothes today," Fitz fought not to visibly cringe.

"I'm sorry?" she said as she quickly glanced around in hopes that no one else was nearby.

"The other day," Mrs. Bellevue said, blocking the path up to the library. "I was afraid there'd been a fire. Why else would you be running by my house with Maximillian Deacon while wearing nothing but your undergarments?"

"It was a sports bra." Of the exact same kind that almost every other woman in town wore to run in. "And running shorts."

Mrs. Bellevue *hmph*ed. "I'd think with your history, you'd have a bit more decorum."

With my history? Fitz wanted to snap. *Would that be the part about my father disappearing in the middle of the night, abandoning Mama Gin and their three young children in order to start a new life with my mother and me?*

Fitz didn't say any of that, of course. Nor did she remind Mrs. Bellevue that she'd been as shocked as everyone else was when that was all revealed on her second day at her new high school. Helluva way to start off her life in Inspiration. Being the biggest story to hit town since, well, since her father had left Mama Gin in the first place, wasn't exactly Fitz's favorite topic of discussion. Yet it still came up on far too regular of a basis. So she drew on the same reserves she'd been drawing on for seventeen years and smiled benignly while saying, "I appreciate your concern."

Those reserves came into play big-time when Mrs. Bellevue leaned forward, and in her still-booming voice attempted to whisper, "I'd just hate to see you make a fool of yourself over him. You know better than anyone how hard it is to live those things down."

Because of people like you! Fitz wanted to shout. And anyway, what was to say Deke wouldn't be the one to make a fool of himself over *her*? As if the subject would ever come up in the first place. Plus, why would Fitz be any more of a fool than any other woman in town? For heaven's sake.

But again, she said none of that. "I certainly do," she answered, keeping her fuming to herself before mumbling something about needing to head inside to meet Dorie. Mrs. Bellevue thankfully nodded vaguely and wandered off across the town green.

Hurrying inside before there were any other encounters, Fitz gave a quick wave to Aunt Laura at the circulation desk and then headed into the office, stopping when she realized Dorie was on a Skype call with Nate. Dorie waved her in, though, so Fitz took a seat at the table in the corner with a sigh of relief. And even more of an incentive to find out more about this job.

Pushing aside a stack of handouts, she got out her laptop and did a search for Sam Price. The only reference she could find was a vague one from an interview he'd given to *Sports Illustrated* about another "big project" on the horizon. Considering the man's last "big project" was to fund the creation of a major league baseball team, the estimate of hundreds of millions of dollars probably wasn't out of line.

She sat back in the chair. So. Wow. Yes, that would definitely be a larger scale than what she was doing now. The Iowa Dream Foundation funds had been built up over the years, but it was nowhere close to what Sam Price was capable of.

Glancing over to make sure Dorie was still on the phone, Fitz clicked on the folder with the packet she'd sent to Doug back in the fall. Since she was big on being anonymous, they'd put together a portfolio that highlighted her day-to-day role rather than the foundation itself. Reviewing it now, Fitz had to admit, it looked damn impress—

"Fitz."

Fitz jumped when she realized Dorie was standing all of two feet away. She slammed her laptop shut. Not the smoothest, by any means, but the last thing she needed was anyone asking about her job search. It would create all kinds of drama, and she'd had more than enough of that in her life.

She looked up as Dorie repeated her name. "Sorry?"

"What do you think about going to the All-Star game?" Dorie asked. "Next month in San Francisco."

"Oh." Fitz had to think about that for a minute.

She'd been to the first All-Star game Nate had played in during his rookie year. It had been an experience, suffice it to say. The parties had been insane, complete with strippers and groupies galore. Plus there had been more alcohol and drugs than Fitz had seen in her entire life, not to mention most of it apparently needed to be consumed in a body shot of some kind. The guys had been so wasted, she wasn't sure they'd realized she'd spent the majority of the trip with Jules, Ella and Mama Gin. *Shopping.*

"Nate's already talking All-Star game?" she asked. "Are they even done with the balloting?"

Dorie turned her phone toward Fitz right in time for her to catch the *puh-leeze* look on Nate's face.

Fitz rolled her eyes. "Right."

With the exception of a rough start to spring training, Nate was playing better than he had at any point in his career, which was saying something. Plus he was even more of a media darling thanks to a comeback story that started with a car accident and ended with his proposal to Dorie, complete with a picture plastered everywhere from *Sports Illustrated* to *People*. Still…

Her reservations must have been obvious, because Nate chimed in with, "I'm thinking it will be a little different this time."

Dorie's "*Hmph*," left no question in Fitz's mind that the other woman was fully aware of Nate's history. "I'd hope so."

The way Nate looked at Dorie in response, though, was neither apologetic nor full of guilt, and Dorie didn't seem upset. Instead, it was clear even to Fitz, who had absolutely no experience whatsoever in these kinds of things, that whatever issues they may have had, they'd gotten past them. Or were at least dealing with them. They loved each other that much. It was so different from anything Fitz had ever experienced that she sometimes actually felt *envious*, an entirely foreign emotion. When Fitz wanted something she went for it, and a relationship of any kind wasn't even close to being on that list.

She didn't want to be tied down. Yes, during the last few months of watching Nate and Dorie fall in love she'd wondered if maybe it wouldn't be so awful to just *once* have someone look at her the way Nate looked at Dorie. But the answer was yes. It *would* be awful. She didn't ever want to depend on someone that much. She'd certainly never let a man become so important to her that the choices he made could disrupt her entire life in the way her father's choices had affected Mama Gin.

Of course, with all that said, it wasn't like Fitz had any expectation of it ever being an issue. And since she didn't have anyone to answer to, not to mention the whole man candy factor she'd managed to notice in the midst of all those body shots, well… Okay. "I would totally be up for that."

A big smile came over Dorie's face as she turned her attention back to Nate. "We're in!" Then she went on to say, "We should invite everyone. Wouldn't that be awesome?"

Nate's immediate response of, "Yeah. I think it would," surprised Fitz a little. She was pretty sure it wasn't the weekend he'd been imagining. It was all good as far as Fitz was concerned, though. As long as Dorie was there to hang out with, she couldn't care less what the guys did. Because then they'd stay out of her business and she could have fun.

Of the dancing on the bar variety.

She smiled. Yep, she was all in.

Chapter Four

The rest of Deke's day didn't go according to plan. Of course, since his plan had been to head up to Ames, drink a *lot*, and then find a woman to hook up with, maybe that wasn't the worst thing. Because as much as he needed it, he wasn't sure he wanted it. But, man, he hadn't had sex in a long time. Too long. And tonight was supposed to be the night he'd get his mojo back. Dirty, anonymous, blow-your-head-off mojo.

Instead he was doing carpool.

He'd packed up all the equipment, turned the field over to the eight-to-ten bracket, and then given in to Si and Matty's pleas to go out for pizza.

This also meant having dinner with Peggy, et al, although, thankfully, also with most of the dads joining them. Being on his own with the women didn't generally bother him, but for some reason it was the last thing he wanted today. And amidst the general grumbling about crazy schedules, honey-do lists, and, yes, the expected comments about Deke's carefree, no-strings-attached life that he shrugged off with a smile, there was a sense of contentment among the couples that he'd never noticed before.

An odd, itchy feeling settled deeply into his chest. It

made him kind of antsy, in fact. By the time he pulled into Lola's driveway, he just wanted to go home. Or, hell, since Ames wasn't happening tonight, maybe he'd go back and find Peggy after all. She'd made it overwhelmingly clear she was interested. Plus, when she wasn't being prissy about her makeup being ruined, she was a hell of a time in bed.

But right now he was definitely in a pissy mood. Foul enough to slam the door of his truck hard and see Lola's flinch as he rounded the back of it.

"I'm so sorry," she said, reaching out for the boys' backpacks when Deke got to the front door. She moved to let him in. "It's your night off. I just…" She tilted her head toward the kitchen island, where Jules sat, shoulders hunched and eyes closed.

Oh, Jesus.

Deke scrubbed his hand over his face. He was an ass.

Here was his widowed, mom-of-four sister, doing what she could to take care of her oldest friend, and here he was, pretty much without a care in the world, in a shitty mood because of an annoying case of heartburn.

He put his arm around Lola's shoulder and kissed the top of her head. "I'm yours for the night, Lo. Whatever you need. Margaritas, beer run… Hell, I can even whip up some cake batter if you want." Lola and Jules's wallowing drug of choice.

Lola's arms went around his waist and she hugged hard. "Oh, we're well past cake batter time," she said. "But I think we can take it from he—"

Her words were cut off by a shriek, followed by a roared, "James… Thomas… *McIntire*!"

A naked, dripping wet three-year-old tore down the second floor hallway. He had a head full of shampoo, his eyes were scrunched shut, and he was wailing like a banshee, a phrase Deke had never fully understood until this particular moment. Three steps behind him was an equally wet, shampoo-wearing Fitz, who was clutching the other two naked triplets, one to each side, as she tore down the hall after James.

With a sigh, Lola closed the front door. "He hates to get his hair washed."

Although Deke spent a fair amount of time with his nephews, he had to admit, whenever he was presented with the opportunity, he made a beeline for Silas and let someone else handle the triplets. "Apparently."

Leaning back against the door, Lola mumbled, "I don't suppose you could…" This time the trailing off of her voice was masterfully coordinated with that pleading look in her eyes. The look she gave him whenever she knew she was asking him to do something he didn't want to do.

Goddamn it.

"You did say anything," she added.

Not technically true. What he'd said was, whatever she needed. He was pretty sure she did not *need* him to take care of the triplets, as Fitz no doubt had it all well enough in hand, banshees notwithstanding. But Lola clearly had no intention of letting him off the hook. So with a muttered, "Hell," Deke turned his baseball cap backward on his head and climbed the stairs. He followed the trail of water down the hallway, through Lola's bedroom, right into the master bath where Fitz was wringing the hem of her shirt.

"Geez, Fitz." He was about to make some snarky comment about her letting the boys run roughshod over her, except when he looked down to see her white shirt was now entirely see-through, all he could see was the girls.

"Really?" she snapped when she looked up and saw him standing there, his eyes where they absolutely shouldn't be. "You've judged about eighteen thousand wet T-shirt contests. You can't honestly tell me this isn't anything you haven't seen."

Well, no. That didn't make it better, though.

"Sit your ass down and help me." She pointed to the spot next to her as she sank to her knees by the tub where the three boys were now playing happily. "I can't believe Lola does this every night."

Given the amount of dirt covering all four of Lola's boys on a regular basis, Deke was pretty sure that wasn't true. In fact, he could have sworn he'd seen Lola just hosing them down one night before putting them to bed.

But reassuring Fitz was a physical impossibility at the moment. She'd just straightened up and it was clear the white bra she was wearing didn't hold up to the water any better than her T-shirt had. He cleared his throat and stared hard at the wall behind her. Nudging her to the side, he took the shampoo she was handing him, while very specifically not looking down. "I can finish up here. Why don't you, uh…"

Damn it to hell, his eyes went straight to Fitz's chest again, completely of their own accord. And because it was Fitz, she was well aware of the transgression and totally pissed off. Hell, Deke was ready to knock his own head into the wall, much less wait around for Nate to do it.

Or Fitz, given that her eyes had gone narrow and her face got all pinched up. Unfortunately, it was accompanied by her folding her arms across her chest in a way that emphasized precisely the thing she was pissed at him about.

Why did women *do* that?

"Look," he said, trying to wrestle the situation into control. "I have no clue, okay? It's like a short circuit somewhere." He turned his cap back around so it was covering his eyes and leaned forward enough so he couldn't quite see her. Waving his hand out vaguely behind him, he managed to finish his thought, even though it was beyond pathetically done. "Just, um, go get some dry clothes on. Give a guy a break."

"I would be happy to 'give a guy a break,'" she muttered. She elbowed him in the gut so he'd move over, leaving no doubt in his mind what kind of break she was talking about. "But you can't even be in the same room with all three of them at once without having a panic attack. Do you honestly think I'm leaving you alone with them in a tub full of water? You can't be serious."

Leave it to Fitz to notice that. He was pretty sure even Lola had no clue the triplets scared the crap out of him.

Fine. He gave the shampoo back to Fitz and then lathered up the first one's hair.

"Uncle Deke is *not* serious," one of them said.

Luke? Maybe that one was Emmet. Deke wasn't entirely sure.

"Uncle Deke is a goofball," another answered. Except in the cute, high-pitched voice they all had going on, it came out sounding more like "poof ball."

"Gee, thanks, Dude," Deke muttered. Christ.

With a smile so sweet it made even Deke want to lay at the kid's feet, the third one looked at Fitz all dreamy-like and said, "Auntie Fitz is *very* serious. I love Auntie Fitz *so* much."

Deke was pretty sure that one was James, because his hair was a mass of dried up shampoo bubbles. Deke was also pretty impressed, because Fitz, who had been ready to kick some three-year-old butt no more than five minutes before, had completely fallen for it. All was forgiven it seemed, as she put her hands on either side of the kid's face and bent down to kiss his forehead.

"And I love James *so* much," she said.

James. Nailed it.

Clearly feeling left out, one of the other two grabbed Fitz's arm, splashing the already sopping T-shirt even more. "I love Auntie Fitz, too," he said. Then, pulling her away from James—and right into Deke, something he was doing everything possible to ignore—the kid plopped down cross-legged into the water. "I also love my penis." Then he moved his hips back and forth. "Look! It jiggles!"

It didn't surprise him at all that Fitz then sweetly said, "Uncle Deke loves his penis, too. *So* much."

Deke snorted. And he felt the laugh ripple through Fitz as she fought to contain it; a giggle so soft he only heard it because he'd turned his head to say...

Nothing. The words died in his throat when his eyes met hers and she looked so...*happy.* He wasn't sure he'd ever seen her eyes sparkle quite like that. That itchy feeling in his chest changed into something entirely different, and he had a sudden urge to lean in. To cup the back of her head and bend down and kiss her.

And, god*damn*, he almost did it. Almost lost every iota of sense he had in his head.

He was saved by a tiny three-year-old voice piping up, asking, "Do you love Auntie Fitz, too?" Followed by a gentle tugging of Deke's hat. "Do you love her penis?"

It took Deke a moment to register the question, a moment during which one of the boys managed to get hold of the shower head and begin spraying with abandon. It was enough to bring Deke back to his senses. He pulled away from Fitz, grabbed the hose and regained control. "Time to rinse you guys off and get you into bed."

And forget any of this insanity had ever happened.

Chapter Five

Fitz sat back on her heels, watching as Deke suddenly became Mr. Mom, rinsing off the boys with the utmost efficiency and speed.

Had he almost just *kissed* her?

Her hand came up to her lips. Granted, she didn't have much experience. There hadn't been a lot of boys around while she was growing up. Coming to Inspiration should have opened up some doors, but the whole Peggy thing had been humiliating enough that she'd never even looked at another boy for the rest of high school. And the downside of hanging out primarily with Nate and Co. during college meant spending far too much time in frat houses playing beer pong. Being damn good at beer pong she'd enjoyed herself immensely. She just hadn't considered it a sufficient form of seduction and therefore ended up alone in her room at the end of the evening more often than not.

So, no. Kissing wasn't exactly her area of expertise. It was possible she'd read the situation entirely wrong.

"For fuck's sake, Fitz," Deke muttered, pulling her out of her head. "A little help?"

She suppressed a nervous giggle as he turned to her, his baseball cap half-forward, half-back, thanks to his attempts to bring the boys under control. Of course now it was hard not to notice his soaking navy-blue T-shirt clinging to his pecs and shoulders…

So okay. Maybe she could forgive him for the wet T-shirt thing. She got it.

"Fitz."

Right. "Sorry." She turned her head away and reached for James. It was time for this bath to be over.

"So, uh, what next?" Deke asked when they'd gotten the three boys out of the tub and wrapped in their towels.

She looked up as he took his cap off and ran his hand through his now thoroughly wet hair. Her mouth went a little dry.

What was her *problem*? Two weeks ago he'd made her judge a burping contest in which extra points were given for substance and tone. Just the other day they'd had an argument over whether it was time to finally burn the tennis shoes in his gym bag. Which, by the way, it was.

How was she possibly finding him even close to attractive?

Shifting her gaze away from him, she said, "Nothing. I've got it from here. Don't you have a harem waiting somewhere?" There had to be *someone* ready to step up to the plate. Why he hadn't been spending more time out there, she had no clue.

Before he could offer any response, Lola appeared in the doorway. "Oh, goodness!" she exclaimed, dropping down to her knees as she gathered her boys into her arms. "Look how clean my babies are! Were you all good listeners?"

At Lola's questioning look, Fitz gave a half-hearted

grin. The triplets were the triplets. No one had any illusions they actually behaved.

In response, Lola gave a big, broad smile. "I can't tell you how nice it was to have a free afternoon," Lola was saying. "That was amazing. Thank you guys so much."

"It was nothing," Fitz said, shrugging. And that was true. Mostly. Peggy Miller wasn't a nothing, not even after all these years, but that had just been a blip of nastiness Fitz was now well used to handling. Although for Deke, the Peggy part was probably the big highlight. He'd even had dinner with her and her whole gang.

Except when Fitz glanced over at him, their eyes met and she saw that look again. Not the look from a few minutes ago, thank goodness. She didn't think she could take that again. This was the one she only saw on his face when he was worried about Lola and thought no one else was paying attention.

It passed through his eyes as she watched, turning into his trademark easy grin as Lola raised her head. "Like I said downstairs, Lo. Anything you need."

"Well, that's good," Lola answered with a grin of her own, although this one somewhat apologetic. "Because I do kind of need one more thing."

Having been the primary designated driver for years, Deke clearly knew where this was heading. He leaned back against the doorframe. "Jules is too drunk to drive herself home."

Lola nodded. "If Fitz could drive Jules's car home, and, Deke, you could bring Fitz back here afterwards…" She shrugged as her voice trailed off.

With a sigh, Fitz straightened up. Jules was her sister. And they weren't exactly besties, but Fitz did love her.

So she smiled and said, "Of course." Without another look at Deke, she headed out the bathroom door.

Deke didn't mind playing chauffeur one bit. He needed some time to get his head straight. He had almost kissed Fitz, for fuck's sake.

He was unlocking the truck when Matty screamed bloody murder. Thinking someone was dead or at least now bleeding profusely, Deke tore around the front of the house, coming to a sudden halt when he realized it was just a tantrum the likes of which Deke had never seen. He took in the scene. No blood, but Jules was kneeling on the ground, trying to contain Matty, while Lola watched from the porch, an upset Silas in her arms.

Deke glanced down at Fitz. "What happened?"

Fitz took a startled step back when he spoke. God almighty, he hoped it wasn't because of what had happened upstairs in the bathroom.

"Matty wants to spend the night here with Si," she said, "but Jules told him his dad is coming to get him in the morning and…"

"*I don't want to go with Dad!*" Matty wailed, pushing away from Jules so hard she had to put her hand behind her in order not to fall.

"Whoa." Deke went over to Jules and Matty and crouched beside them. "Dude, you can't go around pushing girls. You gotta be gentle." Matty and Jules weren't his by blood, but Deke was as much Matty's uncle as Nate was, so he had no problem getting in Matty's face. "What's the problem here?"

The boy's eyes filled with a fresh set of tears and his lip started trembling. "I don't want to—"

"Go with your dad," Deke cut in before the hysteria took hold again. "Okay. But it's one of those things you just gotta do."

"But…but…" Matty sputtered. He looked over at Si and Lola, and then back at Deke. As if Jules wasn't six inches away and couldn't hear every word, he whispered, "Mom and Dad fight all the time. I…" He hiccupped as his gaze shifted to where Si was standing with Lola. "I just want to live here for now and you can be my dad like you are for Si. And I can stay until my dad comes back to live at home."

Well, fuck. Deke had no freaking idea of what to say to that. Jules's heartbreaking hiss of breath didn't help.

"Oh, honey," Jules said, leaning forward and putting her hands on Matty's cheeks. She guided him to look at her. "We've talked about this. Daddy has a new house now. He's not coming back to live with us."

To be honest, Deke never had an issue with Jeremiah the way Nate had. He mostly didn't feel much one way or another. But a married man should keep his goddamn dick in his pants except with the woman he married. It wasn't even close to fair that Jules had to be the one to pick up the pieces. That it spilled over to Lola, and even to Fitz, who had enough bad memories of her own when it came to this shit, made it that much worse. Deke was the town bartender and he did everything possible to keep his nose out of people's business and not choose sides. But in that moment, he hated Jeremiah with more passion than he'd known he had inside him.

Forcing it all back, Deke said to Matty, "Hey buddy, I have an idea," knowing full well Fitz was probably rolling her eyes at what she would say was his typical male need to try and fix things. He gave her a preemptive glare before turning back and saying, "Why don't I take you and Si—"

"Out for ice cream?" Matty said, earning Deke frowns and glares from the moms in the crowd.

"Noooo," he answered, drawing out the word and trying to sound offended they'd even think that was what he'd planned to do. "I have some guy stuff that needs to get done. I need some guys to help me do it."

"Like what?" Matty asked, clearly suspicious.

As he should be. What the fuck did "guy stuff" even mean?

Deke threw another glare over at Fitz, who, with her arms folded across her chest—could no one give the woman a dry shirt?—was trying desperately not to laugh as she obviously thought the same thing.

"Like…" Deke took off his baseball cap and rubbed the back of his neck. "I need to get the paint for Si's front door."

Which was true. Lola had never liked the development she lived in. It had been Dave's idea to live in a neighborhood because of how often he was deployed. And Lola went along with it, thinking one day she'd get her farmhouse when Dave finally came home for good. So much for that idea. But she was finally starting to come out of her grief-stricken shell enough to get things back to where she wanted them. Like having a fire-engine red front door. It was going to piss off the neighborhood association to no end, something Deke fully supported since it meant he was finally getting his feisty, pain-in-the-ass sister back.

"Gotta pick up some lightbulbs for the bar," he added, thinking that as long as he was running around town, he may as well get the rest of his shit done. "And the team shirts for the Father's Day Tournament."

This time when he looked up, the ladies were all staring at him. "What?"

"It's seven o'clock," Lola said, making a point of looking at her watch and then giving an equally pointed look at Matty. "His bedtime is eight thirty."

Bedtime. Right. This was why Deke happily handed off his kids to their parents when practice was done. His idea of bedtime involved a woman and lingerie. Sometimes toys.

He made a show of rolling his eyes as he turned back to Matty. "It's guy stuff. Guy stuff takes half the time girl stuff does." He elbowed Matty's side. "Am I right or am I right?"

He got the giggle he'd been aiming for, which brought the tension down a few notches as planned, and had the boys back in their seats and on the road within five minutes. And sure enough, by 8:30, after taking a ten-minute detour for, yes, ice cream, he was turning into Jules's driveway after dropping Si off at home.

Bringing Matty into the house, he found Jules's older two kids in the family room. "Where's your mom and Aunt Fitz?"

Geo, who was eleven, barely grunted, caught up in whatever device he was playing. Thirteen-year-old Emily rolled her eyes as Matty went to sit next to her on the couch. "They're still in the car. Mom said she had to talk to Aunt Fitz for a while, but she's totally freaking about Dad. Sooo obvious."

Since she was the closest thing to a niece he had, Deke had no problem calling her on her shit. "Maybe you could give your mom a bit of a break."

With a wave of her hand, Emily just focused on the TV. "Whatever."

Rather than get into it with her, he headed back outside.

It was easy enough to see how he'd missed them. Fitz had parked in the shadow of the garage and the glare from the floodlight blocked the view of the front seats.

He went to the driver's side and rested his arms on the open window, realizing too late it put him close enough to Fitz to catch a hint of something citrusy. Since when did she wear *perfume*? Maybe it was just the boys' shampoo. Of course that just made him think about her T-shirt again. The way her breasts would fit perfectly in the palms of his hands.

Christ.

He was saved by Jules, who closed her eyes and leaned back into her seat. "She hates me."

Forcing his attention away from Fitz, he looked up at Jules. "What? Who?"

"Emily. I mean, she's thirteen. She's supposed to hate her mother." She turned to look at Fitz. "Right? Who doesn't hate their mom at thirteen?"

If Deke hadn't been so close to Fitz, he might not have noticed how still she went or the pain that flashed through her eyes. Since Fitz had been about that age when she lost her own mother, Deke figured it was a loaded question. At the same time, he didn't really know what kind of relationship she'd had with her mom. She never talked about either of her parents, and since the subject was basically *Keep the Fuck Out* territory, no one else ever brought it up.

The fact that Jules raised the subject despite how it might make Fitz feel, however, stirred up something

Deke couldn't fully identify. It made him want to get in Jules's face and ask her what the *fuck* she'd been thinking. Fitz had been in the car when her mother was killed, for God's sake. Since Jules was obviously dealing with some shit of her own, he held back.

But as Deke talked himself down, his eyes happened to catch Fitz's. Judging from her expression, she knew where his thoughts had gone and seemed a little surprised.

Well, hell. He was, too. He never lost his shit. *Never.* Right now, though, his heart was actually racing. He almost jumped out of his skin when Fitz gently placed her hand on his wrist.

She wasn't very touchy-feely. Unless she was smacking him in the arm, of course. Rather than calling attention to it by saying anything, though, which would completely piss her off, he straightened up out of his crouch, took a step back and away, and then opened the car door for her. After looking at him for a minute, partly amused, partly wary, she reached down for her purse and got out of the car. She threw an uncertain look at him over her shoulder as she and Jules walked up the path to the door, leaving him to stand there, watching them.

Which was fine. He couldn't quite get a handle on any single one of his senses at the moment. He needed a minute.

That minute didn't do jack, though, because afterward he still didn't know which way was up. He closed the car door and went inside.

Chapter Six

Fitz gave a little tug on Jules's arm and brought her into the house. There was no need to start something that would get both Jules and Emily upset, so they avoided the family room and headed straight upstairs instead. And maybe she was a little bit worried about herself, too. She'd spent a long time keeping her past where it belonged, and the key, she'd found, was to neatly pack her emotions away. But it was like Deke was on a Tilt-A-Whirl and he'd forced her to come along.

No, not forced her—he'd made her want to. She'd wanted to kiss him. She'd wanted to cry when he'd knelt down next to Matty, when he'd reined in his anger over Jeremiah.

And oh, God, when he'd almost gone at Jules because Fitz's feelings might have been hurt… She'd had the urge to throw her arms around him and, well, she didn't know. She had no idea how to handle any of it. This was Nate and Dorie's fault for sure. Their whole happy vibe was so strong it was eating up everyone in its path and making Fitz have all these odd *feelings*.

Fitz kept up a steady patter as they walked, something about Nate's game that day, all the while trying to keep her head from spinning. She got them to the master bedroom and steered Jules to the bed before heading into the bathroom. Her official purpose was to get a cool washcloth in case Jules needed it, but honestly, it was Fitz who needed a minute to splash water on her face.

She'd just turned off the water when she heard Deke come in the room and Jules ask, "Did Emily say anything to you?" Before Deke could respond, Jules went on a bit more about thirteen-year-olds and their mothers. And, honestly, Fitz couldn't take it. She wouldn't cry. She'd learned early on how to keep herself from breaking down under all sorts of circumstances. But that didn't mean she was ready to listen to ramblings about teenage girls and their moms. Preparing herself for however long she needed to wait it out, Fitz sighed and started counting the tiles on the wall, a task she was engrossed in right up until the moment Jules said her name.

"Fitz should hate me, too, you know."

Um... What?

After a slight pause, Deke laughed. "I'm pretty sure she didn't mind driving you home, Jules."

"I wish I could have been like you," Jules continued as if he hadn't said anything. "Always part of that crowd but somehow still removed."

What crowd? Was Jules talking about high school? *Why?*

But if so, there was no way this conversation was progressing any further. That crowd, Deke and Nate excepted, had made Fitz's life even more of a living hell than it had needed to be. She had no interest in reliving even a little of it.

With as much noise as possible, Fitz came into the bedroom. "Here we go." She brought the washcloth over to Jules, pulled back the covers and plumped up the pillows. "Is there anything else you need?" she asked, hoping against hope Jules would just drop it. She could already feel Deke's eyes boring into her.

Jules, however, wasn't cooperating one bit. "How can you be so nice to me?"

Forcing a smile, Fitz said, "You're my sister. Of course I'm being nice."

"Half-sister," Jules corrected gently, "and we never let you forget it back then, did we? Even though what Dad did hurt you as much as it hurt us." She put her arms around herself. "I wanted everyone at school to hate you. Nate's blamed Jeremiah for all this time, but he should have been blaming me."

Jeremiah was a jerk. Fitz had known that from the first time she laid eyes on him, three days after she'd started at her new school. She remembered as clearly as if it had been yesterday, in fact. The tornado happened in July, so the summer itself was mostly a blur, but she'd resolved to move forward as best she could on that first day of school and it had gone much better than anticipated. It was day two when the news about who she was came out and everything crashed and burned. By day three she'd begun to make her list of who to avoid as much as possible, with Jeremiah being at the top, something she'd kept to herself for all of the seventeen years since.

But it was fine. If Jules needed this to process what was going on with the man as part of their divorce, Fitz could handle it. In the scheme of things, it wasn't that big of a deal.

"I'm okay with the nickname, Jules."

The nickname hadn't come until the spring and by

that time Fitz had developed a much thicker skin. No, it hadn't exactly been her favorite moment to sit in her history class and endure an entire discussion on how medieval law handled bastard children. Or to find out that "Fitz" was the surname they'd used at the time. But when her teacher had looked right at her and provided "Fitzpatrick" as an example, Fitz had known the town would never forgive Patrick Hawkins or his illegitimate daughter for what he'd done, and she'd better get used to it. Jeremiah started calling her Fitz and it stuck.

But it was something Fitz had actually come to take pride in. Well, not pride so much as *I don't give a fuck*, a feeling Nate had helped her perfect.

"Really," she said. "I wouldn't have let people call me that for all these years if it was a problem."

Except then Jules teared up. "Not the nickname." She shook her head. "I just found out what Peggy did."

Fitz's first thought was, *That's why you drank so much today?*

But then she realized the ramifications of that statement and all the air left her lungs as she froze in place.

Please do not be referring to the most humiliating moment of my entire life.

Please do not be referring to it in front of Deke, of all people.

The ground dropped out from beneath Fitz's feet and her head started spinning, and not in a happy-ish, Tilt-A-Whirl way.

"I think maybe they did it because of Jeremiah," Jules was saying, "Because he kept teasing you and I didn't make him stop. But I… I didn't know. I swear I didn't kno—"

Deke started toward them, a look of confusion on his

face as he started to say, "Know what?" But Fitz spoke over him and asked, "How did you find out?"

"Tristan told me," Jules said. "Over dinner last night."

Tristan was Tuck's younger brother. He'd been a couple of years ahead in school and a friend of Jeremiah's. More a friend of Jules, apparently, since he'd taken her side in the divorce, but they'd all known each other for a really long time. He'd even dated Peggy for a while after she and Nate broke up. Then again, so had Deke.

Summoning up all the strength in the universe, Fitz briskly said, "It was nothing. Peggy's a bitch." Deke went tense and Fitz was momentarily sorry. That was another sentiment she'd kept to herself for half her life, this time out of deference to Deke and his thing for Peggy. His inexplicable thing, but whatever.

"It's not nothing," Jules persisted. "If Nate hadn't gotten there in time, Lyle might have…"

And now they were entering forbidden waters. "Do you need a glass of water?" Fitz asked, hoping Jules would get the freaking *hint*.

But Jules refused to be put off.

"I watch Emily try and protect Geo and Matt from everything," she said, "and I get so angry because they're getting so battered by this divorce. Then I think about how Ella did that with Nate and with me, but…" With tears streaming down her face, she looked up at Fitz. "It wasn't just that you had no one. That you had lost both your parents in the storm when we'd only lost Dad. But I was so…" A shudder ran through her as she looked away. As the *guilt* came over her face. "So awful."

Fitz had never blamed Jules for any of that high school stuff. Peggy Miller, yes. And Jeremiah for being a complete asshole because he'd wanted to impress Jules, who had made her dislike of Fitz clear way back then? Absolutely. Jules, however? Even back when Jules was being horrible, Fitz had understood how badly she was hurting, too. As devastated and even angry as Fitz had been, she'd never doubted her father's love for her. She wasn't the one he had left. Jules was. Nate and Ella and Mama Gin.

More than ready to leave, Fitz turned to Deke just as Jules, in an entirely un-Jules-like meek little voice, asked, "Did they... Did they touch you?"

"What?" Fitz's head snapped back to Jules. As in *touch* touched? "*No.*"

God, no.

Yes, Peggy was the meanest of mean girls, as far as Fitz was concerned. And Fitz had been a naive, innocent, *broken* fifteen-year-old girl who fell so easily for Peggy's whole "Deke likes you" line that her entire being lit up the moment she heard that the object of her crush, the one freaking ray of light after her parents died, might like her, too. That he wanted to actually meet her back out behind the school. So Fitz had gone out to the shed thinking she'd be seeing Deke, but instead got Lyle Butler, the town bully, along with two of his friends, and she realized she'd been had. She'd been so angry and mortified it hadn't occurred to her until afterwards that they could truly have hurt her. Done so much more.

That day was the first time she'd really understood how alone she was. That she had no one to watch her back, no one but herself to ensure her own survival. Standing there, facing off against three boys, each about twice her size, watching them come at her, getting all handsy and leering at her… She'd taken every ounce of fury at what the world had handed her and unleashed it on them. She'd scratched and hit and kicked enough to startle them, and then Nate had gotten there before they got around to fighting back. They'd been too embarrassed to even look her way again.

But she'd taken care of it. It was done.

"No," she repeated. "They didn't touch me." And she never wanted to talk about this again.

As she was about to say when she felt Deke move beside her. The look on his face was nothing short of murderous.

She'd known the man for seventeen years, sixteen of those as friends. The closest he got to being mad was when his piecrust didn't come out right. He was an insane perfectionist when it came to pastry. But he tended not to get angry. She wasn't sure she'd ever seen him even lose his patience with anyone, much less Jules, who he loved almost as much as he loved Lola. That was even less okay than the weird almost kissing thing. Fitz's very existence had already almost destroyed one family she loved; she had no interest in upsetting another.

She gave Deke a look he'd damn well better take as a warning, before turning back to Jules. "It was a long time ago. We were kids. We're not anymore."

"I don't need you to pretend to forgive me," Jules said, her voice wavering. "I just need you to know I'll make it right someday. Somehow I'll—"

"There's nothing to forgive." Discussion closed. "We both got handed a raw deal. You've booted Jeremiah out of your life, and as far as I'm concerned, that makes us even." Then, with every ounce of strength Fitz had, she smiled. "Please. We need to be done talking about this because Deke's gotten a major overdose of estrogen and God knows how devastating a threat that is to the female population of Inspiration. I think his dick might be shrinking as we speak."

"Hey!" Deke exclaimed as expected while Jules's eyes went wide and she gave a shocked laugh. Fitz wouldn't normally have said something like that in mixed company, but it had to be done. Anything to stop things from getting even more out of hand.

Except Jules surprised them both and said, "It might not be the worst of things for the ladies of Inspiration to get less of Deke," as she gave a vague wave in his direction.

And now Fitz was the one looking at Jules in shock.

"Really?" Deke said, as Fitz and Jules both burst into laughter. But he seemed relieved, too. Turning to Jules, he asked, "Is there anything else you need tonight? Anything with the kids?"

Wiping her eyes with the back of her hand, Jules shook her head. "Thank you, though. For everything."

"Okay, great," Fitz said as brightly as she possibly could. The damage had already been done. "See you tomorrow." Then she walked straight past Deke and to the door. From behind her, she heard Deke say, "Love you, Jules. You take care," but she didn't wait for him. She needed distance. She called out good night to Emily and the boys as she headed out to Deke's truck.

There was a reason she'd spent the last sixteen years hanging out with guys who had no interest in chatting about anything, much less their feelings. Since that fateful conversation with Peggy, in fact. It was a *don't ask, don't tell*, kind of thing and Fitz was good with that.

She'd been pathetic and needy back then. She wasn't now. The last thing she'd needed tonight was a reminder of where she'd been.

It had been a pitiful story, of course; one picked up by the national media over and over again, the tragedy that was the counterpoint to the feel-good story of the scrappy high school basketball team they'd nicknamed The Dream. The fifteen-year-old girl who'd been in the car with her parents on a road outside of Inspiration when the tornado hit. Whose parents had been torn from the car and killed but who herself was left unharmed. Traumatized and unwilling to speak for weeks after that, but with barely even a scrape on her. With no family or even friends to claim her, she'd been placed in the nearest foster home available, with the Jensens on their farm.

That the farm was in Inspiration, the town in which Fitz's father had left a whole other family was just part of the worst luck ever. A family Fitz had no knowledge of and vice versa. That Mama Gin had even considered adopting her, much less gone ahead and done it, had been just another step in the surreal dream over the course of that year. Fitz wasn't at all surprised at how Jules had reacted back in the beginning. She still had days she couldn't believe how soon Nate had come around. Largely, as it turned out, thanks to the Lyle Butler incident. When Nate had come charging around the corner of the shed, she'd even had a moment of thinking he'd been part of it. But then he'd come to a sudden stop and actually smiled when he saw she'd, well, laid them all out. A few days later he made it clear to the entire school that he had her back and he'd been her staunchest supporter ever since.

The irony of it all was supremely satisfying. The very thing Peggy had hoped would put Fitz in her place actually ended up putting Nate squarely in Fitz's corner. That moment after the shed was the first civil conversation she and Nate had ever had. The first time in seven months of knowing about each other and walking the same halls that he'd done anything other than glance in her direction before looking away. But he'd come to find her after the shed to make sure she was okay. She'd said she'd be fine if he could keep it from ever seeing the light of day, and he'd somehow buried it deep enough that Fitz had never heard anyone so much as hint at it.

Until toda—

She jumped when she felt a hand on her shoulder and whirled around to see Deke. She wasn't big on being touched by anyone other than the kids. And Dorie, oddly enough. Dorie was a hugger. It had put Fitz off completely at first, but she'd kind of gotten used to it by now.

"Jesus, Fitz," Deke muttered. "You want to tell me what that was all about?"

"No."

She'd never wanted anyone to know it had even happened, *especially* not Deke. For reasons that changed over time but were as equally important now as they were back then. No way she was about to share the details now.

She went to the passenger side door and grabbed the handle. "Can we just go home?" She knew he was glaring at her, but she refused to look at him, instead staring out her window once she'd climbed inside.

The drive back to Lola's was silent and excruciatingly long. She didn't care. She didn't have heart-to-hearts on a regular basis with *anyone*, and she wasn't about to start now. But when they pulled up to the house and she moved to open the door, he reached out and put his hand on her leg to stop her. Before she could fully register it was there, she felt something stir inside her. Being She Of So Little Experience—and also She Who Had Just Recently Been Reminded How A Once Upon A Time Deke-Crush Had Led To Disastrous Consequences— she just stared at it. But her breath caught and the rush from that almost-kiss flew through her.

She pulled her leg away. Pulled her whole self away.

After everything that had happened earlier she felt raw. Exposed. Flayed and still bleeding. Just like that, this thing she'd kept so carefully contained was suddenly back out in the open again. The idea of going from cool and capable Fitz Hawkins back to poor little Angelica Wade was terrifying.

"You've gotta know," he said, "I'm not letting this go."

No, he wouldn't. He might be the most happy-go-lucky guy in the world, but when he cared for someone it ran deep. She closed her eyes, trying not to cry as long-ago emotions rose up to the surface. Doing everything she could to hide it, she attempted to brush it off with a brisk, "Oh, perfect. So now what, you go all protective on me?"

She was too emotional. Not only didn't she pull it off, it backfired completely.

"What the fuck is that supposed to mean?" Deke actually sounded kind of pissed off.

Unusual for him, but much easier for Fitz to deal with. Unlike him, she got angry regularly. She just didn't tell anyone she did. "It means I don't want your *pity*, okay? It was a long time ago. I'm over it."

"*Pity?*" he asked. He'd gone straight to DEFCON five. Or one. Whatever the bad one was.

It was an entirely new side of him. Fitz watched with fascination as his hands gripped the steering wheel so hard his knuckles went white and his breathing turned shallow. "You think I *pity* you?"

"I think you're looking for something to fix," she snapped, maybe getting a little too up in his face.

"I'm not trying to *fix* anything." His whole body shifted toward her. "I can't fix something if I don't know what's broken."

"I'm not *broken*." She jabbed his shoulder. "That's the whole point!"

"I didn't say *you* were broken, for Christ's sake." He grabbed her hand. "Stop putting words in my mouth."

Pulling back again, she reached for the door handle with her other hand. "Whatever. You don't need to treat me like your little sister. Nate does that well enough on his own."

Deke gave a harsh laugh and, looking down, muttered, "Like my sister. Right."

Which made her realize he was staring down at where his hand grasped her wrist.

The hair on the back of her neck stood up as his head came up and he stared at her. A coil of heat unfurled in her belly and began to work its way down.

And then his hand was cupping her head and he was pulling her to him and his lips were on hers and…

Oh.

Oh, *God*.

Before she could think twice, she straightened up and leaned into him. All those unreliable emotions had her opening her mouth to his. She had every intention of putting a stop to it—she needed to *think* for a minute, damn it—but instead found herself threading her fingers through his hair. Through those tendrils that curled under right there at the back of his neck. She wanted to nuzzle her way into the crook of his shoulder just to have all that softness wash over her.

He cradled her head, tilting it back just so. She opened her eyes and looked into his and…

No.

She wrenched herself away, putting distance between them as she shrank back against the door. Her chest heaved as she gasped in air; her hand shook when she raised it to her lips.

"Oh," she whispered. "My God."

She reached behind her and opened the door, then jumped out before he could say a word.

Chapter Seven

Deke watched as she ran up to Lola's front walk. He felt the sting as he slammed his hands down on the steering wheel.

"*Fuck!*"

What the hell had possessed him? And, yes, he'd been possessed, unable to stop himself from pulling her to him, so desperate and raw that in hindsight he wasn't sure it could even be called a kiss.

God*damn* it.

He should have said something about earlier. Apologized for whatever it was that had passed between them over the boys' bath and told her he'd figure it out and it wouldn't happen again. But now...

No. *Hell*, no.

Apologies, followed by denial. Put it behind them and move the fuck on.

"*Fuck!*" he shouted again to no one in particular, before putting the truck into gear and heading home.

It wasn't even so much the kiss, although that in itself was more than enough. What was truly getting to him was that something had happened to her, in high school it seemed, and he had no idea what it was. He had no idea it had even happened. How the hell had he missed it? They'd barely spent a day apart from each other in years, for Christ's sake.

Deke jabbed the button to close the garage door behind him and pulled the Deacon's truck alongside his Jeep. Times like these, he was glad he lived in a converted warehouse with an entire floor to himself, with only one neighbor—Jason—on the floor above him, and a basement that was half garage and half basketball court. He turned up the music loud, changed into a pair of basketball shorts and grabbed a ball, thinking about Fitz the whole time.

It sure as hell went beyond her goddamned nickname, which, incidentally, he'd hated from the day she'd gotten it. It had been in the early days of the Iowa Dream ridiculousness—late March, probably, since they'd just taken the State title. They'd done one of those morning radio shows up in Ames, and came back to find a commotion at school. In reality, it had probably been only a few kids, but in Deke's memory, almost everyone in the school was lining the hallways, the tribe turning on its weakest link, building nothing into something in the way of high school kids everywhere.

And there was Fitz, her only offense being that she was the bastard child of Patrick Hawkins, throwing her shoulders back in defiance even as tears streamed down her face. As if she hadn't already been through enough. Before he could so much as step forward, though, Lola was already there and pretty much telling everyone else off. But the nickname was there for good.

Well, whatever. As Fitz had said tonight, she was "fine" with it. As vivid as that day was in his memory, it was apparently just a blip on her radar, whereas this other thing Jules had brought up was a whole battleship being blown sky high.

Jesus. What *was* it?

About a hundred free throws later, the only conclusion Deke had come to was that he needed to talk to Nate. He didn't give a shit if it was two in the morning. He shut down the lights on the court and headed up to his loft as he dialed the phone. When Nate picked up, sleepily muttering, "Deke, what the...?" Deke immediately launched into, "You want to tell me what happened to Fitz back in high school and why Jules would feel the need to apologize for it?"

"Are they okay?" Nate snapped, fully awake now.

"Define *okay.*"

"Fuck," Nate muttered. "What happened?"

After Deke gave the short and not-so-sweet rundown, Nate said, "So, yeah, I guess that puts you in need-to-know territory."

"Well, *yeah,*" Deke echoed back. "Considering I love each of them as much as I love my own sister, I would sincerely fucking hope I'm in need-to-know territory." Jesus. He went over to his bar and poured a shot of Jack.

"You remember when we found out about Fitz?" Nate asked.

Deke sat down on his couch, glass in hand. He put his feet up on the slab of concrete that served as his coffee table, and let his head fall back as his eyes closed. "You mean the day you found out she was your sister?"

That was way before the nickname. The second or third day of school. Deke, Wash and Nate had been walking down the hall after Phys. Ed. when, as one, they'd come to a sudden stop at the sight of Mama Gin standing in the hallway with the principal. Her lips were trembling and there were tears in her eyes. "Yeah. I remember."

The tornado had happened in July, but because Fitz's father had been going by the name of Patrick Wade when he died, not Patrick Hawkins, it had taken a month or so for all the pieces to be put together.

"Not my shining moment," Nate said.

Not any of theirs.

The whispers had already begun before the school day was over. Overnight, Fitz went from "Who's the cute new girl?" to "Nate and Jules's father left them for *her*?"

Being all of sixteen years old, figuring out what to say to the best friend who'd just found out his dad had gone and started a new family wasn't exactly in Deke's wheelhouse. Especially because he actually had a bit of a crush on Fitz after seeing her at the Jensens' farmhouse over the course of that summer. Deke liked to think that if he'd been older and wiser, her being Nate's sister wouldn't have rattled him quite as much. But back then, he'd let himself get caught up in other things. Let the rest of his life crowd her out of his mind because her considerable baggage was more than his teenage self could handle. He hadn't just taken the easy route, he'd made a beeline for it and never looked back.

But the guilt Nate still carried was clearly much worse. Nate had never been outright mean during those months—he'd never even gone as far as Jules had, outwardly making his feelings known. But he hadn't done anything to stop the teasing and taunting. Had never so much as told Jules to have Jeremiah tone it down.

"Maybe if I'd done something earlier," Nate said, "they would've let it all go and just left her alone."

They being Peggy and Jeremiah and Lyle Butler and Co., Deke assumed.

Goddammit.

Deke loved Inspiration; it was his own personal Mayberry. Sure there'd been times when folks hadn't exactly been on their best behavior, the treatment of Fitz being an obvious low point. But it wasn't like Fitz had been moping around for all this time. Deke had put those days behind him, and he'd always figured her smile meant she had, too. It was almost too painful to think about that not being the truth she lived every day.

"Tell me the rest," Deke said.

"It was maybe a few weeks after the nickname," Nate answered. "I was in the locker room after practice and I heard one of the guys say something about the equipment shed."

Right. Where Lyle and his friends hung out, usually drinking and smoking whatever they'd been able to score. Not fully Deke's crowd, but close enough, as Jules had ever-so-helpfully pointed out. He leaned forward and squeezed his eyes shut even though he already had a sense of what was coming.

"There were three of them. Butler and his boys," Nate said. "They were pushing her around, telling her no one wanted her there. Pretty much saying it would have been best if she died the day her parents did." A pause, and then… "Trying to get their hands on her and hold her down."

Deke sucked in a deep breath. His eyes stung. "She said they didn't…"

"No," Nate answered, knowing exactly where Deke was going. "She was fighting them off. By the time I got to them, they were, well… Pissed." Except then a smile came into his voice, and there was flat-out pride as he added, "She did some damage. Enough for me to see, even though they were all mostly covered in mud."

Nate paused and took a breath so ragged Deke could hear it over the phone. "They did it because of me, Deke. In *my* name. My own freaking girlfriend told them I wanted Fitz to know her place. I mean, Fitz handled it. She totally took them on. But it made me realize what my uncle had been trying to tell me all along. I could hate my dad all I wanted, but ignoring Fitz only made it worse. It wasn't her fault. And…" His voice trailed off again for a minute. "She was utterly alone."

Which, ironically, was what Jules had also said. Even more ironic since, yes, Nate's family hadn't just taken Fitz in, they'd claimed her officially, with Mama Gin adopting Fitz by the start of the next school year and making sure she shared their last name. But it had still taken a while for Jules and Ella to come around.

It begged the question, "Jeremiah…?"

"No," Nate answered. "He wasn't part of the shed thing. I don't think he even had a clue until after it happened. I mean, I have to believe we would have known if he was *that* bad."

Yeah, Deke had to agree. He'd spent many a holiday sharing a table with both of them and it had never been anything but polite. Even earlier tonight, Fitz hadn't seemed particularly upset by anything Jeremiah had done. Not the way she'd reacted when Jules said…

Oh *shit*.

Shit, shit, shit, shit, *shit*.

With a sinking heart, Deke asked, "What exactly did Peggy do?" Because, yes, that's who Nate had been dating back then. Deke had often wondered why he'd broken it off with her so suddenly and without any explanation to any of them.

There was a long pause before Nate answered, "She's the one who sent Fitz out to the shed."

The air went out of Deke's lungs.

What?

Suddenly unable to sit still, Deke jumped to his feet and ran his hand through his hair. He started pacing. "How did I not know this?"

Nate didn't even sound defensive. "Fitz made me seal that promise in blood."

Finding himself at the windows overlooking the river, Deke let his head fall against the glass. "I can't unknow it."

"I know," Nate said, his voice full of true regret. "I'm so damned sorry. I think that's why Fitz wanted to keep it quiet."

Which, yes, was her right. Absolutely. If she needed the insulation around herself, then more power to her. But…

Wait. That wasn't what Nate had said. With extreme wariness, Deke asked, "What's why?"

Nate hesitated for a few seconds before answering, "Look, she knows how much Inspiration means to you."

"Me?"

Yes, he loved his town. But it wasn't like he didn't know there was a dark side.

And, said the little angel on his shoulder, *he really did think she'd put it behind her.*

What a fucking idiot you are, the little devil on the other shoulder chimed in.

Maybe he was in denial. Maybe she woke up dreading every day. It was clearly something he needed to be more attuned to. For now, though, he wouldn't dwell on the fact that Fitz had never clued him in, *couldn't* let himself even contemplate that his being with Peggy may have hurt her in some way. He just had to make sure he wasn't near anyone who had been a part of hurting someone he loved.

"Are you okay?" Nate asked, reminding Deke they were still on the phone.

The phone that Deke now looked at as if Nate could see the disbelief on his face. "You're asking *me* if I'm okay?"

Not one to beat around the bush, Nate said, "Well, you have been sleeping with her on and off for the last fifteen years."

Just because he was thinking about sleeping with Fitz didn't mean he'd actually done it.

Then he realized Nate meant Peggy. Of course.

And *then* he realized Nate thought there was actually a chance Deke would put Peggy before Fitz. "Are you *shitting* me?"

Yet it was definitely relief in Nate's voice when he said, "Good. Because I need you to make sure Fitz is okay."

"You want me to check on Fitz. *Now?*"

It was the middle of the night. They were nowhere close to nocturnal visits.

And, *Christ*, they were never going to be. Hell, given the way she'd run from his car, he'd be lucky if she didn't straight out slap him the next time they saw each other.

"Fuck, no—it's, what, two in the morning?" Nate was clearly wondering what had gotten into Deke's head. If he knew the truth, however, there was no way he'd be saying, "You are now aware of a situation Fitz has kept under wraps for sixteen years, a situation Jules chose to bring to the surface at a time when there's not a thing I can do about it. When there's not a fucking thing I can do for either of them. Whether you like it or not, you're close to some of the people who made Fitz's life a living hell and who she still has to deal with on a regular basis. So, yes, I would like some goddamn reassurance from one of my freaking best friends in the world that my sisters are not about to implode while I'm playing a fucking *ball game* in Tampa Bay!"

Since Deke felt guilty as hell for all of the above, not to mention fully understanding the reason for Nate's tirade, he made his second mistake of the night, muttering, "Maybe you need to start thinking about coming home for good. Look after your sisters all on your own."

Idiot. The last thing he wanted was Nate swooping in to take care of Fitz. Deke had been her best friend for years. That job was his.

Chapter Eight

Fitz spent the night tossing and turning, alternating between telling herself that the kiss was the biggest mistake she'd ever made, cringing in embarrassment that she'd flat out run away from him, and wondering, *Oh, God, when can we do that again?*

Once she fell asleep, there was no question how her subconscious felt. Her dreams were so X-rated she was an overheated mess when she woke up. She looked around for a minute, disoriented.

She was in her room, one hundred percent alone.

Thank God.

The rest of the morning passed…strangely. On a normal day, Fitz wouldn't think twice about dropping in to see Deke. Today, though, she couldn't decide whether she wanted to pretend the kiss hadn't happened and go about business as usual, or if she should man up, seek him out and have the conversation so they could acknowledge it and move on.

Of course there was also the option of tracking him down at his bar, hauling him into the back room and acting out at least one of those dreams.

Oh, for heaven's sake. She was a grown woman and

he was one of her best friends. They could weather one kiss. Even a spectacular one.

The morning's emails and phone calls weren't nearly interesting enough to get her mind off it, so she left her office thinking she'd go get some coffee at Jules's café. She was almost there when she heard Peggy call her name. Plastering a smile on her face, she turned around. "Hi, Peggy."

"Did you order the extra tables I asked for?" the other woman said, launching into her demands without even a pretense of Iowa nice.

Fighting the urge to grit her teeth, Fitz answered, "Of course I did. The extra chairs, too. I even got them to throw in extra tablecloths at no additional charge." Because that's what she did; she made things happen. It just sucked big-time that as a co-sponsor of Inspiration's Fifty-ninth Annual Father's Day Little League Tournament with the local Jaycees, of which Peggy was chair, Fitz had to make them happen with Peggy Miller. God help her if she was still in Inspiration for the sixtieth.

Trying not to show her irritation as Peggy went through a to-do list of things Fitz had taken care of days ago, Fitz almost didn't notice Peggy's smile had suddenly grown wider, brighter, and sultry in a way Fitz could never pull off. In fact, Fitz was doing everything possible not to be blatant about readjusting her bra strap when…

"Ladies."

The strap snapped into place as she spun around. Peggy smirked and took a step closer to Deke as though it were a requirement to have one golden person standing next to another so they could look down their noses at the little people. To Fitz's deep satisfaction, Deke gave Peggy a bit of a frown and took a step away. A step closer to Fitz, in fact. Although Fitz couldn't work the sultry thing, she had no problem whatsoever with the smug *Take That* smile instead.

Of course, realizing Deke was observing all this with amusement wiped the smirk off her face. She was thirty-two years old. Peggy might stoop that low but Fitz refused to.

Or, rather, she was at least embarrassed about it.

She turned to Deke. "Hi." And that was it. She'd eaten lunch with the man practically every day for sixteen years and she was suddenly incapable of uttering a word.

Really. What was the right thing to say? *Did you mean to kiss me like that last night? Might you be interested in trying again?*

As much as she knew neither of those would fly, she was one hundred percent certain they were both better than the other question running through her mind: *If I ran my tongue around your nipple would you be more likely to groan my name the way you did in erotic dream number one last night, or go the darker route, like in dream number two, and bend me over your knee and spank me a few times because I hadn't asked properly?*

"Fitz," he said, his voice low and raspy and not helping at all. "You okay?"

Not if you keep looking at me like that.

Now it was Fitz's turn to take a step back as she attempted to nod her head. She was feeling flushed and slightly dizzy. Not at all up to what was their usual sparring, although clearly Deke wasn't going there either.

Obviously sensing she was losing the upper hand in the conversation—not that she ever had it but, being

Peggy, she just assumed—Peggy shifted so she was partially blocking Fitz's view and put her hand to Deke's forehead.

"We should be asking *you*," she said. "You're looking a little pale, sugar. Are *you* feeling okay?"

First, the woman wasn't southern. She'd lived in Atlanta for all of two minutes and had no business calling anyone "Sugar." Second, her voice was so sweetly dripping with honey Fitz was concerned about a sudden swarm of bees.

Although Deke was a fan of Peggy's, he wasn't a proponent of PDA. Fitz figured that was due to not wanting to openly play favorites. So his gently but firmly taking Peggy's wrist and pulling her hand away wasn't a surprise. It *was* a surprise, however, that when he said, "I didn't sleep so well last night," He glanced at Fitz and smiled. "Maybe something's going around."

Fitz grinned.

She couldn't help it. The last thing in the world she needed was to be flirting with Deke. No, the last thing in the world she needed was to be doing it in front of Peggy. Yet probably due to that very fact, she found herself saying, "Maybe next time you should call me. I know some excellent relaxation techniques."

With a laugh that held more than a tinge of surprise, he answered, "I'll be sure to do that."

Every one of her cells jumped straight to attention. *Wow.* They seriously did. It was like pop rocks fizzing under her skin.

She barely even registered Peggy trying to figure out a way to work herself into the conversation. It was time to get things back to normal territory. Fitz said to Deke, "What brings you into town so early today?"

Since Deke closed the bar on Friday nights, he usually didn't appear until the lunch rush was over. He spent most Friday mornings helping Wash out on the farm, although Fitz had a sneaking suspicion they shot hoops with some of the farmhands for as much of that time as was humanly possible.

Wash called it team building.

Deke called it a business meeting.

Fitz called it bunk.

With a shrug, Deke glanced across the street at the bar. "Family meeting," he said, his hand going up to his baseball cap and moving the brim from forward to back.

Deacon family meetings at the bar were unusual, though not concerning. The ones at home were the ones to watch out for. Those were along the lines of "Lola's husband just died," whereas family meetings at the bar covered topics more like, "We're thinking of changing the size of the napkins." With the senior Deacons heading out for vacation soon it made perfect sense.

It also meant Deke would be busy. There wouldn't be time for any other conversations about, say, kissing. Good. Having a little more time to digest this wasn't the worst of things. Maybe there would even be time for another dream or two before reality sank in and everything went back to normal.

Because the reality was, she couldn't go around kissing one of her best friends. Not like that, at least. She especially couldn't kiss a man whose idea of a long-term relationship was that he'd slept with the same woman two nights in a row.

Although, come to think of it, maybe he was the best one to be kissing, since she wasn't exactly a big believer in the whole happily ever after thing herself.

Her phone rang right then, and with a glance down she saw it was Headhunter Doug. With a murmured, "I need to take this," she turned her back on Deke and Peggy and walked up the street.

With Peggy in front of him, blocking his view, Deke had to practically crane his head to try and get a sense of who Fitz was talking to. All he heard was, "Hi, Doug," as she turned and walked away.

Who the fuck was Doug, and why did she have to walk away from Deke to talk to him?

Okay, yes, Deke had specifically come into town early to find her. Just tear the bandage off. He couldn't kiss her again—not when she kissed like *that*. Because that would then progress to the next step, sleeping with her, and that would be a huge mistake, even if not for the fact that Nate would probably kill him. Deke was getting entirely ahead of himself, however, since her jumping out of his car last night and hauling ass inside wasn't exactly the best sign. But it all had him off balance enough that when Peggy had put her hand on him and practically pushed Fitz out of the way in order to assert her place, it had taken every ounce of willpower he'd had not to tell Peggy off. Hell, he'd had almost no willpower in the first place because the second he'd seen Fitz it had been almost physically impossible to keep from pulling her to him and doing exactly what he'd promised himself in the early morning hours that he would never do again.

"Are you sure you're okay?" Peggy asked, looking up at him again and sounding like she was genuinely concerned, rather than just trying to get between him and Fitz.

"I said I was, didn't I?" he said, not meaning to bite her head off, yet realizing from the way she took a step back that he had.

Deke looked up the street again to see Fitz had now turned her back on them. What the hell? They didn't keep secrets from each other.

But that wasn't true. Fitz *did* keep secrets from him. Some majorly big ones apparently.

"Hon," Peggy said, her hands back on him, as she looked up. "You certainly aren't acting okay."

He looked down at her as if he were watching from somewhere far above, not quite understanding his reactions. He *liked* having a woman's hands on him. He *liked* women stepping up close and whispering suggestive things in his ear, especially when it was a woman as talented as Peggy Miller. He'd even liked Peggy, up until about ten hours ago.

He grabbed her hands again and pulled them away from his chest and his back—back being a euphemism for ass, of course—realizing belatedly he had no clue how to turn a woman away. He was an expert at deflecting when he wasn't interested, and even better at making sure any woman he was with knew he was in it for the sex, period. But beyond that, not so much.

"Not right now," he said, referring to whatever it was Peggy had just been saying. Something about, well, his cock.

"Seriously, Deke," she snapped, taking a step back. "Being a dick isn't a good look for you."

Oh. Maybe that's what she was saying. He honestly wasn't paying much attention.

Really—who the hell was Doug?

Clearly realizing this conversation wasn't going anywhere, Peggy switched tactics. "Okay, well, I realize you don't exactly have a packed schedule…" He looked down at her sharply. Seriously? "But I'm busy with this weekend's tournament," she continued, "so it's not like I have the time right now anyway." With a huff, she looked over at Fitz. "Will you tell her to call me when she gets off the phone? We have a billion things to go over."

And that almost made Deke laugh. The last thing he was going to tell Fitz was to call Peggy. "Probably not." When Peggy's head came up, he shrugged. "You should probably just call her when you can."

"Call who when who can?" Fitz suddenly asked from right behind him, and parts of Deke snapped to attention in a highly uncomfortable way. Before he could respond, however, Peggy gave a thirteen-year-old worthy sigh, and from out of a huge leather bag she withdrew a planner stuffed with papers. "You. Call me. To make sure you've done everything on your list."

"Really?" Fitz said, the slight snap in her voice the closest Deke had ever heard her to being irritated with anyone outside their circle of friends.

He usually loved it when she got agitated. It was like a little slice of Fitz that only the inner circle got to see and why he took such pleasure in teasing her. Of course, now he was aware there was a part of her he apparently *wasn't* inner circle enough to know, it held less appeal. So, rather than protest when Peggy put her hand on Fitz's arm and turned her toward Jules's café, or be put off by the fact that Fitz didn't seem to be in any more hurry to talk to him than he was to talk to her, he watched the women as they began to walk away from him.

He should've gone into his bar. But he didn't. He couldn't.

"Fitz."

Both women stopped and turned, irritation in Peggy's eyes, wariness in Fitz's.

"A minute?" he asked.

She hesitated before nodding, mumbling something that must've been for Peggy to go ahead, since Peggy headed towards Jules's. Fitz's look turned warier as he neared. As it should have, since this should have been the moment where he said what they both needed him to say. That whatever had been going through his head yesterday was gone, the kiss had been a fluke, and all of his circuits were back to functioning normally.

But when he got to her, all he could think about was how good she smelled.

"Your morning going okay?" he asked, for reasons he couldn't begin to say.

The guardedness on her face disappeared, replaced by downright amusement. "It's going just fine," she answered, her eyes laughing at him. "And yours?"

He took a step closer, getting right up in her personal space for no good reason other than that it meant her hair brushed his arm in the morning breeze.

On his shoulder, his little devil friend was chanting, *Tear the Band-Aid off. Tear the Band-Aid off.* On his other shoulder, his Angel friend joined in, whispering, *It's four little words, my friend. 'We need to talk.' Just four words.*

Ignoring both, he reached out and twisted a strand of her hair around his finger. How could it be so damn soft?

Band-Aid, he heard in one ear.

Four little words, he heard in the other.

And then out of nowhere, a tiny little cherub dropped out of the sky and, Jeremy Renner-style, zapped the devil first and then the angel with his arrows. *All yours*, he said, before disappearing into thin air.

Deke tugged a little on her hair, knowing he was essentially acting like a kid on the playground, crushing on the cute girl in pigtails. Except he was *not* crushing on Fitz. It was just some weirdly misplaced lust. That was all. And the fact that his blood was racing to places it had no business being was a purely physical reaction to the way her eyes widened and her breath hitched when he tugged a little more and her head tilted slightly back.

The arrows must've switched everything up because now the angel was flopping around, frantically crying *Band-Aid! Band-Aid!* And the devil was pulling himself up, groaning, *For God's sake, man—four little words. Four freaking words.*

Hell, there were red lights flashing everywhere and someone shouting, *Abort! Abort!*

But all that did was make Deke's voice extra rough as he said, "I really need to kiss you again."

A chorus of groans went up around him as the angel, devil and Abort! guy all collapsed in exasperation.

Completely unaware of the chaos around her, Fitz gave a nervous little laugh. "Not right here, you don't."

Right. Because they were on Main Street and he was the town playboy and she was Nate Hawkins's baby sister. She was practically *Deke's* baby sister. And if he'd already blown his you-can't-touch-her directive, the very least he could do was not do anything that would make people talk.

She hated it when people talked about her.

He forced himself to let the hair around his finger loosen; to take a step away. "Maybe we should have dinner tonight."

Yes, he was on shift all night, but he could take twenty minutes for dinner.

Her eyes narrowed and she took her own step back. He wasn't sure if that was a good or a bad sign. Then again he wasn't sure if "good sign" meant she'd have been on board with another kiss or the exact opposite. He was that turned around. Then she shook her head. "Dinner meeting tonight for the vendors."

Of course. Because Little League was a Big Fucking Deal in Inspiration, and the tournament was a two day affair with teams coming in from all over the state. Since his Men's League team would be closing it all out on Sunday afternoon, he'd be both a coach and player this weekend, so he'd be seeing her plenty over the next few days. They just wouldn't have a chance to be alone. He took one more step back. That was probably a good thing. "Good luck with that."

"I'm pretty sure I'll be okay." She grinned.

Dude, the devil said.

Oh, fuck me.

He watched as she walked away, waiting until she disappeared inside to twist the brim of his hat back to the front and head into the bar.

Chapter Nine

The Little League tournament was the quintessential baseball and apple pie small town experience and the weather was perfect. Once upon a time, that wouldn't have been a good thing; it was like the universe was piling one injustice on top of another. If Fitz couldn't have her dad around, and she couldn't even openly mourn him on Father's Day, one of the few days per year when she allowed herself to forgive him just a little bit for not-insubstantial sins, then couldn't it at least be miserable outside?

Today, though, even if that hadn't been the case, even if there were tornadoes bearing down from all sides, Fitz was pretty sure she'd still be smiling.

Yes, kissing Deke had been a bad idea. Yes, she knew it could never *ever* happen again. Hell, jumping out of his car and fleeing the other night, as cowardly as that was, might have been the smartest thing she'd done. But she couldn't deny the happy, buzzy feeling she'd had all of yesterday. The way it spiked whenever their paths had crossed or when she'd feel his eyes on her. She'd mostly forced herself not to look his way. To just pretend she wasn't aware. But every once in a while she'd sneak a peek and their eyes would meet and first he'd grin, then she would. It made it hard not to want to go there again.

With a sigh as big as the smile she couldn't keep to herself, Fitz turned her attention back to the table of raffle tickets and pens in front of her, wishing she had last-minute details to distract her. But, no. Everything was completely under control, as always. Yesterday's games had gone great. The vendors had all gotten up and running without too much trouble, and the weather was cooperating fully. She'd even taken pictures and drafted the report Doug had asked her to send along. It had been challenging, to say the least, to find photos of things that showed her off but wouldn't completely scream *Inspiration!* if Nate was among those seeing them. Then again, Nate had bigger issues with Father's Day than even Fitz did and he'd never actually been to the tournament, so maybe it wouldn't have mattered.

"How much time until your break?" Dorie asked from across the tent in between bouts of people.

"Forty-two minutes," Fitz answered, not that she was counting. She actually enjoyed events like this, with all the bustle and noise. She especially enjoyed knowing she'd had a large part in putting it together. It was just the part about people retelling the ironic story of Patrick Hawkins's bastard daughter running the town's Father's Day Tournament that tended to get old. There'd been nine mentions this weekend so far, and that was just the ones said directly to her face. Not that she was counting that, either.

Turning to Dorie, who'd set up a satellite library for the weekend with a baseball theme, she asked, "Fried dough or bomb pop? I can't decide which one to go for first."

Dorie smiled as she straightened out the brochures on her table. "Bomb pop. My brothers are always on my case about those at home so I'm planning a major binge."

"Why would your brothers care about your eating a bomb pop?" Fitz asked. Dorie's brothers never ceased to amaze her. At least Nate wasn't *that* bad.

Rolling her eyes, Dorie frowned. "Popsicles of all kinds. Because I apparently lick them too slow."

Seriously? The thing was red, white and blue. "I'm beyond fascinated by how your brothers manage to make everything about sex."

With a jab of her finger toward Fitz's direction, Dorie said, "This is *exactly* why I needed to leave Boston. At least here there are people who talk sense." She turned back to her brochures.

But of course now Fitz was thinking about it—sex, not bomb pops, although she really did want one of those ASAP—and her thoughts turned back to Deke.

With a groan she barely managed to keep to herself, Fitz let her head fall to the table in front of her. She needed to just stop thinking, period. Easier said than done.

Careful to keep her head turned away from Dorie, Fitz let her gaze travel across the walkway to the Deacon's Bar & Grille tent where Lola and her parents were transitioning from the breakfast rush into the lunch setup while the boys played nearby. It was already close to eleven, which meant Deke would be here any minute now. Fitz assumed it also meant that Peggy, who hadn't been around yet today, would be here soon, too.

She did momentarily wonder if Deke had ended up spending Friday night at Peggy's after all. She didn't *think* so. He'd clearly been thrown by the whole conversation with Jules. At the same time, other than her coming out and saying Peggy was a bitch, no details had been revealed, thank goodness. Plus he hadn't exactly been Flash Gordon when Peggy tried to maul him on the sidewalk. So, no. It wasn't impossible to think that he and Peggy might have hooked up again this weekend even if he'd kissed Fitz on Thursday night. Fitz could easily name several times he'd happily kissed one woman and then spent that very *night* with another entirely.

Straightening back up, Fitz went about reshuffling the pens and postcards on her table. Maybe him going back to Peggy wouldn't be the worst thing. Then she and Deke could go back to being she and Deke and all would be right with the world. Then again, Peggy had been far too crabby yesterday to have had great sex the night before. *Any* sex. Plus Peggy would have taken every possible opportunity to ensure Fitz heard about it.

Realizing there was a ten-year-old boy and his parents patiently waiting to ask a question, Fitz turned her attention to her actual job and did it swimmingly for the next half hour, managing to mostly keep her focus on the people coming by the tent rather than any wayward thoughts about getting down and dirty with too-sexy-for-their-own-good play—

Damn it. She'd just knocked all of her perfectly arranged pens to the ground and had to practically crawl under the table to pick them up.

"Hey, Dorie," she heard from above her. "Do you know where Fitz wants these bottles of water?"

Speak of the devil. Fitz brought her head up a little too suddenly, banging it on the underside of the table.

"Ouch!" She came up frowning and clutching the back of her head.

Oh, *God*, had he been this gorgeous before? Had he always smelled *amazing*?

Doing everything she could to keep herself immune to his physical charms, she spun on her heel. "Back here."

She put all her efforts into acting exactly as she always did around him. Except she suddenly couldn't quite remember how that was. Did she flirt with him? Did she flat out ignore him? Did she generally just go around in a state of low-level irritation? Because right now she had absolutely no clue.

She had even less of a clue as she bent down to open up the cooler and he crouched down next to her, his head so close all he'd need to do was turn it slightly to the left and his mouth would be on her breast.

Oh, hell no, her nipples had not just hardened. She slapped her arms over her chest.

Because they had. And Deke, with his superhero sex god extra sensory perception, had definitely noticed. He at least had the decency to look down at the ground as he grinned.

"It's the cold," Fitz snapped. "From the cooler."

Pushing the bottles down into the ice, Deke just answered, "You'd be amazed at all the bits and pieces I can warm up with my tongue."

And now there was zinging. Little lightning bolts flashed their way down from the tips of her breasts to the juncture of her thighs. For heaven's sake. Fitz dropped down to her knees on the ground next to Deke. "You can't say things like that to me," she whispered, intending it to come out as a declaration but realizing it sounded like a plea instead.

If he'd said something flippant she would have been irritated. If he'd gone with bold, she would have laughed and that would be that. But she didn't know what to do with the look in his eyes as he glanced over at her with a flash of what appeared to be yearning. Or with the set of his jaw as he looked back down at the bottles in the cooler and gruffly said, "I know."

She bit her lip and turned her head away.

Except he didn't let her get away with that. His hand went to her jaw. He tipped her head until she had no choice but to meet his gaze, and everything around them faded away. There were no tents, no other people, just him and her and the way his hand caressed her skin.

It was a good thing she was already down on the ground, because her knees went weak as he said, "Don't hide from me. There's nowhere you can run where I can't find you."

Her lips parted on a sigh. She even managed to get out a soft, "Stalker-y, much?" before she tilted and whirled and found herself stretching up to…

Dorie's shriek pulled her attention back to the front of the tent. Except Dorie wasn't standing there anymore. Instead, she was being swept up into some guy's arms, her arms and legs going around him.

Deke asked, "Is that *Nate*?" not bothering to hide his surprise as he got to his feet.

"Oh, my God," Fitz murmured, standing. It couldn't be.

In all the years she'd known Nate, not once had she laid eyes on him on Father's Day weekend. Even as a teenager he'd disappeared. He'd vanish on Friday night and not be heard from again until Monday morning. To this day Fitz had no idea where he'd go.

Fitz was fine with that. It was the one thing they'd never been able to talk about—he had hated his father and she had loved hers. That it was the same man created a distance far too wide for either one of them to overcome. So she'd grit her way through the day and be grateful she didn't have to make herself pretend in front of Nate, too, because he was the only one who always saw right through her. Except here he was, coming her way, and that wasn't something she could take on this of all days.

Still not quite able to process that, she did register Deke moving so he was standing beside her. A little bit behind, so as not to block Nate, but close enough that she knew he was there if she needed him. Nate knew it too, if the grim look in his eyes as they flicked to Deke and back were any indication. Although Deke and Nate had been friends their whole lives, she knew that, kisses or not, Deke would take her side over Nate's if it ever came to that.

"What are you doing here?" she managed when Nate drew close, forcing herself to focus on him rather than the solid presence at her back.

Something flashed through his eyes before she found herself being pulled hard against his chest.

"Christ, Hawk," she heard from behind her. "Loosen up. She can't breathe."

Although, astoundingly, Nate listened to Deke and loosened his arms, he didn't let go. And since he didn't, Fitz felt the distinct hitch in his chest as his hands gripped her shoulders.

Now he was freaking her out. "Is everything okay?"

As she drew away from him, Fitz's eyes flew from Nate's to Dorie's and even over to Mama Gin, out in the front of the tent. Dorie and Mama Gin didn't look overly upset. Still…

"What happened?" Fitz asked.

"What *happened*?" Nate said. "I came to see you." Before she could even process that—she didn't think anyone had ever dropped everything to see her—he stepped in again, quietly saying, "Are you okay?" And then before she could process *that*, he glanced behind her at Deke.

Warning bells sounded.

"Why?" she asked, as the two men exchanged a look. Taking her own step back, she frowned when she hit the wall that was Deke. Or maybe she frowned at Nate as…

Oh, hold *on*. "You went to Nate?" she snapped, whipping her head around to glare at Deke.

"Angel," Deke murmured, putting his hands in his pockets.

"It was sixteen years ago!" *Why* were they making such a big deal of this?

Her hands flew up to her face as she jerked away from both of them, then crashed right into Dorie, whose arms went around her. "Is everything okay over here?" she asked.

Things were so far from okay, it wasn't even funny. But if Fitz said that, she would probably start crying out of sheer frustration. Nate and Deke would misread it totally and make it ten times worse, so she just squeezed her eyes tight, bringing her hands up to her temples. "Did you tell Dorie, too?"

Not that her life was some big secret, lord knew. It was just that Dorie was the one person in all of Inspiration who didn't know the true extent of the baggage Fitz carried with her. The kindnesses she'd never be able to repay, the resentments she'd never quite get over. The one person who saw Fitz as *Fitz*, and liked her, regardless of how she'd gotten that name.

"Tell me what?" Dorie asked.

Oh, freaking frak. *Perfect.*

Fitz had just let the cat out of the bag. Or, at least, the fact that there was a cat in the bag in the first place.

Ignoring Dorie's question, from behind her Deke said, "I said I wasn't letting it go, Fitz, and you wouldn't tell me. What the hell else was I supposed to do?"

Whirling around, Fitz would have given him a shove but his hands came over her wrists as they made contact with his chest. Even with Nate being so close behind her that she was the middle part of a human sandwich, she found her mind—her body—going back to that kiss.

"You should have come and found *me*," she said, trying to keep a lid on whatever was left of her temper. "Not gone to Nate."

Despite it being nearly impossible, Deke took a step closer. So close she was forced to tilt her head back in a way that hurt. She would have been able to hold back the shiver if his eyes hadn't gone dark as his voice went gravelly. "You ran away from me." Then his eyes went to her mouth and another shiver ran through her.

So not her fault. She hissed, "Because you ki—"

She cut herself off at the last possible second.

"Okay," Dorie said in her firm, no nonsense, librarian voice. "I'm clearly not aware of the subtext, but from what I *have* heard, it's pretty obvious that it's not something you all want shared. So I'll just say now that there's a crowd gathering, and you can do with that what you will."

There was a moment of charged silence as Deke looked at Nate over Fitz's head, face mostly impassive but with his jaw clenched. Nate was practically the mirror image as he looked right back. Though they'd had their occasional disagreements, she'd never seen them angry at each other—hell, until this week she'd rarely seen Deke anything but laid back and happy—and she couldn't stand that it was because of her.

She actually *hated* it. More so even than the fact that a far-too-interested crowd had gathered, and that was saying something. Nate had been Deke's friend since birth. She refused to come between them. Plus, there was the part that they still maddeningly and beyond frustratingly couldn't get out of their heads that she was *over it*.

She yanked her arms out of Deke's hands and stepped away from both of them.

"I'm fine," she snapped. "I am *okay*," she said again, this time specifically to Nate, trying to soften her tone since he'd obviously been worried. She honestly couldn't believe he'd left his team in the middle of a road trip in order to check on her, much less on Father's Day, over… Over… *Nothing*. But he had.

"I *am*," she said again, this time to Deke.

Nate and Deke stared each other down for what felt like forever, although it was probably just a few seconds. But Nate finally looked down at Fitz as his arm went around Dorie and he kissed the top of her head. He nodded.

With relief, Fitz said, "Are you here for the rest of the day?" There was still a long day of baseball ahead, with four Little League games left, then the Men's League game Deke would be playing in to finish out the day. "You can stay for Lola's barbecue?"

She was probably pushing her luck by asking. There was the whole Father's Day thing, of course, but there was also the fact that he played, hello, professional baseball and it wasn't like he could just take off whenever he wanted to. Then again, she wouldn't have put it past him to write some clause into his contract that he could do whatever the hell he wanted to, especially on this of all days.

Sure enough, he nodded again. "I can stay."

"Okay, good." Because she loved her brother to death and was touched he'd come here today for her. It honestly meant a lot. But she was also thrown by how big of a deal this seemed to be to both Nate *and* Deke, and she wasn't quite sure what she was supposed to do about that. She sure as hell wasn't going back to being Poor Little Fitz, the way she'd been back in high school.

"Why don't you make your rounds. We'll catch up later."

Although he clearly wasn't happy about it, he conceded, taking Dorie's hand and pulling her with him as he said, "Later," and walked away.

Once he was out of hearing distance, Fitz whirled back around to Deke, giving him the shove she'd meant to before. Rather than respond properly to her irritation, however, he just smiled and took hold of her wrists again, this time pulling her up against him. She took a moment to appreciate the hard planes of his body against hers before saying, "What the hell was *that*?"

"You know what it was," he said in that damn sexy voice of his. "There's one more thing to be resolved."

She sucked in a breath. For as much as she ached to let her hand travel up his body—or maybe down—she resisted, mustering up the strength to pull herself away yet again. Dragging her gaze away from his mouth, she did what she needed to do. Like she always did. "Can we just get to the inevitable declaration that the whole kissing thing is a really bad idea and say we're not going to do it again?"

If she hadn't been paying such close attention, she might not have seen the muscles at the corners of his mouth tighten. If she could have forced herself not to look at his eyes, she wouldn't have seen them narrow. But she was and they did.

She felt the loss keenly as he let go of her hand and took a step away, transforming back into the easygoing, no flies on me, let's all just be happy-as-can-be Deke she had always counted on.

With a smile that didn't quite reach his eyes, he said, "You are absolutely right." Then he brushed the top of her head with a quick, impersonal kiss before turning and walking away. The fact that it hurt almost more than dredging up some of the most painful memories of her life wasn't something Fitz could dwell on. Instead, she told herself better now than later, when they went too far down that road to ever get themselves back.

She took a deep breath and plastered that damn smile on her face.

Happy freaking Father's Day.

Chapter Ten

She was right. She was absolutely, one hundred percent right.

Not the part about going to Nate. Deke had done exactly what he needed to do in that situation. He had no regrets whatsoever. None.

About the kissing part, though…

"Steee-rike!"

Deke called time as he stepped out of the batter's box, tapped the dirt out of his cleats and adjusted his batting gloves. Then he settled back into his stance and swung the bat up over his shoulder.

Fucking Nate. Of course he'd do the right thing and show up here today. On Father's Day of all days. And, yeah, it put a damper on whatever the fuck was going on, something that, although it probably needed to be stopped, had been pretty freaking fun. Fun in a way Deke didn't usually associate with women, to be perfectly honest.

Not that sex wasn't fun. And until recently he'd had a lot of it. But he certainly hadn't gone out of his way to catch a glimpse of a woman—of one particular woman—or be able to coast for hours on the basis of one tiny smile she'd thrown his way. Nor had he ever been quite so obvious about it, most definitely not in public. So what the hell had compelled him to take hold of her hands? To brush his lips against her hair. To come *this* close to kissing her in front of Dorie. In front of *Nate*, for Christ's sake.

"Strike two!"

Ignoring the calls of the crowd, Deke held his hand up to the ump and stepped out of the batter's box again.

Thank God he was finally on the field himself. He'd been a shit coach today. Yeah, they'd won, but it was kind of hard to do your best when you spent the game staring at the parents of the kids on your team, wondering if they'd been in on giving Fitz hell back in the day. The second the game was over he'd sent the kids off, then gathered up his equipment and headed to the Deacon's tent. Hell, he'd even lied to his parents, telling them he had a headache and would rather man the grills for most of the day than be at his usual place up in the front. He hadn't even checked in with his friends. He clearly couldn't trust himself around Fitz right now. Most definitely couldn't be around Nate. He couldn't decide if he was pissed at Nate for showing up, or if he just wished Nate would beat the crap out of him and be done with it.

Come watch after your sisters yourself.

Fucking *A*.

But now his own team was playing and no one gave a shit if he was smiling. In fact, they were pretty stoked, since he was on fire. He'd already made a ridiculous catch that led to a triple play, and was two for three at the plate with a double and three RBIs. The fact that Jeremiah was pitching for the other team just sweetened the deal. Plus, since Deke's team was actually based in

Ames, there was no one local on it, which meant Deke didn't have to worry that any of these guys had ever hassled Fitz. He'd never had to defend her to any one of them. In fact, the ones who had met her thought she was cute. If he hadn't warned them off, they'd have been all over her.

Do not think about being all over her.

Back in the batter's box, he got back into his stance.

The pitch was low and inside, and he shouldn't have chased it. He got a piece of it, though, and…

"Foul ball! Oh and two."

Goddamn it.

Whatever. She'd given him the out he should have given her, and he damn well needed to take it. They could not get involved. Period. She was one of his closest friends. *The* closest. There was far too much at stake for him to risk it on something that could end so badly.

With a glare at Jeremiah, he shifted his weight back and, as the pitch left Jeremiah's hand, Deke could see the spin of a curveball. It was one of those perfect moments. He didn't even feel the ball hit the bat, just saw the number on the outfielder's jersey moving toward the fence.

A smile spreading over his face, Deke shifted from a sprint to a trot when the outfielder pulled up on the warning track as the ball settled into the trees. Home run, baby. That ball was over the freaking fence. His team cheered him on as they came out to greet him at home plate, and although he wasn't officially playing for the home team, these were his people and they were cheering. Loudly.

He gave a smile and a wave, lingering on the field a bit too long as he scanned the bleachers for Fitz. Hell, the whole point of not doing any more kissing was because they were friends, right? So he had every right to seek her out. And when he finally found her, he decided not to dwell on the fact that he felt it in his chest when her smile went wide as her eyes met his.

He tipped his cap toward her before putting it back on his head, and the good mood carried him through the end of the game. It didn't hurt that they annihilated the other team. Deke hadn't been part of an ass-whipping like that in ages and it felt phenomenal.

"Uncle *Deke*!"

The roar of his name had him turning. It was all of his kids still in their uniforms, running up to congratulate him after the game and throwing themselves at him in one big scrum. Hell, yes. This was what it was all about.

Was it the same for Fitz? Now that he'd been paying closer attention, he could see how she kept herself insulated from the crowd, tucked between Dorie and Lola, with one of the triplets in her lap. The more he thought about it, in fact, the more he realized that with the exception of her family and friends, namely Wash, Jason, Cal and himself, the first time he'd ever truly seen her open up with anyone outside of that circle was when she'd met Dorie.

By the time he showered and dressed and headed back to the Deacon's tent, he'd worked himself up all over again.

Was she really okay? And what did that mean anyway?

Then he started to think about why, exactly, they wouldn't be doing any more kissing. Because, he had to be honest, they'd been pretty great at it so far. Yes, they'd need to keep it contained. Fine. But they had some serious chemistry going on. Everyone in their right minds knew chemistry would blow up in your face if you didn't pay proper attention. So maybe they should just get it on. Let all that combustible stuff catch fire and have a freaking fantastic time. And then they could move on.

He checked in with the bar staff, divided up the things to send back to Deacon's and the things to take to Lola's, and was just about to get into the truck when Fitz came around the side of it, looking more frustrated than he felt.

"I'm riding with you," she snapped. Then she climbed up into the seat, slammed the door shut, and sat with her arms crossed in front of her chest as she glared at something through the windshield.

Probably not the best time to discuss his chemistry theory.

Climbing up into the cab himself, Deke did his best not to think about the last time they sat here together. With intense concentration, he shifted the truck into gear and headed off without a word.

"You were awesome, by the way," she said after a few minutes.

He was awesome in a lot of ways, many of which he'd be more than happy to demonstrate for her. Since she was clearly angry, he thought he'd keep that part to himself. It did, however, raise the question, "That pisses you off because…?"

With a snort, she uncrossed her arms and turned so she was now glaring out the side window. "It's not you. I just…" Then she huffed and threw her hands up in the air. "This is exactly what I didn't want to happen. I swear, if Nate gives me one more of those 'Is she okay?' looks, I might actually kill him."

Oh. Okay, then. Better than her being angry at him, but honestly, Deke was on Nate's side no matter what Fitz said. He kept quiet on that, too.

"I mean, there was a reason I didn't tell anyone, you know? It's bad enough I'm Inspiration's favorite tragedy…"

Were they back to the pity thing?

"Nate *knows* I wasn't…" Her voice trailed off as she visibly shook off what he assumed was the word *raped*. Because that's sure as hell where his head went. The only good side of all of this was that she clearly had *not* had that experience. But, Jesus. The idea of them even…

"They didn't even touch me, for Heaven's sake."

Right. Plus Deke pretty much loved the idea of Fitz putting them down like dogs. That part in itself brought a smile to his face.

Which froze when her hand went to his knee and she squeezed.

He almost swerved off the fucking road.

"I mean, I don't think they were even trying. They were…" Her voice trailed off as she realized where her hand was and pulled it away. Of course, that essentially meant she dragged it over his thigh.

Holy. Fucking. *Hell*.

"They were making fun of me, Deke."

"What? Who?" he asked, attempting to participate in the conversation as he clutched the steering wheel even harder.

"Although the freaking jerks did rip my favorite jeans," she muttered.

Christ.

"But I was like, well, I don't know what I was like. One of those whirling dervish kind of things." Then she laughed. "I'm pretty sure I kicked one of them directly in the junk. And Nate said they were all already bleeding by the time he got there."

Damn it. "Fitz—"

"Don't," she snapped. "Don't give me that 'poor Fitz' look. That's the whole reason I'm riding with you and not Nate. Okay? I mean, for Heaven's sake…" She turned her head away. "You're the last person I want to be alone with right now."

"Gee, thanks," he muttered. "Love you, too, Fitz."

The air went still as they both realized what he'd just said.

"I know," she said a good five minutes later, so softly that his head came up just to be sure she'd truly said something and he wasn't just imagining it. "That's the problem." She reached out to where his hand covered the gearstick and, after hovering there for the most tantalizing of moments, slowly lowered her fingers to his and squeezed. He jerked his head back up to look at the road, trying not to give in to the sudden and desperate desire to pull over to the shoulder.

"Because I do love you," she continued, and he was pretty sure if he looked up at her again he'd see tears in her eyes. He could handle a lot of things. Seeing Fitz cry wasn't one of them. "You're one of my best friends in the world. We can't mess with that, you know? I need you."

His jaw clenched, he turned onto the street that connected with Lola's. Thank fuck.

Then she squeezed—*again*—and the sensation went directly to his dick. Almost as if that's where her hand actually was.

"That's why we can't, um…"

His heart was pounding in his chest. In his throat. He felt like he couldn't breathe.

Fuck.

"…kiss."

Right. Kiss. That's what they weren't supposed to do.

"Or, um, anything else."

Pulling to a stop at the end of Lola's driveway, Deke willed his hand not to shake as he shut off the truck and pulled the keys out of the ignition. He looked down at her hand—felt the heat still pulsing through every part of him, even the parts where he most definitely didn't want it—and then up at her. He had no idea what look he gave her, but whatever it was made her sit back.

Her cheeks turned bright pink and she gave a little cough. "I… So… I'm glad we talked."

That was a talk? Really? He twisted his wrist so that it was his hand on top. Heard her sweet little gasp, which didn't help one bit.

"Could you say something?" she whispered.

No. Or at least he probably shouldn't. But, well, good idea or not, that didn't stop him. "Right now I can't decide which I want more, to fuck those guys over or to just plain fuck. Clearly we're not on the same page on either one of those things."

The angel and devil made their obligatory appearance, but they were both just sitting there with their mouths hanging open. Probably because they knew that, yes, that was the absolute wrong route to go. But her eyes went wide even as they sparked with interest, her gaze very unhelpfully focused on his mouth.

Leaning in close to her ear, he closed his eyes and took in a deep breath. Her hair smelled like lemons. All citrusy and fresh. He turned his head just enough for the skin of his cheek to brush the skin of hers. For her breath to catch in a hitch.

"So I need some time to get my head on straight. We can talk again after that."

Then he pulled back, let go of her hand and got himself out of the truck.

Unsurprisingly, Fitz kept her distance from him for most of the night. And Deke, well, he kept his distance from everyone. Since he and Lola were the only ones at this non-Father's Day barbecue who had a dad nearby and accessible, Deke decided to stick close to his and help man the grill.

It wasn't the best idea since his dad could read him better than he thought. The first thing his dad said was, "You okay?"

His eyes flicked over to where Fitz was taking an active role in a fairly raucous water balloon fight started by Nate and Emily. Was it not possible for the woman to stay dry for once? "Phenomenal," he said.

His father laughed. "Want to try that again, son?"

After a glance at his dad, Deke returned his attention to the grill. "No," he muttered. "I really don't."

His father didn't respond right away. Long enough, in fact, for Deke to think the conversation was over, which was fine by him. He had a good relationship with his dad. They talked about the bar, about Lola and the kids, sports, and even sometimes, when they were being ambitious, town politics. With the exception of "the talk" when Deke was around twelve, it didn't usually get much more personal. Frankly, Deke liked it that way.

So he wasn't at all ready for his father to turn to him, voice rough. "Are you happy, Max?"

Deke honestly didn't know what to say to that. He wasn't ready for the emotion in his father's voice. And, to be honest, he *wasn't* very happy at the moment. That was an entirely new thing, too. But he wasn't about to admit it. "I… Sure. I mean—"

"I know you started taking classes for your MBA."

Deke's head snapped up. He hadn't told anyone about that. And anyway, it hadn't gone anywhere.

"And then Dave died and you put everything on hold to be what Lola needed."

"Anyone would have done that," he mumbled.

"Yeah, for all of two weeks—maybe two months. But two years?" He shook his head and the emotion they'd all felt after Dave's death was written clearly on his face. "I'd give anything to fix that for Lola. I'd sell my own soul." He paused, clearly to get himself under control. When he looked back up again, though, the only thing shining in his eyes was pride. "But I watched my son become a man that day."

Deke looked down at the grill. "Dad…"

"Then something happened about six months back," his father continued as if Deke hadn't spoken. "I'm not sure what it was other than you stopped hopping from bed to bed."

For possibly the first time in his life, Deke's cheeks heated in embarrassment. He'd made his choices and didn't regret them. The life he lived was the life he lived. It might not have been the most profound in terms of giving back to the world, but he was careful in how he treated people. Except right now he couldn't look his father in the eye.

"Yeah," his dad continued. "There was definitely a change in you and it was a good one."

Well, okay then. He didn't have anything to say in response. Especially because the only thing that had changed six months ago, as far as Deke remembered, was that Fitz moved into Lola's house and he suddenly found himself hanging out and watching things like *The Voice*. Though it had done wonders for him trivia night-wise, that was pretty much it.

"Do you want a family, son?"

Deke jerked his head up. Where the hell had *that* come from?

"I've got the boys," he answered. "They're all I need."

"That's not what I asked and you know it," his dad snapped. "Those boys are so lucky to have you. Lola tells your mom how grateful she is every day."

"She does?" That was a…surprise.

But as if he hadn't spoken, his father went on, "You've been the best son a man could have. Watching you grow up has been a gift. I just hoped that by this time in your life…" He paused as his voice caught again. "I'd love to see you with a family of your own. To see you become a husband and father."

"Dad…"

"But mostly I just don't want you to find yourself behind that bar twenty years from now, just you and your regrets."

Regrets? Deke didn't have any regrets.

It wasn't that Deke *didn't* want a family—those kids rushing him today was possibly one of the best things he'd ever experienced. He just hadn't thought about it much. He'd never met a woman he wanted to spend that kind of time with. Hell, part of the reason he hadn't had sex in so long was he preferred poker nights and trivia nights and hanging out with Fitz and the boys to heading out to a noisy bar and making small talk with some woman he'd just end up comparing to…

Well, no, he didn't really *compare* women to Fitz. But he'd be on his way out for a night and then turn around because he'd rather spend his night off with Fitz and the guys. Sometimes he'd even make it as far as a woman's place and he'd be kissing her and…

And, no. Fitz was *not* the reason he hadn't had sex in six months. That couldn't be.

Jesus Christ, he needed to get laid. By someone other than Fitz.

But, fuck. Where had all that come from? "You're not dying, right?" Deke said. "I mean, I know this trip you and Mom have coming up is almost as bad, but you're freaking me out a little."

To be honest, the idea of his parents driving a rented RV and tooling around the Badlands in their T-shirts with the pictures of Lola's kids on them was kind of hilarious. And frighteningly awesome in a way Deke didn't want to think about. Still, it wasn't until his dad laughed and shook his head that Deke breathed easy again.

"It's Father's Day," his dad said. "I get to say whatever I want." Then he laughed, and did that always awkward clap on the back/hug thing before calling out for people to come get their food. Deke, on the other hand, kept his head down and avoided any further conversation. With *anybody*.

He somehow managed until the end of the night. But by the time they reached the end of the evening, with the younger kids in bed and the older ones inside with the grandparents, it was Lola's turn, apparently. With everyone sitting around her fire pit, beers in hand, she kicked him—although she would have said she was just nudging his shin with her foot—and said, "What's up your butt?"

Deke took a drink of his beer. "Nothing. Can't a guy just sit and chill?"

She snorted. "That's not you 'chilling.' That's you getting all broody. After your kids won and you played an awesome game. What's your deal tonight?"

The *deal* was he was in a shitty mood to begin with. And then his dad had put all these crazy ideas in his head, but the only woman on his mind at the moment was Fitz.

"There is no deal," he snapped. "I'm fine." It probably would have been better if he hadn't glanced over at Fitz when he spoke, but that was through no choice of his own. And as long as he was thinking about choice, he definitely wouldn't have chosen for Lola to roll her eyes and say, "Liar," while deliberately ignoring every I-do-not-want-to-talk-about-this-shit vibe he was sending in her direction.

Then Wash picked up the thread. "Christ. It's bad enough when I'm not getting any. But when *you* aren't, that's bad news for all of us."

It wasn't at all helpful when Nate snorted and said, "Works just fine for me," as he glared in Deke's direction.

Deke made sure he stared right ba—

"Oh, for heaven's sake!" Fitz threw her hands up into the air. "It's not about Deke's sex life, okay?"

It, uh, kind of was, but if Fitz was able to get Nate off Deke's case, then all power to her. Except then she looked straight into Deke's eyes, and he could tell from the grim determination in the set of her mouth that she was taking it in a direction *she* didn't want it to go. And it made him feel like shit.

He leaned forward. "Fitz…"

Tell them I kissed you. Tell them I said I wanted to fuck you, for Christ's sake. Call me the shallow asshole they all know me to be and move their attention on to the next thing. He'd honestly rather that than have her put herself out there in a way she didn't want. It was his fault something she'd kept under wraps for so long was all being dragged out again.

But she sat back in her chair, and, with a sigh, said, "Okay. I'm only going to talk about this once."

And then she told them the same story Deke had heard from Nate, although definitely with a different spin. It really did seem like she hadn't been afraid. Like it hadn't crossed her mind they could have done some serious damage and the idea of anyone else thinking along those lines came as a surprise. Clearly, however, it wasn't just Deke. The waves of rage pouring off Nate were so strong, Deke wouldn't have been surprised if he suddenly morphed into the Hulk. Wash and Jason were clearly getting the hint not to make a big deal out of it, but it was obvious they would have been just as happy to hunt Lyle Butler down as Deke was.

"So the *point* of this all," she glared at Nate and Deke before turning to the others—who, incidentally, got re-assuring smiles instead, "is that it's done," she said, her gaze directed at Jules, Ella, Lola and Dorie. "Over," she added, with more exasperation as she turned toward Wash and Jason. "I don't need you to fix this. I didn't then and I don't now." Smiling more for them than for herself, Deke was sure, she added, "I mean, when you guys closed ranks around me, I was the envy of every girl in school. Any fixing to be done got taken care of then."

Yeah, they'd closed ranks. Literally. It was the nickname that had started it, but now Deke understood why Nate had orchestrated an intervention of sorts. None of them had known why, but he was pretty sure the others felt as bad as he did about Fitz by that point, because not one of them had questioned it. And Deke could still remember how alone Fitz had seemed that day as she'd sat in the cafeteria all by herself. How fragile she had been. The hush that had come over the crowd as he, Wash, Jason and Cal followed Nate through the cavernous room.

By the time they'd reached her table, the entire place had gone dead silent. And with the full attention of every person there, Nate put his tray down on her table and reached behind him to pull an Iowa Dream basketball jersey out of his back pocket and then pulled it on over his T-shirt. Then the rest of them put their trays down too and did the same thing. The stunned look on her face when Wash had turned so she could see the "Team Wade" written on the back got him a little choked up even to this day.

With all eyes on them by that point—even the teachers had been staring—Nate's words rang out for everyone to hear. "Next asshole who even thinks about giving my sister shit answers to us first." Then he sat down across from her, waited for the other four to sit down as well, and proceeded to eat his lunch as if it were the most normal thing in the world.

From that day on, it was. She was theirs and they were hers, and they hadn't left her side since. One thing on which Deke was absolutely clear, no matter how things played out between them? He never would.

"I love you all so much," she said now, looking down at the ground. "It took me a little while to get there. I won't lie. But knowing you were all there was what helped make it okay."

No one said anything for a few moments, and even though she was smiling now and staring down Nate until he finally nodded at her in acceptance, all Deke wanted to do was wrap her up in his arms and take her away.

Luckily, before he could give in to that inclination, Wash broke the silence, surprising everyone entirely, by saying, "I hated this place when I came to live here. *Hated* it."

Everyone other than Nate, at least. Nate seemed to know exactly what was coming. Apparently Fitz wasn't the only one whose secrets he'd kept.

"In case you guys hadn't noticed," Wash was saying, "I'm black."

Deke couldn't help but laugh softly as he brought his bottle of beer to his mouth. "Is that so?"

Grinning himself, Wash nodded. "Hate to tell you, it's not just a good tan." After taking a drink of his own beer, he added, "It might shock you, but there aren't exactly a lot of black folk around town. Just Dorie and me, I think."

That got a laugh out of everyone since Dorie, though half Irish, had clearly taken after the Italian side of her heritage, with the olive skin and darker coloring that came along with that. She was not, however, black.

Jason, picking up the thread, smiled and gave a nod

of his head as well. "Inspiration does appear to be lacking families of African-American descent."

Though he smiled again, Wash brought it back to the serious side. "Not sure if you ever realized it, but I didn't have a ton of friends when we were growing up."

That was actually something Deke did remember noticing once upon a time. He talked about it with his parents once he'd been old enough to see that, no, he hadn't been imagining it. But he also hadn't given it too much thought because if people didn't want to hang out with them, that was their problem as far as he was concerned.

Wash looked up at Nate. "Do you remember how it was that I came to be on the basketball team?"

Jason laughed and nodded in a way that made clear that *he* remembered, although, to be honest, Deke had no clue.

"Someone decided that because I was black," Wash continued, "I was obviously good at basketball and wanted to play on the team. And, fuck…" Wash continued, picking at the label on his beer bottle and tearing it, "…don't even get me started on the dating scene."

Now Deke found himself staring at Wash. How could he not have known that? How could he not have had a clue about how Wash had felt growing up?

"At least you could get a date," Jason added, clinking his beer against Wash's. "Try being the biggest nerd ever in a sea of Nordic gods."

"Oh, please," Ella said, rolling her eyes. "You never had a problem getting girls."

"No," Jason corrected. "Deke and Nate never had a problem getting girls. Chicks only hung around me because it meant getting close to them. Until college, at least."

His beer halfway to his mouth, Deke shook his head. "That's not true." Women loved the whole surfer thing Jason had going on: a mop of blond, curly hair, blue eyes and a grin that sucked people in. Deke had been in enough bars with the guy to have seen it firsthand.

But Jason shook his head right back. "Remember how *I* came to be on the basketball team?"

With a bark of a laugh, Wash said, "You were riding your bike past us when we were setting up the basketball hoop that day."

"That day" being the one after the tornado had hit that long ago July, when the photographer had caught Nate and Wash hoisting up the basketball net in the midst of the rubble behind the high school. The picture went on to win a Pulitzer prize, and marked the beginning of the Iowa Dream.

"You guys and Cal needed a fourth," Jason said, still laughing, "because Deke was off getting laid."

Well, yeah. Deke's hand tightened around his beer bottle. Lacey James. But that was seventeen years ago and there was absolutely no reason for him to provide confirmation. So with everyone's eyes on him, Deke forced himself to casually shrug and sit back in his chair.

"The only reason I said yes," Jason went on to say, "was because you were the only guys who had ever been nice to me."

That couldn't possibly have been true. Deke put his beer down on the ground beside him.

But now it was Jules who spoke, her eyes on Nate. "I remember being in second grade, and Nate was in first, and the only kids who would sit with us were Lola and Deke. Everyone else would tease us because our dad was a drunk who'd disappeared into the night and left our mom. They were afraid it would 'catch.'" She put air quotes around that last word.

"Are you all trying to make me feel better?" Fitz said, smiling. "Because it wasn't necessary, but it sure is working."

"Well, good," Wash said. "Because you're obviously not getting anything out of Deke and Lo—"

"Hey," Lola interrupted, holding her hand up. "You're talking to the lonely, widowed single mother of four, don't forget."

Which, of course, meant everyone's eyes swung to Deke.

He had to say something. They were all expecting the off-the-cuff comment that would ease the tension, make everyone laugh. But for maybe the first time in his life, Deke was the one who felt off. Who felt like he was a stranger in his own skin. Who felt like a fucking *idiot* for not having a clue that pretty much every one of his friends had been dealing with all this shit. And that Deke, whose whole freaking job was to pay attention to people's tells, had pretty much been clueless while he was off getting laid.

But they were all looking at him, and he had a role to play. So rather than give in to the sudden urge to jump to his feet with a huge, freaking, What the *fuck*? he pulled on his bartender hat, gave what he hoped appeared to be a genuine smile, and stretched his legs out in front of him as he gave them the response they were waiting for. "Well, Jesus fuck, don't look at me," he said. "I clearly drew the short straw. I'm the one who had to hang out with all you misfits."

As everyone laughed and threw things at him, he

drank from his beer and smiled back, all the while wondering how he had missed every single one of those majorly important things.

Which was why he probably should have avoided being anywhere near Fitz, especially at the very end of the night, after the others had left. It wasn't unusual for them to be the last two by the fire. Deke was always the one to make sure the fire was out, and Fitz would typically hang out with him until the last of the embers died away. It just wasn't a good idea tonight.

"Are you okay?" Fitz asked, her eyes keenly on him.

And he was keenly avoiding looking back. His gaze on the fire, Deke very deliberately misunderstood. "Not usually a woman's response when I tell her we should fuck."

Rather than reply to what he knew was an even more inappropriate response than when he'd said it the first time—which, honestly, was a feat in itself—Fitz's voice went soft. "No, I imagine it's not."

She was quiet for a few minutes as she stared at the fire, too. "I wanted to make it better for you, not worse," she finally said.

Jesus. He closed his eyes and leaned his head back. Of course she'd be the one to call him on that. "I'm a big boy. I can handle my own shit."

Clearly not, but she was kind enough not to contradict him.

Because it wasn't her problem. Hell, he wasn't even sure what *it* was, just that this whole *what-the-hell?* thing was new to him and he was trying to figure it out.

When he heard her get up, putting her Corona on the ground, her clothes rustling as she stood, he assumed she was going inside. But then her hand was on his knee and she was nudging his leg aside and getting up nice and close. He brought his head up just as her fingers brushed his lips.

He wanted to devour her whole. He gripped the armrests so he could at least keep some semblance of control.

"What if I wanted to?" she asked, her hand drifting down his jaw. "Make it better, I mean."

Christ, he couldn't breathe.

"I thought we weren't going to do this," he said, fighting every single cell within him as his body rose up to meet her. Not that he didn't want to, of course; he was even thinking how to go about convincing her she was wrong. He just wasn't sure he was in the best frame of mind at the moment and there was a freaking lot at stake.

"We're not," she whispered, moving even closer, her hands now on his chest. "I am absolutely not kissing you."

Except then she was, and he was letting her, because if he made so much as a move he would go off like a freaking rocket. He dropped his head back and gripped the armrests even harder and tried to keep his heart from bursting out of his chest when her mouth traveled down the side of his neck.

And… Fuck.

He grabbed her by the waist, lifting her up and then settling her in his lap, his hands at her hips. For a second he had enough willpower to keep her hovering over him. To not grind her down against him and ease this godawful six-month-old ache. But then she shifted her hips and every good intention faded away. He pulled her down hard and that moment of first contact was so fucking sweet he wanted to freeze time so he could feel it over and over again. She moaned and pushed against him. Not since his Lacey Jones days had he been so close to losing it while still fully clothed.

As much as he wanted to go there, though—and holy Christ, did he want to go there—he was actually still able to think straight.

So was she. "Oh, *fuck*," she said, her head falling to his chest. "How is it that kissing you is better than sex with any other guy?"

A statement, incidentally, that did nothing to help make things "better" in any way.

She stayed there for a minute, those perfect breasts heaving against his chest as she got her breath back. Then she sat up straight, straddling his thighs rather than his waist. "This would probably be a good time for me to go to bed," she finally said.

"Yeah," he managed. "It would."

But not before he ran his hand up her back, pulled her up against him and kissed her one final time. Open-mouthed and with lots of tongue.

She was the one to pull away this time, panting, although she did it with a smile on her face. "Was that for good luck?"

God's honest truth? "I don't know what the fuck that was for."

Then she gave a low, soft laugh, and a quick brush of her lips to his cheek before she got to her feet and left.

Deke sat there until the sun came up, wondering where they were going to go from here.

Chapter Eleven

The buzz of her phone woke Fitz bright and early on Wednesday morning. Six thirty.

Or, rather, she woke up bright and early on her own. It was the buzz of the phone that put a smile on her face. Deke had texted her each of the last two mornings with a trivia question. Monday morning's had been, What is the brightest star in the sky?

Sirius, Fitz had answered. Go harder next time.

To which Deke had replied, Did you really ask me to go harder? Shit just got real.

'Shit just got real'? she replied. It's amazing you've been able to rack up all those numbers on your belt. Your way with words is…unique.

I happen to be unique in all sorts of ways, he texted back.

Which had both made her giggle and gotten all those pop rocks fizzing again. I think we should probably shut this down right now.

Thankfully, he'd agreed.

Tuesday's question had also been an easy one, but it made her laugh out loud. What's your perfect date?

I'd have to say April 25th, she replied. Because it's

not too hot, not too cold, and all you need is a light jacket.

Miss Congeniality FTW, he'd texted back.

And now you're going soft. Fitz had smirked as she sent that one.

Ouch, he said. Later, Angel.

Reaching over for her phone now, Fitz wondered what this morning's text was. She hated how much she wanted it to be flirty. Logically, she knew that keeping this whole thing going with Deke was the absolute worst idea. But it made her happy in a way she wasn't used to, and she kind of didn't want it to end.

It didn't matter, as it turned out. The text wasn't from Deke, it was from Doug. Things are moving. They liked the package you put together and I think we're heading toward a face to face. Let's talk today.

Wow.

They liked her. They had no idea who she was and they liked her.

She grabbed her pillow and squealed into it, then fell back against her bed, smiling goofily up at the ceiling for a few minutes before forcing herself to sit up and stretch. Not quite ready to get all the way up, she pulled her knees to her chest and wrapped her arms around them, trying to imagine what she'd do with her own place. She'd never had a place of her own, going from Mama Gin's to the apartment Nate owned and then here. As bedrooms went, it wasn't bad. It was in the basement, yes, but Lola's house was on a slope, so Fitz's window looked out over the backyard. Lola was a gardener extraordinaire, and it was a surprisingly nice view.

Not for one minute did she regret moving here. But, yes, signing on with Headhunter Doug had only been the first step. The fact was, she was thirty-two years old and needed to live a life of her own, rather than get comfortable living in other people's houses and taking care of other people's kids.

Although she did kind of love having the sounds and chaos of a family living upstairs. It was something she'd miss when she left, because she didn't see herself with a family of her own. She'd been in therapy for a long, long time. She was pretty confident she was as reasonably adjusted as someone with her past could be. But finding out in the most brutal way possible that her own father had lied to her about being his first child, not his fourth, had the tendency to skew a girl's ideas of happily ever afters. There was a reason she hung out with the guys instead of getting one of her own. Fall in love? No freaking way.

After a quick, I'm free to talk around 1:30, she got herself in the shower.

She was in the middle of drying her hair when her phone lit up with a new text, this one from Deke. Great day for fishing. Pick u up in 20 mins.

Okay, then. No flirty notes, no trivia questions. They were going to have their talk after all.

Which was fine. She'd meant what she'd said to him. That they may as well just move on to the inevitable. Of course, then she'd gone and kissed him again that very night and, well… She'd stayed scarce over the last couple of days; she hadn't entirely minded living in a state of denial.

Not just "hadn't minded," actually. Denial was a great place to be.

So maybe they could put off their chat *just* a little longer. Busy today, she typed. Later this week?

Deke wasn't having it. So get unbusy.

Right. Unfortunately, the man knew far too much about her.

For example, he knew her getting "unbusy" was completely a matter of her deciding it was so. She had complete control over her schedule. There were proposals to consider and checks to write and all sorts of other things. Still, she could do her job in her sleep. Plus, unless she had a meeting to attend or prepare for, she could work anywhere as long as she had her laptop and phone. If she wanted to do it with a fishing pole beside her, it wasn't even a question that she could. Deke knew that as well as she did. Hell, he knew her well enough to know she was standing there right now, trying to figure out how to reply.

It was just that she *really* liked kissing him.

Which was maybe why when his next text came in, saying, You gonna make me beg? the same something that kept possessing her took over and typed, I guess it depends on how good you are on your knees.

Her heart skipped a few beats as she sank down to the floor. What was her *problem*?

Since when did she talk to *anyone* like that?

And what on earth was he going to say back?

I guess it depends on how good you want me to be, apparently.

Oh.

Just the idea made her so hot she actually threw the phone across the room as if it were a potato providing the source of heat.

The phone had nothing to do with it, clearly. It was all Deke.

And fifteen minutes later, when she came up into

the kitchen and saw him standing there, it just took one glance at the look in his eyes and her knees almost gave way. His gaze traveled over her and every cell in her body heated. She couldn't even speak. Her heart started pounding and her breathing went shallow. And then it raced its way down through her, settling dangerously where he had no business being: nestled right there in her very core.

No matter how dangerous this could be—how much damage they could do—she couldn't deny that she *wanted* him there. She wanted him rooted deep inside her and chasing the doubt away.

She closed her eyes and, with a deep breath, focused on the walls that were keeping her safe. The walls behind which she could just happily move through her day the way she had all the others that had come before, ever since the wind had taken her parents away. Except when she opened her eyes up again, she was no longer all alone, secure in her protected space. Nope, he was standing right there.

Her breath caught.

It wasn't fair. It wasn't just the look in his eyes or his almost-too-beautiful face. It was that she knew the taste of him, the feel of him. That she wanted to taste and feel him again. She wanted to reach out and bunch his T-shirt in her hand and pull him that extra step toward her. Bring his body up against hers; lean her head against his chest and know he was hers and hers alone.

Trust that he would never leave.

His hand went to her jaw and he tipped up her chin, that perfect mouth of his curving up into the faintest of smiles. He whispered, "What's going on in that pretty head of yours?" and she nearly fell down to the floor.

When his thumb brushed her cheek she braced her hands on the cabinets behind her just to keep standing. Overwhelmed by the sensation of all that hard muscle right up close against her, she blinked. "Could we maybe just start with 'hello'?"

His eyes narrowed as his lips curved up into a grin. He planted his hands on either side of her and leaned down, sending chills down her back as his lips brushed a wave of her hair. "Hi, Angel," he said, his voice low and raspy as he spoke into her ear. "Morning."

Oh, holy hell. She felt herself melt, felt her body curl into him, completely out of her control. She even, maybe, whimpered a little bit. When he bent his head down to kiss her and paused, his eyes and lips no more than an inch away, she felt herself falling, falling, falling backward into space, unable to do anything other than grab onto him and hold on as his mouth covered hers.

It was too much. Kissing him was one thing; *kissing* him she could do. Very well, as it turned out. Falling into anything, however, was completely off the table. Thank God the boys came clamoring down right then, their footsteps pounding down the stairs from the second floor.

She and Deke parted instantly as they were swarmed, the kids' happy cries—"Uncle Deke's here, Mommy!", "Auntie Fitz!", "Pancake time!"—breaking the spell.

"Okay," she said, trying to keep her world from shifting. She turned her back on Deke as she got out the sippy cups for the toddlers and a bright green plastic cup for Si. "I've got the drinks. Si, you get the napkins; boys, your job is plates and forks."

Her carefully constructed walls, so close to tumbling down, righted themselves again.

Chapter Twelve

He hadn't meant to kiss her. Not like that. Not right
away. But that text she'd sent this morning had messed
with his head. How good was he on his *knees*? If he'd
had ten more minutes, he'd have been happy to give her
a demonstration. After the last two days of not seeing
her, even with the kids coming down it had been hard
to keep his hands to himself.

He wanted her, yes. But he'd wanted a lot of women
in his life and then he'd had them and they'd gone their
merry ways. Sex in itself didn't mean much. It was a
physical thing. This was obviously an entirely different scenario. Risking their friendship for a few hours
of fun wasn't something he was willing to entertain.
He'd spent most of Monday thinking that, yes, shutting
this down was probably the best thing.

Then there he'd been yesterday, standing at his bar
in the same place his parents had worked together for
years, and his grandparents in the years before that. And
he'd begun to think, yeah, maybe it *was* time. Maybe
he'd drunk a little bit too much of the Nate and Dorie
Kool-Aid, but whatever. Maybe his dad hadn't been too
off course and it made sense to stop fighting it. Maybe,
in fact, it would be better to just jump in feet-first and

see how sweet the landing could be. To not worry about how badly a false step could mess everything up between them and instead try and actually make something work.

She was clearly not on the same page, however. Even now, after the best good morning kiss he'd ever had in his life, she was backing away again. Mentally, if not physically, although he could tell she was thinking up ways to get out of fishing as she helped the boys with their breakfast. He could practically hear her thoughts churning. Keeping his back to her, Deke flipped a few strips of bacon and placed a few of the finished ones on a plate as Lola came up next to him.

"What is *up* with you lately?" she asked, leaning back against the counter.

"What?" he said, tearing his attention away from Fitz. For real this time.

Lola grabbed a piece of bacon off the plate. "Fitz, what do you think is going on with Deke?"

"Um, what?" Fitz asked with an almost audible gulp. It was actually kind of cute.

Clearly not noticing that aspect of Fitz's reaction, Lola cocked her head as she stared up at him. "There's been grumbling at the bar," she said. "The speculation is that you're having girl trouble." She took a bite and then folded her arms across her chest, her stare going intense. "But I'm pretty sure I'd know if that were the case, especially because it's never been an issue in your whole entire…"

There was a beat of silence and then her eyes went wide. "Oh, my God. You're having girl trouble."

Proving he was totally off his game, Deke's gaze swung to Fitz. Who, incidentally, had become unnaturally interested in cutting the triplets' pancakes into increasingly tiny pieces. Her head jerked up when, in a tone that was more warranted by, say, a flying saucer landing in the back yard, Lola asked, "Fitz, is Deke having girl trouble?"

For Christ's sake.

If Fitz had been uncomfortable before, she was downright deer-in-headlights now. Recovering just in time, Deke snatched the bacon out of Lola's hand and ate it himself. Served her right. "Jesus, Lola. It's *women* not girls." Since Lola had been drilling that into his head for years, she didn't have as quick a comeback as usual. Taking full advantage, Deke flipped the burner off, deposited the rest of the bacon on the plate, and then dropped the frying pan back on the stove.

Fitz was too honorable to straight out blow him off, but she'd totally seize the moment to give an excuse if he let her. So without even looking in her direction, he grabbed his baseball cap from the hook by the door.

"I'll be in the Jeep," he said to the room.

As he sat there waiting, however, the whole conversation irritated him. *All* of this irritated him. He was still having a hard time with what had happened to Fitz, even if she wasn't. He'd bet a thousand dollars she'd taken more than a weekend to get over it, so he wasn't sure how he was supposed to. But fine. He could deal with that on his own. The real problem was that she'd kept it from him all this time. She'd let him go happily and cluelessly about his business.

He wanted to kiss her again. Hell, he wanted a whole lot more than that. But she was one of his best friends and he was one of hers. If she couldn't trust him with that piece of her life, then what exactly were they playing at here?

The screen door slammed shut and Deke looked up to see her bounding down the steps in a pair of cutoffs he wanted to pull right off her. But he wasn't going to touch her again. Not until they'd talked.

He kept his eyes focused in front as she got in, starting to drive without even saying a word. If she wasn't going to bring up their latest kiss then he wasn't either. In truth, his words had escaped him. He was so afraid whatever he ended up with would be wrong and he'd lose her forever. So he was quiet as they drove out of town, out E63 towards Cambridge, breaking off and taking one of the dirt roads up to Ballard Creek. It appeared to be okay with her since she was quiet, too.

Of course, he definitely didn't win any points when the first thing he said after pulling his Jeep to a stop was an incredulous, "When the hell did you start to knit?"

Looking down at the bag she was holding—with knitting needles tucked in with her laptop—and then back up at Deke, she didn't bother to hold back her grin. "You have a problem with knitting?"

No, he had a problem with Peggy, who knitted her way through every Little League practice and, thanks to Fitz, had also been stuck in his head since last Thursday night. But this conversation was going to be hard enough. No way in hell was he starting there. "You never did it before."

Ah, yes, there he was, quick with the useless statement. Hitting it out of the park, Deacon. Outstanding.

Fitz's amusement turned into an outright laugh, no doubt at his misplaced irritation.

So sue him. He was used to being her go-to guy.

He was also kind of annoyed she had this whole secret past Nate and Jules knew about but he didn't. And he *really* didn't like that he hadn't seen her in two whole days and now that he had her in his sight again, all he could think about was the way the slight citrusy scent set his blood flowing.

Shit.

He was here to *talk*, damn it.

Her eyes left his as she shrugged. "Ella and Jules are teaching me."

He was trying to keep an easy smile on his face. Trying not to let on what he was really feeling: lingering anger at what she'd held back and a nearly disabling desperation to taste her again. He'd never not known what to say to her. He'd never even been tense around her. Not before this past week, at least. But right now his hands were so tight on the steering wheel his knuckles were actually turning white.

Her gaze came back to his. "Are we talking first or are we actually going to get some fishing done?"

She said it as though she knew what was coming. Which was good, because he sure as hell didn't, even though, yes, a conversation was the obvious goal. This was even worse than he'd expected, however. His chest got tight whenever he glanced her way. His throat went dry when his eyes came to a rest on her sitting there in the Iowa Dream T-shirt she wore, fitted a little too perfectly to her curves. He wanted to nuzzle his way up those sleekly muscled legs, all the way up past the dip at the inside of her knees.

"Fishing."

After glancing over at her one more time—a mistake, of course—he got out of the Jeep and went to set up the gear.

"You and your dad seemed to be having a pretty heavy talk the other night," she said. "Everything okay?"

His head snapped up. "We're not here to talk about me."

She raised her eyebrows but didn't call him on it.

He went about his business as briskly as possible, keeping his hands busy as she helped. No telling where they'd go if he wasn't holding on to something already. Like to her hips, for example. Maybe her hair.

But, no, she hadn't just let him go about his business, she was just lying in wait. As soon as he'd sat down on the back tailgate and cast his line, she wedged herself in next to him and said, "Why do you seem so pissed?"

"I'm not pissed." He wasn't. Unsettled, yes, but not angry. It was just that he'd been pretty content with his life all the way up until a week ago. And now he wasn't. He'd been completely and totally thrown.

"Oh, my God," Fitz murmured, looking at him with way too much focus for him to be comfortable. "You're pissed at *me*."

"What?" he said, jerking his head toward her. "No."

"Yes," she answered, with both amusement and surprise. "You totally are." Leaning in closer, not a huge distinction given the tight space, she said, "Please tell me it's not seriously about the knitting."

"Of course not. I just…"

Fuck.

Twisting away from her, he reached back to the cooler and pulled out a beer. So what if it was nine in the morning? And then, because he couldn't keep it inside any longer, he kind of snapped, "I don't know. Are there any other massively big things going on in your life that I don't know about? I mean, it's not like we've been friends for sixteen fucking years or anything." He moved over a little so their sides weren't lined up together, all her curves right up against him. "Jesus, Fitz. Why didn't you tell me? Did you really think I wouldn't want to know?"

Her lip trembled until she bit it and he had to look away. If she started crying, he was done. Under no conceivable circumstances would he be able to keep his arms from going around her if that happened, and once he had her back in his arms God Himself—or Nate; because Nate would probably shove God out of the way whether it earned him eternal damnation or not—would have to pry her out.

Except when she answered, "I'll be sure to let you know if I get a sudden hankering to take up crochet," he realized it wasn't that she was trying not to cry. It was more an attempt not to laugh out loud. Because, yes, he may have been losing his shit just a little bit.

With a glare, he twisted the cap off his beer and took a huge swig.

It was rare that anything truly got to him. This was getting to him.

At least she had the decency to blush a little. Then, knowing full well the distance he'd just put between them, she leaned over again and bumped her shoulder against his before looking away and saying, "They're your people, Deke. You love them and they love you." She reached back for her water bottle. "I wasn't about to take that away from you."

Okay. He'd known that was her way of trying to protect him. But the woman seriously needed to get her head on straight.

"*My* people?" He looked down at her. "I love *you*, Fitz. Anyone who doesn't get that isn't someone I want to know." He wanted to grab her but he forced himself to lean back on his hands instead. "How could you think I'd take Peggy's side over yours?" He took a long pull of beer and then muttered, "For sixteen fucking years."

To his surprise, she laughed, although there was no joy in it. She shrugged a little as she looked away. "Well, it does sound kind of pathetic when you put it like that."

Hell, no. "Don't twist my words. You know that's not what I said."

Rather than give him the comeback he expected, the cocky and confident smartass Fitz he knew, the smile she gave was a sad one. Her head went down and one of the strings trailing off the hem of her cut-offs became the most fascinating thing she'd ever seen, apparently. It certainly took up a lot of her attention. "I can't go back there, Deke," she finally said, so softly he could barely hear her. "I can't be that broken little girl again."

All of the anger seeped out of his soul. It actually hurt to hear her sound like that.

But then her eyes went hard as she slid her gaze out over the water. "I won't ever let people see me that way again."

Well, okay then, he thought, biding his time by taking another drink. "So we're back to the whole not pitying you thing." Which had never been the case in the first place, but whatever.

She looked up sharply. Suspiciously. Then her smile turned wicked as she glanced down at his lips and then back up again. "As in the conversation we had before you kissed me the first time? Maybe we are."

Well, damn.

Yes, she'd sent that text this morning. And, yes, she'd sure as hell kissed him back. In fact, despite her Father's Day declaration that this was a bad idea, she hadn't exactly been sending any stay away signs. If anything, and whether it was intentional or not, she'd been pushing the throttle up steadily, almost as if to see how far it could go.

Deke took another long swallow of beer as every cell in his body went on alert.

If Fitz was any other woman in the world, he wouldn't be thinking twice about any of this. She'd be in his arms already. Her shorts would be off and he'd be going down on her right here in the back of his Jeep.

This was new ground, though. Too important not to tread carefully. Deliberately.

"As in," he confirmed. It took everything he had to hold himself back as he added, "So let me be entirely clear. I don't play games. I tell you exactly what I'm thinking and I expect the same. If I kiss you and you kiss me back, I take that as a sign you want more. Don't tease me about getting down on my knees unless you want my mouth on you for real. If there's some exploring you want to do, I'll draw up the freaking map." Ignoring the hum buzzing through him, he put his bottle down behind him and leaned back. "But you need to tell me where we end up."

Chapter Thirteen

Fitz's heart was beating so hard it was a miracle she was able to think over the sound of it. Her breath caught at his words.

She didn't want to fall—was terrified of being in a place where she had no sense of herself, where he was the only thing keeping her grounded. She never wanted that with *anyone*. Certainly not in a permanent sense. But she couldn't deny how badly she wanted just once to take flight. To let herself go for just that one moment in time.

She wasn't so good with trust, but he was the closest she got to it. And she knew that if she thought too hard, she'd think herself right out of this place, never to reach it again.

"I want you to take me somewhere I've never been," she whispered. "But I need to know you'll bring me right back."

Those eyes that could see so frighteningly far into her soul narrowed. He knew exactly what she was getting at, yet she still needed to say, "You have to promise me this won't change who we are. That we'll still be…us."

"Fitz…" he said in the most tender way as he took her hands in his. Possibly because he could see this scared her out of her mind.

A fuse raced its way through her veins, making it physically impossible to pull away. It was proof of how dangerously close she was to an edge she shouldn't be approaching.

"Promise."

His response to that was to angle up her head so she had no choice but to look directly into his eyes. It was mesmerizing, almost. Hypnotic. "Trust and honesty," he said. "As long as we have that, we'll be fine."

She smiled. A little tentatively, truth be told, yet entirely unable to tear her gaze away. "Sounds kind of like a line to me."

"Not a line," he answered, pulling ever so slightly back. "Not like that."

No, she could see that. It wasn't a line he used for persuasion, it was more the one he wouldn't cross. How he lived the life he did in every way. What you saw was what you got. And, truthfully, it was the only reason she could even consider this. He was probably the one man in the whole world she trusted this much, who she knew with absolute certainty would take care of her until she came back to earth. Who terrified her, yes, but also the only man she felt safe with. Entirely and utterly safe.

So, well, "Okay." She leaned into him and inhaled that perfect, masculine scent.

"Yeah?" he said, smiling after a pause. "I'm not just wishing that up?"

Her reply was to push herself up and brush her lips over his, and then drop her head down to nuzzle his neck. It was something she'd been wanting to do for days.

He groaned. "There is no fucking way that should feel so good."

She agreed entirely. It made no sense that even just

the feel of his skin under her lips sent shivers running down her spine. When he put his hands on her waist, lifting her and moving her over him so she was straddling his lap, she was pretty sure the tremor that ran through her meant this was already the best sex she'd ever had.

His hands went up under her shirt and he lifted it over her head. And...

Oh. Her eyes closed as his hand came up over her breast.

"You do realize," he was saying, "that I've had actual dreams about this."

Considering her own dreams—and the fact that he was slowly brushing his thumb back and forth over her increasingly sensitive nipple—the only response she managed was a whimper when his tongue replaced his thumb. She knew he'd be good—no man could have the reputation he had and not be. But how was it possible to feel *so* good based on so little?

Pushing the cup of her bra aside, his mouth came down over one breast as his hand stroked the other. She arched her back, offering up more of herself to the beautiful wet heat of his mouth. With his tongue still doing magical things, he eased his hand down her back, taking a detour to the snap and then zipper of her shorts. He didn't attempt to take off her shorts, but he did take advantage of their being loose in order to slip his hand inside and come down over the curve of her hip. And now that he had hold of her, he pulled her right in against him and...

"Oh, *God.*" That felt so incredibly *good.*

So good, she didn't think twice about pressing forward. She didn't think, period. She was usually a lot more hesitant, wondering what should go where and if she was doing something wrong. This was Deke, though. As strange as it was in so many ways—her breast was in *Deke's mouth* for heaven's sake—for maybe the first time in her life, she gave in to the raging need to explore.

She pushed him back into the Jeep without thinking twice. "Take this off," she commanded, pushing at his shirt enough for him to pull it over his head.

With a soft chuckle, he said, "I like this side of you," as he shifted farther into the bed of the Jeep, watching her. His eyes roamed over her body as his hands went down to her legs, and he dropped his thumbs down to the inside of her thighs.

"So soft," he murmured, every one of his muscles rippling as he slowly curled up to swirl his tongue around the very tip of her nipple before easing back down again.

She let the shiver run through her and then bent down to do the same to him. Then she set to exploring, running her hands over every single one of those muscles and following with her tongue, pausing finally to say, "Why do you taste so good?"

He laughed. "I live to serve."

"Mmm," she murmured, because, on her hands and knees now and hovering above him, she'd gotten to the good part. He was covered up, but she still closed her eyes and took a deep breath to calm down her racing heart. "Please tell me you have a condom."

Since she hadn't opened her eyes yet, she couldn't see him smile. But she could feel it.

"I sure as hell do," he answered, nuzzling up the side of her neck and setting her to shivering again. "And thank fucking Christ, because with you over me half-naked and staring at my dick…?"

Her eyes flew open and she drew her head back. "I wasn't staring!"

Now he was smiling widely, totally laughing at her. "You absolutely were."

Then he reached down between them. Thinking he was unbuttoning his own shorts, she almost jumped out of her skin when his hand went down the front of hers instead, his fingers brushing over panties that, if she hadn't already been one hundred percent upfront about it, would have proven exactly how ready she was.

Except he wasn't taking any chances, it seemed. "Tell me you want me to touch you," he said, his voice rough. His hand eased down the crease of her thigh. "Tell me this is where you want to be."

Her hips bucked forward as she whimpered. "Yes." She gasped when his fingertips skimmed the edge of the now thoroughly wet cotton. "*Please*."

He'd pulled his head back a little, enough to watch her, smiling as his thumb moved over that ever-so-sensitive bundle of nerves and his finger slipped inside. Her head dropped down and her eyes fluttered closed and she thought she should probably say something sexy or even grateful, but she couldn't actually form any words. He'd barely even touched her, but…

She reared up, reaching back behind her, her hand landing on his thigh as she shamelessly ground against his hand. "Oh, *God*. Deke…" Then everything went sharp and bright and she could no longer breathe. Clearly, she needed a new vibrator. She'd been trying for years and had never managed anything resembling that.

Eyes still closed, she felt his lips at her neck as she

fell down against him and his hand eased away. She was boneless. Entirely spent. How did he *do* that? "Oh, God." She exhaled one more time.

Laying kisses down the length of her collarbone, he eased them both up into a sitting position. Or, rather, he was sitting and she was draped over him, still catching her breath. "Hands up," he said, raising her hands up above her head to the roll bar so she could pull herself up enough for him to strip her shorts and panties off.

And now she was fully naked. Fully naked and with Deke beneath her, his gaze openly taking her in. He stripped the rest of his clothes off, and then reached for the condom, offering an excellent opportunity to appreciate the play of muscles in his arms and chest. Then his hands were on her waist again, and he was pulling her down, and... She clutched the bar with all her might as he slowly eased his way inside her. Sweet *Jesus*. It could not seriously feel that good again.

Moaning as he filled her, she dropped down and wrapped one arm around his back, and stretched the other up so she could run her fingers through his hair. His hand fell down to her waist as he gave her a lazy smile that turned her inside out. When he took her mouth, his tongue touching hers, her entire body surged with want. Her heart did a little dance, sending her blood pulsing through her, all the way down to where she was oh, so very wet, and throbbing desperately with need.

When he started moving inside her she saw stars. "*Deke.*"

"I've got you, baby," he said, his voice gritty and hard and so crazy sexy that it set her off all over again.

She rocked against him, tension building at an almost

unmanageable speed. One hand went to her hip, holding her in place and making it all just so much *more*, while his other hand came up between them to her breast. Along with the feel of him so deep within her, it nearly drove her insane. She rested her hands on his shoulders, and the change in angle drew a low moan out of her.

Deke cupped the back of her neck and pulled her into a kiss, his mouth devouring hers. Between his tongue in her mouth and his hand in her hair and the rough skin of his thighs against the soft skin of hers…

"Oh, *God.*"

Oh, God, oh God, oh God.

He thrust up into her, taking her exactly where he'd promised, over an edge she hadn't even known existed. She exploded in a haze of sensation, all of it intensifying yet again as Deke's hands tightened at her waist and he came as powerfully as she did.

His arm went around her as her entire body went lax.

"It wasn't supposed to feel that perfect," he muttered after the minute it took for both of them to catch their breath.

Fitz wished she didn't know what he meant. She wished it had been just kind of average, maybe even disappointing. Something so it would make sense to never want to do this again.

But it wasn't.

It had been amazing.

She leaned forward and laid a kiss on Deke's shoulder. Okay, maybe three. Then she rested her head against that equally ridiculous chest of his and closed her eyes. Because it had been perfect. So perfect it didn't seem humanly possible, and she was going to hold on to it as long she could.

Chapter Fourteen

The thing about mind-blowing sex was that it was, actually, mind-blowing, and it wasn't until they were halfway back to Lola's house that Deke realized there'd been a point to heading out to the fishing hole and it wasn't to get naked.

Dude, the tiny little devil said, *it was inevitable.*

At least you had a condom, the angel chimed in.

And Jeremy Renner was just hovering over them all with his brawny arms folded across the sash on his chest and a smug look on his face.

"You're all freaking fired," Deke muttered.

"Did you just say something?" Fitz asked.

Well, shouted, because he had the Jeep's top down and that wasn't exactly conducive to conversation. He shook his head.

She looked at him for a minute—he could feel her eyes on him—but he made sure not to meet her gaze. Not out of avoidance. She was very possibly the first woman he'd ever slept with he actually *wanted* to talk to about something other than sex or baseball. For days on end, in fact. But that was the problem. He *had* meant to talk to her. It had been the whole plan. Then he'd fallen into the deep, dark chasm of those glorious eyes and, well, so much for that idea.

Ten minutes later they were pulling to a stop in Lola's driveway. The late morning sun brought out the highlights in her hair, and… Oh, fucking shit. How was it possible for him to go so hard just from a quick glance down at her lips?

Possibly because you're an ass and thinking about what it would feel like to have her mouth on your dick?

Freaking devil.

Deke forced himself to look at Lola's soon-to-be-red front door instead.

"So, how many times have you had sex in this car?" Fitz asked.

Deke turned to her. "*What?*"

"I mean…" She shrugged. "The seats are down in the back so there's all that room, condoms within reach, and there's no way to have any awkward after-sex 'where do we go from here' conversations when you're driving with the top down. It's like the perfect sex-mobile."

She didn't seem upset, just amused.

She was a little bit right, but he wasn't about to admit it. "I don't like clutter, so both my Jeep and my truck are clean…" As she well knew, having spent quite a bit of time in both of them. "Any guy in his right mind always has a condom in his wallet." Duh. "Plus, you've never had a problem talking to me when we're driving in the Jeep with the top down."

Okay, yes, so maybe that last part sounded slightly defensive. But it was as true as the first two.

"I've never had to have an after sex, 'where do we go from here' conversation with you before," she replied.

Right. Which was the conversation they should have

had before it had gotten to the sex part, but here they were. He leaned back in his seat and looked at the steering wheel in front of him. "Just for the record, I usually have that conversation *before* the sex." This was as new for him as it was for Fitz. And because it was Fitz, he could actually admit out loud, "I have no freaking clue what we're supposed to do now."

Because he really wanted to do it again.

She was looking at him again—and he was *not* looking at her, because if he did he would have to eat her up. She quietly sighed when she turned away. "You promised this wouldn't be awkward."

Now he did turn to her. He hadn't been lying. He didn't have a clue where they went from here. But he was a certified expert at leaving the sex behind closed doors. Or at the fishing hole. "No, I promised that no matter what happens, we would still be friends. This is the trust and honesty part of the equation. *Awkward* would be if we couldn't have a conversation right now. I'm happy to talk about anything you want."

He'd actually love to have a conversation with her. Find out what else she was keeping inside, because he had no doubt there was more.

"Anything?" she asked, twisting so she was facing him.

"Hit me." Unlike her, he was an open book.

But when, after staring at him intently for a few seconds she asked, "Why were you so angry with me?" he had to actually look away.

"I wasn't angry with you," he finally said, being not at all honest. So maybe he was a *partially* open book. "I just wish you'd told me about what happened to you." He forced himself to say it without the rage he'd felt when he first heard the story from Nate. And because he couldn't help it, he just couldn't, he added, "You were almost—"

"Oh, my *God*," she said, and not in the good, you've-just-given-me-the-best-orgasm-of-my-life way. Her head fell back against the headrest. "I was not *almost* anything. They were bullies. Pretty much the worst ones ever, in fact. I mean, they practically started crying at the first draw of blood, okay?"

"Jesus, Fitz," Deke answered, making himself turn to her. That urge rose up within him again. He wanted to annihilate anyone who'd even thought about touching her in any conceivable way. "The fact that you had to 'draw blood' is exactly why it is not okay. It's not even *close* to okay."

"You barely even knew who I was back then," she snapped. "I wasn't about to run screaming for your help."

Now he really was pissed. "I knew *exactly* who you were back then." He'd known since the moment he'd first laid eyes on her on a brutally hot July afternoon, her eyes wide and her hair pulled back. He hadn't known she was Nate's sister then; no one had. All he knew was that her name was Angelica and she was the saddest girl he'd ever seen. The fact that he *hadn't* been there for her then—that he'd been just another kid who'd allowed himself not to think about how badly she'd needed a friend—made him angry, too. As furious as he was ashamed. But it didn't negate the fact that, "We've been friends for a long time. I just think maybe you could have mentioned it somewhere along the way."

Proud he was managing to keep the rage he felt out of his own voice, he was taken completely by surprise by the rage in hers as she clutched the door handle and glared at him. "Because I was *humiliated*, okay? I was pathetic and needy and…"

Her voice trailed off and she turned her head away and he was so stunned by her outburst it took him a few seconds to realize there were tears running down her face. It floored him. He was out of his depth in so many ways. He didn't think he'd ever seen Fitz full-out cry. Not since those very early days, at least. He knew she must have. Holy, fuck, she had to have given what she'd been through. But in all the time they'd been friends, she'd never broken down. Never been anything but a calm, kind presence, building up everyone else around her.

Pathetic? *Needy?* That wasn't how they saw her. It never had been.

"Fitz…"

She shied away from him as he reached out.

With an ache so far down deep in his soul he couldn't put a name to it, he pulled his hand back as she wrapped her arms around herself, saying, "I was such an idiot back then. I was just so desperate to believe. They…" She turned away from him again.

Given where his head was at the moment, it took him a minute to process that. To piece together what she'd said the other night at the fire pit, what Nate had told him, and that first night between her and Jules. "They *who*?" Lyle Butler? *Peggy?*

"What did you want to believe?"

She shook her head as she looked out the window and briskly wiped at her tears—that were *killing* him, by the way—before tightening her arms, hugging herself with what seemed like an almost strangling grip. But then, although she kept herself as far away in the seat as she could get from him, she turned back to face him.

"Did you know you were the first person to make me smile after my parents died?" she said, thoroughly stunning him. Again.

Him?

He knew she had no family beyond her parents. That she'd lived a pretty isolated life on a farm before being put into foster care when her parents had died. The Jensens were decent and hardworking, but dour was kind of the name of the game. That they'd been foster parents had been as much of a surprise to Deke as the fact that they'd taken fifteen-year-old Angelica Wade in.

"You gave me back my backpack." She made a noise that was kind of a combination of a sniff and a laugh. "I bet you don't even remember that day."

He did, though. Oh Christ, how he did. He hadn't been nearly the protector he should have been for her, but he'd had some strange Fitz radar, even then. She could be on the other side of a crowded hallway, quietly keeping to herself, and he'd still been able to tell exactly where she was. He'd kept his distance out of deference to Nate, who was still actively avoiding her at that point, but since she'd been a friend of Lola's and since he was always watching out for his own sister, of course, he'd figured even Nate would understand it meant keeping an eye out for Fitz, too.

One day she'd been at her locker and Harry Iverston had pushed up against her and knocked her backpack off her shoulder. Typical asshole move. And it had pissed Deke off beyond words, especially when he'd watched Fitz—still Angelica then, since it was months before the nickname thing—close her eyes and take a deep breath.

By then she'd had enough practice she seemed able to hold back her tears through sheer force of will. So Deke had reclaimed the backpack. Even then he'd wanted to just bundle her up and spirit her away. Since they'd never even spoken to each other at the point, though, he'd instead placed the strap back on her shoulder and given her a wink and a smile before walking away.

Okay, he might have also shoved Harry against the lockers with the promise of a severe beat down if Harry even looked at Fitz the wrong way.

"You made me smile," she added. "I was so…" Her voice broke and she turned to look out the window again. "I was just so alone."

"Jesus," he muttered, hating that she'd felt that way. That it had *been* that way. He looked down at the steering wheel. If he could take even a second of that back, he would. And no, he'd never treated her the way the other kids had, but he'd also never taken the extra step. Not the way Lola had, not until Nate had given the go-ahead all those months later.

If that day with the backpack meant that much to her, it wouldn't have taken much to have been a better friend.

Fuck.

He leaned back against the seat. "You know what kills me? Just grabs me by the throat and takes me down?" He could hear the raggedness of his voice. Knew she could, too. Could even feel his voice break a little. "I thought you were happy. I mean, I figured it took some time to get there, but these last few years…? I thought you were good."

Her breath caught and her eyes were glistening. He kind of hated himself right now. He'd gone through his whole life without a freaking care in the world and never had a clue she hadn't felt the same way. Not about her parents, of course. That was some serious shit. But with Peggy? With Peggy's friends? Fitz had obviously figured out a way to deal with it. They'd just pulled off a perfect weekend and it hadn't been the first time. Still…

"There I was, going about my every day, all happy and go-lucky and shit, and there you were…" He had to stop for a minute. Couldn't actually speak. Finally managed to force out, "It slays me."

And now it was his turn to close his eyes and breathe. He couldn't look her way.

Considering how angry he was at himself, he couldn't imagine she would feel any differently. But instead of getting herself as far away as possible, she sighed. "Oh, Deke." And she reached out for his hand.

He wasn't an idiot. He took what was offered and laced his fingers through hers, looking down at how soft and delicate her skin was against the roughness of his. Focused on that for a minute before he looked up at her again. "What did Peggy do?" he asked, afraid to hear the answer. But he had to. Because there was something she still wasn't saying, something else Nate hadn't told him. Or maybe something even Nate didn't know.

It wasn't a good sign at all that Fitz tensed and started to pull away. But he gripped tighter and it was as if the move made her pull on a suit of armor. She straightened herself up and, after a pause, she said, "Just your usual mean girl stuff. Pretended to be my friend. Got me to tell her all my secrets." She gave a bitter laugh. "Told me the boy I liked liked me, too, and that he was waiting for me. That's the reason I went out to the shed."

Deke's head jerked up. He turned and stared.

Fuck secrets and why she kept them. All of his pro-tective instincts locked into gear. "Do I know him? Was he in on it?" If the fucker was still around and he'd had any idea what was going on… "Did he know?"

And do I have to hurt him? Deke decided not to add.

The strangest look came over Fitz's face. Then to Deke's complete surprise, she reached out and ran her hand down his arm, a gentle caress that came out of no-where and nearly shot him into the stratosphere. He had to fight to stay focused on what she was saying rather than grip her wrist and pull her into his lap the way he was aching to do.

"I was never entirely sure," she said. "I kind of just did that trust thing somewhere along the way."

Yeah, talk about trust. That was a mighty fucking big leap of faith.

Then it hit him.

Oh, Christ, it was one of them. It had to be. Wash, maybe? Cal? He was pretty sure it wasn't Jason, al-though considering the conversation from the other night, he did feel a little bad about even thinking that. But Fitz wouldn't have cared if it were anyone else.

He closed his eyes. That she'd ever put her trust in them was—

"Deke, it was you." she said softly.

He sat there for a minute.

"What?" he said when he was able to speak.

Then the implication of what she'd just said hit him.

He was the reason she had gone out to the shed? That she'd had to actually fight off three guys no matter how fucking stupid and useless they were? That she'd been made to feel so *humiliated* she'd kept it inside for all of these yea—

"Don't you dare," she said, pulling away from him. "I don't want you to feel guilty or that there was something you could've done. I don't need that from you. I don't *want* that from you. If I did I would have told you in the first place."

Shit.

He scrubbed his hand over his face. No wonder she'd kept that from him all this time. Fuck. If it were him, he probably wouldn't have kept him around. "Well, I'm not sure why you didn't hand me my walking papers. Because…"

Except then she got angry. "Don't you get it?" She jabbed him in the chest. "*You* make me happy, Deke," she said, sounding anything but. "You and your happy-go-lucky self."

"Fitz…"

"No," she snapped. "That's all I want from you. That's all I *need* from you. And what happened at the creek was… Perfect. It was perfect. And I'd *really* like to put this whole thing to bed." Her cheeks turned bright red. "I mean, um, stop talking about it. As in, never again."

"Wait…" Which part—him and his happy-go-lucky self or the sex part? Because they were two very different things. Plus… "How did we get to the 'where do we go from here' talk?"

Deke was still firmly in the WTF part of the conversation, truth be told.

"I can't lose you, Deke," she said, shaking her head. "I can't survive that. You mean too much to me. I love you too much."

Okay. Hold the fuck on for a minute. "So you're saying you don't want us to sleep together again no matter how amazing it was?" Which, honestly, was usually his line but he'd never gotten the chance to get there. Obviously. And anyway, it had never been that amazing before so it had never been a consideration.

"It's not that I don't *want* to," she answered, "it's that I can't."

"Because you love me too much." He repeated, just to be clear.

"Exactly."

Well…huh. "That's fucked up."

She didn't deny it. But she also didn't say anything like, *Just kidding, Deke. I so totally want to do it again. Like maybe right now.* Instead she pulled herself away again, retreating into herself. "So, well, we had the talk. By your logic, that means it isn't going to be awkward, right?" she asked.

He turned to look at her. "If I say yes, does that mean you'll sleep with me again?"

She gave a little giggle. Which was beyond cute, but also not at all the reaction he was looking for. He was kind of serious. Then she jumped out of the car. "I do love you, Deke."

She surged forward, gave him a kiss on the cheek, and then got herself out of his reach and headed up the path to the front door.

Well, fuck.

I've got nothing, the devil said.

The angel just shook his head.

And Jeremy Renner was nowhere to be found.

Chapter Fifteen

Late Saturday morning, with Lola at work and Little
League season over, Fitz brought the boys over to Mr.
and Mrs. Deacon's house. She wasn't sure if Deke would
be there. Wasn't sure she wanted him to be.

"Angelica!" Mr. Deacon called over the rose bushes.

She smiled as she turned to him. He was one of the
few people in town she'd never felt...*less*...around. Like
she needed to make some kind of amends. "You can call
me Fitz, Mr. Deacon."

"And you can call me Hank." He laughed.

It was one of their things. He did call her by her nickname occasionally, usually when they were at the bar
and there were tons of other people around. But, yes,
he was one of the few, maybe the only, who regularly
called her by her given name.

She loved him for it.

"Are you here to pick up Deke?" he asked, wiping
the dirt off his hands and coming over to help her un-
buckle the boys from their seats.

There was something in his voice that made her look
up sharply. He was even smiling in a funny way. "Um,
no," she said. "Is he here?" And then, because that might

have sounded a little too eager, she added, "Did he need a ride somewhere?"

"I thought he said something about meeting up with you today," Mr. Deacon said as he lifted James up onto his shoulders. "Must have gotten that wrong."

"Must have," Fitz murmured, watching as he took Luke's hand while Emmet ran up the front walk to the house. "Have fun, boys!"

"We will," Mr. Deacon answered with the Deacon trademark grin.

Since Fitz's car wasn't big enough for all three car seats, she had to exchange Lola's car for her own before heading out for her weekly trip to the cemetery, which left her far too much time to think about Deke.

Things with him had been both normal and strange since Wednesday. Or rather, so normal it had been completely strange. Also, to be honest, a little disconcerting. Yes, she'd been worried it would be awkward. And, yes, she'd been the one to officially put it to rest, so she didn't expect him to fall at her feet. But at the same time, she'd never dreamed sex could be like that. She'd had sex only a few times before, and it had been messy and uncomfortable and not nearly as much fun as she could have had on her own. Not once had any walls been shattered. But Deke had pretty much rocked her world, and now she was wishing for something to make it feel real, even if awkwardly so.

She'd even begun to think maybe it *had* been a dream. She'd had dinner in the bar that very night and he'd smiled and had her Diet Coke ready for her, exactly like he always did. Lunch the next day had been the same. Trivia night on Thursday, lunch on Friday, and early pre-rush dinner with Lola and the kids—

same, same, same. The only thing grounding her in the reality of it all was that he'd glance her way occasionally with a look in his eyes that *incinerated* her. And the trivia questions he'd done the other night had been so bad Wash had to come up with some right on the spot and Deke hadn't even cared. Oh, and that, unlike the usual Deke-mode, he'd barely even smiled at any of the women in the bar. He most certainly wasn't flirting with them.

It wasn't like Fitz *wanted* him to flirt. Not by any means. It was just all kind of *Twilight Zone*.

As she drove out Highway 210, she tried to think about something else. *Anything* else. She failed miserably. It wasn't just the sex. It was all the other things. How caring he was, how tenacious. Even his protective streak.

Well, no. That she could do without.

She settled into the drive, forcing herself to think about the meeting Doug was setting up with Sam in San Francisco during All-Star weekend. Everything was all very hush hush, and Doug was warning her not to get her hopes up because Sam had made clear they weren't officially at the interview stage. Which was absolutely fine with Fitz. She knew everyone would be supportive, but she also knew they would be a little… sad. She couldn't even imagine what Deke would say now that they'd, well, gotten closer than before. But given how unhappy he'd been about something out of her past, she had absolutely no interest in having him dissect her future, too. Plus, she didn't know if anything would come of it. She'd never even had a job interview before. Maybe she'd blow it entirely.

Okay. She was pretty sure that wasn't the case. And

she hoped she wouldn't, because the idea of finally being free of this feeling of everyone always watching just wasn't going away. But thinking about it too much made her stomach turn over.

It's called avoidance, she could hear one of her old therapists say. *Self-sabotage.*

It was also called *survival* as far as Fitz was concerned.

Half an hour later, the gates of the cemetery came into view. So maybe it was a little strange that she spent Saturday afternoons sitting in a folding chair at a cemetery talking to her dead parents. Maybe it was stranger still to bring along her knitting, a thermos of lemonade and snacks, or that she'd never mentioned to a living soul that she even came out here. Still, she was dealing with it, right? Acknowledging that although there was still some anger and bitterness involved, she loved her parents—both of them—and they'd come to an understanding of sorts.

See, Mr. Therapist? There had been so many she couldn't remember this one's name. *Not avoiding. Talking to my dead parents about mutual post-mortem understandings, but not avoiding. Not even a little bit.*

She was so involved in the conversation in her head she'd actually driven past the truck on the side of the road and was turning into the gates before realizing it had the Deacon's logo on the side. She slammed on her brakes, staring into the rearview mirror as she watched Deke get out and walk up to her car.

She turned to him and…

Nope. She was literally speechless.

He crouched down next to her open window. "You need me to leave?"

Uh… *What?*

Shaking her head, she managed, "No."

A smile broke over his face and he gently squeezed her shoulder. Then he came around the front of her car and climbed in.

Driving down the narrow lanes, she took a few moments to process what had just happened. He couldn't have followed her, because he'd already been parked at the gates before she was within sight. With every intention of having a coherent conversation once she came to a stop, all she managed was, "What…? How…?"

It didn't help that unlike the cab of his truck or even his Jeep, her car was small enough that her arm brushed up against his on the center console. She yanked it away as he turned to her.

He didn't say anything right away. He just sat there, looking at her for a minute before looking out the window. "I don't like that you've had to do this alone all this time."

She supposed it shouldn't have surprised her. One of the things she'd come to realize recently about Deke was, when it came to things that mattered to him he didn't hold back. And, yes, she'd known for years she was one of those things.

Entirely unexpected tears sprang to her eyes. Blinking them away, she answered, "Maybe I like doing this alone." Which wasn't necessarily true, but it had never occurred to her to do anything different. Her parents were a sore subject for too many of the people she cared about.

"Okay, Angel," he said, that soft, low voice working its way into her consciousness. "If you truly want to be alone right now, all you need to do is tell me."

She *wanted* to be okay with being alone. Wished it with all her might. But to have him sitting there with her…it made her heart feel like it was bursting in a way she didn't totally understand. She couldn't look him in the eye—couldn't let him see that side of her—but she shook her head. "No." After a few moments of silence, she asked, "How did you know where to find me?"

"I asked Mama Gin."

Her head whipped around. "*What?*"

Mama Gin knew Fitz was here?

He cocked his head and, looking at her like she was crazy, repeated himself. "I asked Mama Gin. Why?"

Why? Was he serious? "Because this is my parents' grave. You know, the guy who cheated on her and left her with three kids to raise on her own—and the woman he did it with."

After a beat of silence, Deke said, "And?"

For heaven's sake. "*And* it's a total insult to ask her about them." The man had to realize that.

But he didn't, clearly. In fact, he just outright laughed. "It's not an *insult*. They're your parents. You loved them. And she loves you. Plus, she's an adult and you're her kid. Of course she doesn't mind."

Now it was Fitz's turn to stare. Then she leaned forward, almost close enough to touch him. Close enough for sure to jab him in the arm. "It is *not* okay to talk to Mama Gin about my parents." She wasn't even going to touch on the part about her only being Mama Gin's "kid" because the woman was too good of a person to let her ex-husband's bastard child stay in the foster system.

Not that Fitz had any issues surrounding that.

"Right," he said, still chuckling as she pulled back. Except then he got serious; his face may even have gone a little pale. "Please tell me you haven't gone your whole life without talking to Mama Gin about your dad."

Well, of course when he put it like that it sounded ridiculous. But it wasn't that simple. "He *left* them. He left *her*. Abandoned them for *me*. That was a horrible thing. I can't just say, 'Oh, can we have a quick chat about him? Maybe over tea?'"

In some kind of shock mode, he just stared at her for a second. Then said, "Of course you can. He's your *father*."

"No, I can't."

Deke leaned forward. "Fitz, your dad did whatever he did for whatever reasons he did it. No one expects you to answer for him. They certainly don't expect you to atone for him."

Had he not learned anything? "Of course they do. You lived it, too. You know the whole sordid story." She wasn't about to remind him Peggy had made her life a living hell *precisely* because of who Fitz's dad was and what he'd done to Nate, Jules and Ella. Deke couldn't be that obtuse. He seriously couldn't be.

Obviously knowing what she was thinking, he glared at her. "Yeah. In *high school*." He looked out at the gravestones as if expecting them to talk before scrubbing his hand over his face. "Jesus, Fitz. We also did drag races up Highway 69 with tractors. We were idiots. But people grow up."

If he'd left it at that, it would have been one thing. Then his face changed, and as he looked at her, she could see the sadness come into his eyes even before he said, "That's part of all this, isn't it? Why you keep so much inside."

Maybe they'd become closer lately with the recent

heart-to-hearts. Maybe he'd seen a side of her no one else had. He was obviously one of very few men to have seen her naked. But, no, she was not having this conversation with him. He was *not* allowed to psychoanalyze her, look into all of the pieces of her past that had already been analyzed and fretted over and discussed by about a billion "specialists" for years on end. Not that she was going to say any of that to Deke, by any means. She'd dealt with the issues she was capable of dealing with. Case closed.

She flung open the door of her car and jumped out. Without even a glance back, she strode down the row of graves, dropped to the ground, then began pulling the dandelions from the base of her mother's headstone.

It took a few minutes for her to calm down, but by the time she did, she realized she'd left both her hat and her thermos in the car. Although it was cooler than usual for June, the temperature was already pretty damn uncomfortable. Already well on her way to becoming overheated, she didn't hear Deke come up behind her so much as realize he was there when her core body temperature rocketed from merely "hot" to "surface of the sun," complete with flares shooting up in the most inappropriate of places, especially considering she was kneeling at her parents' graves.

"I'm fine," she said as calmly as she could manage, especially considering it was something he couldn't seem to get through his head. "I'm not some sad little girl anymore."

"Trust me," he said, his low drawl pure liquid heat. "I am well aware you are one hundred percent woman."

Trying to ignore the tingles running up and down her spine, all she managed in response was, "Hmph."

He brought his arms across that amazing chest of his, six feet worth of solidly muscled sin standing over her and looking down. "I'm sorry. Was that awkward?"

It took everything she had to keep her response a cool, "I'm weeding my mother's grave, Deke. What do you think?"

He crouched down, giving her a close-up and personal view of denim-clad thighs and a hint of what lay between them. Damn him. And then, with a grin that indicated he'd seen exactly where her eyes had wandered, he said, "I think you've spent half your life keeping all this shit bottled up inside, and you don't like me calling you on it."

"I'm sorry," she said, straightening up to her knees. "Exactly what 'shit' do I have bottled up inside?"

"You really want to go there?" He held his hand up and started counting things off on his fingers. "One, your issues with Peggy—"

"To protect *you*."

"Two, the entirely understandable fact that you still love your parents—"

"Because I'd get tarred and feathered if I brought up their names within county lines!"

"Three, the fact that you spend every Saturday afternoon visiting their graves."

"Well... I..." she sputtered. And then, although it was the absolutely least mature thing in the world to do, she reached out and gave him a not-so-gentle shove and sent him sprawling onto his back. Then she made damn sure to turn her attention back to the dandelions so she wouldn't give in to the temptation to crawl right up between his legs until her body was perfectly aligned with his.

Out of pure self-preservation, she didn't look at him when she heard him move. Instead, she turned away a little more so she wouldn't think too hard about the play of his muscles as he sat up, the way he'd felt beneath her when he'd done that very move in order to take her breast in his mouth.

"We're not in county lines right now."

Fitz jerked her head up. "What?"

With his elbows resting on his knees and him twisting a dandelion around his fingers, he looked up at her. "What were they like?"

Her mouth dropped open. She'd lived in Inspiration for seventeen years. It had been a minimum of ten since someone had asked her about her parents.

Then, as if he were entirely unaware he'd just shocked the living daylights out of her, he stretched out on his back, put his hands behind his head and crossed his ankles, looking up at the sky like he was daydreaming in some picture-perfect field full of flowers. "I never met your mom, of course. And I was young when your dad left town, but he and Mama Gin were really close with my parents, so I remember a little bit about him." Then he closed his eyes and smiled. "Mostly that he liked practical jokes."

Yes. Her father had liked practical jokes. It would drive her mother crazy.

And, well… Hell. Deke was right. She'd been so angry at her father for so long, it was hard to remember that part of him. That he was always making her…

No.

"Why are you doing this?" she whispered, trying not to cry.

Even though her gaze was focused on the ground,

out of the corner of her eye she could see him lift his head and look at her. Then he rested his head on the ground again. "I remember this one time Lola and Jules decided they were going to start a fire. They put stacks and stacks of newspaper into the fireplace. There was so much smoke we had to keep the windows open for days in the dead of winter just so the smoke detectors wouldn't go off."

As he spoke, Deke reached out and placed his hand over hers, giving it a gentle squeeze. "My dad was furious. I've never in my life seen him get so mad. But your dad thought it was the funniest thing in the world. I mean, he put the fire out and scared the bejesus out of us with his speech about playing with matches—my dad was practically stroking out, so he couldn't even speak—but there were stacks of newspapers showing up on our porch for weeks after that."

After another squeeze, he pulled his hand away. For a few minutes, neither of them said a word.

Then, for reasons she couldn't have given if her life depended on it, Fitz said, "He was an alcoholic, you know." Like she needed to get that out before anyone else did. Lord knew, the good people of Inspiration had liked to make sure she was aware of that fact.

Deke obviously wasn't one of those people. He only gave her one of those not-falling-for-your-efforts-to-put-me-off looks before resting his head back on his hands and closing his eyes again. "What was he like when you were growing up?"

Her gut clenched.

It felt so strange to be talking about her dad. She didn't even know what to say. Her friends knew her parents had been homesteaders, living off the land. They'd homeschooled her, and although they'd gotten together with other families when the isolation became just too much, they'd primarily kept to themselves.

It all made sense, of course, once Fitz learned about the family he'd left behind. That he'd hidden his existence from them for twelve years. Being too social, even if the town they lived in was a good fifty miles away from Inspiration, would have been dangerous. If you didn't know everyone in the next town over, you at least knew people who did. That he hadn't moved farther away was a risk in and of itself. But even with the full awareness of what he'd done to Nate and Jules and…

She felt the sob rise up and deliberately forced it back down. "He was the best dad." It wasn't exactly something you could go about saying when he'd abandoned the most beloved family in town. It was very possibly the first time she'd ever even admitted it out loud.

"He made everything fun. It was like he lived for making my mom and me happy. Like we were the most important things in the world." She sat back on her heels as she looked at his name carved out in the stone in front of her. Yet for all of the good memories she had of him, she knew there was another side. The part that was broken. The part she was afraid was broken in her.

"I always knew he was really sad," she whispered. The tears came back and this time she couldn't stop them. "I don't know why he left them or why he never came back. But I think he missed them so—"

Before she even realized she'd begun to cry full-out, Deke's arms were around her. And as if it were the most natural thing in the world, she turned into him as he murmured, "Angel," and stroked her hair.

She had no idea how long she cried, just that when

she was done she felt empty in the oddest of ways. Like she had a beginning, and an inevitable end, but nothing quite to fill in the middle. Nothing to fill *her* in. Sitting there at her parents' graves, in the comfort and safety of Deke's arms, she was in a strange kind of limbo, staring into the complete unknown. A future she wished could be like everyone else's, but that she very specifically didn't think about because she couldn't see herself ever trusting a man enough to promise her life to him. Or trusting the universe enough not to throw another tornado in her direction and take everything she loved away. But the idea of living out her days alone was utterly terrifying.

Given her state of mind at the moment, the absolute last thing she should have done was lift her head up. Run her hand up Deke's chest. She most definitely shouldn't have pushed herself up and laid a kiss right there on his lips.

And he knew it.

He didn't kiss her back right away, which was the very definition of awkward and would have been humiliating even if it hadn't been for these particular circumstances. But when she began to pull back, his hand went to the back of her neck and he held her in place. "Don't pull away from me."

They were close enough for her to feel his breath on her skin, to see the lines around his eyes tighten in frustration. She even saw the split second of doubt before he gave in, cupping the back of her head and guiding her the rest of the way to him. She closed her eyes at the dizzying heat as his mouth closed over hers.

The kiss was over almost as soon as it started, but so overwhelming she felt it running through her even after he'd pulled away—while at the same time coming closer, resting his forehead against hers.

"Sometimes I want you so much I can't even breathe," he said once again, shocking her to the point of silence.

Maybe it wasn't that bad of an idea. Maybe they wouldn't be pushing their luck by having sex one more time. Maybe it wouldn't be too complicated to sleep together and still be friends.

Then he muttered, "Fuck," and, oddly, something about Jeremy Renner, before letting go of her and getting to his feet.

"I think I need to take a walk," he said. "You want your things from the car?"

Um, what?

Oh, right. Her hat and her drink. "Sure. Thanks."

Without looking down at her he nodded and, shoving his hands in his pockets, walked off in that direction.

After a few minutes of sitting there in a state of shock, she forced herself to get back to the work of weeding her parents' graves.

Chapter Sixteen

For Deke, everything changed after that day at the cemetery. Pieces fell into place, making sense of something he'd only begun to realize was a puzzle. There was the Fitz he'd grown up with—the one who was the sixth man on their team, who pulled no punches, who came in and ran the show, kicking ass and taking names. Then there was Angelica Wade, the girl who'd had an ongoing thing with Peggy for *years*, who visited her parents' graves every week, and who had all these feelings she'd never let go.

She also happened to be amazing in bed. But when he thought about that, it made things *awkward*, so he concentrated on the other things instead. Like, for example, staying as far away from Peggy and her friends as was possible, which was difficult considering they were in his bar all the time and half of them had kids on his team. Also, getting Fitz to talk about her parents in front of Wash and Jason and Lola. Not Jules—he wouldn't put either of them in that spot—but if there was a chance to get her talking about something from her life before Inspiration, he jumped on it.

She didn't know what to make of it. Hell, neither did he. He just wanted her to be *her*. Both Fitz *and* Angelica.

She was not overwhelmingly happy about it. At least that was his take, given that she'd been a little hands off. Maybe he was just hyperaware and so was paying extra close attention, but she was definitely a little distant. Was certainly keeping her distance by skipping out on their runs and avoiding pretty much any situation where they might end up alone together.

Which was probably for the best. Since he was a true believer in the "any resistance whatsoever means no" directive, he was forcing himself to be hands off, too, even if his dick didn't feel the same—even though it meant walking around with a woody for days on end. Hell, by the time All-Star weekend came around two and a half weeks after they'd had sex, he felt like he was a teenager again. Since he'd actually had more sex at that age than he was having now, that was a freaking problem. It was a bigger problem that, for as much as he tried to psych himself up for being in San Francisco and hitting some of those parties again, he couldn't quite bring himself to get interested in any woman other than Fitz. He'd hoped it would be better by now. But, no. Every piece of him wanted every piece of her.

Yeah, he was screwed. Just not literally.

And now here they were in California, about to spend four days in closer proximity than usual, which wasn't going to help matters one bit.

Keeping his sigh to himself, Deke let his forehead rest against the floor-to-ceiling window with its view of San Francisco Bay.

"Crazy, no?" Wash said from Deke's side as they looked out over the city below.

Would he be referring to the private plane that had brought them to California? The four bottles of complimentary Dom in the bucket on the bar? Nate and Dorie's two-story hotel room, the freaking Presidential Suite, complete with two and a half bathrooms and a baby grand next to the full dining room with a table set for eight? Or maybe it was the dodging in and out of cars as crowds of photographers shadowed them.

"Crazy," Deke repeated. As in, batshit. Exhausting, too. You couldn't pay Deke enough to live like this, not even the hundreds of millions Nate actually earned. Maybe Deke's life was a little too simplistic for most folks, but, comments from the peanut gallery aside, he was happy with it. He liked kicking back with his friends. He liked heading down to the fishing hole with Fitz even when it actually meant fishing, although just in case anyone was paying attention, he liked it a whole lot too when they were naked and kissing.

Shaking his head as he jammed his hands in his pockets and turned to Wash, he said, "Do you miss it?"

"Not even a little bit," Wash answered without hesitation. "It drains your soul." He tipped his head toward Nate, who was over by the bar, pacing as he talked on his phone. "I think Dorie saved his life. No lie."

With a glance over toward Nate, Deke had to agree. For most of the last few years, Deke had been sure they'd lost him for good. Even six months before, Deke wouldn't have sworn Nate was still the same guy he'd grown up with. But then he'd met Dorie and now they had him back.

Dorie, who had, by the way, been dubbed "America's Sweetheart" by the media and was the hit of the weekend, to Nate's complete dismay. In fact, from what Deke could tell that was what the phone call was about.

Something about Nate agreeing to some exclusive interview if the cameras would leave them alone.

"Just bring it down to normal levels of craziness," Nate muttered. After a few more murmurs he hung up the phone and shook his head at Wash and Deke. "Ridiculous," he said, throwing back a full glass of whiskey. Then he went to the bottom of the stairs and called up. "Babe, the later we are, the more access they have. And I already know you look perf…"

His voice faded into nothingness as he took a step back. Then he frowned. "Shit."

Wash raised his eyebrows and grinned at Deke. "This'll be interesting."

Dorie came down wearing a dress with crisscrossing straps that, granted, brought all sorts of possibilities to mind. She looked hot, no doubt. But that wasn't what Nate was commenting on. That became obvious as soon as Fitz came into view.

Ironically, what she was wearing kept pretty much everything covered up. But the way it did so was with black pants that begged you to imagine her curves hugging you in all the places it counted. Though the cherry red shirt she had on was long-sleeved and buttoned up, it was also entirely sheer, and underneath it she wore a black camisole that only highlighted what he was intimately aware was some world-class cleavage. As if that weren't enough, she'd gone on the heavier side with the makeup, her eyes dark with shadow and liner, her cheeks flushed pink and her lips fire-engine red.

"Holy shit," Wash muttered. "That's not Fitz."

If only it weren't.

If asked, Deke would have said his preference was for a less made-up look. But on Fitz, when it was topped off by her hair all long and wild, tousled in a way that couldn't possibly be natural but that looked like she had just been completely and satisfyingly fucked—again, something of which he was keenly aware, well… By now he was used to his dick going rock hard whenever he saw her, but right now he couldn't even think for all the buzzing in his head.

He did register that there was a conversation going on between Fitz and Nate, with Nate clearly trying to get her to change without coming out and stating that under no circumstances was his little sister leaving this room looking like *that*, given the animals who populated those parties. Animals who once upon a time had gone by names like Nate, Wash and Deke. Jason and Cal, too. Being those guys was a whole lot different than being related to a woman guys like that had in their sights. It did give a whole new perspective.

"Are you *serious*?" Dorie asked, jabbing Nate's chest with her finger before getting up in his face, her hands planted on her hips. "Do I need to remind you about playing pool with Tommy?"

Which, clearly meant something to Nate, because, although his nostrils practically flared, you could tell by the set of his shoulders that, even if he'd thought about saying something, he wasn't about to now.

Having obviously already figured out exactly how far she needed to go, Dorie grabbed her bag off the bar and then took Fitz's hand and yanked before heading directly to the door. "Come or don't. We're going dancing."

The door closed behind them before Nate released his stance. When he did, there was no less heat, it was just directed at Wash and Deke. "*Fuck*." Then he whirled on his heel and followed after them.

Yeah. Deke agreed with the sentiment. It was bad enough he was going to have to watch Fitz all night when she looked like that. Considering they were going to a party whose invite list included several hundred of those primates…?

Fuck, indeed.

Lights started flashing and reporters started shouting as soon as they walked out of the hotel. Nate had arranged for private security, which had seemed a ridiculous concept to Fitz when she first heard about it. Given the throngs of people on the sidewalk who were shouting Nate's and Dorie's names, she realized that, if anything, he probably hadn't hired enough.

"Is this for real?" she murmured as a mammoth guy in a black suit held his arms out to keep the people from crowding in too close to Dorie as he led her to the limo.

Nate, who seemed torn between following immediately after them and waiting for Fitz, frowned as his eyes scanned the crowd. "Everyone keeps telling me the craziness will die down." He put his arm around Fitz's shoulder and pulled her up against him. "Next time I pull a stunt like that—" meaning, Fitz supposed, a proposal that went viral within seconds "—tell me I should think twice."

"Awww…" Fitz gave him a big smile. "You know it was the sweetest thing ever." Even Fitz, who wasn't a believer in the whole romance thing, had cried some happy tears when the video appeared on all of her feeds.

Stopping abruptly a few feet away from the limo, Nate frowned down at her as he waited for a different security guy to open up the door. "Sweet" clearly didn't go along with his pro catcher vibe.

She grinned as she climbed in and scooted to the far end of the seat, right across from Dorie. Nate got in next, then Wash next to him. Deke, who seemed on board with the please-stay-far-enough-away-so-I-don't-jump-your-bones-in-front-of-my-brother vibes she was sending, ended up on the seat next to her, but sat far enough away there was no chance of even an inadvertent brushing up.

Which was good. It was their new normal. She was fine as long as she wasn't touching him. She'd even agreed to go fishing a few more times, with the caveat that Silas and Matty come along. She needed the buffer. Although Deke had been entirely aware of what she was doing, he didn't seem to mind. Once he got them set up with their gear, he'd cast his line into the water, sit back and pull his cap down over his eyes, and then ask her something about her mom or her dad or growing up and just generally unlocking all the doors she had slammed shut years ago.

It kind of sucked. She felt like she was in some strange version of *It's A Wonderful Life*, and there was some greater power showing her, *Here. This is what your life could be if you'd only just let it.* But even thinking about those kinds of things made her unsettled. Sometimes even angry. And although she couldn't seem to escape the exceedingly naughty dreams she continued to have about him each night, she worked hard at keeping all those thoughts at bay. Having gotten extremely good at masking her frustration for over two weeks now, she merely turned her head and looked out the window of the limo.

She actually had high hopes for tonight. Resting her head against the seat as the limo pulled out into traffic, she focused on that: fun. Also preparing herself to pretend she wasn't apeshit jealous once Deke put himself out there. She'd been out with him enough to know how this went. He'd walk into a crowded room, women across the land would notice, and then no one would see Deke for—

"Shit. Deke and Fitz, switch sides," Nate muttered and she sat up straight.

"What?" she snapped as Deke's head turned sharply, both of them obviously highly aware of the same thing: maneuvering of any kind would mean actual contact.

Nate was clearly distracted, however, and despite the practical standoff he and Deke had had back on Father's Day, his gaze was on a car full of photographers alongside the limo. There was no other way in the world he'd be forcing a situation like this. But forcing it he was, nudging Fitz's shoe with his foot. "Move to the other side of the seat so you're the one across from us instead of Deke."

Okay, yes, it made sense that Deke should be across from Dorie, and Fitz from Nate and Wash. The back of the limo may have been spacious enough for ordinary people, but it didn't quite have enough room for three six-foot-plus men to be sitting across from each other. But damn. Fitz looked over at Deke, bracing herself against the Earth-halting-on-its-axis moment she still felt whenever his eyes met hers. When he shifted over so she could climb over him, she tried desperately to do so without making things worse than they already were.

The fates were against her. The maneuvering was such that it required not only the climb, but in a moving car it also meant his hands had to go to her hips to keep her steady. And she practically had to strad-dle him in order to get over to the other side. Maybe if his breath hadn't caught as her thighs fell to his, or if his fingers hadn't tightened hard enough to show his strain in keeping her away from where they might otherwise be joined, she'd have been fine. But it had hitched, and his fingers had tightened, and she wasn't fine. She wasn't fine at all.

She scooted away from him the second she could, afraid if she gave herself any ground, she'd strip naked for him right then and there. Thank God he moved away just as quickly.

The rest of the ride was torture. His presence over-whelmed her. Even without looking at him, she could feel his every movement. Wash said something that made him laugh, and she could picture the way the corners of his mouth would turn up just so. The seat shifted, and she nearly shivered at the memory of the way he'd felt beneath her in his Jeep, at the thought of him leaning back and looking up at her as his legs parted enough for her to slide between. As he then parted hers and lifted her up and onto him.

She pushed open the door and jumped out of the limo the second it came to a stop, and was immediately greeted with an explosion of flashbulbs.

"Just get them inside," Nate said from behind her, as she was suddenly being propelled forward by the secu-rity guy and shouldered through the crowd.

"Keep moving." Nate again, with a tight smile on his face as he waved at the reporters. With his arm around Dorie and his hand lightly on Fitz's back, he not only didn't slow down, he was pushing them both forward.

For the first time in maybe *ever*, Fitz was grateful for the simplicity of life in Inspiration. Sure, everyone and their brother knew every last detail of her history, but at least she didn't need security, for Heaven's sake.

As they entered the huge room with its colorful lights flashing and the music pulsing,

Nate's manager/publicist/all-around assistant appeared out of nowhere to guide them toward a roped off area. It was quieter back there, enough to hear Nate's muttered curse when Alexis said, "Like I said on the phone, just a few pictures. I promise. Then you're free for the rest of the night."

Since it was already after ten, that didn't seem the best negotiating point, but Nate appeared resigned to it.

"Okay," the woman said, smiling. "Let's do some Dream shots."

It wasn't the worst thing to see Nate, Wash and Deke hamming it up like old times. Fitz did not, however, like Alexis putting her hand on Deke's arm and pulling him closer to the camera.

Taking a deep breath, Fitz forced herself not to scowl. Or sneer. Or jump on Alexis's back and claw her eyes out from behind. It was a reminder that there were as many gorgeous women out there in the crowd as there were gorgeous men. And Deke was excellent at making new friends.

"What?" he asked Fitz, frowning. The photographer stopped, causing everyone to turn to look at her.

"Nothing." Annoyed with herself for not keeping a better handle on her thoughts, she gestured for them to continue. "Go on. Take your pictures."

But before she could even step back, Deke reached

out and yanked her to him. She came against him with a thud, glaring up at him.

He wasn't paying attention, however, instead smiling at the photographer. "Meet Baby Hawk. The sixth member of The Dream."

Baby Hawk? "Really?" He had to go there?

Well, if that wasn't a clear indication they were back to normal despite sexy times in the back of the limo, nothing else was.

Since no one else seemed to have a problem with her being in the picture, she stayed. And then Nate decided that as long as Fitz was in the picture, it was okay for Dorie to be there as well. Alexis and the photographer clearly loved the just one big happy family vibe of it all, and Fitz ended up squeezed against Deke, trying desperately not to think about how good it felt. There had to be laws against that.

"Uh, Baby Hawk, was it?" the photographer said. Ignoring her glare, he reached out and tugged her arm down a bit. "Yeah, that's it. Around his waist."

"Shit," Deke hissed, his entire body tensing as her wrist brushed his…

"Oh," Fitz gasped, her arm jerking away as she realized he was… *It* was… Hard. So very hard. And Fitz so very much wanted it inside her again.

No. No, she didn't.

She bit her lip.

"Do not… Fucking… Move…" Deke said quietly— painfully—as his hand clamped down on her wrist and held it in place. Not against him, of course, but just out of range.

Blood rushed to her cheeks. Because now she couldn't

get it out of her head. She wanted to close her hand around him. To stroke his length.

To make him come again.

His other hand, the one *not* holding her wrist in a death grip, went to her waist. He gave her hip a warning squeeze.

She had every intention of glaring up at him, but just as she was about to do so, the others shifted, causing Wash to bump into her, which in turn caused her wrist to drop down and push against the tip of Deke's erection.

He gave an almost inaudible groan.

"Are we done?" she asked, her voice unfamiliarly high in pitch.

She immediately began to pull away when the photographer lowered his camera and the others were led away by Alexis, disappearing around the corner. But she found herself being yanked back up against Deke, his hand doing a bit more caressing this time, fingers slipping down to the crease of her thigh.

And she nearly wept. It felt that incredible.

He pulled her closer, forcing her to straddle his thigh. She gasped as he ground her against him. With the music pulsing overhead, he had to bend down to speak to her, right into her ear. "You are the hottest fucking thing I've ever seen," he said, to her complete surprise. "Be careful out there tonight."

Then he let go of her and walked away, leaving her staring after him. She sank back and took a deep breath before pushing off the wall. The first order of business would be a huge freaking drink, followed immediately by a whole lot of dancing to work off this steam.

Chapter Seventeen

All the ground Deke had gained by keeping his distance had evaporated the second Fitz put her hand on his shoulders in the limo. That whole thing with the photographer brought him right to the edge.

And now the woman was pushing him over it and driving him fucking in*sane*.

She'd been at it for an hour now, laughing and dancing with every goddamn guy who asked, which was not a small number. If Nate hadn't been so closely watching her, Deke would have done something about it. He had no idea what, but it would have been something. As it was, he was grateful for a lifetime of being in and around bars, of carefully controlling his reactions. Though he was pretty sure he'd been able to keep all other outward appearances neutral, he'd shredded three coasters and was now working on his fourth.

"Can I get you another?" the waitress said, bending down as she cleared his empty bottle, and displaying what on any other night would be a world of temptation. Her eyebrow arched as she swept up the latest cardboard casualty. "Or maybe just a stack of coasters?"

That earned a grin. Hell, maybe he should be working it as hard as Fitz was. Because she sure as hell seemed determined to go home with *someone* tonight, and given she was keeping her dance card entirely full, odds were it wasn't going to be him.

Which was fine. Whatever. But, *fuck*. He was still hard.

"Let's stick with the beer," he muttered, his eyes traveling back to the dance floor. Now she was dancing with *two* guys. "Christ."

Where the fuck was Dorie? Although she didn't strike him as the clubbing type, she was definitely a bit more worldly. Of course, Deke was part of the reason Fitz wasn't more experienced at any of this. He'd been more than happy to go along with Nate's keep-the-guys-away-at-all-costs plan back in college. Right now he wished he hadn't been so gung ho.

Deke turned to Nate. It was high time for someone to do something about his sister being out there and if it wasn't going to be Nate, then Deke was stepping up. Except before Deke could open his mouth, Dorie appeared in front of them with a look on her face that meant business.

Wariness came into Nate's eyes. "What?" he murmured, sitting up a little straighter.

"Ox is here," she said, plopping down on the seat next to him.

Ox, as in Jack Oxford. All-star pitcher, yes, but also known to the entire world by now as Nate Hawkins's ex-best-friend. Considering the guy had not just slept with Nate's previous fiancée, but had also gotten her pregnant, this had the potential to be ugly as hell and everyone knew it. There was a definite awareness rippling through the crowd, as though everyone was waiting to see if the two men might come face to face.

"Do you want to go?" Dorie asked, as softly as possible given the blaring music.

"Why would I want to go?" Nate asked, seemingly oblivious to the tension. But that was Nate for you. The man could have a mob of angry fans coming at him and he'd most likely just calmly take a sip of his drink as he stared them down.

Deke was familiar enough with the tingling down his spine to know it meant Fitz was nearby; it barely even got to him anymore. Sure enough, she'd left the dance floor, finally, and was about to sit down, bumping him with her hip as she nudged him over and perched on the cushion next to him. "What's going on?"

The waitress, who was clearly well-trained to keep her VIPs happy, appeared almost immediately, her tray balanced on her hand. "Two Dos Equis," she said, placing the beers in front of Deke and Nate, "two Guinness," went to Dorie and Wash. And then, "A Sex on the Beach."

Deke turned to Fitz.

Her cheeks still flushed from dancing, she gave him a little grin as she picked up the drink and took a huge sip from the straw. "What? You never let me order these at home."

"Because their only purpose is to get you drunk," he snapped. He couldn't handle a drunk Fitz. The one time he had served her that drink—too many of them, granted—he'd brought her home and she'd almost stripped in front of him before stretching out on her bed. He'd forced a T-shirt over the bra she'd been wearing and spent the night working on the bar's taxes at her kitchen counter.

Raising her eyebrows, Fitz shrugged and took another sip. "Yep." When she went to put the drink down on the table in front of them, a little bit sloshed over the edge. "Oops," she said, her smile wide. Then she raised her arm and twisted it a bit, letting a drop of the drink slowly work its way down her wrist. She held it up to his lips, leaned in and said, "Wanna lick?"

Which, unlike the presence of the ex-best-friend who had impregnated the ex-fiancée, appeared to be the thing that would put Nate over the edge.

Deke could feel the iciness directed his way. The only thing that surprised him, in fact, was that Nate hadn't killed him yet. For as much as he'd been trying not to be obvious about it and had stayed well away from the subject after Father's Day, he knew Nate was aware something was going on. That there hadn't been an actual throw-down was no doubt due to Nate choosing to keep his focus on his fiancée rather than his sister. But if Fitz kept this up, Deke's days were limited. No doubt.

As gently and impersonally as possible, he moved Fitz's arm aside. "Thanks, but I'll pass." For the health of all concerned.

Second crisis averted, Dorie raised her drink.

Fuck. Deke nearly jumped out of his skin when Fitz's hand went to his thigh as she leaned forward.

"A toast?" she asked, making no attempt whatsoever to keep her breast from brushing his arm. He was going to take her right there, God help him.

With a smile on her face, Dorie said, "I kind of can't believe this is my reality at the moment, but since it is…" She waited for everyone else to raise their glasses before locking eyes with Nate. "To The Dream. The best friends I never thought I'd have and the man I didn't quite realize I had loved all my life. Thank you for making me believe."

There was something about the way she looked at Nate and how he looked back that made Deke a little jealous, truth be told.

Not that he wanted Dorie for himself. She and Nate were so clearly made for each other it didn't even bear thinking about. But the connection between them was so strong it did make a guy think about having a woman who made you feel like that. Because it was obvious to anyone sitting there that despite how quickly they'd gotten together and how whirlwind their romance had been, that love ran deep and true. Nate had never been happier in his life.

Even when she pulled away from the kiss that inevitably followed and said, "I think you should talk to Ox."

She, too, was a little bit drunk. And it was meant for Nate's ears only, most likely, although Wash heard it, too, raising his eyebrows at Deke and muttering, "Oh, shit."

His lips setting into a grim line, Nate answered, "I think maybe not."

Dorie's hand settled over Nate's thigh. "*I* think we should talk about this some more." She leaned in close, and, yes, she was definitely drunk, and this was definitely meant to be private. "You miss him, Nate. And maybe, since you heard Courtney out, you could at least give him a chance to explain."

"Damn it, Dorie," Nate said, his expression changing from hard to soft in the blink of an eye. His eyes flicked to Wash and Deke, both of whom immediately found other things to concentrate on, and then back to Dorie before looking away. "I'll think about it."

"Good," she said, sounding both happy and sad. "Because if you don't, I might have to kne—"

"I know, babe," he said, smiling as he shifted her hand up closer to his knee. "And we all know how that turns out."

Before anyone could ask what "that" was, the DJ's voice rang out loud and clear. "Alright, kids, we've had a request. Although that's not our usual MO, since it's from America's Sweetheart, we thought we'd go along with it. So take a ride with us back to 1993…"

"Oh, *hell*," Wash said, sitting up straight in his seat and echoing Deke's thoughts exactly as the song began to play. Dorie and Fitz jumped up, squealing. Deke shifted in his seat uncomfortably, the image of Fitz dancing to his jukebox that night wasn't ever far from his mind.

"What the hell just happened?" Nate asked, as they all focused on the dance floor.

"So here's the thing…" Wash started to say, looking at Deke in a clear call for help.

But Deke was down for the count on this one. All he could do was shake his head. He buried his head in his hands in hopes it would make him think about something else, make him want Fitz less. But remembering the way she'd demonstrated that lick nearly undid him. He looked up again, catching a glimpse of Fitz just as some guy's arms went around her from behind.

No. Fuck it.

He was done with this shit.

He was on his feet so fast he didn't even think about what it might look like to Nate. Turns out there was no need, since Nate was two steps behind him.

Right before they reached the dance floor, Nate's hand went to Deke's shoulder. "You'd better fucking take care of her tonight."

Which had Deke stopping suddenly despite the dancing that so clearly needed to be put to an end. "What did you just say?" In no universe had Nate just uttered those words.

He had, of course, it was just that Deke had misinterpreted him completely, as was clear when Nate hissed, "You keep her away from all these assholes. Keep her with you or Wash from here on in. If any *one* of them tries to take her home tonight, you kill him and then you come to me. I'll help you bury the body."

The frightening thing was that it didn't seem like he was kidding.

No. The truly frightening thing was that Nate was telling the last man on earth who should be hearing it that he was responsible for getting Fitz safely out of this party and back to the hotel.

"You got it, man," Deke said, knowing he'd just bought his ticket straight to hell. "I'm all in."

Fitz nearly stumbled when Deke stepped onto the dance floor. It was clear he had his sights on someone, and she had to tell herself it didn't matter who he hooked up with tonight. "I'm here for me."

Reminding her that not only was it true but she was doing fine on her own, *thankyouverymuch*, the majorly hot guy who'd just had his hands on her hips shouted down into her ear, "Did you just say something, *cher*?"

Oh, right, majorly hot and *Cajun*. The shortstop from Texas, she was pretty sure.

Before she could answer, however, his warmth was abruptly gone from her back. "Aw, shit," he said, his hands shooting up in the air as though he was being held up. "No more fighting, man."

Right again. Majorly hot, Cajun, and recently making headlines for brawling on and off the field.

"All yours." And he was gone.

Under normal circumstances, it would have pissed Fitz off. But then she looked up and saw Deke glaring as he came closer.

She took a step back.

It was absolutely useless. He reached out and grabbed her hand; turned around and yanked her toward him. She had no choice but to scurry after him.

"What…? Where…?" She finally dug her heels in and pulled out of his grasp. "What are you doing?"

Of course she wished she hadn't when he turned around and came back to her, crowding her in. "What do you think?" he replied, his voice low and yet somehow ringing out clearly over the music.

Okay, yes, he'd pretty much spent the entire night sitting and sulking, but it wasn't her fault he'd chosen that over getting out on the dance floor himself. She was sure it wasn't because of a lack of willing partners. And, honestly, if Nate could keep his act together when his actual *fiancée* was dancing, then Deke had no business having any attitude whatsoever.

But he took her hand again, turned away and pulled her with him as he stalked out of the club. Which was all fine and good until she realized that, while he still had one hand clamped around hers in a death grip, he was raising another to call a cab. Bewildered, she asked, "Where are you going?"

This time when Fitz planted her heels in the ground, she made it stick. And she pulled her hand out of his as she turned back to the doors of the club. Only to be swung back around and right up against Deke when he grabbed her hand again and pulled her back. "Away from here," he muttered.

Oh, no he didn't. Shoving his chest, Fitz had no problem getting up in his business, even if it meant she had to get on tippy toes to do it. "*You* can go wherever you want. *I* am staying right here." She loved him—loved all of them—but, damn it, she was having a good time. An *amazing* time. And the only reason she wasn't in a murderous mood right now was because she'd had just enough alcohol to take the edge off of wanting to kill him. Since she was sobering up quickly, however, his odds weren't looking good.

Deke didn't have the decency to even fight with her about it. When a cab pulled up to the curb, he picked her up by the waist and put her inside. Sliding in after her, he snapped, "Just drive," to the driver. Then he sat back in the seat and looked out the window.

Her mouth dropped open so wide she couldn't even sputter a word.

Had he actually just *removed* her from the club? As if she were a kid he was babysitting rather than a thirty-two-year-old woman who could do whatever she damn well pleased? They were already well on their way when she finally got hold of herself enough to punch him full out, hand-hurt-like-the-devil-but-it-was-worth-it in the arm. "You did not just do that!" Then she leaned forward toward the cab driver and, in the exact same tone, screeched, "Turn around!"

Glaring first at her then the cabbie, Deke was seething. "Do *not* take us back."

The cabbie, a man of no words, pulled the taxi over to the side of the street and got out. Then he turned his back to them, leaned against the door, and took out a cigarette.

Was he freaking *kidding*? She turned to Deke. "You're kidnapping me right now and he leaves me in the back with you?" About to take her not-insubstantial anger out on someone she'd never have to see again, Fitz reached over to open the door, stopping when she felt Deke's hand on her shoulder.

"Anywhere but the club," he said. "*Please*."

Fitz turned to him, surprised at the desperation in his eyes. It was unlike anything she'd ever seen. It sliced through her as if it were a knife through her skin. She stared at him for a minute, closing her eyes briefly only when his hand fell away. Sitting back against the seat again, she knocked on the window. "The Intercontinental," she said when the man got back in.

With the slightest of nods, he pulled back into traffic.

Not to say she wasn't still furious, even more so when they got to the hotel and she realized her clutch, including her phone and key card, was back at the club. Since she now couldn't get to the floor her suite was on, she jabbed the button for Deke's room instead, glaring at him. Just as he opened his mouth to no doubt argue with her, his phone rang. Nate's ringtone. Nate, by the way, who she blamed equally.

With a hiss of breath she crossed her arms against her chest and stared straight ahead.

"At the hotel," Deke was saying. "Yeah. We just realized she left it. Sounds good."

The elevator doors opened as he ended the call. Fitz stormed out into the hallway before realizing she didn't actually know Deke's room number.

It should have been a sign that he wasn't gloating in any way, but it wasn't. Or maybe when he stalked off without even looking in her direction. But, no, she didn't catch on to that, either. So instead, without any regard to the consequences, the second they got in his room she got up in his face once again and shouted, "What is your freaking problem?" She even reached out to give him a little push—okay, yes, maybe an actual shove— just so he knew exactly how pissed she was.

Except he turned toward her right then and caught her wrist in his hand. The air that had merely been crackling turned into a full-fledged electrical storm, lightning bolts and all. He took a step toward her. *Crash!* She took a step back. *Bam!* Her entire body flushed as the bolts came down around her, and she was pretty sure her hair was standing on end.

Her knees may have even actually buckled when he leaned down. "You, Fitz. *You* are my problem."

"I…" Er… "What?"

It wasn't that she hadn't heard him, of course. It was just that she was a bit dazed at the moment, what with him bringing her wrist up to his mouth and running his lips over the sensitive skin.

And then he was walking her backward to the wall until she came up flush against it as he came up flush against her, as big and solid as she remembered him to be. His forehead dropped down to touch hers. With her heart pounding as loudly as it was, she barely heard his muttered, "I can't. I'm sorry," before he started to turn to the door.

She reached out for his hand and stopped him. "Can't what?" she whispered, pulling him back.

He went still. With the exception of where she was touching him, he was obviously working at keeping the rest of him at bay. His eyes traveled down her body and then back up. "Can't be near you." Then he closed his eyes as he leaned in closer, his lips just barely grazing her cheek as he took a deep breath. "Can't keep watching you."

Maybe she was still a little tipsy; she clearly wasn't in her right mind. Because even though she should be in complete support of his leaving this room, the word that came out of her mouth was, "Stay."

His eyes flew open. "What?"

She brought his hand up to her hair, letting go and leaving it there so her own hands were free to run up and down his chest. "Please stay."

She didn't have to say it again. She was suddenly being lifted up. He wrapped her legs around his waist and bent down to kiss her neck while pushing against her and sending her eyes rolling back into her head. Groaning, he let his head fall against hers. "How drunk are you?"

Um… "What?" She was supposed to speak? She opened her eyes to see him staring at her and her heart came to a thudding stop. She turned her head away, both comforted and terrified by the awareness in his gaze. As her friend it was fine. But as her lover…it was too much. She couldn't get that close. Especially not to a man who knew her well enough to get himself inside the deepening cracks in all those supposedly fortified walls.

Yet she found herself entirely soberly saying, "Not nearly enough."

He closed his eyes. "Thank fuck."

His mouth came down on hers, crushing in its intensity. One of his hands tunneled through her hair while the other curved down past the small of her back and he pulled her up against him, her breasts to his chest, her hips lined up with his and all the good parts in between. With a whimper, she grabbed at his belt. She wanted his shirt off, too. About to come apart just from the feel of his tongue against hers, she was nearly delirious with the thought of holding him in her hands. Of having him move inside her again.

He smiled against her lips in agreement, although he seemed a little more focused on her upper body. He'd gotten her down to her camisole without her fully registering it and was now pulling away from her enough to look down between them. He finished unbuttoning his shirt and was down to bare skin. Which was…

Yep. Un-freaking-believably amazing. She ran her hands down his chest, loving the feel of the light dusting of hair over the taut, firm skin. But leaning forward to nuzzle at his neck, meant rocking against that overwhelming heat, reminding her she really just wanted that one thing.

Right now.

She'd already gotten the belt undone and would have been fine with the button and zipper of his pants, except she was distracted by the hard length underneath them and what it did to Deke every time she touched it. Which she proceeded to do, enthusiastically, running her hands up and down, loving the way it twitched and pulsed and how his breath became rapid and shallow. She practically giggled with delight.

"Tease," Deke said as his hands went to either side of her head. There was a smile, too, albeit a wicked one. Shifting so he had her pinned against the wall, he took her hands, bringing them together and raising them over her head, and held her in place while he took care of his button and zipper. Then took care of hers.

Before she could even catch her breath, his hand slipped down beneath the waistband of her panties. But just as he'd done the first time they'd been together, he paused. "You're sure?"

"Are you going to ask me that every time?" she asked, wanting him inside her so badly she was about to come out of her own skin.

His eyes went dark. "Are there going to be more times?"

She didn't have an answer to that. She couldn't think that far ahead. All she could manage right now was, "Just fuck me, Deke," she said as she pulled his head down. "We'll talk after that."

Thankfully, that seemed to be enough for now. His hand lingered at her clit just enough to set off several shockwaves before going down farther and slipping inside, the heel of his hand firm against her. A tremor tore through her, this one forcing a long, low moan as her head fell back against the wall.

"You like that?" he said into her neck while adding another finger to the one already inside.

Beyond a more drawn out moan than the first one and a shifting of her hips, she was incapable of any response other than another whimper.

"Oh, yeah, you do," he whispered as he worked his magic.

Shimmering waves radiated through her, and since he just laughed a little as she tried to free her hands, she arched her back, trying to get closer to him that way instead. Oh, God. "*Deke…*" She pressed her hips forward again.

"I know, baby," he whispered. "I've got you."

Except then he let go of her wrists and his hand was gone from below and he stepped back.

"*No*," Fitz whined, heart pounding as her hands slapped down flat against the wall in order to hold herself up. She was panting now, her breath coming in short little bursts as she watched him grab his wallet out of his pocket and take out a condom. Holding the packet between his teeth, he dropped the wallet to the floor and dropped down to his knees in front of her.

She had that moment of thinking, Hell, no. Not with *Deke*. "You don't have to…"

But the words trailed off as he looked up at her with that wicked smile on his face. He pulled her pants and panties down to her thighs, and then, eyes not leaving hers, leaned forward and licked right up through her folds. She tensed. No one had ever done that to her before. No one had ever made her *feel* like this before.

Then he licked again, and again, and then one more time and all coherent thought ceased. Her head thunked back against the wall. "Oh, God," she gasped. His hands went to the back of her thighs and he pulled her toward him, his tongue delving inside at the same time. Sensation rocked through her and she was trembling, then shaking, and then everything went black and then white and she cried out, maybe screamed, something that may have been his name.

Before she was able to catch her breath, he was standing up, lifting her by the hips, and then bringing her back down, impaling her with a groan and a shudder of his own. "Jesus, Angel. You are so fucking tight."

But she couldn't utter a word because she was back to panting and trembling and pretty much out of her skull with the need to feel that again. "Don't stop. Oh, God, *please*…" She was arching her back, rocking forward against his hips, doing everything she could to have him stroke up against that one perfect spot as he thrust into her, a little deeper each time. Her hands on his shoulders, she clutched at his skin. "Please don't stop."

She cupped the back of his neck and pulled his

head forward so that his forehead was resting on hers. Then she crushed her mouth to *his* and may have even growled as she ran her hands down his back before cupping his ass and pulling him closer. With a groan, he took the kiss she gave him, then gripped her chin, holding her firmly in place as he took control back and amped up the intensity. His mouth dropped down to her neck as his hand went to her breast.

He nipped at her neck as he thrust into her, obliterating everything else that existed in the universe and replacing it with blinding, frantic need. Desperate for his kiss, she pulled his head back up to hers and sought out his lips. Tears started falling as he took her up and over the edge again, her entire body turning into a quivering mass of sheer bliss.

And then he was seeking out her mouth again, his lips on hers as he thrust into her one, two, three times, before letting his head fall against her shoulder and groaning her name.

They stayed like that, with him still inside her, as their breathing steadied. Honestly? She was one hundred percent sure she'd be okay if they never moved. But he finally looked up at her and tenderly brushed a strand of her hair behind her ear. "I can't believe I just took you against the wall of a hotel room." Clearly troubled by that fact, he shook his head and looked away.

She couldn't either, truth be told. And it was probably the worst idea in the world. But that didn't stop her from putting her hand on his cheek and bringing him back to her so she could look into his eyes when she told him, "Well, get over it fast, because we're doing it again."

Chapter Eighteen

They didn't do it again. Not against the wall, at least.
The second time he took her, it was in the bed, and he
happily worshipped every inch of her. He also paid her
back for the torture she'd put him through earlier that
night, driving her right up to the brink more than once
without letting her actually come. He might have done
it a few more times if not for her threatening his life
if he didn't...

Well, he was pretty sure her exact words were,
"Freaking *fuck* me!" Except she didn't actually wait
for him to respond before she flipped him over and
rode him like she was taking the top prize at the goddamn rodeo. His encounters weren't usually quite that
intense. And what intensity there was, was usually sup-
plied by him.

It was the hottest thing he'd ever experienced in his
life.

So the third time, he went so hard and deep that he
was pretty sure *he'd* be feeling it for weeks. He had no
doubt she would.

There hadn't been a fourth time, although, Christ,
he would actually have been willing to try if she made
even the slightest move towards it. For now they'd set-

tled on a bath instead. His room wasn't nearly as nice as the suite she had upstairs next to Nate and Dorie, but the bathtub was big enough for two and there were ceiling high windows looking out over the city. Which, honestly, had seemed a little odd, but Fitz just rolled her eyes and said they had to be one-way and if she didn't have a problem with it, then he had no excuse. Since the view was spectacular, both of the city and Fitz, he figured it wasn't worth the fight. And now she was sitting with her back to his front and it felt so right it actually scared him a little.

Her hands running from his knees down to his hips, she leaned back into him. "No wonder you're happy all the time."

"Hmm?" he asked. He'd been distracted by her breasts. Again. There were freckles there. He'd never noticed them before.

Laughing, she batted his hands away. Took them into hers and pulled them down to rest against her stomach. Which was also good, because he could inch just a little farther down and—

She sat up abruptly and swatted some bubbles at his face. After laughing even harder, she said, "Money where your mouth is, Deke. If I don't get to have you inside me, you don't get to play."

"You've really only been with two other guys?" he asked without thinking. He'd been beyond surprised at her delivery of that news, a declaration between orgasms three and four that she'd now officially come more times with him than she had with all the other guys she'd ever been with combined. Of which there were only two. He also had to admit that for someone who kept so many things so close to the vest, she was remarkably open about sex. Yet another new Fitz fact.

But to her the question apparently meant something else, because now she was frowning. "In no small part thanks to you guys scaring away every guy who even looked my way."

Well, okay, yeah. Deke could see that. He'd never realized they'd been so effective. Nate would be happy to hear that. Until he found out how Deke had become aware of that tidbit of news.

"None of them were good enough for you. We weren't about to let some jerk get his hands on you."

Except, well, three of them *had*, back in that shed, which was still something Deke didn't like to think about. But think about it he did, and the thought that came to mind was, if he'd been her boyfriend at the time, he might have killed them. Whether they actually hurt her or not, he would have killed them dead.

Considering how incensed the whole idea made him as her friend, if he were her boyfriend now? He still might.

Of course he wasn't her boyfriend, and they *were* still just friends, it was just that now they were friends who had slept with each other multiple times.

"Where on earth did you just go?" she said, staring at him while she snuggled up against his chest.

"Nowhere." Which wasn't true, of course, and her eyes narrowed, a clear sign she was aware of that fact. It was a little strange, in fact. Women tended to like the way he made them feel, in bed for sure and sometimes out of it. But that was about as intimate as it got. This was actually a little disconcerting.

"Oh, I'm sorry," she said, while being obviously not

so. "Is that man-slut speak for 'I've been inside your body every which way, but God forbid I let you into my head'?"

"Man-slut?" He sat up straight, which of course meant she was also now sitting up straight, little beads of water racing their way down from her shoulders to those damn perfect...

No. He was *not* going to get distracted yet again. Not when she was insulting him like that. No way in hell.

Her hands went to her hips, which wasn't helping one freaking bit. And then she leaned forward, and since she was straddling his legs, it meant that perfect, tight little bead of a nipple was right where he could—

She stuck her hands in his hair and tilted his head so he had no choice but to look up.

"Well?" she demanded. But then her eyes and voice went soft. "Where did you go?"

He couldn't lie to her, but at the same, he knew exactly how she'd react to what he was actually thinking, so instead he wrapped his arms around her and held her, something he'd been aching to do for the last three weeks. God, he liked the way she felt up against him, all naked and perfect. Then he closed his eyes and leaned back again, bringing her with him and tucking her head against his shoulder, as he said, "Us man-sluts like to chill after sex, not engage in conversation."

Her body went tense at that. "Sorry," she said, her finger tracing the line of his collarbone. "That just came out."

Shifting a little as her tongue took the place of her finger, he said, "No offense taken. I mean, the fact that I gave you your first three screaming orgasms doesn't give me special status or anything."

She laughed. "How do you know you gave me my first three? Who's to say I'm not as good with my hands as you are?"

Okay. No mistaking his reaction to that one. "I am more than happy to help you confirm that statement," he murmured, trying to contain his groan as she rubbed all that nice, wet heat up against his dick. And when she started nibbling and sucking at the base of his neck...? *Damn.*

"You are *really* good at this for a newbie."

She stopped abruptly and sat up again. Then she smacked him on the shoulder.

"Ouch!" he said, not at all softly. She'd sure been spending a lot of time hitting him lately and he had to admit, he wasn't overly fond of it. Not when it was because she was pissed at him for whatever this new reason was. "What the fuck, Fitz? If you want to take it there I'm down with it, but could you give me a little warning first?"

"Why do you do that?" she asked.

As if he had any clue what she was talking about. "Do what?"

Frowning, she reached for a towel. "Change the subject."

For Christ's sake. "You're the one giving me a freaking hickey and rubbing up all over me. How am *I* the one changing the subject?"

She frowned again.

With a deep sigh, Deke leaned back against the cool rim of the tub and rested his arms along the sides. She'd crucify him if he brought up Butler and the shed again, so he didn't. But it might've been better if he had, because instead, lulled into his usual comfort zone around her, he came out and said, "I was thinking about what would happen if I were actually your boyfriend." Meaning he'd have license to beat up anyone who even looked at her funny. An important distinction, though one he couldn't mention.

"*What?*" She was up and out of the tub so fast he didn't have a chance to see any of the good parts.

"Jesus Christ, Fitz," he said, irritated as she wrapped a towel around herself, her back to him as if he hadn't just licked every inch of her skin. "I don't know what those other two guys were like, but if you push me to answer a question, then I'm gonna freaking do it. You know that about me. Or would you rather I revert to freaking man-slut status?" He reached over to grab a towel for himself. "Not that that was offensive, by the way."

"I said I was sorry," she said, with enough of a pause to show she actually was.

So much so she seemed unable to look at him as he got out and wrapped his own towel around his waist.

"It's…" She turned to the sink and reached for a washcloth. "It's nothing personal." Her eyes caught his in the mirror for the briefest of seconds before she looked back down. "I don't want a boyfriend. *Ever.* That's not for me at all. I just don't believe in falling in love. That whole happy ending thing."

Leaning back against the wall, he crossed his arms to watch her run a washcloth under the faucet, not sure he'd heard her right. As she ran it over her face to wipe off whatever makeup they hadn't already worn away, he said, "Come again?"

She shrugged. Then she went back to the face washing. "I mean, think about it. Lola and Dave? Jules and

Jeremiah? Ella and, well, whoever it was she almost got engaged to back in law school?" She shook her head. "I wish Nate and Dorie all the best, but what are the odds of them actually working out?"

What the fuck?

"A hundred percent," Deke answered. Okay, yes, Lola's story was not the one anyone wanted. And Deke was now firmly in the Jeremiah Is A Dick camp. Jules was better off without the guy. But Deke believed wholeheartedly that kind of love was possible. Both sets of his grandparents had been married over fifty years, and his parents had just hit forty. "Angel…"

Putting the washcloth down and turning to him, Fitz glared. "Don't 'Angel' me." She took another towel and used it to dry her hair. "I love them both to death and I think they're great together." She rolled her eyes. "Okay, fine. You're right. Even *I* think they'll probably make it." She shook her head. "But odds are I'm either Mama Gin, who gets left with three kids to raise all on her own, or my own mom, who either finds out after the fact she was the other woman, or who knew it all along. I don't like either of those options." She hung the towel to dry. "Not that there are any guys beating down my door, so it's a moot point anyway."

First of all, the idea of any guy other than him beating down her door wasn't one Deke could handle at the moment. Not without admitting to a streak of jealousy so fierce it was frightening. Second of all, though… Did she not see herself ever falling in love? Did she not even want to? How in the hell had she gotten that one past him, too?

"So you don't see yourself five years from now presiding over trivia night at the bar while I'm home taking care of our babies?"

Holy shit, he did not just say that.

She let out a bark of a laugh. "Not even close." Then she looked at him and her eyes went wide. "You're joking, right? Oh, my God, please tell me you're joking." She turned her back on him and left the bathroom, leaving him to stare after her.

"Of course I'm joking!" he called out, after he'd managed to get his senses back.

And since now he *did* have his senses back, he could admit, yes, she had a valid point about Mama Gin and her own mom. Things weren't black and white, though. There were eight billion shades of gray out there in the world and a whole hell of a lot of other permutations. Plus, she'd never even so much as asked Mama Gin about her father. Maybe there was more to the story than what she knew. He pushed himself off the wall and followed after her.

By the time he came back into the bedroom, she had on her camisole and was buttoning up her pants. Although he should probably leave it alone, he said, "Did it ever occur to you there was maybe another side to the whole thing with your dad?"

Deke had been four, maybe five years old when Nate's father left, but he was pretty sure it hadn't been the happiest of marriages. And, yeah, even before he'd known the term or heard it from the rest of Inspiration for years after the fact, he'd known the man was an alcoholic. Deke had lived it, but he'd been so young that there were very few memories. Of those there were, however, they ranged from the laughter he'd remembered to fits of anger that, unlike the story Deke had told Fitz about their fathers, he'd never joke about. Even at that age he and Nate had known what lines not to cross.

As long as he was bringing it up, however... "Did he ever tell you why you guys were heading into Inspiration that night? He had to know there'd be people who wouldn't be too happy to see him, so he must have had a reason, right?"

Fitz's head jerked up. "What?"

Coming all the way into the room, Deke sat down on the edge of the bed. "I mean, there's twelve steps. Making amends is a big one."

She went a little pale.

Given how she'd responded when he'd asked her about talking to Mama Gin about her father, he held back from saying the words that came to mind, which were, *Please, God, tell me you've thought about this at least once in your life.*

But from the way the color drained out of her face and she said, "You think he was...? Do you think he was going to...?"

Holy fuck. She *hadn't*. She truly had locked all of these things away. Little boxes marked Things Never To Think About and with the keys nowhere to be found.

Jesus. He reached out and gathered her into his arms as she looked up at him, tears forming and spilling over from her eyes. "If he was coming back to see them... That's... That's just so much sadder."

Yeah, it was. It really fucking was.

He took hold of her hips and tugged her toward him until she was standing between his legs. Well, fucking *Christ.* His intention hadn't been to make her feel worse. *Nice one, asshole.*

"Stay here tonight." He couldn't let her leave like

this. He'd wanted her to stay even before this conversation. Now? No question.

She wiped her eyes as she let him pull her in closer. She even gave a little laugh. "Right. And we're going to say what, exactly, when Nate bangs down the door first thing in the morning?"

Yeah, they were skating on razor thin ice. At the moment, though, Deke didn't give a shit. "He knows you're locked out of the suite and with me." Plus, since it was three in the morning and no one had banged down the door yet, Deke figured they'd be safe for the rest of the night. "Use my phone to text Dorie. Tell her you're crashing here."

She cocked an eyebrow.

Sensing she was willing to go with it but needed a nudge in the right direction, he wrapped his arm around her waist and pulled her all the way in. Close enough for him to nestle his head in her chest—okay, so that part was for him—while he brought one hand up to play with her breast. "Tell her I had plans for breakfast but you'll be back first thing."

Well, fuck, if he had the reputation he may as well use it to his advantage. If Nate thought he was meeting up with some other woman in the morning, then even if the man did suspect something, it would make him think twice. At least, Deke hoped Nate would. It wasn't Deke's first choice to deceive his friend, but this was one of those cases where protecting someone was more important than telling the truth. Of course Nate would flat-out kill him when he found out, so whether he was protecting Nate or himself was the question.

When Fitz hesitated, however, he realized he was actually worried maybe *Fitz* wasn't entirely certain. At least that's probably why he sounded a little too sharp when he added, "You know they'll believe you."

Except that wasn't the case. When she tilted his head up it was clear from the look in her eyes she was thinking more about *him*. "You are so much more than that," she said, laying a soft kiss first below his right eye and then his left. "I may not be in the market for a boyfriend," she said, echoing his thoughts a little too closely for comfort. "But I don't doubt you'd be a great one."

Then, as if they did this every night, she pushed him backward so he was lying down on the bed, and crawled up over him. "Okay, lover boy, it's time to go to sleep." She rested her head on his chest. "Can I borrow something to sleep in?"

Now they were talking. "Absolutely freaking not."

Chapter Nineteen

Deke, as it turned out, was a snuggler. To her complete surprise, Fitz was, too. It hadn't been an option with the other two guys she'd been with—one had room-mates, one still lived with his mom and she was so not going *there*—so she'd never really thought about it. If she had, she probably would have said that, after the whole sex thing, she'd want her space back. Her *body* back. It was something physical, as far as she was concerned. To give more of herself than that was too dangerous; overnights came a little too close to that kind of connection. But Deke was different. He already had a huge part of her, so that road had already been traveled.

Plus, she couldn't get enough of touching him. She wanted her legs tangled up in his and his arms around her. God, even first thing in the morning he was perfect. He tasted like coffee and cream and the feel of him against her, hard in all the places she was soft, had her aching for more.

"Babe," he mumbled, pulling her closer as he rolled over, not fully awake.

Which was fine. Perfect. It gave her some time to properly appreciate him, something she hadn't had the opportunity to do last night. She'd been too overwhelmed by the raw sensation of it all for the beauty of him to sink in. He was beyond magnificent to look at. She was compelled to reach out and run her hand over all that sumptuous skin, although she didn't want to wake him. She wanted to savor what had happened, not talk about it. Yet when he cupped his hand around the back of her neck and drew her into a hungry kiss, she couldn't help but respond.

"What time is it?" he eventually murmured.

With reluctance, she lifted her head, saw the time on the bedside clock, and nearly jumped straight up in the air. Eleven a.m.? She *never* slept this late.

Shit. Shit, shit, *shit*. She had her interview with Sam at eleven thirty.

Scrambling for her clothes, she couldn't help but glare at Deke as he chuckled and turned over so that he was now lying on his stomach, head resting on his hands no doubt in preparation to go back to sleep. She was tempted to smack his lazy ass and make him get out of bed, but then there was the potential of him wanting to talk through what had happened between them, something she very much wanted to avoid. Not that they shouldn't be talking it through. As big deals went, having sex with one of your best friends definitely had the potential to be up there, especially when it had already happened once and you'd assured yourself it wouldn't ever happen again. But despite his whole staying home with the babies comment, so far so good.

Also a plus was that she didn't need to explain where she was going. Since her destination happened to be Sam's hotel room, that was definitely a good thing. According to Doug, the reason she was meeting Sam there was that he hadn't even officially announced the foundation, so it was still all in top secret mode. Also a good thing, as far as she was concerned.

Oh, and thank God her key card had been pushed under the door along with a note from Dorie. *You missed our run but I'll forgive you—if you provide details.*

Ha. Not on her life.

Fitz flew upstairs for the quickest shower in the history of man, set a personal record for getting dressed and took the stairs rather than the elevator because Sam's suite was two floors below hers and it was faster that way. Tucking her portfolio under her arm, she knocked on the door.

Sam's assistant opened the door, a polite smile on her face that evaporated the second she saw who it was. "*Fitz?*" Then she smiled broadly as she pulled the door all the way open. "What an incredible pleasure it is to see you here."

"Hi, Hannah." Fitz knew Sam because he had been Nate's friend long before he'd been Nate's boss. But she knew Hannah because they'd worked on several events together over the years thanks to Fitz's job. Getting that response from someone she knew on a purely professional basis was not a bad sign at all.

"Sam will be up in two minutes. He's actually having brunch with Nate right now," Hannah said, pouring Fitz an unsweetened iced tea without even asking.

Oh, hell. Trying to keep her smile calm and serene, Fitz asked, "Will Nate be here, too?"

"No, dear." Hannah's eyes lit up with her smile. "Sam wanted to see for himself who our mystery candidate was before letting any of the investors know." At the sound of the key card on the door the other woman smiled again. "He's been dreading it a little bit, I'm sorry to say. But this is going to be a wonderful surprise."

Fitz certainly hoped so. She wasn't entirely sure since Sam came to a sudden stop right inside the door, a look of confusion on his face. And then came a big smile. "Well, what do you know," he murmured. "Never in my life did I peg 'Jane' as Fitz Hawkins."

"Jane?" Fitz asked, puzzled, as she took a seat on one of the couches at Sam's invitation to do so. She sure as hell hoped it had been her portfolio they'd looked at. Then again, even if it wasn't, her foot was in the door and she wasn't about to let them push it out.

"Jane Doe," Sam said, a smile on his face as he sat down across from her. "That was all Doug gave me. Now I see why."

Okay then. Go, Doug.

Sam leaned forward. "Does Nate know you're meeting with me?"

Fitz shook her head. "I thought it would be better for us to talk first."

And talk they did. Sam grilled her for forty-five minutes, in fact, asking about everything from investment strategies to office management. "I have to be honest," he said as their meeting came to a close, "I took this interview as a favor to Doug."

"Also because you were thoroughly intrigued," Hannah piped up from where she was sitting at a desk across the room. "And because the portfolio blew you away."

"Yes, also because," Sam conceded with a smile. "I was looking for someone with a little more experience, but there was something about your portfolio that kept pulling me back." He cocked his head. "You think you're ready for the big leagues?"

To be perfectly honest? Fitz had no freaking idea. But there wasn't any question he'd thrown at her that she hadn't been able to handle. And if she'd learned anything from having Nate Hawkins as her big brother, it was that confidence went a very long way. "One hundred percent."

It made Sam laugh. "That's the same answer Nate gave me when I asked him if he thought he was good enough to build a baseball team around."

Well. Fitz had to smile at that. "I guess you have your answer, then."

Sam sat back, eyes narrow, even as a smile came over his face. "I guess I do." He stayed like that for a minute, his gaze never leaving hers. Which was pretty damn uncomfortable, but Fitz had been around Nate long enough to know the mind games these guys played, so she knew not to show it.

And it appeared she passed the test. As he stood, Sam said, "I have a group of investors, Nate included, that will be part of the formal interview process. Will that be a problem for you?"

"Absolutely not," Fitz said, standing up as well. Nate would find out sooner or later and if it was because she'd gotten as far as interviewing with the board, then she was okay with that. And other than the oddity of being interviewed by her brother, Fitz had no qualms sitting at a table with big-name players surrounding it. In fact, she loved the idea. "I'd be honored to have the opportunity to show them what I can do."

With a nod to Hannah, Sam said, "Let's set that up then. It won't be for another month or so as we've just begun to gather names. But you will definitely be on the list."

"Great." She tried to keep her smile subdued as she shook hands with him and gave Hannah a hug goodbye.

She waited until the elevator came to do a celebratory dance. It was tempered only when it occurred to her Deke wouldn't be happy about this at all. She didn't for one second think he'd been serious about her having his babies, but, no, he wouldn't be happy.

This hadn't even been an official interview, however. Yes, it had gone well, but who knew how these things worked? Sam might already be having second thoughts. So she'd deal with it later. Compartmentalizing, not avoidance. At least that's what she told herself.

Along those lines, however, she did have to admit this whole thing with Deke had gotten her thinking. And when she got up to her suite and saw Nate and Dorie stretched out together on one of the lounge chairs out on their balcony, she found herself wondering what it would be like to love someone enough to take the risk they might one day leave. To believe strongly enough in the fact that they loved you back.

Nate looked up right then and raised his hand in greeting, shifting in a way that made it clear Dorie was asleep and he was trying not to wake her as he reached down on the ground for something.

A bottle of water, it appeared, as Fitz went through the door that connected their suites and joined them. Water he almost spilled all over himself when he looked up at her and registered the suit she was wearing, before muttering, "No fucking way," as he looked back out over the cityscape below.

Well, okay then. Sooner it was. She supposed she hadn't fully expected to get it by him, especially not after finding out he'd had brunch with Sam. She was just glad she hadn't needed to have a whole long conversation about it before she went.

"Way," she murmured, sitting down in the lounge chair next to him.

He shook his head. "You know I'd practically be your boss."

"You're practically my boss now," she reminded him.

He took a sip of water. "That's different."

"How so? Because you'd be the only one of my bosses who knows I'll run stark naked down the hallway if I see a spider while I'm taking a shower as opposed to five out of five?"

Because she had done that once. March Madness, a few years back. Even Cal had witnessed that one. The worst part? All five guys had looked up at her streaking down the hall and then, as one, turned back to the TV. She'd had to actually grab Jason by the ear—he was the closest—in order to get one of them to help her out.

Nate stared at her for a minute then looked away again. "Why didn't you tell me you wanted a change? We could figure something else out."

Fighting the urge to glare at him, she reminded herself that he was her brother. He loved her. It was in his nature to want to take care of her—which was part of the problem. Maybe she wanted for once in her life do something all on her own. Maybe she *needed* to know she could rely on herself for when the time came. But instead of actually coming out and saying so, she chickened out. "Because I wasn't sure I did. I'm still not sure I *do*. But I'd like to see where it goes."

Nate wasn't happy about it. That was obvious from the way he set his jaw. But he did say, "I can't think of anyone who would do a better job than you would." Then he quietly added, "Sam would be lucky to have you."

Fitz fought off the tears that came to her eyes. "Thanks." It was one thing to think about having a new job, another entirely to consider what it would realistically mean to say good-bye to everyone. She'd never had to do that before. Her parents didn't count because she'd never had the chance to say it. And she talked to them every week. But whatever. She'd be fine.

Changing the subject, Fitz nodded down at Dorie. "You must have tired her out," she said, wishing she could take it back immediately when Nate raised his eyebrows. "With the dancing, I mean. She was totally into the dancing."

With a soft laugh, Nate said, "That she was." Then, a little harder, he said, "You, too."

"Mmm." Fitz decided that was agreement enough. Especially because she wasn't sure if she was pissed at him, since he'd no doubt sicced Deke on her, or grateful, due to what had happened after that. Not that she'd be mentioning any details to Nate, of course. "More parties tonight?"

"Probably." He reached down for the water. "If that's what you guys want to do."

It wasn't. Not if she couldn't dance with Deke, at least. "Maybe we could just do some sightseeing. I bet the view from that park above the bridge is awesome at night." Then again, she was just happy to be somewhere other than Inspiration, so she'd be okay with anything. She shrugged. "Whatever is good."

Nate barely even seemed to be listening. She was pushing herself out of her chair when he said, "Did you sleep with him?"

She jerked her head up so fast she actually hurt her neck. "*Sam?*" Did he seriously just ask her that?

"*No,* for fuck's sake," Nate snapped with the appropriate amount of denial. "With *Deke.*"

Oh.

Fitz felt her cheeks flush and she quickly looked away as Nate swore under his breath. But after taking a deep breath, she turned to meet Nate's gaze head on. "That's your business how?"

Eyes narrowing, because he of course had his answer right there, Nate just looked at her for a minute, not backing off at all. "I don't want to see you get hurt."

Breaking the stare, Fitz fell back into the chair and looked out over the city again. She didn't want to see her get hurt, either. Which was why she'd had sex with Deke, not pledged her life to him. Two very different things.

Since that conversation would have gone over as well as it had with Deke, although for entirely different reasons, Fitz found herself instead asking something she'd never expected to say to Nate. "Do you ever think about Dad?"

Dorie sighed in her sleep and there was the sound of traffic from far below, yet the silence from Nate was overwhelming.

"Do you ever worry that maybe it's in our blood?" Fitz asked, pushing it. "That maybe even trying to be happy is just an all-around really bad idea?"

Maybe not the best thing to ask a man who'd made a majorly public declaration of love to the woman he'd be marrying in a few months. Whatever, though. He was her big brother and he'd obviously figured a way to come to terms with it. She truly wanted to know how.

To her surprise, he laughed. Then he gave a maddening, completely useless answer. "Nope."

When nothing else came, she turned back to him. "That's it?"

He glanced at her and then away, taking another drink of water before putting the bottle back down. "After I left for spring training—" meaning, of course, after he and Dorie had had an epic break-up "—I wasn't thinking much about the future. I could barely even get through each day."

His arms must have tightened around Dorie because she stirred. The look he gave Dorie while she settled again was full of such tenderness that Fitz's own heart ached. "It doesn't matter if it's a bad idea or not," he said. "She's everything. It's not a choice. It just is."

Having never expected words like that to come out of his mouth, Fitz stared at him. He arched an eyebrow in a "what?" kind of way.

Fitz just barely held back a snort. "That was completely unhelpful." Not relevant in any way whatsoever. Honestly. Talking to Deke was, if often maddening, at least productive. Nate gave a vaguely amused shrug, and she glared at her brother before going inside to change.

Nate had heard her about the sightseeing, though, and the next few days were packed with baseball games and tourist traps: cable cars and Fisherman's Wharf, even a nighttime tour of Alcatraz. She got to put her feet in the ocean—her first time—and then her whole body, thanks to Nate and Wash tossing her and Dorie both in. Deke, oddly, wanted nothing to do with that part. It didn't matter, though. Fitz didn't think she'd ever had so much fun.

The last morning they were there, she and Dorie went out for a run, coming back to find the suite unexpectedly full of current and former baseball players, in addition to Deke and Wash and a few more of Nate's friends. Everything between her and Deke was perfectly normal. A better bounceback than their first time together, to her great relief. Things were so normal, in fact, Nate had even stopped giving Deke the evil eye. Hell, to anyone else looking, it would seem as though nothing had ever happened between them. He barely even glanced her way when she came into the suite.

Fine. Whatever. Although it was probably a good thing, since the jeans and T-shirt he was wearing, though perfectly run of the mill, highlighted every single asset he had. Deliberately ignoring the rush she got from seeing him, Fitz went over to Wash instead.

"When did it become a party?" she asked, looking around as Wash put together a plate of fruit from the platters on the buffet.

It was mostly guys who had started out around the same time Nate did, but there were some younger players thrown in. Of the older guys, only a few were still playing. Among the rest of them were three who had gone on to become commentators, two assistant coaches, and one who was rumored to be a hot GM prospect for several teams currently on the lookout. Deke, of course, having spent more than his share of time partying with them all during Nate's first few seasons, fit right in.

Wash shrugged. "You know Nate. Now that he isn't attached to the ice queen anymore, he's back to his old ways."

The ice queen, of course, being his former fiancée, Courtney, who had carefully steered Nate into a much more solitary, head-above-the-rest type of existence. In direct response, Fitz was thinking, to the "old ways" to which Wash had just referred, and it had nothing to do with the partying. Even back in high school, Nate had been that guy who brought everyone together. Who was, yes, heads above the rest in terms of talent, but who was humble about it to a fault, and who excelled at building a team around him. The Dream was a case in point. He didn't even need to work at it—people just naturally gathered around him. When he did retire, something he'd begun to talk about even though it had scared the bejesus out of him until recently, Fitz was pretty sure he was going to do something big. Like maybe achieve world peace.

"Hey, Fitz."

Fitz looked up to see Nate gesturing for her to join him, Deke and a few of the other guys, one of whom was Johnny Whitfield, a former player in town to cover the game for one of the big networks. Plus Sam, who gave her a smile and a nod but didn't in any way acknowledge more than that, which was completely fine with Fitz.

"Johnny's thinking about coming out to Inspiration next month," Nate said when Fitz joined them. "Maybe doing a feature on the foundation."

She put on her professional smile. "That sounds great. I'd love to help set that up."

"Awesome," Johnny said. "You can show me the town during the day…" He clapped Deke on the shoulder. "And Deke, my buddy, can show me the town at night." Then he turned to the other players, laughingly saying to the newer guy, "You wouldn't believe the way the girls used to come out to see Deke. I mean, there we all were with big league contracts, and yet *he's* the one they wanted."

Deke's smile didn't quite reach his eyes. "That was only because I didn't have a curfew like you guys all did."

"Whatever," the other veteran player said. In a high-pitched voice clearly meant to imitate one of the so-called "girls," he added, "'Do you know Max Deacon, baby? I hear there's this thing he does with his—'"

"Or vice versa," Fitz snapped in order to shut them up. Honestly. She'd been around ball players long enough to know they had no problem sharing some pretty intimate details. But she did *not* want to know what some woman said once upon a time about Deke. When they all turned to her in surprise, she said, "How about Deke's the one to show you around during the day and I'll take you out on the town? I mean, we're all about the equal opportunity, right?"

Ignoring Nate and Deke's murderous expressions, Johnny's eyes lit up. "Really," he said.

It was Sam's chuckle, however, that made her glare before she turned back to Johnny with a smile. "Whatever works."

"Or maybe we could team up and do both," Deke ground out, his eyes hard as he went territorial.

Returning her gaze to Johnny, she also ignored both Deke and Nate. "I'll get your contact info from Alexis."

"You got it," he said, the smile on his face growing bigger as Deke grabbed her elbow and, muttered, "Excuse us, guys," as he pulled her away. All the way into the dining alcove, in fact, which was mostly shielded from everyone else.

The second they were out of hearing range, he snapped, "What the hell was that?"

"What?" she said, glaring right back. "Maybe I want

to go dancing again without some caveman carrying me away before I'm done."

"I didn't *carry* you," he said. "I was just removing you from a situation that was not ideal." He went offense rather than defense, backing her up into the sideboard, his hands and arms going to each side of her as he caged her in. "It was either that or killing the next guy who touched you. Jesus, Fitz. Even just a little mercy would have been appreciated."

"Mercy?" She tipped her head back to look up at him. When she saw there was actual pain in his eyes, her voice went soft. "I wanted to be dancing with you."

That clearly surprised him, although she wasn't sure if it was because she'd thought it or admitted it. Then his eyes went down to her lips and for a second she was sure he was going to kiss her, which would have been a seriously bad idea, especially with Nate being on the other side of that wall and the last thing she wanted was a scene of any kind.

As if he'd suddenly remembered where they were, he abruptly pulled his arms away and stepped back. Running his hands through his hair until they met at the back of his head and he clasped them together, he let out a frustrated, "*Fuck*."

Yep. And yet, for as much as she knew it was a bad idea, her body was letting her know in all sorts of fluttery ways it didn't give a damn. It took everything she had to keep from plastering herself against him. Her turn to lean back. Looking down at the floor, she said, "Why does this have to be so complicated?"

Deke didn't answer right away and, to be honest, Fitz deliberately didn't look up at him. Not until she sensed him right in front of her again. But it took him touching his fingers to her chin and tilting her head up for her to be able to look him in the eye.

"I like touching you," he said, his eyes dark. His hands went to her arms and his mouth to her neck and she forgot about Nate entirely. "I sure as hell got the sense that you like touching me." He grinned as she felt her cheeks go hot. Because, well, yes, that was absolutely true. "Maybe it doesn't need to get more complicated than that."

Letting her head fall back, it was hard to ignore the shivers running through her at the feel of his skin against hers. She knew she should make him stop, but all she felt was loss when he took a step back, his eyes going down to the ground. He distractedly ran his hand through his hair. "What if I said I wanted every weekend with you? Maybe even every night."

Her hands went to the table behind her and she went into deer-in-headlights mode. "What do you mean by that?" she whispered. They'd already had this conversation and she was pretty sure she'd made her intentions clear. Just in case not, however, she said, "I don't want a relationship, Deke. I really don't." Especially not now, after this weekend's meeting with Sam and with a ticket out of Inspiration dangling in front of her. This was not the time for distraction.

That damn smile of his came over his face. "I'm not saying a relationship. We already have one of those." Before her frown could turn into a, *That's not what I mean and you know it*, he came up against her again, and nuzzled her neck. "I'm talking sex. Regular, out of this world, I-can't-see-straight sex."

"Regular anything equals a relationship," she managed, closing her eyes.

"No," he said, his voice muffled by her collarbone. "It's like… It's a schmelationship. Sounds like, but not the same thing."

Laughing, she meant to push him away, but only managed to pull him in closer.

"So?" he said a minute later, after driving her nearly to madness, his hand up her shirt and his mouth on her skin.

"Huh?" He was magic. It made it hard to think.

But think she did. In a way, it was the safest thing in the world. God knew they'd already crossed the line in a big way. And she couldn't deny it was exactly what she'd wanted—someone she could be as easy with as Nate was with Dorie. Deke was the only person in the world with whom she'd ever come that close. It was still a major leap, though. And if she actually moved away? Regardless of how tempting it sounded, the answer should be no. Absolutely one hundred percent times ten thousand, *No*.

"Maybe," she said, instead.

His eyes went soft again as he looked down at her mouth. Then he cupped her cheeks with his hands and tilted her head so he could bend to kiss her one more time.

He pulled away again and stepped back. "You should think on it, then," he said, backing away from her slowly. He gave her one final grin before heading back out to the others.

Fitz knew she needed to be talking some sense to herself. Yet all that came to mind was that after every time he touched her, the only thing she could think about was how desperately she wanted him to touch her again.

Chapter Twenty

It was Friday after lunch. Deke hadn't seen Fitz since they'd returned from California early Wednesday morning.

He was not fucking happy about it.

He'd been willing to give her the benefit of the doubt on Wednesday since everyone was lagging, given Nate's game and the early morning flight, even if it was courtesy of Nate's private plane. He'd even been okay with her blowing them off Thursday at lunch because, well, she got a freebie. But with Dorie there both for last night's dinner and for lunch today, the only logical conclusion was that Fitz was avoiding him.

He couldn't blame her.

Yes, she seemed fully okay with how things had been that night. She certainly hadn't held anything back and he'd been more than happy to go along with it. But he'd pushed it too hard. Telling her he wanted to see her every night after the crack he'd made about staying home with their babies? Yeah. "Schmelationship" wasn't exactly going to cut it.

Well, what*ever*. It wasn't like there was anything he could do about it at the moment. He'd said his piece and he wasn't about to take it back. He wanted her; he didn't want anyone else.

"So," Lola said, coming up to the bar with a tray of empties. "Is there a particular thing you're frowning at today, or should I just get used to this new Debbie Downer Deke?"

Deke, yes, frowned before scanning her tray and taking care of the refills. "Debbie Downer Deke? That's the best you could come up with?"

She shrugged as she rested her elbows on the bar, her eyes on the few occupied tables. Late afternoon was downtime, which meant she was handling waitressing duties until the dinner shift came on and she moved over to the hostess stand. Their only customers at the moment, in fact, were their dad and a few of his longtime friends, a group of teachers from the high school who were there for their usual TGIF drinks, and a table full of women who appeared to be starting early on a bachelorette party if the tiara and sashes were any indication.

"Well, I could tell you that one of the games they're playing over there is Which Debbie Gets To Do Deke but that would just be gross."

That wasn't the kind of statement a guy could ignore, of course. His eyes went directly to the table and his smile was automatic. He couldn't help it. When anyone of the female persuasion flirted, he flirted back. At the same time, he had to turn away before it became entirely obvious he had absolutely zero interest in actual engagement.

He finished off the new round of drinks and put them on Lola's tray, not at all expecting her look of surprise. "What?"

"You're not going to take a walk over there?" she

asked, her expression a mix of older sister disdain, with a side order of shock. "Strut your stuff? Put a few more notches on your belt?"

He really wished people would stop talking about his damn belt. Leaning back against the counter, he crossed his arms over his chest. "Oh, so it's fine to objectify my superlative assets, but God forbid a guy says something like that, and then it's all let's go march on Washington time." There. Hopefully that was enough Lola-speak to shut her down.

Unfortunately, she was totally on to him. Although she narrowed her eyes, it was more like she was examining him than glaring. "What planet are you from," she asked, "and what have you done with my brother?"

He pushed the tray in her direction. "You're keeping my fans waiting."

With a distinct, "*Hmph*," she snatched the tray off the bar and went off to deliver the order. If she hadn't had fifteen years' worth of practice slinging drinks while giving off attitude he would have been worried. But she was back ten minutes later, having checked in at the other tables so she could sit down and chat. Great.

She jumped right into it. "So what gives?"

"I have no idea what you're talking about," he said, wishing that someone—*anyone*—would come in for a drink and stay a while. He got really busy wiping down the counter.

"How many blondes are there at that table?" she asked.

Although he had no idea why he was even responding to her, his eyes flicked over to the table with the bride-to-be and her friends. "Three. Why?"

Her eyes narrowed again. "Which ones are wearing wedding rings?"

"Jesus Christ, Lola." With a glare, he grumbled, "How the fuck am I supposed to know?"

Then her gaze went somewhere over his shoulder. "Oh, hi, Fitz."

If he hadn't been so on edge about the woman for, oh, the last *month*, he wouldn't have been caught dead falling for something so obvious. But, goddamn it, he swung his head around, only to swing it back when Lola gave a triumphant smack to the counter. "I *knew* it!"

Fuck.

This time his glare had some serious ice in it. He grabbed the bin of dirty dishes out from under the counter and brought it back to the kitchen, thinking she'd get the hint and get back to her job by the time he returned to the bar. Since it took him all of two minutes, and since not one freaking person in the whole town needed a drink at that moment, it didn't do him one iota of good.

"Does she know?" Lola asked, a gleam in her eye.

She was asking about Fitz. Obviously. What Fitz was supposed to know, however, was the question.

That every minute of their night together had been playing back on an endless loop since the moment she'd left his bed on Sunday morning? That he'd relived every kiss? That he couldn't recall ever, not even once, being so affected by a woman that just getting through the day was a struggle because of how badly he wanted her again?

Fuck, no.

The woman had gone pale at the word *boyfriend*. Since he was having a hard enough time reconciling what was going on inside his own head, he wasn't exactly going to push the point. Nor was he going to utter a word of any of that to Lola. "Since I have absolutely no idea what you're talking about, I'd have to say no."

"Oh, God," Lola whispered, as though the most awful thing in the world were happening. "Please tell me you're not thinking about sleeping with her."

Since Lola was clearly speaking in hypothetical terms whereas Deke most certainly was not, he knew this was dangerous territory. Yet he found it harder than expected to not just come out and ask, Why? Was the idea of him and Fitz being together really that bad of a thing?

"You… You can't, Deke. It wouldn't be like it is with all the rest of your women."

His women? Really?

"She's…"

He leaned back against the counter, his arms across his chest. "She's what?" He loved Lola. He'd lay down his life for her without a second thought. She'd better be careful, however, of what she was about to say.

And she did seem to be choosing her words very deliberately. But the one she came up with was, "Fragile."

"She's not freaking fragile. And I'd recommend not mentioning to her that you think so."

Clearly as taken aback by the vehemence in his tone as he was, Lola sat back, an odd smile on her face. "You're right," she said. "Fragile wasn't the best word. I guess I just meant you need to tread carefully. She deserves someone who will treat her right."

"You think I *won't*?" he snapped. He took care of people. Damn right he would take care of Fitz, whether he was sleeping with her or not. He sure as hell hoped his freaking *sister* would be aware of that.

"Okay, Max," she said softly.

God*damn* it.

Yes, okay, he'd overreacted. Yes, maybe he had a little bit more riding on this—*this* being his ever-so-eloquently proposed extended booty call proposition—than he'd realized. But in no way was he looking for a relationship. He was definitely *not* looking for a relationship with Fitz. Because, yes, he loved her.

And…fuck.

Now he understood what she'd meant when she'd said that very thing to him after that first time in the Jeep.

He turned his back to the room and rested his hands on the counter, leaning heavily. A few seconds later he felt Lola's hand on his shoulder. Then she rested her head on his back as her arm went around him. "You're an amazing person," she said. "Any woman would be lucky to have you."

Deke snorted at that. Fitz clearly didn't agree.

A cheer went up from the bachelorette table and they begin chanting his name. For maybe the first time in his life, he hated his job.

With a sigh, he said, "Duty calls," and made sure there was a smile on his face.

Are we still on for dinner?

The message came late Friday afternoon, reminding Fitz that she had planned to have dinner with Mama Gin. Those kinds of things didn't usually slip her mind, but she'd been on the go since the moment they got back from San Francisco thanks to a conversation with Nate that wasn't even supposed to be a conversation.

It had been specifically meant as a distraction, in fact, since Nate had come upon her standing there after Deke had left her and Nate wanted to know what was wrong, clearly thinking the worst. She hadn't exactly wanted to tell Nate that Deke had told her he wanted to have sex with her every night and that she was actually considering it, so she'd made sure to take the conversation in a different direction. One thing led to another and here she was, sitting on the news that Nate was going to retire.

That was huge. As in, start the *Sports Illustrated* retrospective huge.

And after that he was coming back to Inspiration instead of staying involved with professional baseball in the way everyone expected. Since he wasn't exactly one to be idle, he had big plans for when he was done. He wanted to build a mini-city, it seemed; all sports, all the time. It would have everything from fantasy baseball weekends for the older set right down to a year-round training academy, complete with actual dorms for kids who were there for more than a weekend.

All of which was awesome. Beyond exciting. The only downside was that he was talking about leaving Chicago right as she was beginning to finally get some traction on moving there. Not that it changed her overall plan. It was just that there'd been a reason for choosing a headhunter based in Chicago. She wanted to leave Inspiration, yes. She'd just always assumed she'd be doing it with him nearby. Thinking about it all gave her palpitations, though, so she was more than happy to distract herself with Nate's plans. The past few days had been full of brainstorming with Dorie and Nate, lists upon lists of things to get ready for the board meeting, and the presentation she'd have to make.

"Did you hear that, people?" she called out to the empty office around her. "Year-round. Classes and clubs and everything. It would be amazing!"

Since the office around her was, in fact, empty, she received no response. She didn't expect one—she wasn't actually going crazy. At some point along the way over the last few weeks, however, being alone had begun to bother her. She blamed it on Deke and what he'd said to her that day at the cemetery. She *did* like being alone. When you were alone, no one could disappoint you. It did get a little too quiet sometimes, though, so she'd started to noisy things up.

"That's right," she said, directing her comment to the copy machine. "Noisy it up."

The copy machine refused to respond.

Whatever. She loved this project. It was crazy. Overwhelming. And so freaking fun that she actually looked forward to waking up each day so she could get to work faster. She'd never felt this way before.

Okay. Maybe it was a little bit about Deke, too.

No, damn it. It was more than a little bit about Deke. More like a *lot*.

She shouldn't want him. The idea of being with him felt like opening up herself to everything she'd tried to guard against for most of her life. But he said all the right things, and, God, the things he'd done to her body had been more than right. Plus, although he had his faults, he knew her better than almost anyone in the world.

No. That was *not* a point in his favor.

With a sigh, she looked at the clock. She took the full forty minutes she had left, hoping there'd be enough of a crowd on a Friday that Deke would be fully occupied. And to her shameful yet great relief, he wasn't anywhere in sight when she walked in. Looking around for Mama Gin, Fitz headed to the bar only to be ushered to the back office by Josh, Deke's backup bartender.

As she rounded the corner in the hallway, she nearly ran into Lola.

Lola, who stopped suddenly and gave Fitz the strangest look before gathering Fitz up into her arms. Trying not to noticeably tense up, Fitz just smiled back. "Is everything okay?"

Lola's smile turned overly bright. Kind of forced, which was even stranger because it seemed as though she was also tearing up a bit. Then she gave Fitz another squeeze before releasing her. "Mama Gin's in the office with Deke and my dad. How about I send some dinner back? The usual?"

"Uh, sure," Fitz said. This was…weird. "Thanks."

Lola gave another one of those forced smiles before moving briskly down the hall.

Okay, then. Gearing herself up, Fitz gave a quick knock on the door before opening it and…

"Deke." He was sitting with his hands clasped behind his head, his legs stretched out in front of him and his boots on the desk.

God, she loved those boots.

God, she loved his legs and his head and his hands, too.

Her body's reaction to him was as expected as it was instantaneous. Doing her best to ignore the blood that was stirring up for its inevitable descent to her lady parts, she gave what was probably an overly bright smile.

"Hey, Fitz," he said, dropping his feet to the floor and sitting up straight.

Yep, there all that blood went, stubbornly settling in her core.

She couldn't act on it, of course, because they weren't alone. But the electricity arcing between them was so strong she wouldn't have been surprised if Mama Gin and Mr. Deacon felt it, too. The only thing that pulled her out of it was Mama Gin saying, "Hi, honey. We were just talking about your dad."

Fitz's head snapped up. "What?"

She glared at Deke. He gave a small shrug and raised his eyebrows a bit as he shook his head, kind of a small, *Believe it or not, it wasn't me.* Fitz was *not* inclined to believe it, actually, until Mama Gin nodded her head toward the TV that was on top of the bookshelf. "Hank and I were saying how much Nate looks like him." Fitz's eyes flew up to the TV to see the Watchmen taking the field.

It wasn't that Fitz didn't know what her father looked like, of course. She didn't have any pictures of him, though. The night he'd died she'd been fifteen and in the car on a ride she didn't want to be on. It wasn't like she'd carried photo albums around on a regular basis in the event that her parents were, say, torn away by a tornado before they got home. Since the house Fitz had grown up in had been destroyed that same day, there wasn't much beyond the memories left to pack away.

And no matter what Deke thought, there wasn't any way in hell that Fitz would ask Mama Gin if she had any pictures lying around. Which meant that Fitz had never really had much to compare to. "He does?"

Mama Gin drew her hands into a steeple and raised them to her mouth. With tears glistening in her eyes, she murmured, "Oh, baby." And then she took Fitz's hand and yanked her directly into…

Yes, another hug. Another moment of trying not to tense. An unexpected moment of realizing Deke had touched her over and over again, in all sorts of places, and not once had she minded. In fact, even now, being in his presence after very specifically avoiding him didn't feel even the slightest bit strange. It felt comforting. Safe. As if he'd catch her no matter how far she fell, even if he wasn't happy she'd gone radio silent for two whole days.

There was a small round table in the corner of the office. Deke and Lola had essentially grown up here, and it was where they'd have their family dinners more often than not. Where, someday, Deke could have dinners with those babies of his, too, although the thought of that made Fitz a little sad.

The table was cozy. Fitz had actually loved it when she got to join in because it had reminded her of her own home. It helped now as Mama Gin sat down in one of the chairs and pulled out the other and gestured for Fitz to sit in it. But it wasn't until Deke sat down in the chair next to her, ignoring completely the two other people in the room and murmuring, "Are you okay?" that she truly felt grounded.

She still had no idea what she wanted their relationship to be—was still mostly sure she didn't *want* one. Yet the way he pulled his chair in close to hers, let his legs fall to either side, caging her in almost, while at the same time not getting so close as to make her feel trapped almost made her cry in gratitude. When his hand went to the back of her chair she almost leaned into it, in fact, wanting even just a few seconds of his touch.

That wasn't… It shouldn't…

She pulled away abruptly when Mr. Deacon cleared his throat. "Uh… Max, maybe we should let Gin and Angelica talk."

But she didn't want Deke to go. For as strange as it felt to be talking about her dad to Mama Gin, Deke had been right. This was her father and there were things she wanted to know. It also did occur to her that if she could, say, deal with Peggy freaking Miller on a daily basis, then she could certainly talk about her dad to the woman who had taken over the job of raising her. Especially if the woman in question had brought it up in the first place.

Plus, it wasn't like Mama Gin could unadopt her now, right?

Still, Mama Gin and Mr. Deacon went back a long ways. Having a buffer wouldn't hurt. Fitz smiled. "I'd actually love it if you both stayed."

As she sat back in her chair she realized Mama Gin seemed almost as uncomfortable as she felt. Mama Gin, the most confident, accomplished, amazing woman Fitz knew, seemed unsure. It was beyond reassuring.

With a glance at Mr. Deacon, Mama Gin started by leaning forward and putting a hand on Fitz's knee. "Before I say anything else, I need you to know that I love you."

Tears came to Fitz's eyes before she could stop them.

Dorie said stuff like that all the time. Fitz figured it was one of those big Italian family things. "Love you," as if it was as easy as uttering those two words. In Fitz's experience, it was a much more elusive concept. She'd loved her parents, no doubt about that. She knew what she felt for her family and friends was love, even though she'd fought it for the longest of times, but it wasn't something she could come out and easily say. Nate was the only person she ever said it to regularly, and that was only because he'd said it first—and had gone on saying it until she'd responded in kind, once she'd finally realized he wasn't going away. Except for his two-year interlude with Courtney, but she'd forgiven him for that.

Mostly.

She'd never said it to Mama Gin, though. To the woman who had been betrayed by Fitz's father *and* mother. It had taken Fitz years to even say her adoptive mother's name, and that was only because she'd overheard Deke say it. If he could call the woman "Mama Gin," then she could too. After all, it wasn't like she'd gone and overstepped her bounds by coming out and calling her "Mom." And it would have been safe enough to say even if her own mother had still been alive.

But, no, Fitz had never told Mama Gin that she loved her, and she'd never expected to hear the words in the first place. She couldn't quite say them back, but that didn't seem to bother anyone.

Instead, Mama Gin said, "Your father—"

The tears came back and overflowed immediately. Fitz found herself leaning forward, squeezing her eyes shut as words she'd never allowed herself to say poured out of her. "I loved him so much. I know I shouldn't say that, not after what he did, but I loved him. I still do. My mom, too."

"Oh, honey," Mama Gin said, grabbing onto Fitz's hands. "I loved him, too. He was a good man. He deserved a better life than he had. I wish he could have seen that sooner. And I'm so happy he had you in it."

A sob erupted from somewhere deep inside Fitz. She couldn't hold it back. Not after all this time. Not anymore.

"Fitz... Angelica..." It even seemed like Mama Gin was crying a little, although Fitz couldn't open her eyes enough to see. Instead she turned her head to Deke, knowing he'd be right there.

"Angel," he whispered, stroking her hair and closing his arms around her. "Hear her out, okay?"

It took a few minutes before Fitz could get her emotions under control, but she was finally able to gulp in a breath of air. "You don't mind talking about him?"

"Oh, honey," Mama Gin answered, clasping Fitz's hands extra tight. Leaning in close, she smiled as she brushed a strand of hair away from Fitz's face. "I'm so sorry you thought you couldn't. I never—"

"It's okay," Fitz answered, not wanting Mama Gin to take on that burden, too. It wasn't anyone else's fault. At first Fitz had refused to speak of him because she'd been so angry at what he'd done. Horrified he'd left his family behind; ashamed to admit she'd wondered if he eventually would have done it to her, too.

Once Mama Gin had taken her in, it felt like talking about him would be yet another betrayal no matter what her therapists said. How could she talk about the man to the family he'd left behind? Her friends were Nate's friends. Even Lola wasn't Fitz's to claim; she'd always be Jules's friend first.

Her father had caused so much harm to so many

people she loved, that at first she'd tried to box him out, keeping all her memories locked up and stashed away. It was only in recent years she'd allowed herself to acknowledge him during her Saturday visits, and that had come about because it was really pretty ridiculous to sit and talk to one half of a gravestone but not the other.

But now… "Can you tell me about him?"

This time when Mama Gin smiled there was no sadness in her eyes. Instead she let go of Fitz's hands, sat back in her own seat and glanced over at Mr. Deacon before looking back at Fitz. "He had this razor-sharp wit."

Fitz smiled at that, even as more tears streamed down her face. "I remember."

"He cheated at cards," Mr. Deacon said, relaxing back into his chair, chuckling as he and Mama Gin shared another glance.

"Could talk his way out of anything," Mama Gin added. "Even after getting caught, literally, with an ace up his sleeve." Her cheeks turned a bit pink. "And he was sooooo good-looking."

Mr. Deacon rolled his eyes, making a big show of it as he sat forward in his chair and rested his elbows on the table. "Hell, he could cheat at cards, steal your girl right out of your arms and still walk away and be your best friend."

An actual twinkle in her eye, Mama Gin slapped Mr. Deacon on the arm. "That's only because you stole *his* girl that very same night." To Deke, she said, "You know that's how your parents met, right? That your dad and I decided to set our roommates up with each other?"

With a laugh, Mr. Deacon said, "Didn't quite work out that way."

And the stories went on from there. It was over din-

ner that Fitz—and Deke, apparently—learned Mama
Gin and Mr. Deacon had been high school sweethearts,
thinking they were on the road to marriage, even, when
they'd met each other's college roommates and everything had changed. For the better, they both seemed to
agree despite what Fitz's dad had done.

An hour later, as the food was being cleared away,
Fitz said to Mr. Deacon, "I had no idea you were friends
with him first." It was frightening, in fact, how much
she didn't know.

But even with that thought running through her head,
she was entirely unprepared for Mr. Deacon to say, "I
met your mother once."

"You did?"

Fitz was so surprised it took her a moment to realize
her mouth was hanging open and that she hadn't been
the one to ask the question. It was Deke.

When Mama Gin nodded, Mr. Deacon went on to
say, "I was up in Ames for something. Walked into
a coffee shop and practically ran right into your dad.
There was a woman behind the counter, and he was arguing with her in a way that seemed over the top when it
came to someone getting your order wrong, you know?"

He gave a laugh so rueful, Fitz almost started crying just from the sound of it.

"I even made some joke about him not needing to
get so worked up over a cup of coffee. But he and Gin
were in a tough place, and with Nate and the girls being
so young…" He shrugged. "I passed it off as stress over
how crazy it was for him at home." Then Mr. Deacon
lifted his gaze. His eyes going soft, he looked directly
at Fitz. "You look exactly like her."

This time, Fitz was aware the strangled gasp had

come from her. Her whole body trembled and she had to wrap her arms around herself to keep from falling off the chair.

She had no pictures of her mother, either, and no family from her mother's side. No one else in the world who had ever been able to say those words to her. "I do?"

Even Mr. Deacon, who Fitz had always thought of as Mr. Happy-Go-Lucky, Senior, seemed like he might cry. "It hit me the day the boys graduated from college," he said. "I saw you standing next to Nate. He looked so much like your dad and you looked like…her. I realized that's who he'd been talking to that day. She was pregnant and…" His voice trailed off as he took another moment to glance at Mama Gin. "It was still another year or two before he left, but I think it may have been the day he found out about you."

Mama Gin, who as far as Fitz was concerned had every right to put an end to this conversation, leaned forward and put her hand over Mr. Deacon's. Grimly smiling, she said, "Hank has always had this ridiculous notion that he could have saved my marriage if only he'd said something."

With a glare, Mr. Deacon responded, "I knew that man like a brother." Then he pulled his hand out from under Mama Gin's and looked away. "At least I thought I did."

Although she couldn't believe she was saying the words, Fitz went ahead and asked, "Why do you think he left? How could he…?" Unable to finish the thought, she shook her head. They all got the idea.

Sure enough, Mr. Deacon's eyes went sad and he looked down at the table for a minute before speaking.

"I wish I could answer that. I really do." Leaning forward, he looked at Fitz. "I tried for years to find someone who could tell me what it was that made him just… go." He glanced at Mama Gin again. "I used to wonder if it was something with his parents. He had a bastard of a father. Meanest son of a bitch I ever met. And his mom wasn't much better. The day they dropped him off at college was the last time they ever spoke, as far as I knew. Not sure if he was saddened by it, or just relieved. He never did say."

Dredging up a memory she hadn't even been aware she had, Fitz said, "They came to our house." The icy tension at the dinner table that night came back, too, as did the fight between her parents after the people she'd been introduced to as her grandparents had left. "Once."

The odd part, though, was that she was pretty sure he'd stopped drinking almost immediately afterward. He'd disappeared for a few days, days during which her mother hadn't stopped crying. But things started changing once he got back. He was around the house more, for one thing. He smiled, for another. He hadn't smiled as much before that.

Silence descended, and Fitz knew they were waiting for her to say something. But she was already overwhelmed—with memories, with emotion… The second she opened her mouth she knew she'd start crying again. Yet she so desperately wanted to know if they knew…

"Why was he on his way out here that night?" Deke asked.

Ordinarily, him being so in tune with her would have freaked her out immensely. Tonight, though, she was just grateful.

Mama Gin and Mr. Deacon glanced at each other

again. And again, Mr. Deacon was the one who spoke. "We don't know, son. Not for sure. But I know the man he was. And I have to believe that once he got that demon off his back, he'd do the right thing." Then Mr. Deacon reached forward and took Fitz's hand in his. It was so shocking she didn't even have the chance to pull back before he squeezed tight. "From the day we met you we knew you'd been raised right. Your mom had a hand in that, but I firmly believe your dad did, too. I'd say it was a good bet there was a reason they were on their way here that night. That she'd decided to support him, no matter how hard that road would be to travel."

The tears came back with a vengeance. Fitz had been so angry for so long, and had wasted so many years keeping so much inside that it had crippled her. She knew parts of her were broken. She just didn't know if she'd ever be able to fix them. And she hated that because of those jagged pieces, she hadn't had even an ounce of the amount of faith in her parents that the people who should have hated them the most did.

Now it was Mama Gin's turn to reach out. Scooting closer, she said, "I've had a lot of time to think about this. And don't get me wrong, a good four or five years of that time was full of piss and brimstone. But the last conversation he and I ever had was about him having some things to deal with and if he ever did, I'd welcome him back with open arms no matter what else stood between us." She smiled. "I've come to choose to believe he maybe decided to take me up on that."

"But…" Oh, God, there were so many things running through Fitz's head and her heart. "Nate and Jules and Ella…" Fitz had no idea how they would have handled even the idea of that.

From the grim and stubborn look on Mama Gin's face, it was clear any discussions that may have been had hadn't gone over well. "What matters most to me," Mama Gin said in her my-word-is-law voice, "is that you know you belong to us." Then she leaned forward and took Fitz's hand again. "From the moment I saw you, I knew you were a piece of me—of my family—I didn't even know had been missing."

It was nearly too much to process. Fitz didn't even know what she would have asked if she were capable of speaking. It was as if Mama Gin had said every single word Fitz had ever hoped to hear but Fitz was too overwhelmed to take any of it in.

Mr. Deacon read Fitz's silence as disbelief, it seemed. "Never seen anyone fight for something as hard as Gin fought for you."

And, well, maybe she hadn't believed it entirely. Her head swung over and she met Mr. Deacon's gaze. "What?"

"Tooth and nail," he said. "There were people who thought it was madness. But she used whatever it took to get those doors open and then wouldn't let them close until she'd gotten you."

Mama Gin didn't deny it. She smiled at Fitz's shock. "The Iowa Dream made us a lot of friends. I wasn't above asking for help." Then she let go of Fitz's hand and patted her knee. "I think maybe this was enough for one night." Then she gave Fitz a quick hug, releasing her almost immediately as if she were fully aware too much would put Fitz over the edge. "But this conversation is only beginning. Okay?" she said gently, smiling when Fitz nodded. Then Mama Gin briskly stood up. "Buy me a drink, Hank?"

Taking his cue, Mr. Deacon stood up as well. After a lingering look at Deke, Mr. Deacon gave a nod as well. Then they were both gone.

"Well…" Deke said, as the door closed behind them.

Yes, Fitz thought. Well.

Leaning back against him, she closed her eyes. "Did you have something to do with that conversation?"

He was quiet for a minute before saying, "That depends on how angry you'd be at me if I had."

Furious was what her answer should have been. But the only thing running through her head was that maybe they could figure out a way to make things work. Maybe she could find a way to keep coming back to him after she moved out of Inspiration. But right now she was too drained to think about it. So instead she burrowed her head into the crook between his arm and chest. "Can you just hold me for a little while?" she asked, too tired out to care about any mixed messages she happened to be sending.

He didn't seem to mind. Tucking her up against him, he settled back in his seat. "For as long as you need."

Since right now she was thinking she could maybe make do with forever, she thought it was wise to keep her mouth shut. But, yes. Forever would do.

Chapter Twenty-One

He'd wanted to take her home with him that night. Keep watch over her to make sure she was okay; hold her in case she wasn't. But she'd insisted she was fine and wouldn't even let him drive her back to Lola's. And even if it was his bar he couldn't exactly take off when he wanted to. So he'd had to let her go. Then she'd made herself scarce for the next few days, and Deke was pretty sure if one more person had said to him that they wished they could have a job like his and just shoot the shit all day, he might have hauled off and hit them.

For as much as her episodes of avoiding him had been pissing him off, however, he sensed there was something different about it this time. Or maybe he was coming to understand that maintaining some space was as necessary for her as taking in air. Since she let him get a little closer each time she came back to him, he was starting to think maybe it wasn't the worst thing. But he also realized he had a major problem on his hands: he missed her. He thought about her constantly. It wasn't just that he had absolutely no interest in seeking anyone else out—he actually wanted her more with every passing moment despite any indication from her that she felt the same way. Tonight was going to be flat-out torture since it was poker night and they'd be surrounded by the people who knew them best in the world.

With a frustrated growl, Deke forced himself to think about something else. He was hosting tonight and would soon have some hungry folks on hand, so he'd better get his act together and start cooking. Plus, him thinking about it all so much seemed to be the definition of making it "complicated," which he had specifically told her it wasn't necessary to do.

An hour later he had chili on the stove, nachos ready to go into the oven, and had baked an apple pie. He was taking it out of the oven when the bell for the garage sounded.

With a quick look at the camera he saw it was Dorie's car, with Fitz right behind her, so he buzzed them in, feeling the rattle as the garage door slid open. A few minutes later he heard footsteps on the stairs, and he called out that his door was unlocked once they reached his landing. When the door swung open, however, it was only Dorie who came in. With a quick wave, Fitz continued her way up the stairs to Jason's.

Trying not to show his irritation, Deke turned back to the stove in order to stir the chili. Dorie came up behind him, depositing a cardboard box on his counter. He would have helped her with it, as she well knew, but she was a big stickler on carrying her own things and he wasn't in the mood to argue with her.

Deke glanced down to see what she'd brought tonight. He got the sense she missed cooking for her brothers no matter how much she complained, so she was always happy to feed people and he was always happy to be one of the fed. She made a mean meatball, out of this world tomato sauce—gravy, as she called it—and biscotti that were better, even, than Jules's.

With that said, although Fitz didn't usually cook, she did usually help out when she got there early. That she'd gone to Jason's was telling.

He wasn't about to let on that it was also beyond frustrating. "Hey," he said to Dorie.

"Hi." She started lifting things out of the box: freshly baked cornbread, homemade salsa and guac, and a container full of cookies.

"We're going to be rolling them out of here tonight," Deke said, not unhappily.

"That's what Fitz said," Dorie answered.

When Deke's response was a mere nod as he turned back to the stove, she added pointedly and as if he hadn't already been aware, "Fitz went upstairs to talk to Jason. Something about the financials."

"Okay," Deke said, proud to have kept his voice neutral.

It was a good enough excuse, especially since Fitz had explained her general absence for the week as something having to do with the foundation and Whitfield's visit. It was pretty clear there was something big going on, but they hadn't said anything to anyone else, which made it clear they weren't ready to. And, honestly, Deke was a bartender. He'd been told more than his share of secrets. He had no interest in trying to figure out something someone didn't want to tell him until they were ready to share. The fact it bothered him that it was yet another thing Fitz was keeping from him was something he preferred to ignore.

After all, Jason was the money guy. Hell, it was thanks to Jason and his crazy brain that Deke was a fairly wealthy man. When the Iowa Dream money started coming in, it had been Deke's idea that they invest it in the town. But Jason was the one who said they'd be able to keep investing if they did something beyond just putting the money in the bank. And although he now worked as a math teacher at the high school and was, in fact, head of the math department, he, like Deke, Wash and Cal, could easily have gone without ever working a day in his life. None of them had anything close to what Nate had, of course, but it was enough for Wash to have bought up the land surrounding the farm and make it his, and for Deke and Jason to buy the old Haverson mill and turn it into their lofts. So Fitz chatting Jason up about the money made sense.

But Deke knew Dorie was looking for more. He turned to her. "And?"

She narrowed her eyes, giving him that all-knowing librarian look she had down pat, and, damn, if it didn't make him want to confess *something*. But he wasn't about to. He'd had more than his share of perfecting his look of innocence. He could easily wait her out.

She crossed her arms over her chest. "You think I don't know?"

Damn it, he wanted desperately to know if Fitz had said anything to her, and if so, what. But the second he gave in to that, he'd be turning down a road he didn't want to be on. So he played up the innocence a little bit more.

A smile came over her face, one of those I-know-exactly-what-you're-doing smiles. "I have six older brothers, you know. Don't think you can hide it from me."

Oh, yeah, she was good. But he was, too. "And I have

the nosiest older sister in the world. You think I don't know fishing when I see it?"

For a second she seemed flustered, as if she didn't quite know what to do with that. And then she threw her head back and laughed. Taking a cookie out of the container, she popped it into her mouth. "I do love you, Deke."

Smiling, he grabbed a cookie himself. Dorie had always been a bit of a puzzle to him—or, rather, the fact that he'd never even been attracted to her despite a long list of reasons why he should have been. It had actually scared him a little. Sex was his thing. Not relationships, not the long-term, this-is-leading-to-something connection people shared. Just the purely physical, let's-have-a-great-time-and-then-shelve-the-memory-for-a-rainy-day sex.

That he'd stopped feeling even halfway interested in the women he knew was something he'd pinned on boredom. When Dorie came to town and there hadn't even been a spark between them, it had highlighted how little interest he had in *any*one, which had been more than a little unsettling. Even more so when he'd realized it had been months since a woman had caught his eye, since he'd managed anything beyond the flirting he considered part of his job. He'd been afraid he might never want to have sex again.

Until Fitz.

By the time she and Jason came downstairs twenty minutes later, he'd talked himself into believing he'd be fine. That he wouldn't react to her in any way whatsoever. But he felt it the second she walked in the door, even though his back was to her. And when he turned, when their gazes locked and she seemed as affected as he was, it took everything he had not to go to her right there in front of everyone. With extreme effort, he looked away.

He spent the evening attempting not to look in her direction while also attempting not to make it obvious he was doing that very thing. By the time the night came to an end, he was entirely strung out and in no mood to deal with the teasing about how badly he'd played.

"Earth to Deke."

Deke looked up when Wash spoke, only to see everyone staring at him. "What? Sorry."

"Last hand. You in?"

"Uh, no. I think I'm done." He stood up and left the table.

He'd already packed all the food up by the time they finished and was beginning to wash the dishes. He felt Fitz come up behind him and was just turning when she said, "Want some help?"

Looking down at her, his focus went immediately to her lips. Brilliant. Forcing himself to raise his eyes, he shook his head and turned back to the sink. "I'm good."

But rather than let it go at that, she looked up at him and then away, mumbling, "We, um… We should talk."

Ya think?

Wiping his hands off on the dishtowel, Deke gave her a look before walking the others to the door. He said his good-byes, which included giving Dorie the most innocent, blankest of stares as she raised her eyebrows and smiled, before closing the door behind them. Then he turned and leaned back against it.

His loft took up the entire floor of the building, and a large part of it was open, so there were no walls between the front door and the kitchen area, no walls closing off the living or dining areas. His bedroom had a door, as did the two bathrooms, of course. He was actually grateful for that at the moment, since both a bed and a bathtub were reminders he didn't need, especially not until he knew what she was planning to say.

But first he had to ask, "Are you okay?"

Yes, he understood she needed her space. But the fact that she hadn't been around in days highlighted the fact that, no matter what his intentions may have been, their friendship had been affected. And he hated it. She'd needed him. She'd needed *someone* to talk to after that night with Mama Gin and his dad, and Deke was sure as hell she wouldn't have gone to Nate or Dorie. But because of everything else going on between them, she hadn't sought him out.

He tried to dial back his frustration. She was clearly aware he was unhappy about it, though. With a nervous glance at him, she busily got to work washing dishes. Well, fuck it. "You've been avoiding me," he said.

She shut off the water and planted her hands on the edge of the sink for a minute before turning to him. "I needed time to think."

Pushing off the door, he detoured to the table where he picked up the rest of the dishes and bottles. They'd done this a thousand times, and yet there was something different about it tonight. Something that felt right in a way that Deke didn't want to focus on too much, especially given how she was acting so far. Bringing everything over to where she stood, he placed them on the counter, careful to stay out of reach. "Did you come to any conclusions?"

"I did." Her eyes avoided his, drifting instead to his

mouth, then his chest, then lower, before traveling back up. "Deke…"

She sounded breathless. A little dazed. Or maybe that was just the way he felt.

Then she reached out her hand—ran the tip of her finger down from his shoulder to his waist, watching its path as though she were compelled by some force completely outside of herself and had no idea what it was going to do next.

Deke had no idea either. It could be her way of avoiding saying what she'd come here to say, or an invitation to the next phase of whatever this was.

No *fucking* idea.

"Tell me," he said, his voice guttural and raw as he grabbed her wrist. "Tell me what you want."

Her teeth went to her bottom lip and she pulled it in, still obviously on the fence. It took every ounce of strength he had to stay still as she came to a decision. By the time her tongue darted out to soothe the reddened skin, he was so hard it actually hurt. But it wasn't until she finally whispered, "I need you inside me again," that he muttered, "Thank fucking God," and closed the distance between them.

Shoving the dishes aside, he grabbed her by the hips and lifted her to the counter. She'd already pulled her shirt off and was grabbing at his, her hands all over his skin. His head fell down to hers as he ran his hands up and over the lace of her bra. She'd given up on his shirt and was now fumbling with the button of his jeans.

Jesus *Christ*, he liked it when she fumbled.

He reached back behind him for his shirt and tugged it off, needing to feel her skin against his. And then he unhooked her bra, pretty much tore it from her body, before bending down and curling his tongue around her nipple, something he'd been dreaming about for a week.

With a moan she arched up into him, her hands closing around his waistband, the backs of her fingers nestling into the hollow of his hips, which had him surging up and into her, straining against the clothes that kept them apart. Since that wasn't nearly enough, he dropped his hands to the curve of her ass, second in perfection only to her breasts, and he pulled her up against him.

Sweet *Jesus* that was good.

He reached down for her jeans; no fumbling involved. Caressing, yes. Teasing, definitely, which led to quite a bit of squirming around on her part and a smile on his. "I like making you move," he said.

Though color rose to her cheeks, she had no problem giving him a coy smile as she looked up at him from under those lashes. She reached down into his jeans, cupped him over his boxer briefs, and he almost went off like a shotgun.

"That's good," she murmured into his neck, nipping a little at the skin. "Because I really like when you do it."

He took a minute to let the sensations roll through him—her hand on his cock, her mouth on his throat, her slick heat at his fingertips. He let it settle over him, let it sink in that, yeah, it was as perfect as he'd remembered for almost every hour of every day since the last time he'd had her. He let the tremor take hold at the base of his spine, savoring it, keeping it there until the moment he could let it fully erupt.

Then he pulled her hand up and grasped it; leaned down to kiss her. He was trying not to think about how much he'd missed her particular taste. How much he'd wanted the feel of her lips against his, of the heat of her mouth.

Breaking the kiss, he pulled at her jeans, stripping them off but leaving her panties on, crouching as he brought them down over those beautiful legs and taking his time as he kissed his way back up. Her hips pitched forward and she groaned in anticipation as he worked his way up. He nudged her knees wider with his shoulders, getting himself in there all the way, his hands closing around her thighs.

"I had a dream that went something like this," she managed.

Her, too? He'd take that as a good sign. "Any details you want to share?"

She smiled down at him. "Your tongue," she said. "All over me."

If the scent of her arousal hadn't already drawn him in, her words would have done it. Underneath her jeans and T-shirt she'd worn lacy white lingerie, and he had to force himself to slow down, to take a moment to fully appreciate it. Running his fingers along the rough edge, he said, "Like here?"

"Yes," she gasped from above him, her head falling back. "And then my tongue all over your cock."

Oh, fucking *A*. So much for holding himself back.

He yanked her panties down her legs, laying a kiss right in the middle of all that wet heat, earning himself a low moan. He rewarded her with a lap of his tongue, and then another, and another, until she was gripping his hair and gasping for air. He tightened his hands on her hips as he pulled her closer, sucking and tonguing and kissing until she screamed. Her entire body trembling, she hauled him up and kissed him, too. Then she wrapped her legs around his waist.

"I need you inside me, Deke," she gasped in between kisses. "Inside me now."

And he was almost there when he stopped suddenly, his head thunking down to hers as she whimpered in protest.

"Condom." He gritted his teeth against the pain of denying himself. "Bedroom."

She arched her back, rubbing all that heat against him. "What?" she asked. "You don't have one ready at all times?"

Not entirely minding her version of torture, he ground out, "The idea you have of my life and the reality of it are two very different things." Or, at least, the reality of it lately.

Kicking his clothes away, he lifted her up and carried her to the bedroom. He dropped her down to the bed and came down over her, reaching for the box he kept in his bedside table. Two seconds later he was sinking into her, trying to hold himself back, but having a hell of a time of it thanks to the way she was clutching at him and chanting, "Yes, yes, yes, yes…"

He felt the frenzy of her rise up through his blood, setting everything on fire inside him. "Come for me, Angel." He was as close to begging as he'd ever been, something he was trying not to dwell on. Sex was physical. Controllable. Except, apparently, when it was with Fitz. He tried to hold her steady beneath him, but she refused to stay still, bucking her hips, forcing his slide in and out of her until he was nearly undone.

He went to his elbows, frantic to touch her and taste her, but too overwhelmed by the sensations running through him to actually accomplish that. He'd never been with anyone nearly as…*enthusiastic*, and honestly, it ramped him up.

"Deke," she moaned, arching up to kiss him. "*Please*."

Which was even hotter.

He captured her lip with his teeth, and the bite set her off, fusing her body to his. He sucked and nipped at her neck as he drove into her, harder and harder as she shook beneath him.

The tremor rushed up his spine, the tightness and tension erupting into a wave of all-encompassing heat, his release rocking him to his very core. He came so hard it shattered him. He collapsed on top of her, his chest heaving. But despite having almost no ability to move, he turned his head and whispered into her ear, "The next time you decide not to speak to me for a week, I will fucking hunt you down."

She made a sound that was half laugh, half gasp, as her hand clenched around the back of his neck. "Caveman," she murmured.

He figured that wasn't a bad thing when her inner muscles tightened around him as well. It made him laugh. He even said, "Christ, Angel," stopping abruptly when he realized the second half of that had been about to be, *I love you.*

Since she wouldn't take that well, he kept it to himself.

Chapter Twenty-Two

Deke's bedroom was beautiful. It was mostly done in gray, various shades of it from the faded silver wash on the hardwood floor to drapes that were dark and heavy, the perfect counter to the floor-to-ceiling windows that looked out over the river below. In here, the exposed brick was also gray, but light enough that it was close to white. He had a king-size bed with a wrought iron headboard, two black leather club chairs at the windows facing out, and shag throw rugs that were so thick and luxurious she wanted to roll around on them.

But the focal point was a stunning oversize photograph, maybe four feet wide and almost as tall, of the sun setting over a cornfield. Even in a room lit only by the moon, the colors were so rich that they practically glowed: a cobalt blue sky and emerald green field set apart by glorious yellows and oranges. Fitz had been there when he bought it and still found herself nearly crying over the beauty of it. It was so perfectly *him*. Vibrant and beautiful, shimmering with life. None of the darkness she'd fought so hard to overcome. It was a reminder of why she'd stayed away.

She jumped when his hand went to her hip at the same time she felt his mouth at her neck, sending the most delicious shivers running up and down her spine. Then he pulled his head away—pulled his whole body away, his hand holding her in place when she tried to stay with him.

"No," he murmured. "Let me look at you."

Up on one elbow, he did that very thing, letting his fingers trail slowly up the side of her. Up past her waist, to the underside of her breast, over the peak up to her neck and then her chin, which he tipped up as he leaned forward and kissed her, lingering in a way that had her nervous about what was coming next.

Sure enough, when he pulled away again and rolled over to his back, he brought his hands behind his head and looked up at the ceiling. "Christ, Fitz. The disappearing act is getting old."

Since she didn't have a good answer to that, or an excuse, she stayed quiet, resting her chin on her hands and concentrating hard on the headboard. The headboard that had gorgeously intricate scroll work, yet was so sturdy you could probably…

"Oh, my God," she gasped, her head coming up as she studied it. "You use that for handcuffs, don't you?"

With a glare, he snapped, "Can we maybe focus?"

No, she realized. Not with the idea of that in her head. She found it appealing in a way that frightened her a little.

"Fitz."

"Right," she said. "Focusing." Tearing her gaze away from the headboard only to find that he was staring at her with an intensity that got her all hot and bothered again. "What?"

With a visible attempt to shake off whatever had just been running through his head, he unfortunately came back to, "So is this the plan? You won't talk to me for days at a time and then it will be all, 'Get inside me'?"

"Well, you did say I should tell you what I wanted..." she offered.

She deserved the next glare he gave her. She deserved all of it. But she wasn't playing games. She was just trying desperately to figure out if she could have him like this but still be friends.

Yes, she had stayed away, as he clearly knew. The work stuff hadn't been a lie. She really had been busy. But the conversation with Mr. Deacon and Mama Gin had spooked her. Not what they'd talked about specifically. As draining as that night had been, she'd felt strangely light ever since. It was more about how Deke had been. Or, rather, how she'd been with him and the strength she'd drawn from having him beside her. The way he'd known instinctively when to hold her and when to pull away.

It shook her. *She* took care of her. No one else. Allowing anyone else to step into that role went against everything she believed.

Not to mention that there was the job thing. There was nothing new on that front so it wasn't like anything was imminent. But even that was overwhelming. On the one hand, she knew she should tell him. If they weren't sleeping together she probably already would have. On the other hand, though, she wasn't actually sure that was true. She had no interest in telling Wash or Jason. She'd even rather that Dorie and Nate didn't know, to be honest. She was used to making decisions on her own. To living her life on her own. She didn't want anyone else weighing in on something that was conflicting enough. Right now she was actually think-ing *everything* was conflicting. So, well…

"I don't want a boyfriend, Deke," she got up her nerve to say. She didn't. She honestly didn't. Nothing in the last week had changed her mind about that. But as he sat up and swung his legs over, planting his feet on the floor and turning his back to her, she felt like her heart was actually breaking. She wanted him *so* much, and the thought of him walking away made her feel ill. So even knowing the risk she was taking—how badly it could go wrong and how much they had to lose if it did—she blurted out, "But that thing you said about every weekend, maybe every night?"

He looked at her over his shoulder as he pulled on a pair of sweats, all the while staring directly into her eyes, something she found a bit unnerving. After a pause, he said, "I'm listening."

Sitting up, she held the sheet up against her chest. "What if we kept it like this?" Spent their nights as lovers, their days as friends. "Then when we're done with the sex part," she added, ignoring his frown, "we don't need to worry about breaking up the band. Or, you know, anyone making a big deal of it." Because people would talk. They always did. Since he didn't actually protest, though, she pushed forward. "There's just one thing."

Giving her absolutely nothing to help her gauge what his reaction was to what she was saying, he merely nod-ded for her to keep going.

More nervous than she thought she'd be, her words came out in a little bit of a rush. With her heart pound-ing hard, she forced herself to keep going. "I need to know you won't be sleeping with…" Okay, so she couldn't actually say the name Peggy Miller while she was sitting here naked in his bed, and she certainly didn't want to think about Peggy being in it, too, so she instead ended with, "...other women." And anyway, that seemed a more reasonable request.

But he was quiet for so long she actually began to wonder. She even steeled herself for the answer that she was shit out of luck. So it kind of stunned her when he said, "Until that day in the Jeep, I hadn't had sex in six months."

Um... "Did you say...?"

"Yep." He laughed as he stood up, glancing down at her briefly before going over to the windows and sitting in one of the leather chairs. He rested his head along the back, stretched his legs out in front of him. "Six months."

"But Peggy's always saying..." Well, hell. What *didn't* she say?

"Peggy and I have always had a difference of opinion in terms of what our relationship actually is." He turned and made sure his eyes connected with Fitz's as he added, "And be assured, whatever it was is over as far as I'm concerned," as if he knew she actually needed to hear the words. But then he turned back and looked out at the moon, leaning forward as he rested his elbows on his knees. "I want you more than I want my next breath. I don't know why or how it changed. And I know we're skating on thin ice. But you mean more to me than any other woman I've ever known. My promise still stands. I have faith in us no matter what else happens. What's between us won't ever change."

Oh.

Fitz sat back against the headboard and stared at him.

Well.

"How can you do that?" she asked, truly wanting to know. "Be so sure that it will be okay once all is said and done."

He looked up at her, his hair golden in the moonlight. "That's the definition of faith, Angel."

It was like she could feel the pieces locking into place. His belief was so strong, she could actually let it carry her along. For now, at least.

Tucking the sheet around her, she went to him, pushing herself between his legs. Wary, he looked up at her and sat up a little straighter.

"So," she said, "I guess the whole throw down I was imagining with all those other women was kind of unnecessary."

His jaw twitched. "Well, that all depends on how far you were willing to go. Was wrestling involved?"

Laughing, she shook her head. "I'm not a big fan of unitards."

Reaching his hand out to her, he smiled. "I was thinking more along the lines of Jell-O." He brought her down against him, curling her into his lap. "Wet T-shirt contests are also good. And, you know, you have the most perfect breasts."

She was so surprised by that statement she didn't even realize he'd pulled the sheet down so he could touch them. Except then he rolled her nipples between his fingers and a groan escaped her throat before she could say anything in response.

As soon as she recovered, she straddled him. It appeared he had recovered as well. *Plus* he'd totally been lying about not having condoms everywhere.

"That's not what I said," he replied when she questioned him. "They're just not out in the kitchen. I've never needed to be prepared out there."

"So I'm supposed to believe you've never had counter sex before."

"You have a seriously skewed view of my sex life," he muttered.

Disappointed, she asked, "So no handcuffs, either?"

He went still. "Well let's not get too ahead of ourselves."

It wasn't until much later, when they were back in bed and drifting off to sleep that she said, "So I guess we're doing this."

He took her hand in his, intertwining their fingers. "Yeah. I guess we are."

Faith, she told herself. Believe.

Resting her head on his chest, Fitz closed her eyes. She had no idea what this would mean to their friendship. She had even less of an idea what would happen if this Sam Price thing actually happened. But for the first time in all the nights since they'd first kissed, she had exactly what she wanted in her arms.

Chapter Twenty-Three

So, the devil said, from his perch up on top of Lola's refrigerator. *Why haven't we thought of this before?*

Referring, of course, to the regular and monogamous arrangement Deke and Fitz had been managing for over a week now with no one being the wiser, possibly the first true relationship Deke had ever had. Fitz, too, he thought, although there was no way in hell he was raising that as a topic of discussion.

Deke opened the fridge and took out a carton of orange juice. Lola had taken the kids over to their parents' house for a final sleepover before the big RV trip, so she wasn't here to yell at him for not using a glass. He was in the middle of drinking from it when Fitz walked in the room, decked out in, well, it wasn't a suit, but it was definitely more formal than he was used to seeing her wear for their Iowa Dream Foundation board meetings. And she'd never been quite so out of control sexy. At least not that he'd ever noticed before. A light blue button-down shirt that seemed to be tailored to every curve, and a short gray skirt. And heels. High, high heels.

Va. Va. Voom, the devil said.

"You're wearing *that* tonight?" Deke asked, putting the carton down on the counter beside him.

"Why?" she asked. "What's wrong with this?" Then she frowned and held up her hand with that, *Oh, no, you don't* finger and look on her face. She said, in fact, "Do not for one second think that because we're sleeping together you get to—"

She had absolutely no clue. He grabbed her by the wrist and pulled her to him, ignoring her squealed, "Deke!"

"What's wrong is that I'm going to sit through that whole freaking meeting with a hard-on." His hand on her ass, he pulled her right up against him to demonstrate the issue.

"Oh," she said, her cheeks taking on a little extra pink as she looked away. "That *is* a problem." Reaching down, she took him in hand and he may have growled a little. "I actually have a fix for that."

"Do you now?" He backed her up against the counter and lifted her to it.

Her breath caught as he stepped in close, coming right up against her. She leaned back on her hands and looked up at him with such innocence it was almost as if she didn't know he was suddenly aching to bend down and take a quick nip or two at the bounty she'd offered up. "It might involve handcuffs," she said.

This time he definitely growled. He dropped down into a crouch.

She, in turn, straightened up. "What are you doing?" she asked, laughing, but wary.

"This'll just take a minute." He spread her legs, flipped up her skirt, and went for the panties.

"Deke!" she squealed again, her hand going down

to stop him, but she was too late, catching the back of his head instead.

"That's right," he murmured, nuzzling the inside of her thigh as her fingers tightened in his hair. He loved the softness of all that smooth skin almost as much as he loved the taste of her. He propped one of her legs over his shoulders. "You just hold on." And he took his first, long taste.

"Oh, my God," she sighed. "We don't have time for this." But the muscles in her thighs went slack as she tilted her hips up toward his mouth.

Glancing at her stretched up above him, he smiled as she fell back, her arms going out to either side along the breakfast bar, the counter handily behind her. It hit her right at the shoulders, though, so it made her back arch up as her head dropped back.

He needed her breast in his hand. Needed to feel the weight of it. And since he did have a lot of practice, he was able to reach his hand up, unbutton her shirt and push the cup of her bra aside, all while delving his tongue in deeper.

She moaned as he flicked his thumb back and forth across her nipple. "It should…" she gasped. "*Oh…* It should… Bother me…" She gasped again. "That you are so freakishly good at this." She palmed the back of his head and held him hard against her. "But right now I can't seem to ca…" Her voice trailed off into a full out groan.

He pressed in farther, holding her hips in place so that he controlled her movement, something she seemed to like a lot if the increasing urgency of her pleas were any indication.

"I like the way you beg," he said, pulling back enough

for her to feel him speak the words. Also how she completely gave herself over to him, although he was afraid to think it, much less say it, because it would probably freak her out. So instead he nipped at her clit, nuzzled one or two more times to switch things up, and then released her hips so she could go wild as he took her over the edge.

And she did. Go wild as he took her over the edge. Fuck, he loved that extra rush of sweetness when she came.

She collapsed back against the counter behind her. With one breast exposed and her chest heaving as she gulped in breaths of air, she looked so utterly fuckable he almost dropped trou and went all the way. She even whined a little as she looked down at him.

But she had to get to the library and he wanted to take his time. No matter what, he was going to have a hard time watching her up at the head of the table all night, so either way he'd need to hold himself back from going all feral and laying her out in front of everyo—

"Fitz, are you okay? I thought I heard someone… It sounded like a scream."

It went against every one of Deke's instincts not to shoot up at the sound of Lola's voice from the hallway. But he was still in a crouch and the breakfast bar separated him from her, and given where and how Fitz was sitting, it would be entirely clear what he'd just done to her.

Which might not be the worst of things, as far as he was concerned.

Fitz, of course, didn't concur.

"*Lola?*" she said, her head whipping around. She'd gotten her bra back on, but it was pretty obvious she was buttoning up her shirt. "I, uh… What are you doing here?"

"I forgot my jacket," Lola answered, her voice coming closer.

Fitz was down off the counter so fast that Deke felt the breeze. He yanked her panties from off the floor where Lola might see them and shoved them into his pocket as Fitz walked around to the front of the breakfast bar and then past it, presumably so that Lola wouldn't come far enough around to see him sitting there.

Sure enough, it sounded as though Lola had stopped over by the dining room table as she added, "Jules and I are going out tonight after the meeting and I think it's supposed to rain." Being Lola, however, she wasn't deterred from her original line of questioning. "Were you, uh, crying?"

Hell, yeah, she was.

"*What?*" Fitz asked, so flustered that she was totally about to give them away all on her own. They were going to need to work on that if she wanted to keep this a secret. "Uh, no. Vocal exercises. You know, to get ready for the presentation tonight."

Then she made some ridiculous noises that sounded like the horrible impression of an opera singer that they were.

The devil and angel recoiled in horror. *That was awful*, the angel said.

Yep. They were definitely going to need to work on her evasive techniques. He sat back against the fridge and rested his arms on his knees.

"Your shirt's not buttoned right." Lola had actually been an expert at evasive techniques back in the day.

Deke was pretty sure she and Dave had actually had sex in the pantry during her eighteenth birthday party—while his mother was in the kitchen lighting the candles on the cake. He wouldn't put it past her to call them out right now.

Fitz was getting her act together, though, smoothly saying, "Oh, my God. Thanks. I spilled juice on my other shirt—that totally must have been the scream you heard—and had to make a last-minute change. That would have been so crazy embarrassing. Just like me, huh?"

It wasn't. Apart from Jules, Fitz was the most put together person they all knew. Part of why he'd had no clue there was so much buried underneath that shell of hers. Lola, however, decided not to comment on that.

"I'm glad you guys are coming to the meeting, by the way," Fitz said, steamrolling right past it. "You know we have dinner for you and everything, right?"

"Yes." Deke could hear the smile in Lola's voice. Because, well… "We're catering it."

Oh, *man.* As good as outed, Deke was about to stand up when Lola gently said, "Are you sure everything's okay? I know you and Jules haven't always been the closest, but it's an open invitation for you to join us at any time. You know that, right?"

If Deke hadn't been riding on such a high from the taste still on his lips, his heart might have broken a little bit at the way Fitz's voice faltered as she asked, "What?"

"I mean," Lola went on to say, "I'm not sure if I ever said it before. And with Dorie here, you and she have gotten so close, plus you've always hung out with the guys. But if you ever need some extra girl time…"

"I, um…" Fitz actually sounded a little choked

up. That alone made Deke want to jump to his feet. "Thanks. I'll take you up on that sometime." Then she cleared her throat and, sounding almost back to normal, said, "But I, uh, have some things to do after the meeting."

Deke being one of them, for damn sure.

"Okay," Lola answered. Though the suspicion was still there in her voice, she let it go. "So where's Deke?"

Or not.

"Huh?" Fitz snapped, from zero to flustered in oh point oh seconds flat.

"His truck's parked outside. Is he here?"

"Oh. Yes. I'm not sure where. Maybe in your bathroom? Between you and me, I think he goes up there for the *Cosmos*."

She did not just say that. And anyway, Lola kept her *Cosmos* stashed under her bed.

Lola laughed. "Well, if you happen to think of it, can you tell him his registration is about to expire? I keep forgetting."

Freaking A, Lola. He had two more days.

"I will be happy to let him know." Fitz's last word was a muffled squeal. Not as good as the ones he got out of her, but he liked it nonetheless.

He also liked that it was because Lola was giving her a hug. It had been a subtle shift, but it seemed like ever since San Francisco, or maybe, since the talk with Mama Gin, Fitz had been letting her walls down, little by little. It was still incredible to him she'd kept so much bottled up inside for so long, and he was happy to see he wasn't the only one working at breaking her down.

After a quick "Thanks," Lola left the room and there was the sound of the closet door opening and then closing before a called out, "See you in a bit!" Then the front door slammed shut, leaving him and Fitz alone again.

She came back around the end of the island, leaning her hip against the counter and folding her arms across her chest. "Do you think she knows?"

If Lola hadn't warned him off Fitz, he'd say yes. Especially after that performance. "Babe, we have some work to do. That was, well…"

Pathetic, the devil suggested.

"I know," Fitz sighed, her chin dropping to her chest. Then she cocked her head to the side and gave him a wicked grin. "But I'm really good at everything else." She reached her hand out to help pull him up.

He pulled her down instead and she fell against him. "Yeah, you are."

"Too bad we need to go," she whispered, her voice all husky as she nuzzled his neck.

Yes, unfortunately. Because of this big presentation she and Nate were doing tonight, and because they had invited a whole host of extra folks, the meeting was going to be in the media room at the library and there was some extra set up to be done. And although Josh was entirely capable of running things for a night, it wouldn't hurt for Deke to check in and make sure all the food was set.

"Can I have my panties back?" she asked sweetly as they both reluctantly stood.

"Nope," he said, taking her held out hand and pulling her behind him as he headed to the front door.

"You're joking," she answered, although she didn't actually protest.

"Panty lines are totally unbecoming." He barely stopped long enough to grab her purse and computer bag before opening the door and giving her a little nudge so she was in front of him.

"But… I…"

Though still not actually protesting, she sputtered similar things all the way into town, right up to the moment he pulled in front of the library. "Think of it as payback for the crack about the *Cosmos*." But he was completely about to give them back to her when Nate walked right up then with…

"Sam," Fitz said in surprise as she climbed down from the truck, her hands clamping down over her skirt as a breeze caught the hem. "I didn't realize you'd be here tonight."

Very carefully, she reached up to give Nate a quick hug and kiss on the cheek, taking a moment to glare at Deke along the way.

Which Deke of course noticed, but he was paying more attention to the flare of appreciation in Sam's eyes as the man's gaze fell down to Fitz's heels, no doubt also taking in her grabbable ass and outstanding legs.

It didn't escape Nate's notice, either, who gave a clear, *What the fuck, Dude?* look over Fitz's head. To which Sam raised his hands and lowered his eyes to the ground, an equally clear, *Sorry. Noted. But I'm a guy and she's a seriously fine woman and some of the parts operate on their own.*

Focused on Sam, it took a minute for Deke to swing his head back to Nate, whose icy stare was now directed at him. That one could be read from the international space station. *You and I have already had this discussion, bro, and I am seriously going to pound you into the ground.*

Having a great deal of practice dealing with Nate

over the years, it was easy enough to pull back and smile in pure It's All Chill mode. With a wave, he left them all on the sidewalk as he pulled away, reminding himself that other guys could appreciate all they wanted. He was the one who had just made her scream. Hell, he could still taste her. Which, uh, was a problem. He took a quick detour into the men's room to wash his face—thank fuck he'd been in the car when Nate walked up—and then headed back to the kitchen.

Thinking it would probably be better to avoid any pre-meeting-hanging-out conversation with Nate, Deke spent the next forty-five minutes in the office taking care of some bookkeeping, even allowing himself a few moments of thinking about what it would be like if they did come clean. If they were an official couple, her running the foundation from the back office while he ran the bar. Yeah, he was pretty sure he could get into that idea.

Because there was too much food to carry, Josh was taking it over on a cart, which left Deke to go over some last minute things with the kitchen staff before heading over to the library. He ran into Lola and Jules as they were going into the building.

"So do you know why we're here?" Lola asked as they got to the top of the stairs.

He didn't in fact. Because Fitz lived at Lola's, he obviously couldn't spend the night with her. And Lola was too perceptive for Fitz to spend too many nights away. Since they spent pretty much all the rest of their time with Wash, Jason, Dorie and/or occasionally Tuck, there wasn't much opportunity to talk. By the time they were alone together, conversation was the last thing on their minds.

Lola and Jules didn't need to know any of that, of course. Nor would it be unusual for him to shrug and say, "No clue," since he rarely felt a need to ask. But, well… What *was* she working on so much? It was still like pulling teeth to get her to give details on anything, much less something he hadn't come out and asked about.

Well, details on anything other than sex. She had no problems talking about all sorts of things there. She was remarkably open about that.

About everything else? No.

It was actually beginning to bother him a little bit.

Especially when he walked into the room and saw her standing at the head of it, her eyes all sparkly and bright as she smiled at something Nate said. Nate was leaning back against the table with Dorie settled up against him, her back to his front. And Sam was standing there right with them, his arms across his chest and his head bent down and tilted toward Fitz as he listened intently to what she was saying.

Yeah, Deke was definitely bothered by that. And that was before Josh brought Fitz the bill for the meal that had just been set up. It wasn't the handing of the bill that was the problem, of course. Rather it was the way Josh smiled down at her as she took it and signed for everything and the way she smiled right back. Deke felt irritation rise up through his chest and it took everything he had not to let it escape.

It wasn't like they needed to declare their everlasting love or anything like that. But, hell. He'd slept with Peggy maybe ten times in the last few years and pretty much every living soul in Inspiration over the age eighteen was well aware of that fact. He'd never snuck around behind closed doors before and he was finding he really didn't like it. They were sleeping together. So what? They were both consenting adults. It shouldn't matter to anyone else.

And now he hesitated. If she were any other woman in the world, he'd have already gone over to her; he definitely would have with any other woman he'd slept with. He'd never had a problem with the way he was with women because he honestly didn't give a shit. His body wasn't sacred. They were welcome to whatever they wanted to take on that front. But they didn't get his heart or his head.

So maybe the problem he was having at the moment was that Fitz was the first woman he'd ever been with who had all three—and he wasn't allowed to tell anyone he had even a little part of her.

Chapter Twenty-Four

Fitz knew the second Deke walked in the room.

She was showing Sam the parts of the presentation that might end up being relevant to his foundation, and she actually stuttered for a second before deliberately turning her back to the doorway and looking down at her laptop. Not reacting outwardly to Deke whatsoever was getting harder to do with each passing day, especially when her reaction tended to be as obvious as it was uncontrollable.

"You're thinking about how many scholarships?"

Sam. Laptop screen. Right.

"Our goal for now is fifty percent, although ultimately we'd love to bring that up to a hundred," she answered.

"Ambitious," he nodded.

"Have you ever known Nate to think small?" she asked.

Crisis averted. She paged to the next slide, trying to decide whether she should just come out and ask if this was part of her interview. Except someone might overhear her and since she already knew it wouldn't go over well, she at least wanted Deke to be the one she told first. But other than a vague "things are moving forward and we'll be in touch soon" type statement, Sam hadn't even talked about the job, so saying anything might be bad on that front, too.

Goddamn it. She would be a lot more comfortable if she was wearing underwear at the moment. Well, if she could manage this, she'd have absolutely no problem with the interview.

Fitz looked up at Nate and smiled at whatever he'd just said and then realized Josh was standing in front of her with the bill for dinner. She gave him a smile, too, remembering not to be a total imbecile in time to say, "Thanks."

"Any time," he answered. "Deke said you or Jason could settle up tomorrow but you'd need this for your records."

She wondered if her skin actually flushed at the sound of Deke's name or if that heat was all internal. Hopefully the latter. "Sounds good." And although there was no need whatsoever, as soon as Josh left, she went over to check the trays of food in order to have a minute to pull herself together.

All of her cells snapped to attention right before Deke said quietly into her ear, "I am one hundred percent sure none of this tastes as good as you do."

She whirled around, hissing, "You did not just say that!" as a look of complete innocence came over his face and he smiled over her shoulder.

"Hi, Mama Gin," he said.

"Max," she said, wrapping her arm around him and giving him a hug. After turning to Fitz and doing the same, she asked, "So do I get a hint about why I've been invited tonight?"

Things had been remarkably easy with Mama Gin since the night at the bar. They'd talked about Fitz's father a few times since then; Mama Gin had even come out to the cemetery one afternoon. It was wonderful and strange all at the same time. Another new normal. But not what Fitz should be thinking about now, either.

Happy to have an excuse to put some distance between her and Deke, Fitz smiled brightly. "Nope." Then she turned to the assembled group. "Why doesn't everyone grab some dinner so we can get started."

Between Deke, having Sam here unexpectedly, and the meeting itself, dinner wasn't even a possibility, so Fitz took full advantage of the fifteen minutes to go through the presentation one more time. When everyone was finally settled, she looked around the room. There was nothing to be nervous about. These were the people she loved most in the world: Nate and Dorie; Jason and Wash; Ella, Jules, Lola and Mama Gin. Even Tuck was there today.

And, of course, Deke.

Her gaze lingered on him, despite how dangerous it was. The slow smile he gave her now was as soothing as that amazing drawl of his, the whispered, "Angel," in the middle of the night. She looked down at her notes, not even caring she had the same grin on her face that he wore on his.

"Thanks, everyone, for coming tonight," she said. "I know we're a larger group than usual. What we have to say will impact everyone so we want to give you a chance to put the brakes on now."

And since she wanted this as much as Nate did, she hoped they'd see the good in it, too. With a nod, she handed it over to Nate.

He wasn't nervous like she was—at least not visibly so. She was kind of happy, though, to see that he needed some fortification, too. Or at least that's how she was reading Dorie's smile and squeeze of his hand before he stood up and took Fitz's place and then launched right into it.

"So I guess this is kind of my dress rehearsal for officially announcing my retirement from baseball after next season."

Although it wasn't the surge of reporters jumping forward as it would be on the actual day, he'd definitely gotten everyone's attention. "I'm of course hoping," he said, "the rest of this season will be as good as the first half was, and that next year will be the same. But even if not, I've had a good run and I'd rather go out on a high note than be one of those guys who doesn't know when to pack it in." He glanced down at Dorie and brightened visibly when she smiled. "Plus, now that I've been spending more time in Inspiration again, it's clear to me that someone needs to start talking sense around here. I mean, Christ, just the other day someone said to me that if Mom decides to stop running for mayor one day, Deke might actually be next in line."

That got Deke's attention. He even seemed flustered for a minute, which he shouldn't be. As far as Fitz was concerned, it was a role he'd been born to play. But, per usual, he made a joke. "Must have been Si. He'll do anything to ride in that convertible for the Founders Day parade."

Everyone laughed, of course, because that was something Si had been pretty vocal about after Jules's kids got to ride with Mama Gin last year. But Deke was the only one who seemed even halfway surprised when Mama Gin smiled as she leaned forward and said, "Actually, Max, that would have been me. But we can talk about that later."

Obviously happy to have facilitated that little bomb being dropped, Nate brought the attention back up to the front of the room. "As you all know, Johnny Whitfield will be in town to tape his show in a few weeks. I'll make the official announcement then. And since I expect he'll want to know what I'm planning to do next, I thought it would be the perfect platform to, well…" He nodded at Fitz before sitting back down.

Which was her cue to stand up. "We actually have two things to talk about today." She dimmed the lights and pulled up her presentation, the first slide of which was the Iowa Dream Foundation logo. "One of the reasons Johnny is coming to Inspiration is because he loved the story behind the foundation, and he loved even more what we've done with it." Because, yes, after Deke had pulled her away from Johnny that day in San Francisco, thereby prompting the conversation with Nate, it had come back full circle to Johnny again. "But as we talked, both Nate and I realized we've got things running really well here at home."

"*You've* got things running well at home," Nate interjected. And thanks to the chorus of cheers now it was Fitz who was flustered, unused to such enthusiastic praise. Also a little irritated, because she had a feeling that was Nate's way of pushing her to stay. She was pretty sure the only reason he was supportive of her ideas to expand the foundation was because he thought it would keep her there. But even that would be a big change, given what she was about to propose.

"Um, thanks," she mumbled before picking up where she'd left off. "Last week I spent some time talking to

Nate's friends in Chicago and it turns out there are more than a few of them who like what we're doing, too, and who would love to be a part of it. With their investments and Jason's talent, we could begin branching out and helping other towns that may have been hard hit in the same way Inspiration was with the tornado." A mission she believed in wholeheartedly, but that also gave her a way out of Inspiration even if she didn't get Sam's foundation job. As Fitz spoke, Dorie distributed folders to each of the official board members. "This will mean a change of bylaws and mission, of course, so it will need a board vote."

Carefully not looking at Sam because she was afraid she'd screw it up, she also, as agreed upon, added, "The reason Sam is here tonight is because he was part of the initial conversation and because he's been in the exploration stages of starting a private foundation of his own, which, incidentally, hasn't yet been publicly announced and therefore needs to stay in this room." And whether it was officially part of her job interview or not, she knew he was paying close attention to everything she was doing tonight, including how well she stuck to the script.

"He's interested in being one of those investors," she said. "Because this is a pretty major change, we thought we'd put it out there for you to begin thinking about. We'll have another board meeting next week so we can answer questions and talk it through." She glanced down at Nate, waiting for his nod before continuing, "Then there's this next part."

She nodded to Dorie so the second round of folders could be distributed. "If we do end up expanding the foundation's mission, it will take up some of Nate's newly freed time because it will be partly up to him to drum up investors. But he'd like to spend most of his time here in Inspiration running the—" she brought up the next slide "—Iowa Dream Academy."

Having some kids come out to play sports during the summer wasn't a stretch. The scale of it, however, was obvious on the slide. And since it bordered Wash's land, not to mention the land and the farmhouse that Lola had had her eyes on since she was a kid, there were definitely going to be questions.

"Before I go forward, I want to say we are well aware that this would have an impact on everyone in the room whether personally," like with Wash and Lola, "professionally," like with the increased demand on city services and resources that Mama Gin and Tuck would have to deal with, "or both. So the packets you have present three options, ranging from a year-round operation that brings kids of all ages here from all over the country for both academics and athletics, down to a much more basic, summer-only baseball and basketball camp."

She spent the next half hour going through the various plans, including financial projections, architectural drawings and the various lists of people Nate wanted involved. Knowing they'd thrown a whole heck of a lot at everyone, she closed with, "We understand this could change the entire landscape of Inspiration. And we know that, even if every single one of you here is fully on board with the project, we'd still have a long way to go in terms of approval from the town." It did occur to her that she might not be part of that "we," but that wasn't something she chose to dwell on.

"Therefore, the only way we'd move forward with

the full-scale option is if we have complete agreement from everyone in this room. And since it's a lot to take in, not to mention a lot to ask, each packet includes an anonymous ballot addressed to the foundation's mailbox with a simple vote: 'Option One' for the full-scale, 'Two' for in-between, or 'Three' for the scaled down version. We only go with Option One if it's unanimous. If that's not the case, then we go with one of the lesser versions and Nate gets an actual retirement."

No one even smiled at that, which Fitz didn't think was a good sign, but they were definitely looking through the materials, so who knew? She wasn't sure how to take it, though, when Deke sat back in his chair and looked at her and then Nate. "With the full-scale option, who in this room is directly involved?"

From the way he asked, she couldn't tell whether he was leaning toward it or against it so her heart was pounding even more than usual when she brought up the org chart she and Nate had spent an entire plane ride talking through. Their ideal roster, as Nate had called it, would include Jason being the main advisor on academics, Wash on community collaboration, and Deke on—

"Youth and family programming?" he asked, shaking his head and laughing. "That's a joke, right? I mean, I'm a freaking *bartender*."

Since he seemed to be the only one in the room who didn't see himself as more than that, no one else laughed. He sat back and cocked his head. "What? You need someone to drive one of those trains around the whole place and to keep the rest of the family occupied while little Jimmy plays baseball?"

Nate, who made clear how unhappy he was with

Deke every time Fitz brought his name up, sat back in his chair. "I love that."

Managing not to give him an I-told-you-so slap on the shoulder, Fitz couldn't help but give a smug smile. It was exactly why she'd insisted. Whatever anyone else could do, Deke would take it somewhere no one else had thought of. "Any other questions?"

She and Nate fielded some easy ones, as did Jason. Even Wash and Lola seemed interested, if not overly enthusiastic. Although Lola did seem to be genuinely smiling when she sighed and said, "So I guess it really is time for me to find an actual nanny."

To Fitz's surprise, that threw her more than anything else that had come up. "Um... No, I don't think so." They were still months away from any of this.

Which only made Lola laugh before gently saying, "Fitz, you do realize that if this all goes through, everything in your life changes. I mean, you'd be the one in charge of all this, right?"

"Um... Well..." Fitz looked down at Nate, but he was no help. In fact, as Fitz began to answer, "Not really," he leaned forward and spoke over her, saying, "I'd like her to be." His gaze shifted first to Sam, then to her with a completely neutral look on his face while somehow still making his opinion entirely clear.

Having Sam there didn't help, of course. Hell, maybe if he'd done anything other than sit back with an equally bland expression, Fitz might have come out and said something. But with both of them just sitting there, she realized that she was totally on her own here. As always. And since she was well used to it by now, it should have been something she could easily handle. Instead, and for the first time in years—since the moment she'd realized she'd never see her parents again—she felt actual panic. She couldn't breathe.

She hoped to God it wasn't obvious. She could *not* lose her shit here, at her *job*. Not in front of Sam, of all people.

As her heart started racing, her eyes flew up to Deke's.

And he saw it. Saw it and reacted immediately, drawing everyone's attention away from her by saying, "Forget about Fitz, people. What about me? *Jesus*, you've got me driving a train, advising on programming, whatever the fuck that means, plus I've apparently got to set up a campaign fund. This is some serious shit."

By the time he was done—well by the time everyone else was done giving him a hard time—Fitz's breathing was almost back to normal and her heart had stopped racing. *Almost*. But whatever. She was about to take back control of the meeting when she realized Nate was staring at her.

Then he turned, and although his expression didn't change, she could tell by the way he focused on Deke he knew exactly what had just happened. Maybe he even felt a little bit guilty. Either way, he decided to let her off the hook by saying loudly enough to get everyone's attention, "So I don't like that whatever I do means you all pay for it one way or another, which is why it only moves forward if you all give the go ahead. Because of Johnny's visit, unfortunately, we do need to have a sense of what you're thinking so we'll need your ballots back by next Wednesday. Fitz will send out an email for a time to meet next week."

His gaze moved back to hers and her response was automatic. "Anything else?"

There were a few more questions, actually, and she

was grateful for it because it meant she could end on a high note. By the time they'd adjourned the meeting, she was pretty sure she'd managed to get past it. She was even able to smile when Lola came up to her afterward and said, "I'm sorry. I didn't mean to put you on the spot. And I know the nanny thing was a stopgap to help me out. Deke's been telling me I need to figure out something official for a while now. It's just that I love having you live with us so much—" She did? Fitz's heart started picking up its pace again. "It was what came to mind. It was entirely selfish of me to even—"

"Lola."

Fitz's entire body warmed at the sound of Deke's voice. She looked up to see him very deliberately keeping his distance, but his eyes were burning into hers and she got the sense that he was as ready to take her in his arms as she was ready to be there. But she couldn't. Not yet. Not until later tonight.

Then he smiled. Although he wrapped his arm around his sister's shoulders, his gaze never left Fitz's when he said, "It's not selfish. I can't imagine anyone living with Fitz would ever want her to leave."

Did he mean that? Really? Because now that she mostly had hold of herself again, she wasn't feeling at all okay with the fact that he'd been the one to step in and help and yet she'd given him not one bit of a heads up as to what was going on. If she weren't so scared of how it might change things between them, she would pull him out of this room and tell him right now. But it would change things. He *would* be angry. And since he was possibly the only person in the world who believed in her enough to jump in and take her back without even a second's hesitation, the idea of upsetting him scared her so much that her heart went into full-out race mode again. She clutched the table. This time she felt like she might actually throw up.

Except, no. He'd said it as part of the joke. Or at least that's what she told herself as he looked down at Lola and went on with what he was saying. "You, on the other hand, are a total slob and, personally, I'd kick you out in a second."

Lola turned to him and pounded him in the arm. "I have four kids. I have *triplets*. Who are *three*."

"Blah, blah, blah," Deke said, rolling his eyes, ignoring her outraged laugh. "Next thing you're going to tell me is that you have a job and a personal life. What*ever*. The fact of the matter remains you've been a mess for a long time, Lo."

With a smack on the arm, Lola spun him around and pushed him toward the now decimated trays of food. "Okay, Mr. Clean. Show me how it's done."

He glanced back at Fitz over his shoulder and winked.

And Fitz felt a surge of…love.

But friend love. Because that was all it was. And she'd loved him forever, so it wasn't like anything had changed.

Well, um… The sex part. That was obviously different.

She looked down at the table and began gathering her things together. After a minute, Nate came over and leaned back against the conference table. He folded his arms across his chest. "Want to tell me what that was about?"

Fitz glared at him as she shut her laptop down. "*Really?* How about you tell me?"

"I want you to be part of this," he answered, not at all apologetic. "I won't pretend otherwise."

Other than a huff, Fitz had no response to that. So she ignored him while she went about her business. She'd gone as far as putting the extra portfolios into her bag when he said, "So you're still sleeping with him."

And there went all the folders right onto the floor. "*Damn* it." With a glare at Nate, she flounced down to pick them up, feeling the air in all sorts of odd ways just in time to keep her skirt from flying up. Sam crouching down next to her to help didn't make it at all better.

Oh, for heaven's sake.

Except, well… She did want to work for him. Panic attacks and other ramifications aside, she really wanted the job with Sam's foundation.

Damn it. How obvious had her near-breakdown been?

Not very, apparently, if Sam's saying, "That was a fantastic presentation," meant anything. "Do you have time to talk a little bit?"

They weren't strangers. They weren't friends, either, of course, but thanks to his longstanding relationship with Nate, she figured she could at least take advantage of that fact.

She smiled. "Of course. Could we maybe meet over at Deacon's in fifteen minutes or so? You guys can grab a table." Probably not the best way to handle the high-powered owner of the Chicago Watchmen and potential new boss, but she needed a minute. Big time. "I'll see you in a few."

Chapter Twenty-Five

Deke spent the rest of the evening watching Fitz have drinks with another man.

Yes, it was work, but that didn't make it suck less. And it was a damn good thing Sam had gotten control of his eyes and was being completely professional. Overly professional, it seemed, given they all went back a ways, but maybe that was because Nate was there with them the whole time.

Well, most of the time. There was the two-minute interlude when Nate came over to get a round of drinks. While Deke was drawing a draft, Nate smiled and said in the most conversational tone ever, "You do realize the only reason I'm not kicking the ever-living shit out of you is because Dorie seems to think you and Fitz are good for each other. She made me promise to be nice. She's also made it clear I'll never see her naked again if I play the baby sister card so make no mistake—if I have to kill you and end up never having sex again in my life, yours will be the slowest, most painful death you can possibly imagine."

"Dorie," Deke called out, his eyes never leaving Nate's, "your drinks are on the house tonight."

With a laugh, Dorie called back, "No worries, Deke. I've got your back."

Actually, Fitz seemed happy, his friends were all having a good time and his bar was full. It wasn't the worst of nights.

Plus, with Lola's kids at his parents' and Lola herself with Jules, Fitz was coming home with him. Not only did she stay until closing, as the crowd dwindled down to the final stragglers, she actually offered to help close out Betsy's tables so the other woman could get home to her kids. Hell, she'd actually sat and talked with Tristan Tucker and his date for a while, something Deke didn't think he'd ever seen. If it hadn't been for Josh still hanging around, well, it wouldn't have been the first time Deke had had sex in his bar, but it would have been the best, he had no doubt. She'd done amazing at that board meeting, even with that moment at the end. He might not like the idea of Fitz's job getting more intense, but if it meant she wore those suits and heels every day? There were some definite perks. The idea of it made him so hot for her that, once he got her home, he barely made it to the bedroom before tearing her clothes off. Yep, he damn well ravished her. She didn't mind one bit.

Which was why, when he was woken up by the click of metal in the middle of the night and realized it was the sound of her handcuffing him to the bed, he was taken a little bit by surprise. Before he could even process it, she took his other wrist and cuffed that one as well.

"You," she said, "have been a very naughty boy."

Deke—and his dick—came to full attention. "I have?"

Now that he was fully secured, she climbed off him and went over to the overnight bag she'd stashed by the windows. Her hair was all teased out, kind of the way it had been the first night they'd been together in San Francisco, and she was wearing something flimsy enough for the moonlight to shine through. Grabbing hold of the headboard, he hiked himself up enough to see…

Well, he wasn't sure what you'd call it. An overshirt of some sort, dark but completely sheer, floating behind her as she walked toward him, not even coming close to covering up the corset she was wearing. Or the garters. Or the knee-high boots. Where the fuck had those come from?

"You, uh… Want to turn the lights on?" He hated when she hid from him, no matter what form it took. But there was also the part where the dominatrix thing was working for him big time. And, damn it, he wanted to see her. *All* of her.

She stopped at the end of his bed, completely out of his reach. She'd cuffed his hands down close to the mattress, so it wasn't the easiest thing to even keep his head high enough up to see her. Especially because there was some tenting going on and it was entirely in the way.

His head dropped back down when the tips of her fingers trailed lightly up to his knee. "Nope," she said. "You're being punished."

All the parts that weren't already throbbing, started. He had no freaking idea what was going on but, holy fuck, was he happy to play along. "I'm pretty sure the prisoner has the right to know the charges against him."

"True," she said, her palm grazing the head of his cock and, even with the sheet between them, the heat of her hand had him surging up.

Completely ignoring his efforts to get closer, she pulled the sheet down past his waist to the top of his thighs. Got herself wedged between his knees so he had no choice but to open his legs up a little wider, although it wasn't the easiest with his legs mostly trapped by the sheet. But, God, he wanted her on him. He grabbed hold of the headboard again, tried to flip her under him. She wasn't having it. And all efforts came to a screeching halt when he felt the first stroke of her tongue—wet and slow, from base to tip.

Oh, *fuck*. "Fitz… Baby…"

"Mmm?" she murmured, letting the vibration roll over her tongue as she swirled it around and then down again. Then she sat back on her heels and her hand took the place of her tongue. Rather than a nice strong grip, however, she let her fingernails skim his skin, the sensation of them sharp enough to have him on edge, but light enough for him to want more. He clenched his jaw so as not to start begging.

Not at all concerned, she kept those fingernails grazing as she sternly said, "The charge is theft and indecency. Stealing a woman's panties comes with major penalties."

If not for the thought of her bare through that meeting, he might have been able to keep his hips from rearing up again. God*damn*. "Defense states all items of clothing were returned," he said.

She smacked the inside of his thigh. "The prosecution stipulates that is technically correct," she answered, "however, the motivation was questionable."

Okay, yes. So she'd come up to him while he was doing the food cleanup with Lola, jabbed his arm and said, "You. Come with me." Then she'd grabbed him by the wrist and pulled him out of the media room and into the stairwell.

"Sex in the library? Isn't that illegal?" he'd asked.

Not caring if it was, mind you, it was just that if he was going to be mayor he'd need to know things like that.

"No touching," she'd said, smacking his hand away. "My underwear. *Please.*"

Even that had been hot.

Staring at her now as her hand trailed up and down his leg, he said, "Defense pleads temporary insanity."

Her hand came back up and gave a way too light stroke up his shaft. "Explain."

With a groan, he said, "Stairwell sex was implied. In the *library.*" He wasn't generally into sex in public places, but that was now on his bucket list for damn fucking sure.

She lost her composure for a second, a grin breaking through, possibly because he may have whined. Then she got her lawyer face back on. "Hmmm… The prosecution can see the point." To his surprise, she even brought her eyes up to meet his, something she rarely did when nakedness was involved. "The prosecution is also taking into account the fact that the prisoner came to the rescue of a damsel in distress earlier this evening, and she's petitioned the court for lenience."

Yes, maybe she was mixing her metaphors a little, but he wasn't about to call her on that. Not when she sounded a little more emotional than usual in these circumstances. "Fitz…"

But she didn't reply as she settled her shoulders between his legs again and let her hair fall teasingly over his skin right before her mouth closed over him.

Okay, fine. He was happy to go with that for now. Especially when she'd come up with an excellent alternate use for her tongue. Sweet *Jesus.*

But he wanted his hands on her. He wanted his mouth

on her. He'd never been restrained—he'd never had any woman be with him the way Fitz was. And hell, fucking, yes he was getting off on it, as was overwhelmingly obvious. But he wanted to *see* her. Look into her eyes and have her look right back. With her down between his legs, the only thing he could do was jerk his head up.

Or maybe not. With a frustrated huff, he let his head fall back down to the bed. "Hell, Fitz. If we're gonna do this again, at least put the cuffs a little higher so I can see you. Or come closer for fuck's sake."

She laughed, goddamn it. Actually laughed before taking him all the way to the back of her throat and then releasing him. Teasing him the way he'd teased her more than once before—and he wasn't sure how he felt about it. Not in a physical sense. He wanted inside her so much he was actually sweating. But he'd never not been the one in control before; he'd most definitely never been handcuffed. Hell, if it was any other woman, he still wouldn't be.

Still playing her part, she shook her head regretfully, her hand going back down now, from his thigh to his knee to his ankle. "The jury finds the defendant guilty of the original charge. Punishment will proceed."

Trying to pull his head up again, he said, "Unless you're into whips and chains—" and he was ninety-nine percent certain that wasn't the case although, God knew, she was always doing something she wasn't telling him about so there was always that slight chance "—I'm not sure anything else you can dream up will be nearly as effective."

Because he was already in pain. Pulsing, throbbing, *serious* pain.

Completely unexpectedly, she gave him a wet kiss on the inside of his thigh and then pulled away. Then he felt something drift over his foot that was far too light to be anything but...

Oh. Fuck. God. Damn. It was the flimsy thing, which she was taking off, deliberately out of view. It was followed by the sound of a zipper, a slow, seductive slide he could only listen to. His dick jumped to attention like she was pulling it on a string. Fuck, fuck, fuck.

She laughed again, and this time something with a bit more substance, something a little lacier, landed on his knee. He sucked in a breath as it continued its course right on up. "You know...?" she said. "Seeing you like this sure does make me wet."

Jesus fucking Christ.

She came crawling up over him on all fours, letting her breasts graze his stomach and chest. Then she let out a quiet gasp as she dragged that slick, wet heat over the length of his pulled-way-too-tight skin. But rather than sink onto him—as he so fucking required—she lay down, her hand slowly making its way down her own body. Down the curve of her neck, down between her breasts... It disappeared from his sight just as she let her head fall back. "*So* wet," she moaned.

The growl erupted out of him and he was pretty sure he'd be bleeding by the end of the night if she didn't take these handcuffs off him, but he didn't give a shit as he twisted and hooked his leg over hers, dragging her toward him as she squealed in surprise.

She'd pinned him down for a reason, however, and clearly had no intention of giving up control. She flipped him back over and straddled his thighs. "Take your punishment like a man, Prisoner Deacon." Then she leaned down and kissed him, murmuring, "Time for *you* to show a little bit of that trust."

He tried—oh, fuck, he tried—working on getting his breathing back to normal as she sat back up and over him, what little clothes she still had on in disarray.

Then all bets were off when she bent down again and had her way. She took him in hand and mouth, torturing him with long, slow strokes before coming up for air. She knew exactly how wet to get him, exactly how hard to squeeze and stroke, exactly where to swirl her tongue. In the brief moment of sanity before his eyes rolled back in his head, he realized no other woman had ever made him feel this way—or ever even tried to.

He wanted to touch her. *Needed* to get his hands back so he could run them over every single centimeter of her skin.

Her hand cupped his balls, then her finger trailed underneath, and the whole world collapsed around him, falling and crashing left and right, every cell coming together in one big mass, pounding and pulsing right *there*. At the very last moment before the entire universe detonated, she pulled away.

Again.

She sprawled across him, her hand fumbling with the drawer of the bedside table and then jerking back when he caught her nipple with his teeth in a not very gentle tug. She cried out and came back to him, knocking the drawer out of the table as she did, but managing to snag a condom as everything else spilled to the floor. Which was good because he was past the point of caring whether he had one or not.

And it was even worse now, because he could see her. Every goddamn gorgeous inch of her from her ruddy red lips right down to the tips of her still-boot-clad toes. *Fuck*, those boots… "Get up over me."

"What?" she asked, cheeks flushed, eyes glazed over.

He flattened out so as to give her enough room to swing her leg over his chest and straddle him. "Higher."

Eyes widening, she shook her head. "I…"

She was so fucking close he could practically taste her arousal. With a groan he jerked his head up close enough to get a nip of her inner thigh. "Hands up high on the headboard, Angel. I want to see all of you stretched out above me."

Finally he could do something with his hands: grab hold of her knees and splay them open hard enough for her to fall against him. He took full advantage by getting his tongue on her clit and then his teeth, just enough for her to scream. It was abso-fucking-lutely perfect.

He couldn't touch her breasts but he could see them, and he enjoyed every single second it took to drive her to the point where she was writhing and moaning his name in a constant chant before shattering, slumping against the headboard as she gasped for air above him.

When she finally came down, literally and figuratively, he nearly exploded when she drew the condom over him, and then looked directly into his eyes. Held his gaze. He came harder than he ever had within seconds of her sinking down. She collapsed against him, both their chests heaving as they gasped for air.

"Oh my God," she finally murmured into his chest. "That was… It was…"

"Intense," he finished for her. As in, hands down, the freaking most amazing sex he'd ever had.

Ever.

God*damn* it. He wanted her to have his babies.

Oh, fuck, he was screwed.

Chapter Twenty-Six

To Deke's utter astonishment, the sex kept getting better. That was a new experience for him. Yes, he'd had years-long relationships of a sort with more than a few women. But never more than a few nights at a time, and definitely never in a way that made him think he might be interested in something permanent. He and Fitz had been sleeping together for almost a month now and not once had he thought it was time to move on.

On this particular night, everything was going great. The bar was crowded for a weeknight, and Deke liked seeing folks having a good time and enjoying themselves. Seeing the bar thrive made him appreciate the legacy his father had built, and his father's father before him. And, yes, he'd begun to think about Fitz alongside things like family and ongoing generations. It should have been terrifying but wasn't.

But he wasn't quite ready to fully admit that. He sure as hell knew she wasn't.

A roar of laughter erupted from one of the tables in the room and he looked up.

Well, okay. Maybe not *everything* was perfect.

Shunning an entire table of regulars wasn't good for business, yet that was exactly what he was doing.

It was doubly hard because it was Peggy and her crew, which meant the Cosmos flowed and shit got loud. It also usually meant Deke playing along. Although he'd managed to keep his distance so far, the natives were getting restless. With Little League season long over, he wasn't seeing Peggy as often as he had then. But there'd been a shift in the wind it seemed, and although they hadn't been together in quite some time now, she'd been turning up the heat. Occasional texts had turned into a regular stream that, looking back, wasn't entirely unusual yet now seemed beyond extreme. He was finding it harder and harder to turn her down without making a big thing of it.

And it really would be a big thing. If he ever did have another conversation with Peggy, what she'd done to Fitz would be the first topic they covered. He didn't think he'd ever in his life straight-out disliked someone. Now, though, he felt an unfamiliar ugliness inside. Considering his livelihood, he was hoping to hell it didn't come out.

Thankfully, tonight was busy enough that Deke could play dumb without too much trouble, and he'd acknowledged Peggy's wave with a nod and then turned away. It was only a matter of time, however, before that came to a head.

He scanned the bar, checking on empties and refills, his eyes, as always, landing on Fitz. She was happy tonight in a way he didn't think she'd ever been. She hadn't warmed up to Peggy by any means, but she and Dorie had spent some time at a table with a few of Peggy's friends, one of whom had just started working for Dorie. And then when Dorie and Jules took the kids out on the dance floor tonight, Fitz had gone with them. Except for the night of the prom and in San Francisco, he didn't think he'd ever seen her dance. He'd most certainly never seen her let go like that here in Inspiration.

All thoughts stopped abruptly when the door to the bar swung open and Sam Price walked in. Sam Price, followed by Johnny Whitfield.

What the hell? Whitfield wasn't filming his show for at least another week, and Sam… Well, Deke had no freaking idea what Sam would be in Inspiration for, but it sure as fuck better not be to check out Fitz's ass again. Or any other part of her. Without realizing he was doing it, Deke yanked a tray of dirty dishes out from under the counter hard enough that two of the glasses almost broke.

"Geez, Deke. What did those dishes ever do to you?"

He turned to see Lola coming up behind him. She wasn't hostessing tonight but her attention was on the front door, too. They both watched as Dorie approached, a welcoming smile on her face, yet one that showed she hadn't been expecting them either.

Nor had Fitz. That was clear the second Deke got his wits about him enough to turn to look at her. She seemed downright shocked. She had a handful of play-ing cards and two three-year-olds vying for her atten-tion, but she was just sitting there, eyes wide as she stared at Dorie and the two men.

Deke ran his hand through his hair. Jealousy wasn't an emotion he was used to. He'd never cared enough about a woman to want to stake a claim. But whether he was ready to admit his feelings to or even about Fitz, they were sure as hell there. Seeing that she didn't seem particularly happy to see Sam was a relief of frightening proportions. She managed to recover by the time Dorie led the others to the table, standing up and smiling during the round of introductions. They knew Mama Gin and Jules, of course, but they hadn't met Aunt Laura or Uncle A it seemed, nor, of course, Deke's own parents, who were back in town in between stops on their road trip, or any of the kids.

As the evening wore on, however, whereas Fitz became more relaxed, Deke got more and more irritated. Seriously, if Whitfield didn't stop putting his arm around the back of Fitz's chair, Deke would take his fucking head off.

Deke snapped his towel against the side of the sink.

Lola, who was back at the bar to get a round of drinks for the table, reached for some limes and smiled. "Have you ever seen Fitz look so *happy*?"

That wasn't Fitz happy, that was Fitz playing a part. Deke was surprised Lola couldn't tell the difference; it was clear as day to him. She'd been happy dancing earlier. She'd been happy having dinner and playing Go Fish with the boys. Hell, just this morning he'd had her tied spread-eagle to his bed, and all he'd had to do was breathe and she'd arced up like she'd been hit by a thousand bolts of pure electricity. She'd sure as hell been happy then.

"Ecstatic," he answered.

"Dude," Jason said from his regular seat at the bar. "Why are you so stressed out?"

"What?" Deke dragged his attention away from Fitz's table. Sure, Jason could talk. Being that there wasn't room to squeeze anyone else in at the table, both Price and Whitfield had made a point to come over to the bar and say hi. After a round of high-fives and some small talk, everyone had happily gone about their business. Everyone except Deke.

"I'm not stressed out," he said. "Life couldn't be better."

Fuck. That wasn't any better than Fitz had been with Lola before the board meeting last week.

Then Wash muttered, "Do not even fucking tell me…"

With a jolt, Deke realized he'd been watching Fitz again, so he made sure to pull his attention away. But Wash was already staring at him.

"*Fitz?*" he asked.

Looking down quickly, Deke thought maybe Wash's comment had been about something else entirely. Just because Wash had honed his observation skills under the tutelage of Nate and Mama Gin didn't mean he'd figured anything out. Then again, Wash had been the one to call Nate and Dorie first, so it wasn't a complete surprise to look back up and meet Wash's stare and know he had to handle this carefully.

Drying off the glasses he'd taken out of the sink, Deke stared right back, refusing to give anything up. Jason was not an observer by any means, but even he would catch on to that, especially with Wash practically blaring a horn in his ear.

Too late. Jason's eyes went over to Fitz and then back. "No fucking way. *Fitz* is the one who has you all locked up?" A look of horror came over his face. "I mean, yeah, she's hot. But that's just gross. It's like doing your own sister."

If only Deke felt that way, these whole last few months would have been a hell of a lot simpler.

"Uh, no offense, Lo," Jason added. "If you weren't Deke's sister, I'd totally do you."

"Really," Lola said, not bothering to hide her amusement. "I'm, um...not sure what to say. Although, if I had to be honest, I'd most likely go for one of Nate's baseball friends. If, of course, I ever had sex ag—"

"Whoa!" Deke held up his hands. He was entirely unprepared for Lola to go into the monologue about how she was not, in fact, ever having sex again, at least not until all of her eggs had shriveled up and died. For one thing, she was, actually, his sister. For another, the words "eggs" and "sex" did not belong in the same sentence. He took appropriate precautions every single time. As far as he was concerned, that was all that needed to be said.

"It has nothing to do with Fitz." But the fact that he might have maybe wanted it all out in the open meant he wasn't a little more forceful in his denial.

"What has nothing to do with me?"

Deke's, "Nothing," was about as smooth as the motion of his head when he jerked it up to see her standing there.

Since he was staring into her eyes, it was impossible to miss them go wide as Jason ever-so-helpfully answered, "Well, thank Christ, because you two being together makes about as much sense as, hell, I don't know..." He shrugged. "Deke having an actual meaningful relationship."

It was called a *schmelationship*, thank you very much. "Gee, thanks, Jase. It's nice to know my best friends think so highly of me." Deke tried to somehow telegraph to Fitz that, no, he hadn't said anything to anyone and that this conversation had taken on a life of its own. But he also wasn't too happy the look in her eyes was something akin to horror.

Of course, that was the moment Peggy decided to make her way over to the bar and call out his name. "Deke, baby, we need a little sugar. You think maybe you can oblige?"

Again, not anything she hadn't said a hundred times before. It was just that now it made him cringe.

She was a regular, he had to remind himself. A not very nice person, but his job required he play a role. And Fitz, who he was actually beginning to think of as his girlfriend even though a total of two other people in the world were aware of their connection, had looked like she'd rather face another tornado than acknowledge to their friends there was something between them. So maybe it wasn't his best move, but he looked up at Peggy and did what he had to do. "Give me five minutes and I'll make it real sweet."

Her satisfied smile—not to mention her glance at Fitz, although he may have imagined that part—was a blaring red sign that, not only wasn't it his best move, it was probably one of his worst ever. And when he turned back to look at Fitz, she was gone.

Chapter Twenty-Seven

Bitch.

Screaming, out-of-control, hate-isn't-a-strong-enough-word bitch.

Fitz grabbed one of the trays of drinks and whirled around to bring them to the table. One of these days she was going to say something like, "Guess who's having spectacular sex with Deke *now*, Miss Has-Been Cheerleader from Hell."

Oh, God. No she wasn't.

She was on edge, though, thanks to Sam's surprise visit, so she didn't trust herself.

We were in the neighborhood. Sam had laughed, fully acknowledging Inspiration, Iowa, wasn't "in the neighborhood" for anyone unless they lived there. Or had a fleet of private planes at their disposal. Which, given his family's fortune came partly from getting in on the whole airline business early on, Sam did.

Fitz knew this from her research. She also knew Johnny was one of his investors thanks to a lot of piecing together she and Dorie had done based on things Nate had said. Nate who, incidentally had decided it was all fine and good that Fitz had decided she wanted to do this on her own, and was therefore going to support her one hundred percent in that effort.

What Fitz didn't know was why Sam and Johnny were here tonight when Johnny wasn't scheduled to be in Inspiration for another week and as far as Fitz knew the formal interview process for the job still hadn't begun. She was actually wondering if it ever would. With all that going on, the last thing she could reasonably handle was Peggy being all over Deke.

Well, no. The *actual* last thing Fitz could handle was that she'd gone over to the bar to get a dose of Deke of her own. It bothered her immensely that she wanted one of his smiles to help settle her. Not just wanted one, needed it. She wasn't ready to feel like this.

"Here are the refills," she said, all efficient and crisp, as if she wasn't teetering on the edge of losing it in all sorts of ways.

She passed the beers around as Lola came up behind her with the kids' drinks. Deliberately ignoring any conversations happening on the other side of the room, Fitz picked up the new cards she'd been dealt and sat back in her chair as Johnny leaned in.

She also had to admit Jason's comments had thrown her. She'd been lulled into this whole Deke-wonderland, but Jason's reaction was exactly what she'd worried about. It was bad enough they'd be the talk of the town. That in itself made her feel sick to her stomach. But even worse was how it would change things with the others. Look at how things were between Deke and Nate. What had almost happened with Jules. The idea of any more relationships changing because she and Deke liked to get naked together…

Well, maybe it was time to start winding it down.

It would definitely make things easier. Plus she was coming to count on him too much. With a glance at Deke, who was now distributing drinks to Peggy and her friends, three of whom Fitz knew for a fact he'd been with and two more of whom she suspected, it was clear he'd have no problems bouncing back. He was probably more ready to end this than she was.

But for as much as she knew that would make things easier all around, it was yet another thing she wasn't ready to think about.

"Tough hand," Johnny said, drawing her attention back to the game. She looked down to see the "tough" hand was actually a fantastic one in the Go Fish world. But he was exactly right. Fitz didn't like winning outright when there were toddlers involved.

So she ignored the three kings in her hand and instead said, "James, do you have any sixes?"

"Eight!" James answered.

Though Johnny tried to keep his laugh inside, Sam's own attempt was obviously making it difficult. And to be honest, seeing two grown men trying to keep straight faces was quite entertaining.

"Eight sixes?" Fitz asked, arching one eyebrow. "Or did you mean one eight?"

Sam leaned in to point something out to James while whispering in his ear.

"Three!" James replied.

Since this was pretty much the pattern for the night, Fitz said, "Perfect. I'll take it."

But James shook his head and pulled his cards in close. "You can have Emmet's car."

That was unexpected. And unpopular. Rather than just say no, however, Emmet decided to throw said car directly at James's head, where it would have done some damage if Deke hadn't appeared right then and snatched it out of the air. "Okay, buddy. Mom says you guys have been great but it's time to go home."

"Already?" Silas whined, coming up from whatever game he and Matty had been playing on Mama Gin's phone.

Fitz had to admit, she felt entirely the opposite. She was so ready to not be here with all these Deke and Peggy thoughts swirling around in her head. And although she suspected Sam and Johnny had come to Inspiration to see her, they hadn't come out and said anything to that effect and she was more than happy to use the kids as an excuse to leave.

But that plan flew out the window when Lola said, "Any chance you can catch a ride back if you stay? My mom said she needs to get in as much baby time as possible while they're here. I thought she could drive with me back to the house."

No. Fitz tried to keep the panic from showing in her eyes. Being an adult who did, in fact, want to make a good impression on the man she'd told she was ready for the big leagues, however, she forced a smile and said, "Sure."

Dorie, who seemed to have as little a clue as to what Sam and Johnny were doing here as Fitz did, raised her eyebrows before turning to Sam. "Are you guys in town for the night? Do you need a ride somewhere? Fitz and I can drop you off along—"

"I'll drive her home," Deke snapped, cutting Dorie off as he lifted Emmet out of his seat.

Dorie's eyebrows went higher. "Fine by me," she said, grinning over at Fitz.

Fitz smiled back, although her heart wasn't entirely in it.

It definitely wasn't in it when, fifteen minutes later, after the older and younger sets had cleared out and Wash and Jason had taken their places and everyone was now thoroughly involved in a discussion about the Watchmen's chances of making the World Series, Fitz looked up to see Deke back at the bar, talking to Peggy. Who, of course, chose that moment to put her hand on his arm. Nope. The word *hate* wasn't nearly strong enough. Fitz turned her attention back to the baseball discussion.

No more than two minutes later, she could feel his presence. She didn't need to raise her head to know he was there.

"So," he said, the sharpness still in his voice surprising her as he slid into the seat James had occupied, diagonally across from her. "You guys are in town for how long?"

Well, that was…rude. *Again.*

Fitz shifted as Johnny tensed and then straightened up beside her.

Gathering up the cards she could reach, Fitz's smooth-it-over instincts were blaring, but she couldn't bring herself to say anything that might give her away. Not sharing the same concerns, Wash was the one to say, "And what brings you here?"

Although he was perfectly cordial about it, downright friendly when compared to Deke, the unasked part of the question—*And why are you here in town when Nate isn't?*—was clearly heard by all.

Fitz wanted to hear the answer as much as she dreaded it. She really wasn't ready to tell anyone about the job. At the same time she *did* want to know why they were here. Was it an interview? Had Sam brought

Johnny here to feel her out? Or had Johnny just decided to come check out Inspiration earlier than planned and Sam decided to tag along? She truly had no idea.

Not one thing became any clearer when Johnny smiled down at her. "I was thinking I'd take you up on that offer to show me around."

And now it was Fitz's turn to straighten up. Wait, was he coming on to her? It would be a pretty dumb move since all it would do was make Deke mad. Something she wished wasn't so obvious, by the way, but that was so far down the list of concerns right now it wasn't even funny. Because if Johnny was coming on to her it meant she wasn't a serious contender for the job and they were just stringing her along. The fact that the possibility made her almost overwhelmingly sad and angry was, she guessed, a sign of how much she wanted it.

When Johnny cleared his throat, she said, "Oh," and glanced at Dorie. "Sure." Then, although she'd made that offer only to keep from hearing about Deke's history of sexcapades, she added, "We'd love to." And then stared at Dorie with as strong a you-are-doing-this-with-me vibe as possible.

Dorie got the hint, thank God. "We totally would," she said without even a second's hesitation. She pulled out her phone. "I have a meeting at 9:30, but maybe we could head out to Ella's farm after that. I think Nate mentioned possibly filming from there. Her porch has a fantastic view."

Fitz tried not to openly show her relief, but from the way Johnny glanced at her and then Sam before turning to Dorie, she had a feeling he could tell. But he didn't make a big deal of it and Sam took it totally in stride as well, so that was good. And, hopefully, all above-board because she liked him and would very much like to work for him and it would suck big time if he was, in fact, a total jerk. So maybe this was a test of some kind. See how the potential candidate handles all the good-looking player types who'll be coming at her each and every day.

Deke, in the meantime, tipped his chair back, for the most part appearing completely unfazed. But she could see the white of his knuckles as he clutched the back of the chair next to him, and his jaw was clenched so tightly she was afraid he might actually break it.

"Well on that note…" Wash said, standing once the arrangements had been made. "I've got an early morning, as usual. 'Night, all."

Jason stood up as well, nodding at Sam and Johnny. "Nice to see you guys. Let me know if you want a tour of the high school. I've got some fantastic senior projects I'd be happy to show off."

Wash put his hand on Jason's shoulder. "The frightening thing is that he's entirely serious."

"What?" Jason asked, as Wash steered them toward the front door. "You should see what one of the kids did with graphing…"

With an almost apologetic smile, Dorie said to everyone still at the table, "They really are good. I think we should rope in the high school kids with some kind of contest to help us with the designs for Baseball City."

Which was what they'd all been calling the Iowa Dream Academy since the votes had come in last week and it was unanimously decided to go full speed ahead. It was keeping Fitz busy at the moment and she was good with that.

After a long and somewhat awkward moment of silence that even Fitz didn't try to fill, Sam said, "I guess we'll call it a night, too. We'll see you ladies in the morning," and then nodded at Deke.

Dorie also got up, saying, "I'll walk out with you." She reached over and gave Deke a hug. With a wave toward Fitz, Dorie said, "I'll call you," over her shoulder as she joined Sam and Johnny. And before Fitz could even register what had happened, they were out the door, too, leaving Fitz alone with Deke.

"So…" she mumbled, glad to have a minute to catch her breath.

Except then Deke said, "What the hell was that?"

Fitz went still.

"What?" she asked. Because, honestly, there were so many things, not one of which she wanted to address.

And she had no idea which one he'd pick until he came out and, every muscle in his body tense, asked, "Would it really be so bad? Telling people we're a thing?"

Maybe another man wouldn't have seen the downright terror in her eyes. Maybe another man wouldn't have cared. But Deke had and he did, and there was a sting of disappointment in the air all around them when she didn't answer right away. Before she could say or do anything to fix it, though, he muttered, "Right," and stared down at the cards in front of him. Then he suddenly leaned forward and gathered them up. "I've got to get back to work. If you're sure you want to hang around, I'll be ready to go in about an hour."

Of *course* she wanted to hang around. That was the whole problem. She wanted to be with him all the time. She'd even begun to think about what it would mean to be away from him if she got this new job.

Well, pretty much everyone she cared about, but

mostly him, which went against almost everything she'd spent her entire life believing. She would not rely on a man. She would not change her life for anyone. But it had never occurred to her that she'd be here in this completely unfamiliar place with *Deke*.

She couldn't say any of that, of course. She could barely even think it. Especially not when he was so obviously unhappy. She couldn't handle her own emotions; she didn't have the first clue how to handle his.

"Okay," she mumbled, looking down. By the time she managed to raise her eyes again, he was up and headed to the bar, not even glancing back in her direction.

Which was when it fully hit her. It wasn't just the way he was with Nate, or how he'd almost lost it with Jules. There were actual changes in him. His reaction to Johnny. The way he was nodding at something Josh was saying, friendly but not actually interacting with the regulars. He let Josh handle the bar and instead began busing tables. It even bothered Fitz a little that he didn't give Peggy's table a second glance, as crazy as that seemed.

She'd changed him. She'd broken *him*.

Although she finally got up to help and got a smile in acknowledgement, it wasn't until they were in his truck and on their way that she finally got the nerve to say something. "I want you to be happy."

Deke glanced over at her before turning his attention back to the road. "Is something going on with you and Price?"

"Sam?" Leave it to Deke to figure out Johnny wasn't even close to being a problem despite being front and center.

"Because if you want to sleep with him," Deke said,

his voice so even it almost didn't even sound like him, "then I'd rather you just come out and say it."

Sleep with *Sam*? "*No.*"

His eyes came to hers quickly, as if searching to make sure she was telling the truth. But he had to know she wouldn't lie to him. And, yes, his expression softened as he looked back out at the road. Which was when she should have told him about the job. She absolutely needed to tell him. But he was already upset. Plus at this point, with the completely random Sam/Johnny visit, she had even less of a clue if they were seriously considering her for the job, so telling him now would make it all that much worse.

Which was the worst excuse ever, but she was going with it for now. Especially when he looked over at her one more time and said, "Then I'm good."

That wasn't even close to true. "Not the way you used to be."

He frowned, proving her point exactly, although she wasn't about to mention it.

"Well, yeah," he said. "Finding out the woman I've been sleeping with off and on for years used me as bait and that I've been completely oblivious to all the other bullshit going on around here for pretty much my entire life… It's been getting to me."

Yes. It was even worse than she'd thought. She'd taken the best thing in her entire life, the best *person* she'd ever known, and she'd burned out his light.

She should have been humble about it. She should have been quiet, for damn sure. But instead it was like all of her emotions swirled up, out of control, and every reservation she'd ever had came tumbling out.

"*See?*" she snapped, afraid she might actually burst

into tears. "That's *exactly* why I didn't tell you about what Peggy had done. Because it would change the way you felt about *everything*. 'It doesn't need to be complicated,' you said. But it *is* complicated. Everything's totally different already."

He pulled to the side of the road, leaving the engine on but leaning back and resting one arm along the open window. "So you'd rather I be clueless, happy-go-lucky Max Deacon, without a freaking care in the world."

"No. That is *not* what I said. I just hate that tonight you were so…"

His eyes narrowed. "So *what*? Pissed off?"

Well, yes. But if she said that he'd be even more so. "It's like you were totally happy with life until you started being with me."

He turned to fully face her. "*That's* what you get out of this?" Then he looked back out through the windshield. "Yeah, I'm pissed. Forget the part about walking around in some freaking daze for my whole life. Or that it's like pulling teeth to get you to tell me even the slightest thing."

"That's not—"

"I'm pissed," he said, speaking over her, "because Peggy is texting me ten times a day and I would love more than anything to tell her to back off, but you don't want me to tell her why. Or that I kind of hate her guts at the moment, which is a pretty strange place to be, considering that, as far as she knows, my bed is completely empty and waiting for her."

Wait. "What?" Peggy was texting him? Ten times a *day*?

"But that doesn't even hold a candle to the fact that I can't put my arms around you and kiss you or kick the ever-living shit out of any other guy who looks at you twice."

Her lips formed an "Oh," but she was pretty sure no word actually came out. She looked down. She honestly didn't know what to say. Other than she wanted to open up a can of whup ass and throw it Peggy's way.

Except then he added, "And because I saw the look in your eyes when Jason said what he did."

Letting her head fall back against the seat, Fitz closed her eyes. Right. There was that.

She may have even flinched when he said, "I know what this is supposed to be. I know what I told you it was, but I think I might have been wrong."

How so? she wanted to say. *What were you wrong about?*

Except she knew. She knew exactly.

They were falling in love.

It should have been a happy thing. It was what every normal person in the world wanted. But Fitz couldn't speak. She couldn't breathe. And this was supposed to be the *good* part.

"I don't know how to do this," she finally managed to say. "I don't know how to sleep with you and still have you be my friend." Because that, above all, was the most important thing.

"Is that what we're doing here?" he asked after the most awful pause ever. "Sleeping together? Because I've slept with a hell of a lot of women and it was never like this."

Another thing she should be happy to hear, yet all she could do was clutch the armrest and say, "I'm afraid I can't be what you want me to be."

She could feel the air around them change. It took

a minute before he asked, "Is that your way of saying we're calling it quits?"

Now it was her turn to go still. No. That wasn't what she was saying at all, even though it would probably be for the best. But being with him was the one thing she *was* sure of; she just didn't know how to make it fit with everything else. "Is that what you want?" she whispered.

He draped his arms over the steering wheel and leaned forward. Keeping his distance, yet saying, "What I *want* is to call you my girlfriend."

The air rushed out of her lungs. She felt like she was being torn in two. All the pieces she'd taped up together, her little Humpty Dumpty of a soul, actually breaking apart.

"Oh, Angel," he sighed as he turned to her, reaching out and putting his hand in her hair and making it all that much worse. He couldn't be so tender. He couldn't *love* her. "Why does that scare you so much?"

The tears finally fell. They had nowhere else to go. "I don't know."

Except that *was* a lie. Possibly the first one she'd ever told him. She just wasn't ready to admit she needed him. She could barely admit it to herself, much less to him.

His hand went down to her waist and she felt the seatbelt release, felt herself being lifted up onto his lap, something that should have been physically impossible to do. But she didn't question it because even with her fighting against it with everything she had, it felt so right to lean her head against the solid and warm wall of his chest.

"Babe," he said, his voice catching.

Tightening her arms around him in a desperate attempt to hold on, she said, "Is it really different for you? Being with me?"

It took him a few minutes to answer, and when he did his voice was quiet. "It really is."

She took a deep breath. He meant so much to her. No matter how much that scared her she could at least admit that much. "How do you do this? How can you believe?"

He didn't answer right away. When he did, his voice was as ragged as she felt. "Because I know what I feel is so strong there's nothing that would stop me from fighting my way back to you. No matter what stands in our way."

That made her cry all over again.

Because she couldn't do this. She didn't *trust* this.

But she couldn't let him go.

"What if we did this in baby steps?" she asked, practically giving herself a panic attack as the words came out of her mouth. But the thought of losing him was even worse. Losing the part of him that no one else knew she had.

Well, not *no* one…

She raised her head. "Like maybe we could have dinner with Dorie and Nate. Kind of like a double date."

When he didn't answer right away she was afraid she'd gotten it wrong. Maybe he was just talking it all through because they were, actually, friends. But then he brushed the hair back off her forehead and a wicked look came into his eyes. "Can I kiss you in front of Nate and make him want to tear my head off?"

Never would she have thought she could end one of the most draining evenings of her life with a laugh. But she did. "No tongue."

"That, my friend, is a deal." He shifted and placed her back in her seat, saying, "Let's go home."

Chapter Twenty-Eight

It was easier than she'd ever expected. They had Dorie and Nate to dinner at Deke's one night a couple of weeks later. Fitz's first official baby step. With Deke stealing amused glances at her from over by the stove, Fitz buzzed around the room rearranging things and probably resetting the table four times.

"Not sure why you're bothering," he finally said. "Nate will probably try and knock me around a few times, and then I'll go all MMA on him and it will all get messed up anyway."

Sure enough, when Fitz opened up the door before they'd even rung the bell, Nate was basically hissing at Dorie, "The second we get home you're naked. That's the only reason I'm here."

Now hold on a minute. Fitz folded her arms across her chest. "Why are you allowed to say that to her but I'm not allowed to say anything like that about—?"

She snapped her mouth shut when Nate turned to her in full-on glare mode.

With a sigh, Dorie gave Fitz a hug. "It's like some big brother handbook. Word for word." She took Nate by the hand and pulled him inside Deke's condo before planting a kiss directly on his lips. The fact that he was still glaring down at her didn't faze Dorie one bit. "For Fitz's Christmas present this year, I'm going to make sure to get her in the same room with Tommy and Sean while they're giving you hell."

Although Nate hadn't kissed Dorie back, he smiled. "And what's my Christmas present?"

Reaching up, Dorie placed her hand on the back of his neck and drew his head down. "I'll make up for every single minute of it in whatever way you want."

"Oh, for heaven's sake," Fitz muttered. She hadn't been kidding when she'd told Deke Nate and Dorie were possibly the only two people in the world she truly believed were that much in love. But it wasn't something she needed to witness firsthand.

With a smile, Dorie broke away and went over to Deke, handing him a bottle of wine before giving him a hug, too. "I am so happy to be here tonight."

Smiling down at her, Deke said, "Well, I am very happy to have you here. But we're going to whip your asses in Trivial Pursuit."

Which was genius, of course. Because no matter how unhappy Nate may have been, the man was physically incapable of ignoring a taunt like that. After a lingering look at Fitz, Nate turned to Deke and smiled. "Bring. It. On."

It was one of the happiest nights of Fitz's life.

There hadn't been much time for any more baby steps after that, with Fitz traveling more often than not with her newly expanded Iowa Dream Foundation duties. It helped keep her mind off what was happening with Sam's job—or not happening, since she'd heard absolutely nothing further. It probably wasn't a good sign that she was seeing the man fairly often as their paths kept crossing and he'd said not one single thing. Doug kept assuring her these things took time so she shouldn't worry. Nate, whose team was now heavily into the race for first place, mostly shrugged it off, and Dorie just commiserated, pointing out that no news was good news since there were no hard decisions to make. Or conversations to have.

True. And Dorie's outlook allowed Fitz to exist in this strangely happy state that was almost too much to wrap her head around. Lola had found a college student to help out with the boys, so whatever time Fitz did have in Inspiration, she spent with Deke. Since he was crazy with things at the bar, most of that time was spent there. She'd bring her laptop so she could do work as she'd watch him go about his night, totally in his element, back to his happy-go-lucky self.

It did surprise her no one had called them on anything yet, because it seemed to her they were more, well, together. They were still officially a secret, but the looks he gave her practically set the room on fire as far as she was concerned. And although they were careful about it, there was definitely some inappropriate touching. One night, with all their friends right there in the bar, they'd even done it on the desk in his office. She'd been helping him design a new website and he'd had some bills to pay and, well…

"You do realize every time you smile like that it makes me want to kill him a little bit more," Nate said from the driver's seat, reminding Fitz that, yes, maybe it was time for the next baby step.

"Will you be here for poker night next week?" she asked, ignoring his statement as the Mustang pulled up in front of Deke's building. "I think it's time to tell Wash and Jason about Deke and me."

It was midnight, and no one knew she and Nate would be back tonight. The Watchmen had clinched their division, though, so Nate had an unexpected day off. He'd agreed to drop her off even though he wasn't happy about it, knowing full well what would happen the second Fitz was inside Deke's loft.

"Honestly," Nate muttered, looking at the building in front of them. "How does Jason not already know?"

Noise cancelling headphones, Deke had told her one night—or, rather, breathed into her neck. Jason would put them on whenever he heard the doors open up at night, apparently.

But Fitz wasn't about to tell Nate that because, well, it was Nate and that was TMI. But also because he'd use it as an excuse to remind her that Deke had a history of middle-of-the-night visitors that Jason had been dealing with for years.

So she just shrugged.

As she started to reach for the door handle, Nate said, "He's going to offer you the job."

Her thoughts on seeing Deke, it took Fitz a minute to realize what Nate had said. "I'm sorry?"

He turned to look at her. "Sam. He told us this morning."

Fitz's mouth dropped open as she turned to stare. "But... I mean..." Her heart, which had come to a sudden stop, started hammering. She wasn't... She wasn't even close to ready. "There's supposed to be an interview. I'm supposed to meet everyone. Answer their questions."

Wasn't she? That was how these things were supposed to work, right?

Nate laughed. "He's been interviewing you for the past month and a half, Fitz."

"No," she whispered, shaking her head. "I was working."

Nate raised his eyebrows. "Didn't it occur to you that you were seeing a lot of Sam?"

"Well, *duh*." And some other majorly high-profile people, but whatever. "Because he's interested in investing in our foundation."

"No, Fitz," Nate said gently. "He's interested in *you*. He had three other people in mind and never got past a first interview."

Fitz's eyes flew up to the windows of Deke's apartment. She'd been dreading telling Deke she'd be on the road for six weeks straight. How was she going to tell him she was about to be offered a new job? A job she hadn't even told him she'd applied for—that she'd actively sought out. And deliberately kept from him.

"You couldn't have mentioned this before?" she asked, almost crying.

"I didn't want to freak you out," Nate said, looking at her strangely. "Why are you freaking out *now*?"

She dropped her head into her hands. "Oh, God."

It only took a few more seconds for Nate to read the signs. "He doesn't know?"

Unable to speak, Fitz shook her head. "I thought I had at least a few more weeks. Sam said there'd be a formal interview."

Well, that and because she knew she should have brought it up by now and Deke was going to be mad.

Really, *really* mad, even after she gave him what she

felt was the perfectly sane explanation that the very existence of Sam's foundation still wasn't officially public.

And she hadn't wanted to jinx it.

And she wasn't even sure she was going to take it.

And, damn it, they hadn't even been in a *schmelationship* when the whole thing started. And once they were it seemed too late anyway and she wasn't good at sharing *anything* and how the hell was she supposed to know that *this* was a big thing—until all of a sudden it was—except she'd been dealing with a whole lot of *really freaking big things* all at the same time. Like high school secrets and talking about her father and falling in love with her best friend—even though she'd sworn to herself she would never *ever* allow herself to fall in love—and she wasn't even equipped to handle one of those things.

She squeezed her eyes shut and leaned her head back against the headrest. Deke was not going to take this well.

"Is it better if I come in with you?" Nate asked.

"God, no." That would be the worst possible thing.

"It will probably be fine," Nate offered, not sounding any more confident than Fitz felt.

"Probably," Fitz repeated, gathering the strength needed to get herself out of the car, up the stairs, and let herself in with the key Deke had given her. But the second she slipped between the sheets, he turned to her and said, "Christ, I missed you so much." And then he had her clothes off and scattered every which way.

She put it off for another day.

By the time morning came, she felt sick to her stomach. Forcing herself to open her eyes, she rolled over, hoping for at least a moment to fully appreciate the man before opening up the ugliest can of worms ever. She sat up straight when she saw not just that he was gone, but that there was a note on the pillow.

Nate's in town but I'm guessing you know that. Jason and I are meeting up with him at Wash's. See you at lunch.

D.

P.S. Keys to the truck are on the hook by the door if you need wheels.

No, no, no. She fell back to the bed.

The rest of the morning took forever and she was completely useless at work. She texted him a few times, hoping he'd check his phone and come by her office before heading to the bar. But he generally turned his phone off when he was with the guys, knowing that anyone who needed to reach him could track him through one of them.

So not happening.

She counted down the minutes until it was time to head over for lunch, the weather not soothing her nerves one bit. The clouds were so thick they obscured the sun entirely, and the wind was enough to whip everything up into a frenzy. Nate's pilot had told him they were getting in in time to beat the thunderstorms coming up through Kansas and Nebraska, but they'd be in for a rough couple of days. Freaking perfect.

Wash and Jason greeted her with big smiles when she got to the bar, Dorie with a hug, and Deke, who was actually taking a shift at the moment, with a head nod and grin from the other side of the bar. That Peggy had moved from her usual table to a barstool was just a minor irritation at this point.

"Not that I doubted you," Wash said, pulling her attention away from Deke, "but you guys made the right call with Nate's announcement. Guys I haven't heard from in years have been hitting up my phone."

That, at least, brought a genuine smile to Fitz's face. As they'd planned, Nate had announced his retirement on Johnny's show and within an hour of it airing, they'd fielded almost a hundred phone calls about the expansion of the foundation and the development of the academy, and that was just from people who had their direct phone numbers. Fitz had lost count of the number of Nate's teammates who were interested in becoming involved, not to mention acquaintances of his, ranging from this year's Oscar winner for Best Actor all the way to the lead singer of the band of the moment. Requests for information had reached into the thousands.

"Want to come to Miami with me?" she asked Wash now. So caught up in the job thing, she'd completely forgotten she hadn't told Deke about her travel plans.

"You're going to Miami?" Deke asked. He'd come over to their end of the bar and was fiddling with something under the counter. Although he wasn't looking at her, she could see the tension in the way he held himself. The tight pull at the corners of his mouth and eyes.

"In a few weeks," she mumbled. "I didn't have a chance to tell you last night." Given that both Wash and Jason were paying close attention, she tried not to blush in any way since the reason she hadn't had that chance was because she'd been naked and underneath him and she had a really hard time talking to him once he got her clothes off. She tried to smile. "Want to come with?"

He straightened up and looked at her. "I could maybe get away for a couple of days."

Which was...fine. He seemed a little tenser than usual, but, yes, mostly fine.

What she wasn't ready for at all, however, was for Dorie to lean forward and say to everyone, "Wait, I thought Sam said you'd be heading to Boston with us."

Deke's eyes shot to Dorie's and then back to Fitz. "You're going to Boston? With Sam?"

Okay, yes. So that sounded...bad. "With Dorie and *Nate*," she corrected. Maybe the thing about the new job was going to be worse than she thought.

But then, because Jason, though completely oblivious to so many things around him, also had an uncanny ability to see connections between things before anyone else even knew there was anything to connect, her entire life blew up in front of her.

"Sam?" Jason asked. "Sam Price? Holy shit. You're up for that job, aren't you?"

Feeling the floor drop out from underneath her, Fitz's eyes went to Deke.

That was all it took.

When she opened her mouth to explain, he cut her off, saying, "You've got to be fucking kidding."

"Deke," she said, reaching out to him, not even caring how obvious it was. "I—"

"Don't," he said, cutting her off so sharply she jerked her hand back.

He grabbed something off the counter behind the bar and didn't even glance her way as he said, "Josh, I've got to fix this hose. I'll be back in a few."

Her heart thudding in her chest, Fitz knew he didn't want her to follow, yet she was off her stool and on her way to the back in a shot. The only problem was that Peggy was faster. And closer to the hallway Deke had disappeared down.

On her feet and heading toward them, however, Fitz stopped abruptly right before she turned the corner. What exactly was she going to do? Get into a catfight with Peggy in the back hallway of Deacon's Bar and Grille? No.

She would talk to Deke. After he cooled down.

Determined to turn and march herself directly back to the bar, she pushed off the wall, completely intending to leave, only to catch a glimpse of Deke and Peggy in an embrace, Peggy flush up against him, her arms draped around his neck. Fighting back the bile that had just risen in her throat, Fitz took a huge step back so she was well on the other side of the corner again. She braced herself against the wall in hopes they hadn't seen her.

She closed her eyes and let her head fall back to the wall when she heard him say, "We're not doing this here."

"That never bothered you before," Peggy purred. And Fitz had no doubt she was plastering those boobs right up against his chest.

"Not what I meant," he muttered.

The air turned about thirty degrees colder when Peggy answered, "Then what *did* you mean?"

"You know exactly what I mean," Deke said, clearly not in the mood to talk to Peggy either. Hopefully he was also taking this moment to disentangle himself from Peggy's arms and push her to the side, although Fitz had no leg to stand on at the moment.

There was a moment of silence before Peggy's satisfyingly astounded, "You aren't seriously still having your summer fling, are you?" Then her voice turned sultry again. "It's been too long, baby." Despite the noise of the bar behind her, Fitz could hear the sound of a zipper being pulled down loud and clear.

And then, thank all of the gods that were out there, the sound of it going decidedly back up.

"Okay, then," he muttered. "So we're doing this here after all."

Peggy practically squealed in delight, only to have Deke cut her off with, "Not *that*. We…" He paused and took an audible breath. "We're not having sex again, Peggy. We're done."

"We'… *What?*" Peggy went from incredulous to furious in no time at all. "It's Suzie, isn't it. She's the one you've been with all summer. I *knew* you were sleeping with her, that little bitch."

"It's not Suzie," Deke sighed. And over Peggy's next question, he added, "And it's not Rayna."

Who the hell was Rayna?

"Jesus, Peggy, it's not about any of them. Just…" He sounded tired. *So* worn down. "Look, what we had was good and I'd like to remember it that way. But there's a lot working against you right now, and believe me when I say it's in your best interest to let this go."

Fitz had known Deke for a long time. She'd seen a lot of different sides of him over the years, even more so in the last few months. But never once had she known his voice to sound so *scary*. Cold. She was so taken aback, in fact, her heart pounding so loudly, she almost missed Peggy's quiet, "What exactly do you mean by that?"

And his response was so low and quiet back, Fitz

could barely hear it. "It means that you hurt people I care about—"

"Oh my, God. *Fitz?*" Peggy said, with that special sneered emphasis on the name that even Jeremiah had never added.

"Yes, Fitz. Jesus, Peggy," he said, "you used *my* name to get her alone with three assholes who were twice her size. You knew exactly what those guys were like, and yet you lured her there like the fucking big bad wolf."

"They didn't rape her," Peggy snapped, as if that made everything all right. "And I already paid for that. Nate broke up with me and hasn't spoken to me since."

Deke snapped right back, "Because what you did was *heinous*. I wouldn't have spoken to you since that day, either, if I'd known."

"But you didn't know, Deke, did you? Nate knew. Jeremiah knew... And no more than three weeks after it happened, you were balls deep inside of me and making me scream."

"Jesus," Deke muttered, echoing Fitz's thoughts exactly.

But Peggy wasn't done. "I'm thinking it's more that you didn't want to know. You *like* everyone at a distance. You keep them there. You watch over them from behind that bar, but you never get too close. Honestly? I always expected your precious Fitz would have told you a lot sooner. But you can tell her right back for me that she needs to get over it. It was sixteen years ago."

Bitch.

Fitz hated her. *Hated.* Never in her life had Fitz wanted so badly to physically hurt someone. But before she could do so much as take a step forward, she heard Deke's voice, menacing and low. "Fitz *is* over it. She is so fucking over it, it kind of pisses me off."

Yes, he'd made that clear.

"But *I'm* not. I won't ever be. I liked you, Peggy. We've spent a lot of years having a really good time. But what you did—what you used *my name* to do? That's not something I can forgive you for. And I'll go to my grave knowing I'm the reason she could never quite be free of you."

Oh, God. Oh, *Deke*.

"Don't do this," Peggy warned. "The things I can say about you… It will make standing behind that bar every night pretty damn uncomfortable."

No. Fitz closed her eyes. This was exactly what she didn't want; what she'd wanted to protect him from. The reason she'd sworn Nate to secrecy all those years ago. This bar was his home. His *life*. It meant everything to him. With a deep breath she pushed herself off the wall again, this time with every intention of finally stepping forward and redirecting Peggy's hate back where it belonged, no matter how uncomfortable it was.

Except Scary Deke came through again. "You say whatever you want to who-the-fuck-ever you want. I'm not ashamed of anything we ever said or did together. I honestly don't give a fuck. There's no one in this town that I care about who chooses you over me."

And with that, he suddenly came around the corner, his head still turned back to Peggy, but so close that all Fitz needed to do was reach her arm out to touch him. Yet she couldn't. Not the way he'd reacted before. She pulled her arms in tight.

It was enough to draw his attention to her, and he jerked to a halt. When their eyes met, the entire world came to a stop. Then it shifted, and Fitz hoped with everything she had she could hold on. The spell wasn't even broken as Peggy came around from behind him and pushed past Deke, obviously angry as hell. Out of the corner of her eye, Fitz could see the other woman straighten up a bit as she muttered, "Perfect," before passing right between them and moving away.

"I'm…" Fitz whispered. "I'm so sorry."

He was the one to break the stare, looking down at the floor. When he spoke, his voice was gruff in a way she'd rarely heard. "Am I delusional? Am I the only one who thought we were actually moving towards something we both wanted to explore?" Then he took a step closer. "Is there not something kind of big going on here?"

"I…" She bit her lip again so that it would stop quivering long enough for her to actually speak. "Yes. You know I think there is."

"Then why in the *fuck*," he spat out, "did you not tell me you're up for a new job?" He came right up to her, angrier than she'd ever seen him. "A job that I'm pretty sure means you'll have to move away, for *fuck's* sake."

Yes, he was angry. Yes, he deserved to be. "I'm…"

All the reasons she hadn't told him ran through her head. Not a single one of them made one bit of sense now.

"I am an *idiot*," he muttered, pacing back and forth. "Here I am, walking around on Cloud Nine because seeing you in my bar made me start to think about what our future might look like. You and me and some kids to pass it all along to one day."

Wait. *What?* She panicked at the thought of coming

out to Jason and Wash. Marriage was the *last* thing on her mind. *Kids?*

"I never said…"

"That's right, Fitz," he hissed. "You never said. But the thing is, you don't ever actually say *anything*, so I'm kind of used to figuring it out on my own. Guess I got a big F on that one."

"I know, *okay*?" she said, needing him to stop. "I know I should have told you! I know I handled it all wrong! But I…" But she *what*? Even she had no idea what came at the end of that. She fell back against the wall, her hands against it, holding her up. "Nate and Dorie were the only ones who knew. And only because Nate's on the interviewing committee. It's not like I was going around telling everyone else. You would have been the *first* person I told."

He stared at her for a minute. Then he shook his head. "How do you not get this?" He took a few steps closer. "I don't give a *shit* if you told everyone else. You can take out an ad in the *Chicago Tribune*, for all I care. What matters is that you didn't tell *me*. That you actually *kept* it from me." He took a step back. "Is that what was going on with Price and Whitfield that night?" His eyes went to the floor before he looked up at her again. "The worst part is that I actually knew there was something you weren't telling me." He shook his head and gave the most bitter laugh ever. "I'd actually convinced myself it was that you were falling as hard as I was, you just couldn't quite get up the nerve to—"

"I was," she said, stepping toward him and trying not to cry when he took a step back. "I *did*." She felt back for the wall, needing it to keep her upright.

Not coming any closer he shook his head. "Did it not occur to you I might just want to freaking know?"

"Why?" she asked. "So you could talk me out of it? Tell me I should stay here in Inspiration? That you'd be the one to take care of me? That you're the one who would *fix* me?"

That seemed to make him even angrier than before. "Where the fuck do you get these things?" His hand came down on the wall next to her head as he leaned in close. "No, Fitz," he said, his voice quiet and cold. "So that I could be *happy* for you. So that I could cheer you on. So that I could tell the fucking *world* that the woman I am goddamn in love with is about to head up Sam Price's new foundation."

Oh.

"You... You're in love with me?"

Okay. So, yes, she'd been pretty sure that's what had been happening, as frightening as the idea of it had been.

"Yes, Fitz. I love you. I think maybe I've been a little bit in love with you since the first day I saw you at the Jensens' farmhouse. If Peggy had told me that day Angelica Wade was out behind the equipment shed, I would have been out there in a second."

"You would have?" That was good... Right? All these things he was saying were good.

So why did she feel like her whole world was about to be torn apart?

Probably because she knew the next words out of his mouth would be, "But I can't do this anymore."

And it felt exactly as she'd expected it would. Like somewhere inside of her, something had been ripped out. *Torn* out, no less devastating than the sudden loss of her mother's arms around her, that last grasp of her hand. It took everything Fitz had to stay standing. *Breathing.*

He gave not one bit of ground as his eyes went hard. "I love you, Fitz. I do. I want to spend my life kissing you. Watching your eyes come alive whether it's because you're under me in my bed or at the head of a boardroom running Sam Price's freaking show. I needed two things, Fitz. Just two. Honesty and trust."

If the sob hadn't frozen in her throat along with every other cell in her body, it would have erupted right out of her. Especially when he looked down for a minute— maybe ten; everything was frozen at the moment—and when his eyes came back to hers he seemed nearly as torn up as she was. "I hate that you feel the way you do. I would do anything to make you happy. Anything I could to make you feel like you don't need to do this alone. I honest-to-God would."

He took a step backward. Still close enough to touch, yet he held himself back. "I'm not going to try to talk you into something you don't believe in, but I can't keep giving everything I have to someone who won't even meet me halfway." Then he shoved his hands into his pockets and his eyes went down to the floor. "Yeah, I'm done."

He turned and walked away.

"Wait…" She started to go after him, stopping only when she saw the way his shoulders tensed when he stopped a few feet away.

He was truly going to do this then? Just go like her father had?

"You're *leaving* me?" She wrapped her arms around

her body, trying to keep her insides from falling out. "That's it? The end?"

His head dipped down for a minute as he answered, "I'm not the one leaving, Fitz. If you ever want to find me, you know exactly where I'll be."

Right. Because she did know him. She trusted him. Deke was the only man she trusted as resolutely as she had her dad, in fact, up until her father's past transgressions had blown it all away. But for the first time since the day she'd learned what her father had done, she realized it wasn't the men in her life that were the problem. They weren't who she couldn't trust, the ones who would disappoint her the way her father had.

S*he* was.

And she stood there, stunned, as he disappeared from sight.

Chapter Twenty-Nine

It did strike Deke as ironic that after a lifetime of making sure his relationships with women weren't strong enough to require severing them, he'd essentially broken up with two in the span of five minutes.

Christ.

He hadn't meant to end it with Fitz. He didn't *want* to end it. And it took everything he had not to turn and go back to her.

Resisting the urge to walk right out, the feeling of defeat he'd never before experienced until this very moment, Deke looked around and realized he'd taken himself back out to the bar, and was now just standing there while Josh looked at him as though he had two heads. He wasn't quite up to speaking to anyone yet so he was about to make the rounds of busing tables when Wash and Dorie both spoke, practically at the same exact moment.

"Did you give her the boot?" Wash asked as Dorie snapped, "What the...?"

Deke looked up to see Wash staring across the room at Peggy while Dorie looked over his shoulder at Fitz. Dorie acted first. With a scathing glare, she was off the stool before Deke even realized she was moving, and on her way to Fitz. Wash, on the other hand, as with just about every other person in the place, had turned his attention to the scene taking place between Peggy and Lola.

It was a beauty. Since Peggy had decided he'd done her wrong, it apparently gave her license to tear up her bill and throw it in the waitress's face. She had no shame whatsoever about letting the entire place know she was *not* paying for today's lunch because, "Your brother's an asshole!" Which was freaking perfect. Peggy, of all people, was the one throwing a hissy fit. She was chewing out Lola, chewing out the waitress, spewing her hate on everyone except the one person she should: him.

Jesus Christ. Within the hour, the whole freaking town would be talking about him and *Peggy* when what he really wanted was to shout out that Fitz was the one he was in love with, and—

Yes. He was in love with Fitz.

Goddamn, fucking, kicking the shit out of you, love.

He yanked the bin of dirty dishes out of its place.

But even if he had come to that particular revelation, it didn't change a damn thing. There was no way he could take back what he'd said. No way to fix it, either. He was who he was and Fitz was who she was. She was never going to go against everything she believed to be true—or, for that matter, break down any of those walls. Even for him.

"God*damn* it!"

The words exploded out of him in such a roar that everything around him came to a screeching halt. Heads turned, mouths dropped open, even Peggy stopped what she was saying, midstream. It was like Godzilla himself had appeared and was crashing and thrashing his way through town.

Except it wasn't Godzilla thrashing around, it was him. Easygoing, let-everything-roll-off-his-back Max Deacon had just slammed down a bin full of dishes—*slammed* it—and was now stalking his way across the room. He felt strange in his own skin even as he came to a stop in front of Peggy. "Get out."

"What?" she asked, as though no one had ever called her on her shit.

Well, probably, no one ever had. He sure hadn't.

"Get your bag…" He stepped in close enough for her to have to tip her head back. "Take your jacket…" And he was quiet enough that only he, Lola and Peggy's friends could hear him, although that was a freaking favor she did not deserve. "And get. The *fuck*. Out." Another step, and now she was stepping back as well.

Her surprise turned to attitude. "This is a public place. You can't tell me to leave. Your father would never—"

Ignoring her protests, he hissed, "And don't fucking *ever* speak to my sister or our staff like that again."

Her mouth gaped open. She shut it, opened it and then shut it again. She glared at him. "Fine," she said, snatching her bag and tucking it under her arm. Then she went on the offensive, stepping right up to him this time. "I sure hope she's worth it because you've just lost a hell of a lot of business."

Yeah, he probably had. Peggy's father was president of the Rotary Club, her mom was second only to Mama Gin in terms of town matriarchs, and Peggy headed up the Jaycees. Plus, Peggy's crowd tended to frequent the bar more often than not. Between the three of them, they brought him a lot of business and he'd clearly put an end to that.

He didn't give a freaking shit.

Ignoring the concerned looks of Lola and his friends, not to mention the not-at-all-contained curiosity of a large portion of the rest of the crowd, he turned his back on her. Threw his apron down on the table and said to Josh, "You have the bar. I'm going fishing."

Peace the fuck out.

Fitz was numb. She felt hollowed out—no heart to beat, no lungs to breathe. She barely had enough air to speak, much less scream.

Oh, how she wanted to scream.

"I…" she gasped, feeling Dorie's arms go around her and pull her into a hug. "I can't…"

Breathe. She couldn't breathe.

Before she knew what was happening, she was being propelled through the back hallway.

One minute she was standing there watching Peggy yell at Lola, and the next she was in the alley behind Deke's bar.

"Oh, God."

Tears spilled out of her eyes and she didn't know why. She expected nothing from him. She expected nothing, period. No one to answer to, no one to make promises he wouldn't be able to keep, no one to count on other than her own reliable self.

And then, suddenly, all the feelings she hadn't been able to feel came to her in an all-consuming roar. Her heart started pounding, her lungs burned and the scream she couldn't get out filled her head. She was trembling— *sobbing*—and still completely unable to breathe.

"It's okay, sweetie," Dorie was murmuring in her ear. "It's going to be okay."

No, it wasn't. Nothing was going to be okay.

She wished she were different. That she'd grown up the way everyone else had—fighting with her mom. Hating her dad for giving her a curfew. Complaining that the dinner wasn't what she wanted, that her clothes were all wrong, that…

She wanted her mother, goddamn it. Her dad. She wanted her family back.

She wanted all the things that could never be.

She felt her legs buckle beneath her, felt her body curl into itself. Felt the light she'd had for such a short while fade to black.

"What the hell happened?" she heard Nate ask and then a murmured response as Dorie answered.

Completely unable to deal with any of it, she rested her head against something solid, realizing belatedly it was Nate's chest, and that he'd picked her up off the stairs outside Dorie's apartment, where she'd apparently come to a stop before sinking down to the floor.

She remembered even less after that. There was the sense of dark clouds whirling around her, of falling through space, of fear and chaos and an overwhelming roar as everything around her was shaken and tossed. When her eyes snapped open, she saw her father sitting there, across the room, smiling and looking down at her mom with such tenderness that she felt her whole being swell with joy as she woke up from the horrible nightmare of…

Yes, she'd fallen asleep, but this wasn't a nightmare she could wake out of. There had been a tornado. It *had* taken them away. And that wasn't her father in front of her, it was…

Nate's head snapped up. Smile gone, he pulled away from Dorie. "You're awake. What the hell did Deke—"

"Oh, my God." Mama Gin was right. Nate looked exactly like their father. How had she never seen it before, not once, in all these years?

Maybe because she'd never allowed herself to remember the way their father had looked at her mother, the same way Nate looked at Dorie. Because they *had* been in love. What he'd done had been horrible enough for Fitz to not be able to get past it. Before all that, though. Before she'd become part of the scandal he'd created, what was there between her parents had been strong enough for them to face whatever lay ahead of them. Together.

And Fitz's heart broke all over again. For all this time, she'd refused to even consider the possibility of falling in love. The idea of what it meant both to have and to lose something so utterly profound had scared her too much. So she'd used her anger as an excuse to play it safe, to sit there in her comfort zone while Deke took a running jump straight off the edge of the cliff.

For her.

She looked up to see Nate still watching her, his eyes cold and his lips settled into a grim line. His voice tight with anger, he repeated, "What did Deke do?"

With his hands at his side and his eyes radiating fury, Fitz was afraid he might kill Deke. Maim him, at the very least.

Dorie was clearly also ready to lay into Deke, although she had a much softer touch. Coming over to the

couch and putting her arm around Fitz, she said, "It's
okay if you don't want to talk about it, we—"

Her gaze flew up to Nate's as he cut her off, saying,
"*I* want to talk about it," fists clenching. "As soon as I
can find him, at least."

Fitz leaned forward, a tiny bit of panic flaring up as
she looked out the window at the sky that seemed omi-
nously darker than it had only a moment before. "He's
not at the bar?"

The grim look came over Nate's face again as Dorie
frowned and said, "He apparently decided to go fishing."

Fishing? Images from her dream came rushing back.
The helplessness of being caught in the storm. "Call
Lola," she demanded, the fear taking over.

With an apologetic look, Dorie shook her head. "Lola
says there must have been some kind of misunderstand-
ing because, I quote, 'Deke and Fitz are totally in love,'
end quote, and that the two of you need to figure this
out."

The sob rose up through Fitz's chest so quickly that
she had to gulp in air in order to breathe. And gulp it
in again.

Yes, she should have told him about the job. She
knew that. But she hadn't been ready for *anything* to
happen the way it did. Not the job, and definitely not
him. "He... He changed the rules." They would have
been fine if it had all stayed the way it was supposed to.
"It was..." She buried her head in her hands; there was
no way she could meet Dorie's eyes, much less Nate's.
"It was just supposed to be..."

Before she could muster up the courage to say the
word, however, Dorie made a sound that was half gasp,

half laugh, while Nate sighed. When Fitz looked up, she could see he'd put his hand to his forehead and had his eyes closed. Pinching the bridge of his nose, he said, "If the ending to that fucking phrase is 'sex,' I am seriously going to…"

Dorie snorted as his voice trailed off and he glared at her. Fitz was obviously missing something, but she wasn't about to interrupt.

"And I suddenly find myself in Deke's corner," he muttered.

"Oh, honey," Dorie said, pulling Fitz into a hug. "It will all work out. I honestly believe that."

Well, of course *Dorie* believed. Dorie had a man who worshipped the ground—

"Did you hear that?" Dorie asked, cocking her head at the sound of sirens in the distance.

"Shit," Nate muttered, going for the remote and turning on the TV.

"My phone," Fitz snapped, jumping to her feet. "Where is it?"

"We turned them off…" Dorie's mouth dropped open as she stared at the image on the TV. The one showing a map with Inspiration in the middle of it and flashing red all around it.

Shutting off the TV, Nate was already in motion, grabbing Dorie's hand and pulling her from the couch. "We need to go."

Right. Because for some ridiculous reason, over half the buildings in town didn't have basements even though they lived in freaking tornado alley. And although almost all of the buildings in town had been damaged by the last tornado, not nearly enough of them had been bad enough to require rebuilding from the ground up.

Deacon's was one of the few in this part of town with
a basement because they'd run a bar there during Pro-
hibition.

But Fitz couldn't move. Standing there staring at the
TV, the map was imprinted on her mind even though
the TV was now off. If he'd really gone fishing, then he
was right there in the middle of all that red.

"God*damn* it, Fitz," Nate yelled from the doorway.
"Come on!"

She ran out after them, down the stairs and out onto
the street. She even turned to run toward the bar right
along with Nate and Dorie and every other person who
had any sense, when the sight of the sky stopped her
cold. It wasn't the way she remembered it. She'd always
had a picture in her head of a disaster movie-type funnel cloud, but the reality was that she'd never seen it.
She'd been so scared she'd just huddled in the backseat,
her eyes squeezed shut as the winds battered the car.

This could barely even be called a cloud, it was that
big. Still in the distance, but huge and pitch black as it
crowded the color out of the sky. She honestly wouldn't
have been surprised if a cow came flying across the
road.

Yes, she had screwed things up. Yes, *she* was the one
who'd come close to destroying the best thing she'd ever
have. *But you want faith, Deke? Here you go. Angelica
Hawkins is fighting her way back to you no matter what
stands in the way.*

Even if it was a tornado. A big one.

But what-the-fuck-ever.

She ran across the street to where Nate's car was
parked, because, yes, thank you, God, he kept his keys
tucked in the visor. It drove Dorie crazy.

She got in and powered it up and… Holy *cow* that was a lot of engine.

Well, good.

You know what, Universe? *No.*

No. Freaking. *Way.*

Chapter Thirty

Two hours after leaving the bar, Deke found himself
still sitting in his Jeep, staring out over the creek. He
had no idea what he'd been thinking. He wasn't fishing, that was for damn sure. It had been raining all day
and the temperature had dropped about twenty degrees
in the last hour alone, plus the thunderstorm that had
just started was making it clear this was not the best
day to be out here. But he was at a complete loss as to
what to do.

He couldn't go back to the bar right now. He had no
interest in seeing another living soul, to be honest. Hell,
the way he was feeling right now, he could see himself
getting back on the road and driving right up Highway
35 until Inspiration was so far behind him that it wasn't
even a speck on a map. The rest of the world be damned.

Keeping what had happened to her in high school a
secret, yeah, he got that. He even understood why she'd
wanted to keep what they'd been doing from everyone
else—he couldn't imagine facing either Nate or Dorie
right now, much less Wash or Jason once they heard
the whole story.

At the same time, though, he was…*pissed*. How long
had she known she was up for this job? How long since

she'd decided to leave? He let his head fall back against the seat. Doesn't need to be complicated, my ass. What a fucking idiot he'd been.

Damn it, Fitz. Give me something.

Of course he'd fallen in love with her. How could he have expected anything else? But she was also the most infuriating creature on the face of this earth. She'd pushed him right up and over the breaking point. Hell, up until today he hadn't even known he *had* a breaking point. But there it was. If only he didn't love her so much. If only he didn't want to see her happy, honest-to-God happy, for once in her life.

Yeah. If only. Things would be a hell of a lot easier, that was for fucking sure.

He was so lost in his own thoughts, and okay, maybe he was blasting AC/DC as loud as his speakers could go, that it took him a minute or two before he heard it.

He turned the music down for a second and…

Fuck. Tornado sirens. He leaned forward in order to see more of the sky as he powered his phone back on. It practically blew out of his hand the second it came to life. There were no less than five tornado watch alerts, and another came up right then, except this one was a warning. Which meant there wasn't a chance of a tornado, there *was* one. If the sudden influx of voicemails and texts meant anything, it was that it was heading right toward Inspiration.

Although the last thing he should do was get back on the road, he threw the Jeep into gear and backed out of the brush faster than a bat could work its way out of hell. Two seconds later he was barreling down the highway into town, watching the huge black cloud off in the distance, the sky pea soup green all around him.

There was no way he was stopping until he had Fitz in his arms. She may not be in love with him—she may not ever have the capacity to be—but no matter how fucked up things were right now, he cared more deeply for her than anyone he'd ever known. There was no way he was letting her ride this out alone.

He glanced up to his left, pausing for a split second as the power of what he saw registered. It was still out over the fields, a massive wedge of a cloud ready to unleash its fury. Tendrils dropped down out of it, swirling along the ground. He'd never actually been in a tornado. He and Lola had been up in Ames with their grandparents when the one that destroyed the town hit seventeen years before and, to be honest, it was mesmerizing. From this far away, at least. But it wasn't exactly the time to be in awe of Mother Nature. He slammed his foot down on the gas, cranking it up to ninety.

The streets were deserted by the time he got into town, an apocalyptic scene with cars pulled haphazardly to the sides of the road as their occupants escaped to the nearest shelter. When he turned off the main road and towards the town center, right there on the sidewalk were Nate and Dorie, standing and arguing, despite it seriously not being the time for that. Nate looked like he was restraining Dorie so she couldn't turn back. Deke pulled up next to them and leaned out the window.

Without even a word of hello, Nate said, "We were at Dorie's when the sirens went off. Fitz was right there with us. I have no fucking clue where she went."

There wasn't even time to wonder. Deke nodded, ready to move forward again.

"We'll help you find her," Dorie said—well, shouted, in order to be heard.

Hell, no. Fitz would kill them all if something happened to Dorie. Deke looked at Nate. "I've got this."

To his complete surprise, Nate didn't even attempt to fight him on it. Instead, he nodded before turning back to Dorie and saying, "We're going to the bar. You're either walking on your own or I'm carrying you."

Deke didn't even look to see which way Dorie chose. He floored the gas.

Those last few blocks were the longest trip Deke had ever taken in his life. He didn't have time to go slow and he had to pay extra close attention to driving, but he did his damnedest to keep his eyes out for Fitz along the way. She had to be somewhere close by, and one glance in the rearview mirror was enough to tell Deke he was running out of time. He screeched around the corner onto Dorie's street...

And came to a sudden halt.

If not for the particular circumstances it would have been comical to watch Fitz wrestle with Nate's Mustang as it bucked back and forth. She was actually attempting to maneuver out of a parking spot without hitting the cars to her front or back.

During a *tornado*.

He pulled to the side of the road and jumped out of his Jeep, his eye on what now seemed like a much more rapidly approaching cloud. He got to the Mustang and was about to wrench the door open when she looked up and smiled.

Smiled. And waved.

No fear, not even anger. She just got out of the car and said, "Oh, good."

He truly was delusional. Good?

"Are you out of your fucking mind?"

She looked up at him. "I didn't think it would be that hard to drive a stick."

What?

Then she looked past him, her hand over her eyes as the wind whipped her hair around.

"Oh," she said, taking a step back. Her eyes widened. "Oh, wow."

He looked over his shoulder to see the cloud was a lot fucking closer. And its tendrils had joined together into a funnel that was now zig-zagging its way toward town. There was the roar of a train, and then the rat-a-tat-tat of machine gun fire as the hail began to fall. Big freaking balls of hail. And they *hurt*.

He grabbed her hand and they ran toward the building. They were only twenty feet away from the door leading up to Dorie's apartment, thank God, because even that seemed too far away. The stairway had only a few small windows along the ceiling, but the hail was so loud Deke was sure it was strong enough to break the glass. The apartment door was wide open. He pushed Fitz ahead of him into the living room when the drop of pressure made his head feel like it was going to explode and the sound of the loudest train whistle he'd ever heard suddenly seemed about ten times louder.

So this was what it was like to be in the middle of a tornado. Holy freaking fuck.

With a burst of speed he didn't know she had in her, Fitz ran straight back to the bathroom while Deke detoured to the bedroom to pull the mattress off the bed. He was right behind, jumping into the bathtub after her, pulling the mattress over them just as the windows blew out. And then he clung with all his might, his arms straining as he fought the wind, as she curled into him and buried her head against his chest.

Afraid that it all might be too much for Fitz, he chanced a look down at her. She didn't seem even the least bit scared. Just kind of…calm. Serene.

"What the fuck were you doing out there?" he asked at one point.

"Coming for you," she answered.

"That was, uh…" How to put it best? "…fucking crazy."

"It's called faith, Deke," she said, a smile on her face as she tucked her head into his neck.

She was clearly in shock.

Even if they made it through this it was, without doubt, the end. Of course she was going to take that job—after Mother Nature's repeat performance, she might not even come back to visit.

Deke would figure out a way to live with it, though. Eventually. Right now, buffeted by the wind and knowing he was the only one standing—well, lying in a tub while holding the mattress over the top of them—between Fitz and a tornado, he decided he could do all his figuring out later. He'd found her. That was enough for now.

Fitz took a sledgehammer to a lot of walls as she lay there in Deke's arms.

She loved him.

It wasn't just the lover he was, coaxing her body into bliss, night after night, or the friend he'd been to her for over half her life, nor was it the brother he was to Lola, the uncle he was to every kid in the Deacon and Hawkins clan. It was the man he was—the man who had changed because of her, but refused to be fully broken in order to keep her. Refused to let *her* break *him*.

She was, actually, broken.

It wasn't that she was dead inside, but she had been wounded. Almost mortally so. The life had drained out of her and she'd existed as a shell for seventeen years. She didn't even realize it until these last few months. Until she felt the pain of him walking away and realized the only one standing in the way was *her*.

She didn't need to be happy for her life to come crashing down around her.

It could happen while she was miserable and heartbroken, while she was cursing all the years she'd wasted because she was afraid of what might happen if she tried to step out into the light.

She'd hurt him. Disappointed him. She'd be lucky if he even thought about giving her another chance. But she also knew what she had to lose if she couldn't get past this overwhelming fear of what lay ahead in order to just live every day with him.

As the wind died down and she could feel Deke begin to relax as he no longer had to struggle to hold the mattress over them, she looked up at him. "You came back for me." As she'd known he would.

She'd just planned to get to him first.

"I always will," he answered, and for the first time in seventeen years, Fitz felt true peace. But she had a long way to go before she could count on that lasting.

Sure enough, even as he smiled his eyes grew dark. "But, Fitz—"

His phone rang, startling both of them, although she supposed she could thank their own foundation for that.

They'd helped the town put up extra cell towers for this very purpose—and she was grateful for the reprieve.

"Yeah, I got her," Deke said once he answered. "She's fine. Dorie?"

Fitz closed her eyes, tightening her arms around Deke as she rested her head on his chest.

"Okay," he was saying. "I have to call Lo—" Fitz felt his whole body release its tension. "Oh, thank fuck. Jules and…" His head fell back against the edge of the tub as he shoved the mattress off to the side. "That thing was massive. I've never seen anything like it… Yeah, probably not my greatest idea." Knowing he was looking down at her, Fitz smiled as his hand brushed through her hair. "The fishing hole. Pretty damn stupid… It wasn't exactly a choice."

Fitz could hear Nate's laugh over the phone and she smiled. Nate and Dorie knew. She hadn't been in any state to admit it to them, but they knew. Now she just had to figure out how to tell Deke. Especially because, odds were, he wouldn't believe her. He'd think it was because of the tornado. Maybe even that she'd gone a little crazy.

Maybe she had.

"Everyone's okay?" she asked, as Deke put down the phone.

He let his head fall back again and closed his eyes, his fingers playing lazily with her hair. "They had a big old party in the basement of the bar, Lola and Jules and the kids. They picked them all up when the first watch was issued. Everyone else is either there or checked in."

"And everyone's houses?"

He shrugged. "Unclear. But houses can be rebuilt." And there was nothing they could do about that at the moment. Truly nothing, because he added, "Police said to stay put while they figure everything out."

"Really?" she asked, a smile coming over her face even though this was so not the time. "As in, we're not allowed to move out of this nice, big tub?"

His head came up and his eyes flashed a warning. "Fitz…"

"I know," she said, burrowing her head in his chest even though she wasn't sure she still had the right. She brought her hand up to play with the button on his shirt. "I'm…" Her voice caught. "I'm so sorry. I don't even know what else to say."

He didn't answer at first. He didn't try to put distance between them, or even stop her hand, but he held himself so still beneath her. And when he did speak, it wasn't exactly what she wanted to hear.

"Here's the thing," he said. "I know you, Fitz. With the exception of song lyrics—" she pulled back in order to glare at him, not the easiest thing to do given the twinkle in his eye "—you're really good at everything you do."

But then even the slightest hint of a smile left his face, his gaze growing intense as he stared at her and then looked away. "It makes me think that you loving me isn't something you want to be good at."

She wanted to deny it. She wanted to tell him that she'd suddenly changed her mind and she couldn't care less about this job because all she wanted in life was to give him the happily ever after he deserved.

But she couldn't.

"You're right," she said, voice raw. "I don't. I really don't want to be in love with you." He tensed up again.

Pulled back even as she held on. "But it turns out I suck more at fighting it."

It wasn't a choice. Just like Nate had said—like Deke had. Not that that helped matters in anyway.

To her surprise, he laughed softly as his arms tightened around her. "I think that might be the most honest thing you've ever said to me."

She straightened up suddenly. "That's what you need from me?"

His eyes went dark as his hands framed her face. "I need you not to lie to me because you think I won't like the truth." She started to pull away, but he held her in place. "Can you do that, Fitz? Because I can't—"

"I think I'd rather die than watch you walk away from me again," she whispered, cutting him off. She didn't even realize she was crying until she tasted salt on her lips.

Apparently that was a good next step because she was suddenly being hauled up the length of his body and he was kissing her and his hands were on her and it felt like maybe she *had* died and gone straight to heaven. Except, as long as she was on a roll with this honesty thing she needed to see it through.

"Wait," she managed, bracing her hands against his chest. Pulling back from him felt like one of the hardest things she'd ever have to do, as hard, almost, as saying, "I want this job, Deke. And I don't know if I can give you the things you want."

His face completely unreadable, he asked, "What exactly would those things be?"

With a deep breath, she eased back a little farther. "Staying in Inspiration. Helping you with the bar."

Her voice caught at the unexpected lump in her throat. "Having a family."

He was so quiet for a minute that she was pretty sure she'd done it. Gone and ended the best thing that ever happened to her because of all those broken pieces bouncing around inside. But then his hands were in her hair again and he was tilting her head up.

"Maybe I don't want the things you think I do." Gruffly, he added, "Maybe I just want you."

This time she knew full well the tears were coming. She could feel them build up inside her so suddenly they had no choice but to overflow. "What?"

He seemed a little emotional himself. "And maybe we could actually *talk* about the things we want instead of assuming." He grinned. "And by 'we' I mean you."

Completely unexpectedly, she laughed. Given all the tears involved, it probably wasn't very pretty. And it didn't stop her from hitting him in the chest. "Well, *maybe*," she said, "we could also acknowledge I'm not the only one in this relationship with things to talk about."

His eyes went mockingly wide. "Did you just say we were in a relationship?"

"Schmelationship is too hard to pronounce," she answered. Then she hit him again. "And you're deflecting."

This time his reply was utterly serious. "You're the only one who's ever called me on that."

Given the look in his eye, she went still. "Is that a good thing or a bad one?"

His eyes drifted down to her lips and then came back up. "I guess it depends on how you look at it."

Now it was her turn to stare, especially as she felt

him go hard beneath her. As his hand traced its way over the curve of her breast. "And how exactly are you looking at it?" she asked. Kind of breathless, truth be told.

"Right now?" He tipped her chin up. "As a good thing. A very good thing."

The smile that came over his face was one of the best things she'd ever seen. "Okay," he said. "We can talk about anything you want."

They would. Later. At the moment, though, there was only one question on her mind. "Could we be done talking for now?" She tilted her hips ever so slightly. Since they were, in fact, still crammed together in this tub, she felt every glorious inch of him against her.

He laughed. "Did you have something else in mind?"

She took his hands in hers and pushed them up over his head. Stretching out along the length of him, she savored the feel of his body against her. "I'm thinking right now I need you to make love to me."

Almost since the moment they'd begun sleeping together she'd been waiting for the moment it would end. For the first time, she allowed herself to believe that it was only the beginning.

"Love, huh?" He grasped her hands tightly. "You can look me in the eye and say that?"

She nodded, making sure not to so much as even blink as she whispered, "Love."

For a minute he stared at her and the fear came crashing over her again. Until he smiled and said, "Well, okay, then."

That he had a condom didn't surprise her. But how the man managed to strip her of the rest of her clothes and most of his in the confines of the tub while holding her wrists in his hand she'd never know. He did have his talents. But she didn't care. Because the moment he slid into her, she knew she was home.

Chapter Thirty-One

Three days later, Deke was still marveling that the damage the tornado had left in its wake had been minimal.

Well, manageable. Roofs had come off a bunch of buildings downtown, and windows were blown out everywhere. The hail made its mark. But it was mostly the southwest corner of town that had been hit, which was largely farmland. A few old barns had been taken out, a grain silo, and about eighty percent of Ella's fences, although her house and barn were still standing and her horses had been spared. All the buildings out there had damage of some kind, irrigation systems would need to be replaced, and mid-September was a pretty fucking bad time for entire crops to be gone. But the foundation would help with all those things and people would get through it.

The fear of what could have happened if Fitz had driven through that tornado reared up and hit him at unexpected times, even as the details faded away. She had survived, though; they both had. Things might not be moving forward the way he wanted them to, but they were still here on this earth and he was beyond grateful.

They hadn't talked yet. Not the way they needed to. They'd both been so busy over the last few days that they'd fallen into bed exhausted, barely even having the energy to, well…

Okay. He'd never not have the energy to make love to her, especially while he was still living on borrowed time in terms of her being in his bed. Though she'd postponed her trip, she hadn't called it off. She'd also been talking to Sam off and on for days and in front of Deke. She did seem to have gotten the message about opening up. He knew from Lola, though, that she was looking at condos in Chicago. Signs of a happy future weren't good. But he'd decided to live in the dream for a little bit longer. No need to force it, right?

And if that wasn't a load of bull, there was a bridge that had landed in the middle of a cornfield he'd be happy to sell.

"Deke!"

He looked up to see Mama Gin standing with some-one in a suit, probably another one of the insurance adjusters. Turning the food truck over to Josh—if this wasn't a time for a good old-fashioned barn raising, complete with free food and beer, then when was?—he headed over.

"This is who I was telling you about," she said, her hand going to Deke's shoulder. "Max Deacon, I want you to meet Dan Samson."

Shaking hands, Deke nodded as the other man said, "Gin's been telling me about you for a while, but I haven't had the chance to meet you before now."

Deke resisted the urge to ask what on earth Mama Gin had been telling this guy, not to mention who the guy actually was. Instead, he said, "Well, I guess I'm glad to hear that. I hope most of it is good."

"What I hear is that she's grooming you to be Inspiration's next mayor," Dan said.

Deke still wasn't entirely sure she'd been serious about that. She had put him in charge of the town's disaster recovery task force, though, which had him leaning toward yes. To his surprise, he was finding he actually liked it—was pretty good at it. Even according to Peggy's dad, who had come up to him this morning and clapped him on the back while saying so.

Plus it would help him be somewhere other than his bar 24/7 once Fitz left town. So that was good.

Deciding to stay as neutral on the subject as possible, however, Deke smiled. "I can't imagine anyone filling her footsteps."

Which earned him a sharp laugh from Dan as the man nodded past the food truck. "Looks like a party, not a disaster area."

Deke just smiled. "My sister loves little kids." Which was a lie. Lola actually wasn't a big fan of anyone under the age of ten, unless she was related to them or close enough to it, i.e., Jules's kids. But she was great with them. Between her and her new nanny, they practically had a camp going while the adults worked at picking up debris and rebuilding the barn.

"She actually doesn't," Mama Gin said, blowing his lie out of the water. "Deke can be pretty persuasive."

Now he did raise his eyebrows. "No more so than the next guy."

They made a little bit more small talk before Mama Gin and the man moved on. Shaking his head, Deke had turned back to the food truck when Fitz came up next to him.

"Why were you talking to Dan Samson?"

"You know him?" Deke asked.

A frown on her face, she nodded. "He's the governor's chief of staff."

That made Deke do an actual double take. "The governor? Of Iowa?"

"Uh-huh." She looked around, her eyes surveying the progress. She'd been the one to come up with the idea of bringing everyone together as soon as the police said it was okay to go ahead; he'd been the one to propose using the barn raising party as a theme. They made a good team. They really did.

"This really doesn't bother you one bit, does it?" she said.

He looked down at her, not sure what she was referring to at first. But then he saw the way her eyes uneasily skimmed the crowd. Because, yes, everyone had turned out today. Even Peggy and her parents, all the Rotary Club and the Jaycees. And pretty much down to the last of them, they were obviously curious about him and Fitz.

Rumors were rampant as one would expect given the various scenes in the bar the day of the tornado. And God knew, Fitz hated being the center of attention. So, well, Deke knew exactly how to take the focus off her. Having spent nearly his whole life playing that part, he went ahead and put on the required show. Raising his arms up over his head in a stretch, he said, "The ladies love it when I take off my shirt, too, but I'll save that for later. A nice little pick-me-up for the end of the day."

He dropped his arms when Fitz gave a surprisingly sharp jab to his side. "You're awful."

But she laughed, and that was all he wanted. "I know, baby," he said, running with it. "You want it for yourself, but sometimes you've got to think about the greater good."

That time she almost snarfed the water she was drinking. After wiping her mouth with the back of her wrist, though, she got very serious, very fast. In fact, he was pretty sure she'd started crying. "Angel…"

"Oh, God, please don't," she said, ducking her head and turning toward him so no one else would see. It took everything he had not to wrap his arms around her and pull her all the way in. Since she was deliberately keeping from touching him, though, he'd give her the courtesy of the same no matter how hard it was.

He wrapped his arms around himself instead. "Peggy hates you, you know," he said, ignoring the pain that flashed through her eyes as her head suddenly came up. He nodded. "Suzie and Rayna, too, I'm pretty sure."

"I seriously have no freaking idea who Rayna is," she muttered before her eyes came to his with a glare. "Is there a point to this?"

He nodded at that as well. "I'm pretty sure that with those three exceptions, you are Inspiration's most beloved citizen."

"What?" This time her gaze went to the crowd— who were all, yes, still watching—before coming back to him.

"They revere Nate," he said. "They think Jason's great with the kids, if a little spacey. Some of them might still think Wash is a scary black dude, but mostly they're grateful he's kept the Hawkins farm local. And me, well…" He shrugged. "Mostly they think it's time for me to grow up and maybe do something with my life."

"*Seriously?*" she snapped. "Do they not get what

you put on hold so you could help Lola? That you're probably the best Little League coach this town has ever seen?" Her voice got louder as she built up momentum. "That you almost single-handedly take care of the people in this tow—"

"Fitz," he said, a little surprised at how fiercely she'd leaped to his defense. Because that wasn't what he'd been going for, not one bit. He couldn't deny it gave him a bit of a rush as he got back to his point, though. Which was, "But you? They pretty much just love you."

She shook her head. "They don't, Deke. And it's oka—"

"I'm the town bartender," he said, smiling down at her. "I hear things." As in pretty much everything, including the odds of Fitz staying in town. Mrs. Bellevue was one of the few holdouts, declaring that Fitz came from strong if not entirely trustworthy stock. But everyone else expected she'd be gone by Harvestfest. The good-bye party they were planning had the potential to be the biggest event this town had ever seen. That wasn't something he wanted to dwell on, however. "I'm pretty sure everyone out there is just waiting on my signal to give you a huge, town-wide group hug."

"Oh, God," she said. "That sounds awful." But she was smiling as she looked up at him, even though her eyes were brimming with tears. "Are you telling me this to make me stay?"

And now he was the one who needed to turn away. He wouldn't do that. No matter how much he wanted to, he'd never be the one to hold her back. He shook his head. "I didn't want you to leave without knowing how much you're loved. That you'll never be alone."

She didn't answer right away. He had no idea if that

was a good or a bad thing. But he wasn't sure he had the strength to look down right now and not give in to the urge to drop down to his knees and beg, so he just stood there, waiting for her to respond.

"About that," she finally said.

And here we go.

With a sigh, he told himself he was ready for this. He had to be. "I'm leaving for Miami on Monday," she said, not unexpectedly. "And I'll be on the road for six weeks, two of them in Boston with Sam."

He couldn't keep the grimace from coming over his face. "Yeah, I got that the other day."

"Will you meet us there?" she asked. "For a few days, at least?"

He looked down at her, wanting desperately to say yes. But he couldn't do this with her. Not if she couldn't—

"Because I've been thinking," she said, turning to him and taking his hand.

Without even realizing it, he looked up, his eyes gauging how close they were to everyone else, who could see them...

Except then it occurred to him the reason for that was because she was the one who didn't want people to know about them. Was afraid they might talk.

Then her hand went to his chest and she stepped up so close to him he had to put his arms around her to steady himself. The fact that Jason, of all people, noticed was something she needed to know. "*Fitz...*" Especially because now Wash was avoiding all pretense and openly staring, as were Mama Gin and Lola beside them. Dorie was grinning her head off.

"In case I wasn't clear enough about it the other day," Fitz said, "I've fallen completely in love with you."

His attention zoomed right back to her. Screw everyone else. "What?"

Her hand moved up to his shoulder, to the back of his neck. "I'm not sure when exactly. Maybe that time in the car." She smiled. "Maybe all of them."

His mouth fell open.

"I have to go away, because that's my job. But it turns out that since I really love you, too, I'm coming back afterwards and staying, whether I take the new job or not."

She hadn't accepted the job?

"I actually made a proposal to Sam that would partner our expanded foundation with the one he wants to build. Pending board approval, of course." She smiled apologetically. As if Deke gave a flying fuck about approval right now. "But only if the home-base of operations is here." Her grin grew wider. "I was wondering what you thought about maybe building out the space above the bar."

Deke's head was spinning. "But…" He actually felt dizzy. "Lola said you were looking at condos in Chicago."

For a second she seemed confused. Then her head fell against his chest and she laughed. "I am. With Dorie. For her and Nate." When she looked back up, though, her smile was gone. The look on her face, in fact, was scared and unsure in a way that didn't seem encouraging. Considering she was now standing with her arms around him, he decided it would be okay to kiss the top of her head and tighten his arms around her just in case it helped. It sure as hell helped him.

"Were you serious the other day?" she asked. "About wanting to spend your life kissing me?"

Still a little stunned at the turn this had taken, Deke looked down at her as she began to pull away.

"Could you please say something before I have another freaking panic attack?" she practically hissed.

She did look a little pale. Kind of like she was about to face a runaway train. Or a tornado. "Completely serious," he said, only able to get the words out because he didn't want to make her feel worse. He pulled her to face him and brushed the hair out of her eyes. "Are you asking what I think you're asking?"

She shook her head and, yeah, his blood may have run a little cold. At least until the moment she said, "I'm not asking anything. I'm telling. Honesty and trust, right?"

For possibly the first time in his entire life, Deke was completely unable to speak. He did manage a nod, however.

"Okay, then," she mumbled before taking a deep breath. "The fact that everyone is staring right now makes me feel like I might faint. But when I look into your eyes—when I feel your arms around me—somehow it all fades away."

Deke had been a pretty happy guy all his life; in the bigger scheme of things, at least. But he hadn't known his heart could soar—not like this. He could not get this fucking smile off his face. And that was before she added, "I want to be with you, Deke. I want to spend my life with you, even if that means I end up married to the mayor of this whole damn town. To my complete surprise, I don't give one iota of a crap if that's the biggest story to hit Inspiration since the last time

I was big news." The tears that had been brimming in her eyes overflowed as she looked up at him. "As long as I'm with you."

His smile was so big it was probably being picked up by satellites right now. "That's one freaking hell of a baby step, Angel," he said, pulling back a little. "I can tell this to the world?"

"No more secrets." She looked happier than he'd ever seen her.

So he lifted her up, wrapped her legs around his waist and in front of the whole town, he kissed her—and she let him. Then, loud enough for the entire town to hear him, he said, "I'm therefore declaring to the entire universe that I belong to Angelica Wade Hawkins."

He touched his forehead to hers. "And she belongs to me."

* * * * *

Acknowledgments

If the first book takes a village, then the second book takes a *lot* more support from that village. So first, I must give a huge THANK YOU to Kelley, for the countless nights, weekends, and pretty much otherwise round-the-clock taking the reins at home (yes, I did that one on purpose) so that I could write. Thank you also to Mom, who gave up Sunday-morning crossword-puzzle time—you are one of the three best grand/mothers in the world. And to Dad, for going along with it all, as well as Lucy, Will and James for all of your patience and love. Maybe someday you will read my books, but not today.

Thank you also Jess, Jenny T. and, again, Mom, for your early and ongoing support, as well as to Bobbi L. and Bobbi D. for the absolute perfect feedback at the most crucial time.

To Jon and Billy for keeping an eye out for my baseball facts, Heather for the Inspiration perspective, Jenny #2 from behind the bar and Emma for, well, some important research that will not be named. I am deeply grateful for all of your comments; any errors are mine alone.

I'm also especially grateful to Christine W. for coming back into my life just in time (on all fronts).

And a tremendous shout-out to Jonathan and Jenny

at J. Stevens Salon for helping to start this journey off with a bang, not to mention Jess (yes, again!), Rachel, Jaime, Colleen, *plus* Jen Hallock, Bobbi Lerman, Kristen Drew and Nicole Michaels for that amazing first week and all of the cheerleading along the way.

None of this would have been possible without Sarah E. Younger and Alissa Davis. I am forever grateful to both of you for seeing The Dream and turning it into the reality.

About the Author

Award-winning author Jen Doyle is a big believer in happily-ever-afters—so she decided it was high time she started creating some. Jen holds an MS in library and information science from Simmons College GSLIS and, in addition to her work as a librarian, has worked as a conference and events planner as well as a communications and enrollment administrator in both preschool and higher education environments. Some might say that there is very little difference between the two; Jen has no comment regarding whether she is one of the "some." She currently lives in the Boston area with her husband, three children and three sometimes problematic cats. Visit her at jendoyleink.com, Facebook.com/jendoyleink.

Get 4 FREE REWARDS!

We'll send you 2 FREE Books plus 2 FREE Mystery Gifts.

FREE
Value Over
$20

Both the **Romance** and **Suspense** collections feature compelling novels written by many of today's best-selling authors.

YES! Please send me 2 FREE novels from the Essential Romance or Essential Suspense Collection and my 2 FREE gifts (gifts are worth about $10 retail). After receiving them, if I don't wish to receive any more books, I can return the shipping statement marked "cancel." If I don't cancel, I will receive 4 brand-new novels every month and be billed just $6.74 each in the U.S. or $7.24 each in Canada. That's a savings of at least 16% off the cover price. It's quite a bargain! Shipping and handling is just 50¢ per book in the U.S. and 75¢ per book in Canada.* I understand that accepting the 2 free books and gifts places me under no obligation to buy anything. I can always return a shipment and cancel at any time. The free books and gifts are mine to keep no matter what I decide.

Choose one: ☐ **Essential Romance**   ☐ **Essential Suspense**
                      (194/394 MDN GMY7)   (191/391 MDN GMY7)

Name (please print)

Address   Apt. #

City   State/Province   Zip/Postal Code

Mail to the **Reader Service:**
IN U.S.A.: P.O. Box 1341, Buffalo, NY 14240-8531
IN CANADA: P.O. Box 603, Fort Erie, Ontario L2A 5X3

Want to try 2 free books from another series? Call 1-800-873-8635 or visit www.ReaderService.com.

---

*Terms and prices subject to change without notice. Prices do not include sales taxes, which will be charged (if applicable) based on your state or country of residence. Canadian residents will be charged applicable taxes. Offer not valid in Quebec. This offer is limited to one order per household. Books received may not be as shown. Not valid for current subscribers to the Essential Romance or Essential Suspense Collection. All orders subject to approval. Credit or debit balances in a customer's account(s) may be offset by any other outstanding balance owed by or to the customer. Please allow 4 to 6 weeks for delivery. Offer available while quantities last.

Your Privacy—The Reader Service is committed to protecting your privacy. Our Privacy Policy is available online at www.ReaderService.com or upon request from the Reader Service. We make a portion of our mailing list available to reputable third parties that offer products we believe may interest you. If you prefer that we not exchange your name with third parties, or if you wish to clarify or modify your communication preferences, please visit us at www.ReaderService.com/consumerschoice or write to us at Reader Service Preference Service, P.O. Box 9062, Buffalo, NY 14240-9062. Include your complete name and address.

STRS19R

Get 4 FREE REWARDS!

We'll send you 2 FREE Books plus 2 FREE Mystery Gifts.

Harlequin® Medical Romance™ Larger-Print books feature professionals who navigate the high stakes of falling in love in the world of medicine.

FREE Value Over $20

Get 4 FREE REWARDS!

We'll send you 2 FREE Books plus 2 FREE Mystery Gifts.

Harlequin® Romance Larger-Print books feature uplifting escapes that will warm your heart with the ultimate feel-good tales.

FREE
Value Over
$20

Get 4 FREE REWARDS!

We'll send you 2 FREE Books plus 2 FREE Mystery Gifts.

Harlequin® Desire books feature heroes who have it all: wealth, status, incredible good looks... everything but the right woman.

FREE
Value Over
$20

YES! Please send me 2 FREE Harlequin® Desire novels and my 2 FREE gifts (gifts are worth about $10 retail). After receiving them, if I don't wish to receive any more books, I can return the shipping statement marked "cancel." If I don't cancel, I will receive 6 brand-new novels every month and be billed just $4.55 per book in the U.S. or $5.24 per book in Canada. That's a savings of at least 13% off the cover price! It's quite a bargain! Shipping and handling is just 50¢ per book in the U.S. and 75¢ per book in Canada.* I understand that accepting the 2 free books and gifts places me under no obligation to buy anything. I can always return a shipment and cancel at any time. The free books and gifts are mine to keep no matter what I decide.

225/326 HDN GMYU

Name (please print)

Address   Apt. #

City   State/Province   Zip/Postal Code

Mail to the **Reader Service:**
IN U.S.A.: P.O. Box 1341, Buffalo, NY 14240-8531
IN CANADA: P.O. Box 603, Fort Erie, Ontario L2A 5X3

Want to try 2 free books from another series? Call 1-800-873-8635 or visit www.ReaderService.com.